IL OSE AUSSI DOUTER

Quinton

D1580054

RODMOOR

RODMOOR

A Romance

JOHN COWPER POWYS

O they rade on, and farther on,
And they waded rivers abune the knee.
And they saw neither sun nor moon
But they heard the roaring of the sea
                    ANONYMOUS

A New Edition with a Preface by
G. Wilson Knight

MACDONALD . LONDON

First published in the United States of America in 1916 by
G. Arnold Shaw
First published in Great Britain in 1973 by
Macdonald & Co (Publishers) Ltd.
49 Poland Street
London W1
Printed in Great Britain by
Whitstable Litho,
Straker Brothers Ltd.

ISBN 0 356 04532 3

PREFACE

Powys is rather like Shakespeare in that his early work shows no faltering, but springs out, like the birth of Athene, ready-armed. *Rodmoor* was his second novel, and the only one that has never been published in England. It has nevertheless a quality all its own. It is a strange book, but grips the reader, holding him with a keen suspense. It is the most dramatic of all Powys's books.

I have called it 'strange'. The hero, Adrian Sorio, has been in a mental home and is engaged in writing on destruction as the key to existence; a theme to be taken up again, with differences, in Powys's next story, *Ducdame*, and, much later, in *The Inmates*. These rather mind-staggering simplicities mean much in Powys. He is fascinated by the phenomenal universe and also by the strange possibility of a universe composed of not-being, perhaps of what we today would call 'anti-matter'. His last published work was, with exact purpose, entitled *All or Nothing*.

In human affairs, this poses the question of life and death. What is death? In *The Art of Happiness* Powys says that we should enjoy the prospect of death and alters Wordsworth's famous line (Michael 77) to read, 'the pleasure which there is in life and death'. We should enjoy the prospect of not-being, rather as we enjoy a dreamless sleep. The more, however, that we think of such blissful 'not-being' the more it assumes a positive quality, like the 'Nirvana' of Buddhist philosophy. Throughout Powys's life-work this problem, in various forms, continues to teaze. The gist of it all is, rather amazingly, already perfectly expressed in *Rodmoor*. Here we are told that there is something 'beyond the point where every living thing ceases to exist and becomes nothing'. It is as a 'blinding white light' that is yet 'neither light nor darkness'. All normal terms are inadequate except one: here Adrian will be reunited with his idealised son, the seraphic Baptiste.

It is natural that so strange a story should have human figures that are also strange. Our story is set by the sea, in East Anglia, the only Powys novel—with the exception of the opening chapters of *A Glastonbury Romance*—to be so located. Here the sea is, or seems, fearful, a threat, almost malignant. Of the people, Brand Renshaw is a Gothic monster of dark, mysterious, evil. The girl Philippa is an elfin creation at home with the elements and bisexually conceived. True, we have on the other side the wise Mrs Renshaw and the faithful Nance who stand for sanity as normally understood, but the balance favours the strange ones and is preceded by a vision of an ambisexual figure 'seeking amid the dreams of all the great perverted artists of the world for the incarnation it has been denied by the will of God.'

The hero all but ends with Philippa, but drawn on by his visionary 'Nirvana' he leaves her for the sea, now blessed part of a serene infinitude, and after the exultant cry 'Baptiste!', he dies.

G. Wilson Knight

1973

CONTENTS

CONTENTS

RODMOOR

I

THE BOROUGH

IT was not that he concealed anything from her.

He told her quite frankly, in that first real conversation they had together — on the little secluded bench in the South London park — about all the morbid sufferings of his years in America and his final mental collapse.

He even indicated to her — while the sound of grassmowing came to them over the rain-wet tulips — some of the most secret causes of this event; his savage reaction, for instance, against the circle he was thrown into there; his unhappy habit of deadly introspection; his aching nostalgia for things less murderously new and raw.

He explained how his mental illness had taken so dangerous, so unlooked for a shape, that it was only by the merest chance he had escaped long incarceration.

No; it was not that he concealed anything. It was rather that she experienced a remote uneasy feeling that, say what he might,— and in a certain sense he said too much rather than too little — she did not really understand him.

Her feminine instinct led her to persuade him that she understood; led her to say what was most reassur-

ing to him, and most consolatory; but in her heart of
hearts she harboured a teasing doubt; a doubt which
only the rare sweetness of these first love-days of her
life enabled her to hide and cover over. Nor was this
feeling about her lover's confessions the only little cloud
on Nance Herrick's horizon during these memorable
weeks — weeks that, after all, she was destined to look
back upon as so strangely happy.

She found herself, in the few moments when her passionate emotion left her free to think of such things,
much more anxious than she cared to admit about the
ambiguous relations existing between the two persons
dependent upon her. Ever since the death of her
father — that prodigal sailor — three years ago, when
she had taken it upon herself to support both of them
by her work in the dressmaker's shop, she had known
that all was not well between the two. Rachel Doorm
had never forgiven Captain Herrick for marrying
again; she felt that instinctively, but it was only quite
recently that she had grown to be really troubled by the
eccentric woman's attitude to the little half-sister.

Linda's mother, she knew, had in her long nervous
decline rather clung than otherwise to this grim friend
of the former wife; but Linda's mother had always been
different from other women; and Nance could remember how, in quite early days, she never interfered when
Miss Doorm took the child away to punish her.

To Nance herself Rachel had always been something
of an anxiety. Her savage devotion had proved over
and over again more of a burden than a pleasure; and
now that there was this increased tension between her
and Linda, the thing began to appear invidious, rapa-
cious, sinister.

She was torn, in fact, two ways over the situation. Her own mother had long ago — and it was one of her few definite recollections of her — made her swear solemnly never to desert this friend of former days; and the vows she had registered then to obey this covenant had grown into a kind of religious rite; the only rite, in fact, after all these years, she was able to perform for her dead.

And yet if loyalty to her mother kept her patiently tender with Rachel's eccentricities, the much warmer feeling she had for her other parent was stirred indignantly by the thought of any unkindness dealt out to Linda.

And just at present, it was clear, Linda was not happy.

The young girl seemed to be losing her vivacity and to be growing silent and reserved.

She was now nearly eighteen; and yet Nance had caught her once or twice lately looking at Rachel Doorm with the same expression of frightened entreaty as she used to wear when led away from her mother's side for some childish fault. Rachel's father, a taciturn and loveless old man, had recently died, leaving his daughter, whom he had practically cast off, a small but secure annuity and a little house on the east coast.

It was now to this home of her ancestors, in the village of Rodmoor, that Rachel Doorm was anxious to transport both sisters; partly as a return for what Nance's mother, and more recently Nance herself, had done for her support, and partly out of fanatical devotion to Nance.

The girl could not help experiencing a feeling of infinite relief at the thought of being freed from her uncongenial work in the dressmaker's establishment. Her pleasure, nevertheless, had been considerably marred, in the last few days, by the attitude of her sister towards the projected change.

And now, with the realisation of this thrilling new passion possessing her, her own feeling about leaving London was different from what it had been at first.

None of these questions interrupted, however, on that particular afternoon, the girl's dreamy and absorbed happiness.

In the long delicious intervals that fell between her and her lover with a perfume sweeter than that of the arrested rain, she let her mind wander in languid retrospect, from that seat in Kensington Park, over every one of the wonderful events that had led her to this.

She recalled her first sight of Adrian and how it had come over her, like an intimation from some higher sphere of being, that her fate was henceforth to lie, for good and for evil, in that man's hands.

It was quite early in April when she saw him; and she remembered, sitting now by his side, how, as each day grew milder, and the first exquisite tokens of Spring penetrated one by one — here a basket of daffodils, and there a spray of almond-blossom — into the street she traversed to her work, she felt less and less inclined to struggle against the deep delicious thrill that suffused itself, like a warm indrawing wave, through every pulse of her body. That it should never have come to her before — that she should have lived absolutely fancy-free until so near her twenty-third birthday — only made her abandonment to what she felt now the more sweet and entire.

" It is love,— it is love," she thought; " and I will give myself up to it!"

And she had given herself up to it. It had penetrated her with an exultant inner spring of delight. She had immersed herself in it. She had gone through her tedious drudgery as if she were floating, languidly and at ease, on a softly rocking tide. She had lived entirely in the present. She had not made the least movement even to learn the name of the man whose wordless pursuit of her had stirred her senses to this exultant response.

She had felt an indescribable desire to prolong these hours of her first love, these hours so unreturning, so new and so sweet; a desire — she remembered it well now — that had a tinge of unformulated fear about it; as though the very naming, even to herself, of what she enjoyed, would draw down the jealousy of the invisible powers.

So she had been careful never to stop or linger, in her hurried morning walks to the historic bridge; careful — after she had once passed him, and their eyes had met — never so much as to turn her head, to see if he were following.

And yet she knew — as well in those first days as she knew now — that every morning and night he waited, wet or fine, to see her go by.

And she had known, too — how could she not know? — that this mute signalling of two human souls must change and end; must become something nearer or something farther as time went on. But day by day she put off this event; too thrilled by the sweet dream in which she moved, to wish to destroy it, either for better or for worse.

If she had doubted him; doubted that he cared for her; all would have been different.

Then she would have taken some desperate step — some step that would have forced him to recognise her for what she was, his one of all, ready as none else *could* be ready, to cry with a great cry — " Lord, behold thine hand-maid; do unto her according to Thy will!" But she had known he did care. She had felt the magnetic current of his longing, as if it had been a hand laid down upon her breast.

And in answer she had given herself up to him; given herself, she thought, with no less complete a yielding than that with which, as she heard his voice by her side, reaching her through a delicate mist of delicious dream-ing, she gave herself up to him now.

She recalled with a proud gladness the fact that she had never — never for a moment — in all those days, bestowed a thought on the question of any possible future with him. In the trance-like hours wherein she had brooded so tenderly over the form and face of her name-less lover, she always pictured him as standing waiting for her, a tall, bowed, foreign-looking figure, clothed in the long weather-stained Inverness — the very tex-ture of which she seemed to know the touch of — by that corner curb-stone where the flower-shop was.

Just in that manner, with just that air of ardent ex-pectation, he might be found standing, she had felt, through unnumbered days of enchantment, and she pass-ing by, in silence, with the same expectant thrill.

Such a love draught, not drained, not feverishly drunk of, but sweet in her mouth with the taste of a mystic consecration, seemed still, even now that she had him there beside her, to hold the secret, amid this warm breath of London's first lilacs, of a triumphant Present, wherein both Past and Future were abolished.

It seemed to the happy girl on this unique April afternoon, while the sliding hours, full of the city's monotonous murmur, sank unnoticed away, and the gardeners planted their pansies and raked lethargically in the scented mould, as though nothing that could ever happen to her afterwards, could outweigh what she felt then, or matter so very greatly in the final reckoning. With every pulse of her young body she uttered her litany of gratitude. "*Ite; missa est*" her heart cried — "It is enough."

As they walked home afterwards, hand in hand through the dusk of the friendly park, she made him tell her, detail by detail, every least incident of those first days of their encountering. And Adrian Sorio, catching the spirit of that exquisite entreaty, grew voluble even beyond his wont.

He told her how, in the confusion of his mind, when it was first revealed to him that the devastation he was suffering from did not deny him the sweet sting of "what men call love," he found it impossible to face with any definite resolution the problem of his doubtful future. He had recognised that in a week or so every penny he possessed would be gone; yet it was impossible — and his new emotion did not, he confessed, alter this in the least — to make any move to secure employment.

A kind of misanthropic timidity, so he explained to her, made the least thought of finding what is popularly known as "work" eminently repellant to him; yet it was obvious that work must be found, unless he wished, simply and quietly, to end the affair by starvation.

This, as things went then, he told her, giving her

hand a final pressure as they emerged into the lighted streets, he did not at all urgently want — though in the first days of his return from America he had pondered more than once on the question of an easy and agreeable exit. It was as they settled down side by side,— her hat no longer held languidly in her gloveless hand,— to their long and discreet walk home through the crowded thoroughfares, that she was first startled by hearing the name " Rodmoor " from his lips. How amazing a coincidence! What a miraculous gift of the gods!

Fate was indeed sweeping her away on a full tide.

It seemed like a thing in some old fantastic romance. Could it be possible even before she had time to contemplate her separation from him that she should learn that they were not to separate at all!

Rachel Doorm was indeed a witch — was indeed working things out for her favourite with the power of a sorceress. She kept back her natural cry of delight, " But that is where we are going," and let him, all unconscious, as it seemed, of the effect of his words, unravel in his own way the thread of his story.

It was about a certain Baltazar Stork she found he was telling her when her startled thoughts, like a flock of disturbed pigeons, alighted once more on the field of his discourse. Baltazar, it appeared, was an old friend of Sorio's and had written to offer him a sort of indefinite hospitality in his village on the North Sea. The name of this place — had she ever heard of Rodmoor? — had repeated itself very strangely in his mind ever since he first made it out in his friend's abominable hand.

At that point in their walk, under the glare of a great provision shop, she suddenly became conscious that he was watching her with laughing excitement. "You know!" she cried, "you know!" And it was with difficulty that he persuaded her to let him tell her how he knew, in his own elaborate manner.

This refuge — offered to him thus out of a clear sky, he told her — did in a considerable sense lend him an excuse for taking no steps to find work. And the name of the place — he confessed this with an excited emphasis — had from the beginning strangely affected his imagination.

He saw it sometimes, so he said, that particular word, in a queer visualised manner, dark brown against a colourless and livid sky; and in an odd sort of way it had related itself, dimly, obscurely, and with the incoherence of a half-learnt language, to the wildest and most pregnant symbols of his life.

Rodmoor! The word at the same time allured and troubled him. What it suggested to him — and he made her admit that his ideas of it were far more definite than her own — was no doubt what it really implied: leagues and leagues of sea-bleached forlornness, of sand-dunes and glaucous marshes, of solitary willows and pallid-leaved poplars, of dark pools and night-long-murmuring reeds.

"We'll have long walks together there!" he exclaimed, interrupting himself suddenly with an almost savage gesture of ardent possession. If it had been any one but Baltazar Stork, he went on, who had sent him this timely invitation, he would have rejected it at once, but from Baltazar he had no hesitation in accepting anything. They had been friends too long to make any other attitude possible. No, it was no scruple of pride that led him to hesitate — as he admitted to her

he had done. It was rather the strange and indefinable reaction set up in his brain by those half-sinister
half-romantic syllables — syllables that kept repeating
themselves in his inner consciousness.

Nance remembered more than once in a later time the
fierce sudden way he turned upon her as they stood on
the edge of the crowded square waiting the opportunity
to cross and asked, with a solemn intensity in his voice,
whether she had any presentiment as to how things
would turn out for them in this place.

"It hangs over me," he said, "it hangs over us
both. I see it like a heavy sunset weighted with purple
bars." And then, when the girl did nothing but shake
her head and smile tenderly, "I warn you," he went
on, "you are risking much — I feel it — I know it.
I have had this sort of instinct before about things."
He shivered a little and laid his hand on her arm as
if he clung to her for reassurance.

Nance remembered long afterwards the feelings in
her that made her turn her face full upon him and
whisper proudly, as if in defiance of his premonitions,
"What can happen to us that can hurt us, my dear,
as long as we are together, and as long as we love one
another?"

He was silent after this and apparently satisfied, for
he did not scruple to return to the subject of Rodmoor. The word gave him in those first days, he said,
that curious sensation we receive when we suddenly say
to ourselves in some new locality, "I have been here; I
have seen all this before."

Had he at that time, he told her, been less distracted
by the emotions she aroused in him, he would have
analysed to the bottom the dim mental augury — or

was it reminiscence? — called up by this name. As
it was he just kept the thing at the back of his mind
as something which, whatever its occult significance, at
least spared him the necessity of agitating himself about
his future.

Nance's thoughts were brought back from their half-
attention with a shock of vivid interest when he came
to the point, amid his vague recollections, of his first
entrance into her house. It was exactly a week ago, he
reminded her, that he found himself one sunny morning
securely established as a new lodger under her roof.
In his impatient longing to secure the desirable room
— across the narrow floor of which, he confessed to her,
he paced to and fro that day like a hungry tiger — he
had even forgotten to make the obvious inquiry as to
the quarter of the London sky from which his particular portion of light and air was to come.

It was only, he told her, with a remote segment of
his consciousness that he became aware of the fine,
full flood of sunshine which poured in from the southern-
opening window and lay, mellow and warm, upon his
littered books and travel-stained trunk.

Casual and preoccupied were the glances he cast,
each time his mechanical perambulation brought him
to that pleasant window, at the sun-bathed traffic and
the hurrying crowd. London Bridge Road melted into
his thought; or rather his thought took possession of
London Bridge Road and reduced it to a mere sound-
ing-board for the emotion that obsessed him.

That emotion — and Nance got exquisite pleasure
from hearing him say the words, though she turned her
face away from him as he said them — took, as he
paced his room, passionate and ardent shape. He did

not re-vivify the whole of her,— of the fair young being whose sweetness had got into his blood. He confined himself to thinking of the delicate tilt of her head and of the spaciousness between her breasts, spaciousness that somehow reminded him of Pheidian sculpture.

He hadn't anticipated this particular kind of escape — though it was certainly the escape he had been seeking — amid the roar of London's streets; but after all, if it did give him his cup of nepenthe, his desired anodyne, how much the more did he gain when it gave him so thrilling an experience in addition? Why, indeed, should he not dream that the gods were for once helping him out and that the generous grace of his girl's form was symbolic of the restorative virtue of the great Mother herself?

Restoration was undoubtedly the thing he wanted — and in recalling his thoughts of that earlier hour, to her now walking with him, he found himself enlarging upon it all quite unscrupulously in terms of what he now felt — restoration on any terms, at any cost, to the kindly normal paths out of which he had been so roughly thrown. He thrust indignantly back, he told her, that eventful morning the intrusive thought that it was only the Spring that worked so prosperously upon him. He did not want it to be the Spring; he wanted it to be the girl. The Spring would pass; the girl, if his feeling for her — and he glanced at the broad-rimmed hat and shadowy profile at his side — were not altogether illusive, would remain. And it was the faculty for remaining that he especially required in his raft of refuge.

Up and down his room, at any rate, he walked that day with a heightened consciousness such as he had

not known for many clouded months. "The Spring"
— and in his imaginative reaction to his own memories
he grew, so Nance felt with what was perhaps her first
serious pang, almost feverishly eloquent —" the Spring,
whether I cared to recognise it or not, waved thrilling
arms towards me. I felt it "— and he raised his voice
so loud that the girl looked uneasily round them —
" in the warmth of the sun, in the faces of the wistful
shop girls, in the leaves budding against the smoke of
the Borough. It had come to me again, and you —
you had brought it! It had come to me again, the
Eternal Return, the antiphonal world-deep Renewal.
It had come, Nance, and all the slums of Rotherhithe
and Wapping, and all the chimneys, workshops, wharves
and tenements of the banks of this river of yours could
not stop the rising of the sap. The air came to me
that morning, my girl! "— and he unconsciously quickened his steps as he spoke till, for all her long youthful
limbs she could hardly keep pace with him —" as if it
had passed over leagues of green meadows. And it
had! It had, Nance! And it throbbed for me, child,
with the sweetness of your very soul." He paused for
a moment and, as they debouched more directly eastward through a poor and badly lit street, she caught
him muttering to himself what she knew was Latin.

He answered her quick look — her look that had a
dim uneasiness in it — with a slow repetition of the famous line, and Nance was still quite enough of a young
girl to feel a thrill of pride that she had a lover who,
within a stone's throw of the " Elephant and Castle,"
could quote for her on an April evening that " *cras amet
qui nunquam amavit* " of the youth of the centuries!

The rich, antique flavour of the words blent well

enough as far as she was concerned with the homely houses and taverns of that dilapidated quarter. The night was full of an indescribable balm, felt through the most familiar sounds and sights, and, after all, there was always something mellow and pagan and free about the streets of London. It was the security, the friendly solidity, of the immense city which more than anything just then seemed to harmonise with this classical mood in her wonderful foreigner and she wished he would quote more Latin as they went along, side by side, past the lighted fruit stalls.

The overhanging shadow of Adrian's premonitions, or whatever they were, about Rodmoor, and her own anxieties about Rachel Doorm and Linda withdrew themselves into the remotest background of the girl's mind as she gave herself to her happiness in this favoured hour. It was in a quiet voice, after that, that he resumed his story. The sound, he said, of one of the Borough clocks striking the hour of ten brought a pause to his agitated pacing.

He stretched himself, he told her, when he heard the clock, stretched his arms out at full length, with that delicious shivering sensation which accompanies the near fulfilment of deferred hope. Then he chuckled to himself, from sheer childish ecstasy, and made goblinish faces.

Nance could not help noticing as he told her all this, how quaintly he reproduced in his exaggerated way the precise gestures he had indulged in. "Per Bacco! I had only three pounds left," he said, and as he shrugged his shoulders and glowered at her under a flickering lamp from eyes sunken deep in his heavy face, she realised of what it was he had been all this while vaguely reminding her — of nothing less, in fact, than one of those saturnine portrait-busts of the Roman decadence, at which as a child she used to stare, half-frightened and half-attracted, in the great Museum.

The first thing he did, he told her, when the sound of the clock brought him to his senses, was to empty his pockets on the top of the chest-of-drawers which was, except for the bed and a couple of rickety chairs, the only article of furniture in the room. An errant penny, rolling aside from the rest, tinkled against the edge of his washing basin. "Not three pounds!" he muttered and leered at himself in his wretched looking glass.

It was precisely at that moment that the sound of voices struck his ears, proceeding from the adjoining room.

"I had spent half the night," he whispered, drawing his companion closer to his side as a couple of tipsy youths pushed roughly by them, "lying awake listening. I felt a queer kind of shame, yes, shame, as I realised how near I was to you. You know I knew nothing of you then, absolutely nothing except that you went to work every day and lived with some sort of elderly person and a younger sister. It was this ignorance about you, child, that made my situation so exciting. I waited breathlessly, literally petrified, in the middle of the room."

Nance at this point felt herself compelled to utter a little cry of protest.

"You ought to have made some kind of noise," she said, "to let us know you were listening."

But he waved aside her objection, and continued: "I remained petrified in the centre of the room, feeling as though the persons I listened to might at any moment stop their conversation and listen, in their turn, to the frantic beating of my heart. I heard your voice. I knew it in a moment to be yours — it had the round, full sweetness "— his arm was about her now —" of your darling figure. 'Good-bye!' you called out and there came the sound of a door opening upon the passage, 'Good-bye! I'm off. Meet me to-night if you like. Yes, soon after six. Good-bye! Look after each other.'

" The door shut and I heard you running down the stairs. I felt as though that ' Meet me to-night ' had been addressed to myself. I crossed over to the window and watched you thread your way through the crowd in the direction of the Bridge. I knew you were late. I hoped you would not be scolded for it by some shrewish or brutal employer. I wished I had had the courage to go out on the landing and see you off. Why is one always so paralysed when these chances offer themselves? I might easily have taken a fellow-lodger's privilege and bidden you good morning. Then I found myself wondering whether you had any inkling that I had been sleeping so near you that night. Had you, you darling, had you any such instinct? "

Nance shook her head, nor could he see the expression of her eyes in the quiet darkened square, across which they were then moving. They came upon a wooden bench, under some iron railings, and he made her sit down while he completed his tale. The spot was unfrequented at that hour, and above their heads — as they leaned back, sighing tranquilly, and he took possession of her hand — the branch of a stunted beech-tree stretched itself out, hushed and still, enjoying some secret dream of its own amid the balmy perfumes of the amorous night.

"May I go on?" he enquired, looking tenderly at her.

In her heart Nance longed to cry, "No! No! No more of these tiresome memories! Make love to me! Make love to me!" but she only pressed his fingers gently and remained silent.

"I took up a book," he went on, "from the heap on the floor and drawing one of those miserable chairs to the window, I opened it at random. It happened to be that mad lovely thing of Remy de Gourmont. I forgot whether you said you had got as far as French poetry in that collection of yours that Miss Doorm is so suspicious of. It was, in fact, 'Le livre des Litanies,' and shall I tell you the passage I read? I was too excited to gather its meaning all at once, and then such a curious thing happened to me! But I will say the lines to you, child, and you will understand better."

Nance could only press his hand again, but her heart sank with an unaccountable foreboding.

"It was the Litany of the Rose," he said, and his voice floated out into the embalmed stillness with the same ominous treachery in its tone, so the poor girl fancied, as the ambiguous words he chanted.

"*Rose au regard saphique, plus pâle que les lys, rose au regard saphique, offre-nous le parfum de ton illusoire virginité, fleur hypocrite, fleur de silence.*"

The strange invocation died away on the air, and a singular oppression, heavy as if with some undesired spiritual presence, weighed upon them both. Sorio did not speak for some minutes, and when he did so there was an uneasy vibration in his voice.

"As soon as I had read those lines, there came over me one of the most curious experiences I have ever had. I seemed to see, yes, you may smile,"— Nance was far from smiling — " but it is actually true — I seemed to see a living human figure outline itself against the wall of my room. To the end of my days I shall never forget it! It was a human form, Nance, but it was unlike all human forms I've ever beheld — unless it be one of those weird drawings, you know? of Aubrey Beardsley. It was neither the form of a boy nor of a girl, and yet it had the nature of both. It gazed at me with a fixed sorrowful stare, and I felt — was not that a strange experience — that I had known it before, somewhere, far off, and long ago. It was the very embodiment of tragic supplication, and yet, in the look it fixed on me, there was a cold, merciless mockery.

" It was the kind of form, Nance, that one can imagine wandering in vain helplessness down all the years of human history, seeking amid the dreams of all the great, perverse artists of the world for the incarnation it has been denied by the will of God." He paused again, and an imperceptible breath of hot balmy air stirred the young leaves of the beech branch above them.

" Ah! " he whispered, " I know what I thought of then. I thought of that ' Secret Rose Garden ' where the timid boy-girl thing — you know the picture I mean, Nance? — is led forth by some wanton lamp bearer between rose branches that are less soft than her defenceless sides."

Once more he was silent and the hot wind, rising a

little, uttered a perceptible murmur in the leaves above
their heads.

"But what was more startling to me, Nance," he
went on, "even than the figure I saw (and it only
stayed a moment before disappearing) was the fact
that at the very second it vanished, I heard, spoken
quite distinctly, in the room next to mine, the word
'Rodmoor.'

"I threw down the 'Book of Litanies' and once
more stood breathlessly listening. I caught the word
again, uttered in a tone that struck me as having something curiously threatening about it. It was your
Miss Doorm, Nance. No wonder she and I instinctively hated each other when we met. She must have
known that I had heard this interesting conversation.
Your sister's voice — and you must think about that,
Nance, you must think about that — sounded like the
voice of a little girl that has been punished — yes, punished into frightened submissiveness.

"Miss Doorm was evidently talking to her about this
Rodmoor scheme. 'It's what I've waited for, for
years and years,' I heard her say. 'Every Spring that
came round I hoped he would die, and he didn't. It
seemed that he wouldn't—just to spite me, just to
keep me out of my own. But now he's gone—the old
man—gone with all his wickedness upon him, and my
place returns to me—my own place. It's mine, I tell
you, mine! mine! mine!' It was extraordinary, Nance,
the tone in which she said these things. Then she went
on to speak of you. 'I can free her now,' she said, 'I
can free her at last. Aren't you glad I can free her?
Aren't you glad?'

"I confess it made me at that moment almost indignant with your sister that she should need such pressing on such a subject. Her voice, however, when she murmured some kind of an answer, appeared, as I have said, quite obsequious in its humility.

"'O my precious, my precious!' the woman cried again, evidently apostrophising you, 'you've worked for me, and saved for me, and now I can return it — I can return it!' There was a few minutes' silence then, and I moved," Sorio continued, " quite close to the wall so as to catch if I could your sister's whispers.

"Miss Doorm soon began once more and I liked her tone still less. 'Why don't you speak? Why do you sit silent and sulky like that? Aren't you glad she'll be free of all this burden — of all this miserable drudgery? Aren't you glad for her? She kept you here like a Duchess, you with your music lessons! A lot of money you'll ever earn with your music! And now it's my turn. She shall be a lady in my house, a lady!'"

Nance's head hung low down over her knees as she listened to all this and the hand that her lover still retained grew colder and colder.

"I remember her next words," Sorio went on, " particularly well because a lovely fragrance of lilacs came suddenly into the window from a cart in the street and I thought how to my dying day I should associate that scent with this first morning under your roof.

"'You say you don't like the sea?' Miss Doorm went on, 'and you actually suppose that your not liking the sea will stop my freeing her! No! No! You'll have the sea, my beauty, at Rodmoor — the sea and the wind. No more dilly-dallying among the pretty shop windows and the nice young music students. The

Wind and the Sea! Those are the things that are waiting for you at Rodmoor — at Rodmoor, in my house, where she will be a lady at last!'

"You see, Nance," Adrian observed, letting her hand go and preparing to light a cigarette, "Miss Doorm's idea seems to be that you will receive quite a social lift from your move to her precious Rodmoor. She evidently holds the view that no lady has ever earned her living with her own hands. Does she propose to keep a horde of servants in this small house, I wonder, and stalk about among them, grim and majestic, in a black silk gown?

"I must confess I feel at this moment a certain understanding of your sister's reluctance to plunge into this 'milieu.' I can see that house — oh, so clearly! — surrounded by a dark back-water and swept by horribly cold winds. I'm sure I don't know, Nance, what kind of neighbours you're going to have on the Doorm estate. Probably half the old hags of East Anglia will troop in upon you, like descendants of the Valkyries. And the North Sea! You realise, my dear, I suppose, what the North Sea is? 'I don't blame little Linda for shivering at the thought of it."

For the first time since she had known him Nance's voice betrayed irritation. "Don't tease me, Adrian. I can't stand it to-night. You don't know what all this means to Rachel."

Adrian smiled. "Your dear Rachel," he said, "seems to have got you both fairly well under her thumb."

"She was my mother's best friend!" the girl burst out. "I should never forgive myself if I made her unhappy!"

"There seems more chance, as I see it now," observed Sorio, "that Miss Doorm will make Linda unhappy. I think I may take it that Linda's mother wasn't much of a favourite of hers? Isn't that so, my dear?"

"We must be getting home now," the girl remarked, rising from the bench. But Sorio remained seated, coolly puffing wreaths of cigarette smoke into the aromatic night.

"There's not the slightest need to get cross with me," he said gently, giving the sleeve of her coat a little deprecatory caress.

"As a matter of fact, when I heard that woman scold Linda for not wanting to set you free I felt, in a most odd and subtle manner, curiously anxious to scold her, too; I quite longed to overcome and override her absurd reluctance. I even felt a strange excitement in the thought of walking with her along the edge of this water, and in the face of this wind. O! I became Miss Doorm's accomplice, Nance! You may be perfectly happy. I made up my mind that very moment that I would write at once to Baltazar and accept his invitation. Indeed I did write to him, the minute I could hear no more talking. I was too excited to write much. I just wrote: 'Amico mio: — I will come to you very soon.' and when I'd finished the letter I went straight out and posted it. I believe I heard Linda crying as I went downstairs, but, as I tell you, Nance, I had become quite an accomplice of Miss Doorm! It seemed to me outrageous that the selfish silliness of a child like that should interfere with your emancipation. Besides I liked the thought of walking with her by the shore of this sea and calming her curious fear."

He threw away his cigarette and, rising to his feet, drew the girl's arm within his own and led her homewards.

The beech-tree, as if relieved by their departure, gave itself up with more delicious abandonment than ever to the embraces of the warm Spring night. They had not far to go now, and Nance only spoke once before they arrived at their door in the London Bridge Road.

"Had that figure you saw," she asked in a low constrained voice, "the same look Linda has — now that you know what she is like?"

"Linda?" he answered, "Oh, no, my dear, no, no! That one had nothing to do with Linda. But I think," he added, after a pause, "it had something to do with Rodmoor."

II

DYKE HOUSE

NANCE HERRICK stood at her window in the Doorm dwelling the morning after their arrival thinking desperately of what she had done. The window, open at the top, let in a breath of chilly, salt-tasting wind which stirred the fair loose hair upon her forehead and cooled her throat and shoulders. At the sound of her sister's voice she closed the window, cast one swift, troubled look at the river flowing so formidably near, and moved across to Linda's side. Drowsy and warm after her deep sleep, the younger girl stretched out her long, youthful arms from the bed and clasped them round Nance's neck.

" Are you glad," she whispered, " are you glad, after all, that I made you come I couldn't have borne to be selfish, dear. I should have had no peace. No!—," she interrupted an ejaculation from Nance, " — it wasn't anything to do with Rachel. It wasn't, Nancy darling, it really and truly wasn't! I'm going to be perfectly good now. I'm going to be so good that you'll hardly know me. Shall I tell you what I'm going to do? I'm going to learn the organ. Rachel says there's a beautiful one in the church here, and Mr. Traherne — he's the clergyman, you know — plays upon it himself. I'm going to persuade him to teach me. O! I shall be perfectly happy!"

Nance extricated herself from the young girl's arms

and, stepping back into the middle of the room, stood contemplating her in silence. The two sisters, thus contrasted, in the hard white light of that fen-land morning, would have charmed the super-subtle sense of some late Venetian painter. Nance herself, without being able precisely to define her feeling, felt that the mere physical difference between them was symbolic of something dangerously fatal in their conjunction. Her sister was not an opposite type. She too was fair — she too was tall and flexible — she too was emphatically feminine in her build — she even had eyes of the same vague grey colour. And yet, as Nance looked at her now, at her flushed excited cheeks, her light brown curls, her passionate neurotic attitude, and became at the same time conscious of her own cold pure limbs, white marble-like skin and heavily-hanging shining hair, she felt that they were so essentially different, even in their likeness, that the souls in their two bodies could never easily comprehend one another nor arrive at any point of real instinctive understanding.

Something of the same thought must have troubled Linda too at that moment, for as they fixed their eyes on each other's faces there fell between them that sort of devastating silence which indicates the struggle of two human spirits, seeking in vain to break the eternal barrier in whose isolating power lies all the tragedy and all the interest of life.

Suddenly Nance moved to the window and threw it wide open.

" Listen! " she said.

The younger sister made a quick apprehensive movement and clasped her hands tightly together. Her eyes grew wide and her breast rose and fell.

"Listen!" Nance repeated.

A low, deep-drawn murmur, reiterated, and again reiterated, in menacing monotony, filled the room.

"The sea!" cried both sisters together.

Nance shivered, closed the window and sank down on a chair. With lowered eyes she remained for some seconds absorbed and abstracted. When she lifted her head she saw that her sister was watching her and that there was a look on her face such as she had never seen there before. It was a look she was destined to be unable to thrust from her memory, but no effort of hers could have described it then or afterwards. Making an effort of will which required all the strength of her soul, Nance rose to her feet and spoke solemnly and deliberately.

"Swear to me, Linda, that nothing I could have said or done would have made you agree to stay in London. I told you I was ready to stay, didn't I, that night I came back with Adrian and found you awake? I begged and begged you to tell me the truth, to tell me whether Rachel was forcing you into going. I offered to leave her for good and all — didn't I? — if she was unkind to you. It's only the truth I want — only the truth! We'll go back — now — to-morrow — the moment you say you wish it. But if you don't wish it, make me know you don't! Make me know it — here — in my heart!"

In her emotion, pressing her hand to her side, she swayed with a pathetic, unconscious movement. Linda continued to watch her, the same indescribable look upon her face.

"Will you swear that nothing I could have done

would have made you stay? Will you swear that, Linda?"

The younger girl in answer to this appeal, leapt from her bed and rushing up to her sister hugged her tightly in her arms.

"You darling thing!" she cried, "of course I'll swear it. Nothing — nothing — *nothing!* would have made me stay. Oh, you'll soon see how happy I can be in Rodmoor — in dear lovely Rodmoor!"

A simultaneous outburst of weeping relieved at that moment the feelings of both of them, and they kissed one another passionately through their falling tears.

In the hush that followed — whether by reason of a change in the wind or simply because their senses had grown more receptive — they both clearly heard through the window that remained closed, the husky, long-drawn beat, reiterative, incessant, menacing, of the waves of the North Sea.

During breakfast and the hours which succeeded that meal, Nance was at once surprised and delighted by the excellent spirits of both Miss Doorm and Linda. They even left her to herself before half the morning was over and went off together, apparently in complete harmony along the banks of the tidal stream.

She herself, loitering in the deserted garden, felt a curious sensation of loneliness and a wonder, not amounting to a sense of discomfort but still remotely disturbing, as to why it was that Adrian had not, as he had promised, appeared to take her out. Acting at last on a sudden impulse, she ran into the house, put on her hat and cloak, and started rapidly down the road leading to the village.

The Spring was certainly not so far advanced in Rodmoor as it was in London. Nance felt as though some alien influence were at work here, reducing to enforced sterility the natural movements of living and growing things. The trees were stunted, the marigolds in the wet ditches pallid and tarnished. The leaves of the poplars, as they shook in the gusty wind, seemed to her like hundreds and hundreds of tiny dead hands — the hands of ghostly babies beseeching whatever power called them forth to give them more life or to return them to the shadows.

Yes, some alien influence was at work, and the Spring was ravished and tarnished even while yet in bud. It was as if by an eternal mandate, registered when this portion of the coast first assumed its form, the seasons had been somehow thwarted and perverted in the processes of their natural order, and the land left, a nuetral, sterile, derelict thing, neither quite living nor quite dead, doomed to changeless monotony.

Nance was still some little distance from the village, but she slackened her pace and lingered now, in the hope that at any moment she might see Adrian approaching. She knew from Rachel's description only very vaguely where Mr. Stork's cottage was and she was afraid of missing her lover if she went too far.

The road she was following was divided from the river by some level water meadows and she did not feel certain whether the village itself lay on the right or the left of the river mouth. Miss Doorm had spoken of a bridge, but among the roofs and trees which she made out in front of her, she was unable at present to see anything of this.

What she did see was a vast expanse of interminable

fen-land stretching away for miles and miles on every side of her, broken against the sky line, towards which she was advancing, by grey houses and grey poplars but otherwise losing itself in misty horizons which seemed infinite in their remoteness. On both sides of the little massed group of roofs and trees and what the girl made out as the masts of boats in the harbour, a long low bank of irregular sand-dunes kept the sea from her view, though the sound of the waves — and Nance fancied it came to her in a more friendly manner now she was closer to it — was insistent and clear.

Across the fens to her left she discerned what was evidently the village church but the building looked so desolate and isolated — alone there in the midst of the marshes — that she found it difficult to conceive the easily-daunted Linda as practising organ music in such a place. She wondered if the grey building she could just obscurely distinguish, leaning against the wall of the church, were the abode of Mr. Traherne. If so, she thought, he must indeed be a man of God to endure that solitude.

She had wandered into the wet grass by the road's edge and was amusing herself by picking a bunch of dandelions, the only flower at that moment in sight, when she saw a man's figure approaching her from the Rodmoor direction. At first she assumed it was Adrian, and made several quick steps to meet him, but when she recognised her mistake the disappointment made her so irritable that she threw her flowers away. Her irritation vanished, however, after a long survey of him, when the stranger actually drew near.

He was a middle-sized man wearing at the back of his head a dark soft hat and buttoned up, from throat to ankles, in a light-coloured heavy overcoat. His face, plump, smooth, and delicately oval, possessed a winning freshness of tint and outline which was further enhanced by the challenging friendliness of his whimsical smile and the softness of his hazel eyes. What could be seen of his mouth — for he wore a heavy moustache — was sensitive and sensuous, but something about the way he walked — a kind of humorous roll, Nance mentally defined it, of his sturdy figure — gave an impression that this body, so carefully over-coated against the cold, was one whose heart was large, mellow and warm. It was not till after a minute or two, not in fact till he had wavered and hovered at her side like an entomologist over a newly discovered butterfly, that the girl got upon the track of other interesting peculiarities.

His nose, she found, for instance, was the most striking feature of his face, being extremely long and pointed like the nose of a rodent, and with large quivering nostrils slightly reddened, it happened just then, by the impact of the wind, and tilted forward as the man veered about as though to snuff up the very perfume and essence of the fortunate occasion.

From the extreme tip of this interesting feature hung a pearly drop of rheum.

What — next to the man's nose — struck the girl's fancy and indeed so disarmed her dignity that even his entomological hoverings were forgiven, was the straight lock of black-brown hair which falling across his forehead gave him a deliciously ruffled and tumbled look, as if he had recently been engaged in a rural game of " blind man's buff." The forehead itself, or what could be seen of it, was weighty and thoughtful; the forehead of a scholar or a philosopher.

Nance had never in all her life been treated by a stranger quite in the way this worthy man treated her, for not only did he return upon his steps immediately after he had passed her, but he permitted his eyes, both in passing and repassing, to search her smilingly up and down from her boots to the top of her head, precisely as if he were a connoisseur in a gallery observing the " values " of a famous picture.

And yet, for she was not by any means oblivious to such distinctions, the girl was unable to feel even for one second that this surprising admirer was anything but a gentleman — a gentleman, however, with very singular manners. That she certainly did feel. And yet, she liked him, liked him before he uttered a word, liked him with that swift, irrational, magnetic attraction which, with women even more than with men, is the important thing.

Passing her for the third time he suddenly darted into the grass, and with a movement so comically impetuous that though she gave a start she could not feel angry, picked up her discarded flowers and gravely presented them to her, saying as he did so, " Perhaps you'll be annoyed at leaving these behind — or do you wish them at the devil? "

Nance took them from him and smiled frankly into his face.

" I suppose I oughtn't to have picked them," she said. " People don't like dandelions brought into houses."

" What an Attic chin you have! " was the stranger's next remark. There was such an absence in his tone of all rakish or conventional gallantry that the girl still felt she could not repulse him.

"You are staying here — in Rodmoor?" he went on.

Nance explained that she had come to live with Miss Doorm.

"Ah!" The stranger looked at her curiously, smiling with exquisite sweetness. "You have been here before," he said. "You came in a coach, pulled by six black horses. You know every sort of reed and every kind of moss in all the fens. You know all the shells on the shore and all the seaweed in the sea."

Nance was less puzzled than might be supposed by this fantastic address, as she had the advantage of interpreting it in the light of the humorous and reassuring smile which accompanied its utterance.

She brought him back to reality by a direct question. "Can you tell me where Mr. Stork lives, please? I've a friend staying with him and I want to know which way a person would naturally take coming from there to us. I had rather hoped," she hesitated a little, "to have met my friend already. But perhaps Mr. Stork is a late riser."

The stranger, who had been looking very intently at the opposite hedge while she asked her question, suddenly darted towards it. The queer way in which he ran with his arms swinging loosely from his shoulders, and his body bent a little forward, struck Nance as peculiarly fascinating. When he reached the hedge he hovered momentarily in front of it and then pounced at something. "Missed!" he cried in a peevish voice. "Damn the little scoundrel! A shrew-mouse! That's what it was! A shrew mouse!"

He came hurrying back as fast as he went, almost as if Nance herself had been some kind of furred or feathered animal that might disappear if it were not held fast.

"I beg your pardon, Madam," he said, breathlessly, "but you don't often see those so near the town. Hullo!" This last exclamation was caused by the appearance, not many paces from them, of Adrian Sorio himself who emerged from a gap in the hedge, hatless and excited. "I was on the towpath," he gasped, "and I caught sight of you. I was afraid you'd have started. Baltazar made me go with him to the station." He paused and stared at Nance's companion.

The latter looked so extremely uncomfortable that the girl hastened to come to his rescue.

"This gentleman was just going to show me the way," she said, "to your friend's house. Look, Adrian! Aren't these lovely?"

She held out the dandelions towards him, but he disregarded them.

"Well," he remarked rather brusquely, "now I've found you, I fancy we'd better go back the way we came. I'm longing to see how Linda feels. I want to take her down to the sea this afternoon. Shall we do that? Or perhaps you can't both leave Miss Doorm at the same time?"

He stared at the stranger as if bidding him clear off. But the admirer of shrew-mice had recovered his equanimity. "I know Mr. Stork well," he remarked to Sorio. "He and I are quite old friends. I was just asking this lady if she had ever been in the fens before, but I gather this is her first visit."

Adrian had by this time begun to look so morose that Nance broke in hurriedly.

"We must introduce ourselves," she said. "My

name is Miss Herrick. This is Mr. Adrian Sorio."
She paused and waited. A long shrill cry followed by a
most melancholy wail which gradually died away in the
distance, came to them over the marshes.

" A curlew," remarked the intruder. " Beautiful
and curious — and with very interesting mating habits.
They are rare, too."

" Come along, Nance," Sorio burst out. But the girl
turned to her new acquaintance and extended her hand.

" You haven't told us *your* name yet," she said. " I
hope we shall meet again."

The stranger gave her a look which, for caressing
softness, could only be compared to a virtuoso's finger
laid upon an incomparable piece of Egyptian pottery.

" Certainly we shall meet," he murmured. " Of
course, most certainly. I know every one here. My
name is Raughty — Doctor Fingal Raughty. I was
with old Doorm when he died. A noble head, though
rather malformed behind the ears. He had a peculiar
smell too —not unpleasant — rather musky in fact.
They called him Badger in the village. He could drink
more gin at a sitting than any man I have ever seen.
He resembled the portraits of Descartes. Good-bye,
Miss — Nance ! "

As soon as the lovers were alone Sorio's rage broke
forth.

" What a man ! " he cried. " Who gave him leave
to talk like that of Mr. Doorm? How did he know
you weren't related to him? And what surpassing
coolness to call you by your Christian name ! Confound him — he's gone the way we wanted to go. I
believe he knew that. Look! He's fooling about in
the ditch, waiting for us to overtake him ! "

Nance could not help laughing a little at this. "Not at all, my dear. He's looking for shrew-mice."

"What?" rejoined the other crossly. "On the public road? He's mad. Come, we must get round him somehow. Let's go through here and hit the tow path."

They had no more interruptions as they strolled slowly back along the river's bank. Nance was perplexed, however, by Adrian's temper. He seemed irritable and brusque. She had never known him in such a mood, and a dim, obscure apprehension to which she could assign no adequate cause, began to invade her heart.

They had both become so silent, and the girl's nerves had been so set on edge by his unusual attitude towards her, that she gave a quite perceptible start when he suddenly pointed across the stream to a clump of oak trees, the only ones, he told her, to be found in the neighbourhood.

"There's something behind them," she remarked, "a house of some kind. I shouldn't like to live out in that place. How they must hear the wind! It must howl and moan sometimes — mustn't it?" She smiled at him and shivered.

"I think I miss London Bridge Road a little, and — Kensington Park. Don't you, too, Adrian?"

"Yes, there's a house behind them," Sorio repeated, disregarding her last words and staring fixedly at the oak trees. "There's a house behind them."

His manner was so queer that the girl looked at him with serious alarm.

"What's the matter with you, Adrian?" she said. "I've never known you like this —"

"It's where the Renshaws live," her lover continued. "They have a kind of park. Its wall runs close to the village. Some of the trees are very old. I walked there this morning before breakfast. Baltazar advised me to."

Nance looked at him still more nervously. Then she gave a little forced laugh. "That is why you were so late in coming to see me, I suppose! Well, you say the Renshaws live there. May one ask who the Renshaws are?"

He took the girl's arm in his own and dragged her forward at a rapid pace. She remarked that it was not until some wide-spreading willows on the further side of the river concealed the clump of oaks that he replied to her question.

"Baltazar told me everything about them. He ought to know, for he's one of them himself. Yes, he's one of them. He's the son of old Herman, Brand's father; not legitimate, of course, and Brand isn't always kind to him. But he's one of them."

He stopped abruptly on this last word and Nance caught him throwing a furtive glance across the stream.

"Who are they, Adrian? Who are they?" repeated the girl.

"I'll tell you," he cried, with strange irritation. "I'll tell you everything! When *haven't* I told you everything? They are brewers. That isn't very romantic, is it? And I suppose you might call them landowners, too. They've lived here forever, it seems, and in the same house."

He burst into an uneasy laugh.

"In the same house for centuries and centuries! The churchyard is full of them. It's only lately they've taken to be brewers — I suppose the land don't pay for their vices."

And again he laughed in the same jarring and ungenial way.

"Brand employs Baltazar — just as if he wasn't his brother at all — in the office at Mundham. You remember Mundham? We came through it in the train. It's over there," he waved his hand in front of him, "about seven miles off. It's a horrid place — all slums and canals. That's where they make their beer. Their beer!" He laughed again.

"You haven't yet told me who they are — I mean who else there is," observed Nance while, for some reason or other, her heart began to beat tumultuously.

"Haven't I said I'd tell you everything?" Sorio flung out. "I'll tell you more than you bargain for, if you tease me. Oh, confound it! There's Rachel and Linda! Look now, do they appear as if they were happy?"

Favoured by the wind which blew seawards, the lovers had been permitted to approach quite close to their friends without any betrayal of their presence.

Linda was seated on the river bank, her head in her hands, while Miss Doorm, like a black-robed priestess of some ancient ritual, leant against the trunk of a leafless pollard.

"They were perfectly happy when I left them," whispered Nance, but she was conscious as she spoke of a cold, miserable misgiving in her inmost spirit. Like a flash her mind reverted to the lilac bushes of the London garden, and a sick loneliness seized her.

"Linda!" she cried, with a quiver of remorse in her voice. The young girl leapt hurriedly to her feet, and

Miss Doorm removed her hand from the tree. A quick look passed between the sisters, but Nance understood nothing of what Linda's expression conveyed. They moved on together, Adrian with Linda and Nance with Rachel.

" What do they call this river? " Nance enquired of her companion, as soon as she felt reassured by the sound of the girl's laugh.

" The Loon, my dear," replied Miss Doorm. " They call it the Loon. It runs through Mundham and then through the fens. It forms the harbour at Rodmoor."

Nance sat silent. In the depths of her heart she made a resolution. She would find some work to do here in Rodmoor. It was intolerable to be dependent on any one. Yes, she would find work, and, if need be, take Linda to live with her.

She felt now, though she would have found it hard to explain the obscure reason for it, more reluctant than ever to return to London. Every pulse of her body vibrated with a strange excitement. A reckless fighting spirit surged up within her. Not easily, not quickly, should her hold on the man she loved be loosed! But she felt danger on the horizon — nearer than the horizon. She felt it in her bones.

They had now reached the foot of Rachel's garden and there was a general pause in order that Adrian might do justice to the heavy architecture of Dyke House, as it was called — that house which the Badger — to follow Doctor Raughty's tale — had taken into his " noble " but " malformed " head to leave to his solitary descendant.

As they passed in one by one through the little dilapidated gate, Nance had a sudden inspiration. She seized her lover by the wrist. "Adrian," she whispered, "has there been anything — any one — to remind you — of what — you saw — that morning?"

She could not but believe that he had heard her and caught her meaning, yet it was hard to assume it, for his tone was calm and natural as he answered her, apparently quite misunderstanding her words:

"The sea, you mean? Yes, I've heard it all night and all day. We'll go down there this afternoon, and Linda with us." He raised his voice. "You'll come to the sea, Linda; eh, child? To the Rodmoor sea?"

The words died away over the river and across the fens. The others had already entered the house, but a laughing white face at one of the windows and the tapping of girlish hands on the closed pane seemed to indicate acquiescence in what he suggested.

III

SEA-DRIFT

THE wind had dropped but no gleam of sunshine interrupted the monotonous stretch of grey sky, grey dunes and grey sea, as the sisters with their two companions strolled slowly in the late afternoon along the Rodmoor sands.

Linda was a little pale and silent, and Nance fancied she discerned now and again, in the glances Miss Doorm threw upon her, a certain sinister exultation, but she was prevented from watching either of them very closely by reason of the extraordinary excitement which the occasion seemed to arouse in Sorio. He kept shouting bits of poetry, some of which Nance caught the drift of, while others — they might have been Latin or Greek, for all she knew — conveyed nothing to her but a vague feeling of insecurity. He was like an excited magician uttering incantations and invoking strange gods.

The sea was neither rough nor calm. Wisps of tossed-up foam appeared and disappeared at far distant points in its vast expanse, and every now and then the sombre horizon was broken in its level line by the emergence of a wave larger and darker than the rest.

Flocks of gulls disturbed by their approach rose, wheeling and screaming, from their feeding-grounds on the stranded seaweed and flapped away over the water.

The four friends advanced along the hard sand, close to the changing line of the tide's retreat, and from the blackened windrow there, of broken shells and anonymous sea refuse they stopped, each one of them, at different moments, to pick up some particular object which attracted or surprised them. It was Nance who was the first to become aware that they were not the only frequenters of that solitude. She called Adrian's attention to two figures moving along the edge of the sand-dunes and apparently, from the speed with which they advanced, anxious to reach a protruding headland and disappear from observation.

Adrian stopped and surveyed the figures long and intently. Then to her immense surprise, and it must be confessed a little to her consternation, he started off at a run in pursuit of them. His long, lean, hatless figure assumed so emphatic and strange an appearance as he crossed the intervening sands that Linda burst into peals of laughter.

" I wish they'd run away from him," she cried. " We should see a race! Who are they? Does he know them? "

Nance made no reply, but Miss Doorm, who had been watching the incident with sardonic interest, muttered under her breath, " It's begun, has it? Soon enough, in all conscience! "

Nance turned sharply upon her. " What do you mean, Rachel? Does Adrian know them? Do *you* know who they are? "

No answer was vouchsafed to this, nor indeed was one necessary, for the mystery, whatever it was, was on the point of resolving itself. Adrian had overtaken the objects of his pursuit and was bringing them back with him, one on either hand. Nance was not long in making out the general characteristics of the strangers.

They were both women, one elderly, the other quite young, and from what she could see of their appearance and dress, they were clearly ladies. It was not, however, till they came within speaking distance that the girl's heart began to beat an unmistakable danger-signal. This happened directly she obtained a definite view of the younger of Adrian's companions. Before any greeting could be given Rachel had whispered abruptly into her ear, " They're the Renshaws — I haven't seen them since Philippa was a child, but they're the Renshaws. He must have met them this morning. Look out for yourself, dearie."

Nance only vaguely heard her. Every fibre of attention in her body and soul was fixed upon that slender equivocal figure by Adrian's side.

The introduction which followed was of a sufficiently curious character. Between Nance and the young woman designated by Rachel as Philippa there was an exchange of glances when their fingers touched like the crossing of two naked blades. Mrs. Renshaw retained Linda's hand in her own longer than convention required, and Linda herself seemed to cling to the brown-eyed, grey-haired lady with a movement of childish confidence. Nance was calm enough, for all the beating of her heart, to remark as an interesting fact that her rival's mother, though oppressively timid and retiring in her manner towards them all, seemed to exercise a quelling and restraining influence upon Rachel Doorm, who began at once speaking to her with unusual deference and respect. The whole party, after some desultory conversation, began to drift away from the sea towards the town and Nance found herself in spite of some furtive efforts to the contrary, wedged closely in between Mrs. Renshaw and Rachel — with Linda walking in front of them — as they followed the narrow uneven path between the sand-dunes and the heavy sand of the upper shore.

Every now and then Mrs. Renshaw would bend down and call their attention to some little sea plant, telling them its name in slow sweet tones, as if repeating some liturgical formula, and indicating into what precise colour its pale glaucous buds would unsheathe as the weather grew warm.

On these occasions Nance quickly turned her head; but do what she could, she could only grow helplessly conscious that Adrian and his companion were slipping further and further behind.

Once, as the tender-voiced lady touched lightly, with the tips of her ungloved fingers, a cluster of insignificant leaves and asked Nance if she knew the lesser rockrose the agitated girl found herself on the point of uttering a strangely irrelevant cry.

" *Rose au regard saphique*," her confused heart murmured, " *plus pâle que les lys, rose au regard saphique, offre-nous le parfum de ton illusoire virginité fleur hypocrite, fleur de silence.*"

They approached at last the entrance of the little harbour, and to Nance's ineffable relief Mrs. Renshaw paused and made them sit down on a fish-smelling bench, among coils of rope, and wait the appearance of the missing ones.

The tide was low and between great banks of mud the water rushed seaward in a narrow, swirling current. A heavy fishing smack with high tarred sides and red, unfurled. sails, was being steered down this channel by two men armed with enormous poles. Through the masts of several other boats, moored to iron rings in the wooden wharf, and between the slate roofs of some ram-shackle houses on the other side, they got a glimpse, looking westward across the fens, of a low, rusty-red streak of sombrely illuminated sky. This apparently was all the sunset Rodmoor was destined to know that evening and Nance, as she listened vaguely to Mrs. Ren-shaw's gentle voice describing to Linda the various "queer characters" among the harbour people, had a strange, bewildered sense of being carried far and far and far down a remorseless tide, with a heavy sky above her and interminable grey sands around her, and all the while something withheld, withdrawn, inexplicable in the power that bore her forward.

They came at last — Adrian and Philippa Renshaw, and Nance had, in one heart-rending moment, the piti-less suspicion that the battle was lost already and that this fragile thing with the great ambiguous eyes and the reserved manner, this thing whose slender form and tight-braided, dusky hair might have belonged to a masquerading boy, had snatched from her already what could never for all the years of her life be won again!

As they left the harbour and entered the main village street, Adrian made one or two deliberate efforts to de-tach Nance from the rest. He pointed out little things to her in the homely shop-windows and seemed sur-prised and disappointed when she made no response to his overtures. She *could* not make any response. She could not bring herself so much as to look into his face. It was not from any capricious pride or mere feminine pique that she thus turned away but from a profound and lamentable numbness of every emotion. The wound seemed to have gone further even than she herself had

known. Her heart felt like a dead cold weight — like a
murdered, unborn child — beneath her breast, and out
of her lethargy and inertness, as in certain tragic
dreams, she could not move. Her limbs seemed formed
of lead, and her lips — at least as far as he was concerned — became those of a dumb animal.

A man, viewing the situation from outside, the slight-
ness and apparent triviality of the incident, would have
been astounded at the effect upon her of so insubstantial
a blow, but women move in a different world, a world
where the drifting of the tiniest straw is indicative of
crushing catastrophes, and to the instinct of the least
sensitive among women Nance's premonitions would have
been quite explicable.

It was at that moment that it was sharply borne in
upon her how slight her actual knowledge of her lover
was. Her absorption in him was devoted and complete
but in regard to the intricacies and complications of his
character she was as much in the dark to-day as when
they first met in London Bridge Road.

Strangely enough, in the paralysis of her feelings,
Nance was unconscious of any definite antagonism to
the cause of her distress. She found she could talk
quite naturally and spontaneously to Miss Renshaw
when chance threw them together as they emerged upon
the village green.

" Oh, I like those trees! " she cried, as the row of
ancient sycamores which gave the forlorn little square
its chief appeal first struck her attention.

The cottage of Baltazar Stork, it turned out, was
just behind these sycamores and next door to the building which, with its immense and faded signboard, offered the natives of Rodmoor their unique dissipation.

" The Admiral's Head!" Nance repeated, surveying
the sign and thinking to herself that it must have been
under that somewhat sordid roof that Miss Doorm's
parent had drunk himself to death.

" Don't look at it," she heard Mrs. Renshaw say,
" I feel ashamed every time I pass it."

Philippa gave Nance a quick and rather bitter smile.

" Mother is telling them that it is our beer which they
sell there. You know we are brewers, don't you?
Mother thinks it her duty to remind every one of that
fact. She gets a curious pleasure out of talking about
it. It's her morbid conscience. You'll find we're all
rather morbid here," she added, looking searchingly into
Nance's face.

" It's the sea. Our sea is not the same as other
seas. It eats into us."

" Why do you say just that — and in that tone —
to me?" Nance gravely enquired, answering the other's
gaze. " My father was a sailor. I love the salt-
water."

Philippa Renshaw shrugged her shoulders. " You
may love being *on* it. That's a different thing. It remains to be seen how you like being *near* it."

" I like it always, everywhere," repeated Nance obstinately, " and I'm afraid of nothing it can do to me!"

They overtook the others at this point and Mrs.
Renshaw turned rather querulously to her daughter.

" Don't talk to her about the sea, Philippa — I know
that's what you're doing."

The girl with the figure of a boy let her eyes meet
Adrian's and Nance felt the dead weight in her heart
grow more ice-cold than before, as she watched the effect of that look upon her lover.

It was Rachel who broke the tension. "It wasn't so very long ago," she said, "that Rodmoor was quite an inland place. There are houses now, they say, and churches under the water. And it swallows up the land all the time, inch by inch. The sand-dunes are much nearer the town, I am sure of that, and the mouth of the river, too, than when I lived here in old days."

Mrs. Renshaw looked by no means pleased at this speech.

"Well," she said, "we must be getting home for dinner. Shall we walk through the park, Philippa? It's the nicest way — if the grass isn't too wet."

In the general chorus of adieus that followed, Nance was not surprised when Sorio bade good-night to her as well as to the others. He professed to be going to the station to meet the Mundham train.

"Baltazar will have a lot of things to carry," he said, "and I must be at hand to help."

Mrs. Renshaw pressed Linda's hand very tenderly as they parted and a cynical observer might have been pardoned for suspecting that under the suppressed sigh with which she took Philippa's arm there lurked a wish that it had been the more docile and less difficult child that fate had given her for a daughter.

Linda, at any rate, proved to be full of enthusiastic and excited praise for the sad-voiced lady, as the sisters went off with Rachel. She chattered, indeed, so incessantly about her that Nance, whose nerves were in no tolerant state, broke out at last into a quite savage protest.

"She's the sort of person," she threw in, "who's always sentimental about young girls. Wait till you find her with some one younger than you are, and you'll soon see! Am I not right, Rachel?"

"She's not right at all, is she?" interposed the other. Miss Doorm looked at them gravely.

"I don't think either of you understand Mrs. Renshaw. Indeed there aren't many who do. She's had troubles such as you may both pray to God you'll never know. That wisp of a girl will be the cause of others before long."

She glanced at Nance significantly.

"Hold tight to your Adrian, my love. Hold tight to him, my dearie!"

Thus, as they emerged upon the tow path spoke Rachel Doorm.

Meanwhile, from his watch above the Inn, the nameless Admiral saw the shadows of night settle down upon his sycamores. His faded countenance, with its defiant bravado, stared insolently at what he could catch between trees and houses, of the darkening harbour and if Rodmoor had been a ship instead of a village, and he a figurehead instead of a sign-board, he could not have confronted the unknown and all that the unknown might bring more indifferently, more casually, more contemptuously.

IV

OAKGUARD

THE night of her first meeting with Adrian Sorio, found the daughter of the house of Renshaw restless and wakeful. She listened to the hall clock striking the hour of twelve with an intentness that would have suggested to any one observing her that she had only been waiting for that precise moment to plunge into some nocturnal enterprise fraught with both sweetness and peril.

The night was chilly, the sky starless and overcast. The heavy curtains were drawn but the window, wide-open behind them, let in a breath of rain-scented air which stirred the flames of the two silver candles on the dressing table and fluttered the thin skirt of the girl's night-dress as she sat, tense and expectant, over the red coals of a dying fire.

A tall gilt-framed mirror of antique design stood on the left of the fireplace.

As the last stroke of midnight sounded, the girl leapt to her feet and swiftly divesting herself of her only garment, stood straight and erect, her hands clasped behind her head, before this mirror. The firelight cast a red glow over her long bare limbs and the flickering candle flames threw wavering shadows across her lifted arms and slender neck. Her hair remained tightly braided round her head and this, added to the boyish outlines of her body, gave her the appearance of one of those androgynous forms of later Greek art whose am-

49

biguous loveliness wins us still, even in the cold marble,
with so touching an appeal. Her smooth forehead and
small delicately moulded face showed phantom-like in
the mirror. Her scarlet lips quivered as she gazed at
herself, quivered into that enigmatic smile challenging
and inscrutable which seems, more than any other human expression, to have haunted the imagination of certain great artists of the past.

Permitted for a brief moment to catch a glimpse of
that white figure, an intruder, if possessed of the smallest degree of poetic fancy, would have been tempted to
dream that the dust of the centuries had indeed been
quickened and some delicate evocation of perverse pagan
desire restored to breath and consciousness.

Such a dream would not, perhaps, have survived a
glance at the girl's face. With distended pupils and
irises so large that they might have been under the influence of some exciting drug, her eyes had that particular look, sorrowful and heavy with mystery, which
one feels *could not have been in the world* before the
death of Christ.

With her epicene figure, she resembled some girl-
priestess of Artemis invoking a mocking image of her
own defiant sexlessness. With her sorrowful inhuman
eyes she suggested some strange elf-creature, born of
mediæval magic.

Turning away from the mirror, Philippa Renshaw
blew out the candles and flung open the curtains.
Standing thus for a moment in the presence of the
vague starless night full of chilly earth odours, she
drew several long deep breaths and seemed to inhale the
very essence of the darkness as if it had been the kiss of
some elemental lover. Then she shivered a little, closed

the window and began hurriedly to dress herself by the
fire-light. Bare-headed, but with a dark cloak reaching to her feet, she softly left her room and crept silently down the staircase. One by one she drew the
heavy bolts of the hall door and turned the ponderous
key.

Letting herself out into the night air with the movements of one not unaccustomed to such escapades, she
hurried down the stone pathway, passed through the
iron entrance gates, and emerged into the park. Catching up the skirt of her cloak, and drawing it tightly
round her so that it should not impede her steps, she
plunged into the wet grass and directed her course towards the thickest group of oak trees. Between the
immense trunks and mossy roots of these sea-deformed
and wind-stunted children of the centuries she groped
her way, her feet stumbling over fallen branches and
her face whipped by the young wet leaves.

A mad desire seemed to possess her, to throw off
every vestige and token of her human imprisonment and
to pass forth free and unfettered into the embrace of
the primeval powers. One would have thought, to have
watched her as she flung herself, at last, on her face
under one of the oldest of the trees and liberating her
arms from her cloak, stretched them round its trunk,
that she was some worshipper of a banished divinity invoking her god while her persecutors slept, and passionately calling upon him to return to his forsaken shrine.
Releasing her fierce clasp upon the rough bark of the
tree, not however before it had bruised her flesh, the
girl dug her nails into the soft damp leaf-mould and
rubbed her forehead against the wet moss. She shuddered as she lay like this, and as she shuddered she

clutched yet more tightly, as if in a kind of ecstasy, the roots of grass and the rubble of earth into which her fingers dug.

Meanwhile, within the house, another little drama unrolled itself. In the old-fashioned library collected by many generations of Renshaws, where the noble Rabelaisian taste of the eighteenth century jostled unceremoniously with the attenuated banalities of a later epoch, there sat, at the very moment when the girl descended the stairs, a tall powerfully built man in evening dress.

Brand Renshaw was a figure of striking and formidable appearance. Immensely muscular and very tall, he carried upon his massive shoulders a head of so strange a shape that had he been a mediæval chieftain he would doubtless have gone down to posterity as Brand Hatchet-pate, or Brand Hammer-skull. His head receded from a forehead narrow and high, and rose at the back into a dome-like protrusion which, in spite of the closely-clipt, reddish hair that covered it, suggested, in a manner that was almost sinister, the actual bony substructure of the cranium beneath.

The fire was out. The candles on the table were guttering and flickering with little spitting noises as their wicks sank and the cold hearth in front of him was littered with the ashes of innumerable cigarettes. He was neither reading nor smoking them. He sat with his hands on the arms of his chair, staring into vacancy.

Brand Renshaw's eyes were like the eyes of a morose animal, an animal endowed perhaps with intellectual powers denied to the human race, but still an animal, and when he fixed his gaze in his concentrated manner upon the unknown objects of his thought there was a weight of heavily focussed intensity in his stare that was unpleasantly threatening.

He was staring in this way at the empty grate when, in the dead silence of the house, he caught the sound of a furtive step in the hall without, and immediately afterwards the slight rasping noise of bolts carefully shot back.

In a flash he leapt to his feet and extinguished the guttering candles. Quietly and on tip-toe he moved to the door and soundlessly turning the handle peered into the hall. He was just in time to see the heavy front door closed. Without the least token of haste or surprise he slipped on an overcoat, took his hat and stick and went forth in pursuit of the escaped one.

At first he saw only the darkness and heard no sound but the angry flutterings of some bird in the high trees, and — a long way off, perhaps even beyond the park — the frightened squeal of a hunted rabbit. But by the time he got to the gate, taking care to walk on the flower-beds rather than on the stone pathway, he could make out the figure of the girl no great way in front of him. She ran on, so straight and so blindly, towards the oak trees that he was able without difficulty to follow her even though, every now and then, her retreating figure was absorbed and swallowed up by the darkness.

When at last he came up to her side as she lay stretched out at the foot of the tree, he made no immediate attempt to betray his presence. With his arms folded he stood regarding her, a figure as silent and inhuman as herself, and over them both the vague im-

mensities and shadowy obscurities of the huge earth-
scented night hung lowering and tremendous, like powers that held their breath, waiting, watching.

At intervals an attenuated gust of wind, coming from
far away across the marshes, moved the dead leaves
upon the ground and made them dance a little death
dance. This it did without even stirring the young
living shoots on the boughs above them.

The darkness seemed to rise and fall about the two
figures, to advance, to recede, to dilate, to diminish, in
waves of alternate opacity and tenuity. In its indraw-
ings and outbreathings, in the ebb and flow of its fluctuating presence, it seemed to beat — at least that is how
Brand Renshaw felt it — like the pulse of an immense
heart charged with unutterable mysteries.

This illusion, if it were an illusion, may have been
due to nothing more recondite than the fact that, in the
silence of the heavy night, the sound of the tide on the
Rodmoor sands was the background of everything.

It was not till the girl rose from the ground that she
saw him standing there, a shadow among the shadows.
She uttered a low cry and made a movement as if to
rush away, but he stepped quickly forward and caught
her in his arms. Tightly and almost savagely he held
her, pressing her lithe body against his own and caressing it with little, deep-voiced mutterings as if he were
soothing a desperate child. She submitted passively
to his endearments and then, with a sound that was
something between a moan and a laugh, she whispered
brokenly into his ear, " Let me go, Brand, I was silly to
come out. I couldn't help it. I won't do it again. I
won't, I swear."

" No, I think you won't ! " the man muttered, keeping his arm securely round her waist and striding swiftly towards the house. "No, I think you won't!"

He paused when they reached the entrance into the garden and, taking her by the wrists, pressed her fiercely against one of the stone pillars upon which the gate hung.

"I know what it is," he whispered. "You can't deceive me. You've been with those people from London. You've been with that friend of Baltazar's. That's the cause of all this, isn't it? You've been with that damned fool — that idiotic, good-for-nothing down at the village. Haven't you been with him? Haven't you?"

The arms with which he pressed her hands against her breast trembled with anger as he said these words.

"Baltazar told me," he went on, "only this morning — down at Mundham — everything about these people. They're of no interest, none, not the least. They're just like every one else. That fellow's half-foreign, that's all. An American half-breed, of some mongrel sort or other, that's all there is to be said of him! So if you've been letting any mad fancies get into your head about Mr. Sorio, the sooner you get rid of them the better. He's not for you. Do you hear? He's — not — for — you!" These last words were accompanied by so savage a tightening of the hands that held her that the girl was compelled to bite her lip to stop herself from crying.

"You hurt me," she said calmly. "Let me go, Brand." The self-contained tone of her voice seemed to quiet him and he released her. She raised one of her wrists to her mouth and softly caressed it with her lips.

"You'll be interested, yourself, in these people before very long," she murmured, flashing a mocking look

at him over her bare arm. "The second girl is very
young and very pretty. She confided in me that she
was extremely afraid of the sea. She appealed to
mother's protective instincts at once. I've no doubt
she'll appeal to your — protective instincts! So don't
be too quick in your condemnation."

"Damn you!" muttered her brother, pushing the gate
open. "Come! Get in with you! You talk to me as
if I were a professional rake. I take no interest — not
the slightest — in your young innocents with their engaging terrors. To bed! To bed! To bed!"

He pushed her before him along the path, but Philippa knew well that the hand on her shoulder was
lighter and less angry than the one that had held her a
moment ago, and as she ascended the steps of Oakguard — the name borne by the Renshaw house since
the days of the Conqueror — there flickered over her
shadowy face the same equivocal smile of dubious meaning that had looked out at its owner, not so long since,
from the mirror in her room.

When the dawn finally crept up, pallid and cold out
of the North Sea and lifted, with a sort of mechanical
weariness, the weight of the shadows, it was neither
Brand nor Philippa who was awake.

Roused, as always, by the slightest approach of an
unusual sound, the mother of that strange pair had lain
in her bed listening ever since her daughter's first emerging from the house.

Once she had risen, and had stood for a moment at
the window, her loose grey hair mixed with the folds of
an old, faded, dusky-coloured shawl. That, however,
was when both of her children were away in the middle
of the park and absolute silence prevailed. With this

single exception she had remained listening, always silently listening, lying on her back and with an expression of tragic and harassed expectation in her great, hollow, brown eyes. She might have been taken, lying there alone in the big four-posted bed, surrounded by an immense litter of stored-up curios and mementoes, for a symbolic image of all that is condemned, as this mortal world goes round, to watch and wait and invoke the gods and cling fast to such pathetic relics and memorials as time consents to leave of the days that it has annihilated.

Slowly the dawn came up upon the trees and roofs of Oakguard. With a wan grey light it filled the pallid squares of the windows. With a livid grey light it made definite and ghastly every hollow and every wrinkle in that patient watcher's face.

Travelling far up in the sky, a long line of marsh-fowl with outstretched necks sought the remoter solitudes of the fens. In the river marshes the sedge-birds uttered their harsh twitterings while, gathered in flocks above the sand-dunes, the sea-gulls screamed to the inflowing tide their hunger for its drifted refuse.

Wearily, at last, Helen Renshaw closed her eyes and it was the first streak of sunshine that Rodmoor had known for many days which, several hours later, kissed her white forehead — and the grey hairs that lay disordered across it — softly, gently, tenderly, as it might have kissed the forehead of the dead.

V

A SYMPOSIUM

ADRIAN SORIO sat opposite his friend over a warm brightly burning fire.

Baltazar Stork was a slight frail man of so delicate and dainty an appearance that many people were betrayed into behaving towards him as gently and considerately as if he had been a girl. This, though a compliment to his fragility, was bad policy in those who practised it, for Baltazar was an egoist of inflexible temper and under his velvet glove carried a hand of steel.

The room in which the two friends conversed was furnished in exquisite and characteristic taste. Old prints, few in number and rare in quality, adorned its walls. Precious pieces of china, invaluable statuettes in pottery and metal, stood charmingly arranged, with due space round each, in every corner. On either side of the mantelpiece was a Meissen-ware figure of engaging aspect and Watteau-like design, while in the centre, in the place where a clock is usually to be found, was a piece of statuary of ravishing delicacy and grace representing the escape of Syrinx from the hands of Pan.

The most remarkable picture in the room, attracting the attention at once of all who entered, was a dark, richly coloured, oval-shaped portrait — a portrait of a young man in a Venetian cloak, with a broad, smooth forehead, heavy-lidded penetrating eyes, and pouting disdainful mouth. This picture, said to have been painted under the influence of Giorgione by that incomparable artist's best loved friend, passed for a portrait of Eugenio Flambard, the favourite secretary of the Republic's most famous ambassador during his residence at the Papal Court.

The majority of these treasures had been picked up by Baltazar during certain prolonged holidays in various parts of the Continent. This, however, was several years ago before the collapse of the investment, or whatever it was, which he inherited from Herman Renshaw.

Since that time he had been more or less dependent upon Brand, a dependence which nothing but his happy relations with Brand's mother and sister and his unfailing urbanity could have made tolerable.

" Adrian, you old villain, why didn't you tell me you'd seen Philippa. Brand informed me yesterday that you've seen her twice. This isn't the kind of thing that pleases me at all. I don't approve of these clandestine meetings. Do you hear me, you old reprobate? You don't think it's very nice, do you, for me to learn by accident — by a sort of wretched accident — of an event like this? If you *must* be at these little games you might at least. be open about them. Besides, I have a brotherly interest in Philippa. I don't want to have her innocence corrupted by an old satyr like you."

Sorio contented himself by murmuring the word " Rats."

" It's all very well for you to cry ' Rats! ' in that tone," went on the other. " The truth is, this affair is going to become serious. You don't suppose for a moment, do you, that your Nance is going to lie down, as they say, and let my extraordinary sister walk over her?"

Adrian got up from his seat and began pacing up and down the little room.

"It's absurd," he muttered, "it's all absurd. I feel as if the whole thing were a kind of devilish dream. Yes, the whole thing! It's all because I've got nothing to do but walk up and down these damned sands!"

Baltazar watched him with a serene smile, his soft chin supported by his feminine fingers and his fair, curly head tilted a little on one side.

"But you know, mon enfant," he threw in with a teasing caress in his voice, "you know very well you're the last person to talk of work. It was work that did for you in America. You don't want to start *that* over again, do you?"

Adrian stood still and glared at him.

"Do you think I'm going to let *that* — as you call it — finish me forever? My life's only begun. In London it was different. By God! I wish I'd stayed in London! Nance feels just the same. I know she does. She'll have to get something, too, or we shall both go mad. It's this cursed sea of yours! I've a good mind to marry her, out of hand, and clear off. We'd find something — somewhere — anywhere — to keep body and soul together."

"Why did you come to us at all, my dear, if you find us so dreadful?" laughed Baltazar, bending down to tie his shoe-string and pull up more tightly one of his silk socks.

Adrian made no answer but continued his ferocious pacing of the room.

"You'll knock something over if you're not careful,"

protested his friend, shrugging his shoulders. "You're the most troublesome fellow. You accept a person's offer and make no end of a fuss over it, and then a couple of weeks later you roar like a bull and send us all to the devil. What's the matter with us? What's the matter with the place? Why can't you and your precious Nance behave like ordinary people and make love to one another and be happy? She's got all her time to herself and you've got all your time to yourself. Why can't you enjoy yourselves and collect seaweed or starfish or something?"

Adrian paused in his savage prowl for the second time.

"It's your confounded sea that's at the bottom of it," he shouted. "It gets on her nerves and it gets on mine. Little Linda was perfectly right to be scared of it."

"I fancied," drawled the other, selecting a cigarette from an enamelled box and turning up the lamp, "you found little Linda's fears rather engaging than otherwise.

"It works upon us," Sorio went on, heedless of the interruption, "it works upon us in some damnable kind of way! Nance says she hears ·it in her sleep. I'm sure *I* do. I hear it without a moment's cessation. Listen to the thing now — *shish, shish, shish, shish!* Why can't it make some other noise? Why can't it stop altogether? It makes me long for the whole damned farce to end. It annoys me, Tassar, it annoys me!"

"Sorry you find the elements so trying, Adriano," replied the other languidly, "but I really don't know what I can do to help you — I can only advise you to

keep out of Philippa's way. She's an element more
troublesome than any of them."

"Tassar!" shouted the enraged man in a burst of
fury, "if you don't stop dragging Philippa in, I'll
murder you! What's Philippa to me? I *hate* her —
do you hear? I hate the very sound of her name!"

"Her name?" murmured Stork, meditatively, "her
name? Oh, I think you're quite wrong to hate that.
Her name suggests all sorts of interesting things.
Her name has quite a historic sound. It's mediæval in
colour and Greek in form.. It makes me think of Eurip-
ides."

"This whole damned Rodmoor of yours," moaned
Adrian, "gets too much for me. Where on earth else,
could a man find it so hard to collect his thoughts and
look at things as they are? There's something here
which works upon the mind, Tassar, something which
works upon the mind."

"What's working on *your* mind, my friend," laughed
Baltazar Stork, "is not anything so vague as dreams or
anything so simple as the sea. It's just the quite definite but somewhat complicated business of managing
two love affairs at the same time! I'm sorry for you,
little Adrian, I'm extremely sorry for you. It's a situation not unknown in the history of the world, in fact,
it might be called quite common. But I'm afraid that
doesn't make it, any pleasanter for you. However, it
can be dealt with, with a little skill, Adrian, with just a
little skill!"

The man accused in this teasing manner turned furiously round, an angry outburst of blind protest trembling on his tongue. At that moment there was a low
knock at the outer door. Baltazar jumped to his feet.

"That must be Raughty," he cried. "I begged him to come round to-night. I so longed for you to meet him." He hastened out and admitted the visitor with a cordial welcome. After a momentary pause and a good deal of shuffling — for Dr. Raughty was careful to wear not only an overcoat but also goloshes and even gaiters when the weather was inclement — the two men entered the room and Stork began an elaborate introduction.

"Dr. Fingal Raughty," he said, "Mr. Adrian —" but to his astonishment Sorio intervened, "The Doctor and I have already become quite well acquainted," he remarked, shaking the visitor vigorously by the hand. "I'm afraid I wasn't as polite as I ought to have been on that occasion," he went on, speaking in an unnaturally loud voice and with a forced laugh, "but the Doctor will forgive me. The Doctor I'm sure will make allowances."

Dr. Raughty gave him a quick glance, at once friendly and ironical, and then he turned to Stork. "Mother Lorman's dead," he remarked with a little sigh, "dead at last. She was ninety-seven and had thirty grandchildren. She gurgled in her throat at the last with a noise like a nightingale when its voice breaks in June. I prefer deaths of this kind to any other, but they're all pitiful."

"Nance tells me you were present at old Doorm's death, Doctor," said Adrian while their host moved off to the kitchen to secure glasses and refreshment.

The Doctor nodded. "I measured that fellow's skull," he remarked gravely. "It was asymmetrical and very curiously so. The interesting thing is that there exists in this part of the coast a definite tradition of malformed skulls. They recur in nearly all the old families. Brand Renshaw is a splendid example. *His* skull ought to be given to a museum. It is beautiful, quite beautiful, in the anterior lobes."

Baltazar returned carrying a tray. The eyes of Dr. Raughty gleamed with a mellow warmth. " Nutmeg," he remarked, approaching the tray and touching every object upon it lightly and reverently. " Nutmeg, lemon, hot water, gin — *and* brandy! It's an admirable choice and profoundly adapted to the occasion. May I put the hot water on the hob until we're ready for it? "

While Baltazar once more withdrew from the scene, Dr. Raughty remarked, gravely and irritably, to Sorio that it was a mistake to substitute brandy for rum. " He does it because he can't get the best rum, but it's a ridiculous thing to do. *Any* rum is better than no rum when it's a question of punch-making. Are you with me in this, Mr. Sorio? "

Adrian expressed such complete and emphatic agreement that for the moment the Doctor seemed almost embarrassed.

On Baltazar's return to the room, however, he hazarded another suggestion. " What about having the kettle itself brought in here? "

Stork looked at him without speaking and placed on the table a small plate of macaroons. The Doctor glanced whimsically at Sorio and, helping himself from the little plate, muttered in a low voice after he had nibbled the edge of a biscuit, " Yes, these seem perfectly up to par to-day."

The three men had scarcely settled themselves down

in their respective chairs around the fire than Adrian began speaking hurriedly and nervously.

" I have an extraordinary feeling," he said, " that this evening is full of fatal significance: I suppose it's nothing to either of you, but it seems to me as though this damned *shish, shish, shish, shish* of the sea were nearer and louder than usual. Doctor, you don't mind my talking freely to you? I like you, though I was rude to you the other day — but that's nothing — " he waved his hand, " that's what any fool might fall into who didn't know you. I feel I know you now. That word about the rum — forgive me, Tassar! — and the kettle — yes, particularly about the kettle — hit me to the heart. I love you, Doctor Raughty. I announce to you that my feeling at this moment amounts to love — yes, actually to love!

" But that's not what I wanted to say." He thrust his hands deep into his pockets, stretched his legs straight out, let his chin sink upon his chest and glared at them with sombre excitement. " I feel to-night," he went on, " as though some great event were portending. No, no! What am I saying? Not an event. Event isn't the word. Event's a silly expression, isn't it, Doctor,— isn't it — dear, noble-looking man? For you do look noble, you know, Doctor, as you drink that punch — though to say the truth your nose isn't quite straight as I see it from here, and there are funny blotches on your face. No, not there. *There!* Don't you see them, Tassar? Blotches — curious purply blotches."

While this outburst proceeded Mr. Stork fidgeted uneasily in his chair. Though sufficiently accustomed to

Sorio's eccentricities and well aware of his medical
friend's profound pathological interest in all rare
types, there was something so outrageous about this
particular tirade that it offended what was a very
dominant instinct in him, his sense, namely, of social
decency and good breeding. Possibly in a measure because of the " bar sinister " over his own origin, but
much more because of the nicety of his æsthetic taste,
anything approaching a social fiasco or *faux pas*
always annoyed him excessively. Fortunately, however, on this occasion nothing could have surpassed the
sweetness with which Adrian's wild phrases were received by the person addressed.

" One would think you'd drunk half the punch already, Sorio," Baltazar murmured at last. " What's
come over you to-night? I don't think I've ever known
you quite like this."

" Remind me to tell you something, Mr. Sorio, when
you've finished what you have to say," remarked Dr.
Raughty.

" Listen, you two! " Adrian began again, sitting
erect, his hands on the arms of his chair. " There's
a reason for this feeling of mine that there's something
fatal on the wind to-night. There's a reason for it."

" Tell us as near as you can," said Dr. Raughty,
" what exactly it is that you're talking about."

Adrian fixed upon him a gloomy, puzzled frown.

" Do you suppose," he said slowly, " that it's for
nothing that we three are together here in hearing of
that —"

Baltazar interrupted him. " Don't say ' shish, shish,
shish ' again, my dear. Your particular way of imitating the Great Deep gives me no pleasure."

"What I meant was," Sorio raised his voice, "it's a strange thing that we three should be sitting together now like this when two months ago I was in prison in New York."

Baltazar made a little deprecatory gesture, while the Doctor leaned forward with grave interest.

"But that's nothing," Sorio went on, "that's a trifle. Baltazar knows all about that. The thing I want you two to recognise is that something's on the wind,— that something's on the point of happening. Do you feel like that — or don't you?"

There was a long and rather oppressive silence, broken only by the continuous murmur which in every house in Rodmoor was the background of all conversation.

"What I was going to say a moment ago," remarked the Doctor at last, "was that in this place it's necessary to protect oneself from *that*." He jerked his thumb towards the window. "Our friend Tassar does it by the help of Flambard over there." He indicated the Venetian. "I do it by the help of my medicine-chest. Hamish Traherne does it by saying his prayers. What I should like to know is how *you*," he stretched a warning finger in the direction of Sorio, "propose to do it."

Baltazar at this point jumped up from his seat.

"Oh, shut up, Fingal," he cried peevishly. "You'll make Adrian unendurable. I'm perfectly sick of hearing references to this absurd salt-water. Other people have to live in coast towns besides ourselves. Why can't you let the thing take its proper position? Why can't you take it for granted? The whole subject gets on my nerves. It bores me, I tell you, it bores me to tears.

For Heaven's sake, let's talk of something else — of any damned thing. You both make me thoroughly wretched with your sea whispers. It's as bad as having to spend an evening at Oakguard alone with Aunt Helen and Philippa."

His peevishness had an instantaneous effect upon Sorio who pushed him affectionately back into his chair and handed him his glass. "So sorry, Tassar," he said. "I won't do it again. I *was* beginning to feel a little odd to-night. One can't go through the experience of cerebral dementia — doesn't that sound right, Doctor? — without some little trifling after-effects. Come, let's be sensible and talk of things that are really important. It's not an occasion to be missed, is it, Tassar, having the Doctor here and punch made with brandy instead of rum, on the table? What interests me so much just now," he placed himself in front of the fire-place and sighed heavily, "is what a person's to do who hasn't got a penny and is unfit for every sort of occupation. What do you advise, Doctor? And by the way, why have you eaten up all the macaroons while I was talking?"

This remark really did seem a little to embarrass the person indicated, but Sorio continued without waiting for a reply.

"Yes, I suppose you're right, Tassar. It's a mistake to be sensitive to the attraction of young girls. But it's difficult — isn't it, Doctor? — not to be. They're so maddeningly delicious, aren't they, when you come to think of it? It's something about the way their heads turn — the line from the throat, you know — and about the way they speak — something pathetic, something — what shall I call it? — helpless.

It quite disarms a person. It's more than pathetic, it's tragic."

The Doctor looked at him meditatively. "I think there's a poem of Goethe's which would bear that out," he remarked, "if I'm not mistaken it was written after he visited Sicily — yes, after that storm at sea, you remember, when the story of Christ's walking on the waves came into his mind."

Sorio wrinkled up his eyes and peered at the speaker with a sort of humorous malignity.

"Doctor," he said, "pardon my telling you, but you've still got some crumbs on your moustache."

"The one word," put in their host, while Dr. Raughty moved very hastily away from the table and surveyed himself with a whimsical puckering of all the lines in his face, at one of Stork's numerous mirrors, "the one word that I shall henceforth refuse to have pronounced in my house is the word ' sea.' I'm surprised to hear that Goethe — a man of classical taste — ever refers to such Gothic abominations."

"Ah!" cried Sorio, "the great Goethe! The sly old curmudgeon Goethe! He knew how to deal with these little velvet paws!"

Dr. Raughty, reseating himself, drummed absent-mindedly with his fingers upon the empty macaroon plate. Then with a soft and pensive sigh he produced his tobacco pouch, and filling his pipe, struck a match.

"Doctor," murmured Sorio, his rebellious lips curved into a sardonic smile and his eyes screwed up till they looked as sinister as those of his namesake, Hadrian, "why do you move your head backwards and forwards like that, when you light your pipe?"

"Don't answer him, Fingal," expostulated Baltazar,

" he's behaving badly now. He's ' showing off ' as they say of children."

" I'm not showing off," cried Sorio loudly, " I'm asking the Doctor a perfectly polite question. It's very interesting the way he lights his pipe. There's more in it than appears. There's a great deal in it. It's a secret of the Doctor's; probably a pantheistic one."

" What on earth do you mean by a ' pantheistic ' one? How, under Heaven, can the way Fingal holds a match be termed ' pantheistic '? " protested Stork irritably. " You're really going a little too far, Adriano mio."

" Not at all, not at all," argued Sorio, stretching out his long, lean arms and grasping the back of a chair. " The Doctor can deny it or not, as he pleases, but what I say is perfectly true. He gets a cosmic ecstasy from moving his head up and down like that. He feels as if he were the centre of the universe when he does it."

The Doctor looked sideways and then upon the ground. Sorio's rudeness evidently disconcerted him.

" I think," he said, rising from his chair and putting down his glass, " I must be going now. I've an early call to make to-morrow morning."

Baltazar cast a reproachful look at Adrian and rose too. They went into the hall together and the same shufflings and heavy breathings came to the ears of the listener as on Raughty's arrival. The Doctor was putting on his goloshes and gaiters.

Adrian went out to see him off and, as if to make up for his bad behaviour, walked with him across the green, to his house in the main street. They parted at last, the best of good friends, but Sorio found Baltazar seriously provoked when he returned.

" Why did you treat him like that? " the latter persisted. " You've got no grudge against him, have you? It was just your silly fashion of getting even with things in general, eh? Your nice little habit of venting your bad temper on the most harmless person within reach? "

Sorio stared blankly at his friend. It was unusual for Mr. Stork to express himself so strongly.

" I'm sorry, my dear, very sorry," muttered the accused man, looking remorsefully at the Doctor's empty glass and plate.

" You may well be," rejoined the other. " The one thing I can't stand is this sort of social lapse. It's unpardonable — unpardonable! Besides, it's childish. Hit out by all means when there's reason for it or you're dealing with some scurvy dog who needs suppressing but to make a sensitive person like Fingal uncomfortable, out of a pure spirit of bullying — it's damnable! "

" I'm sorry, Tassar," repeated the other meekly. " I can't think why I did it. He's certainly a charming person. I'll make up to him, my dear. I'll be gentle as a lamb when I see him next."

Baltazar smiled and made a humorous and hopeless gesture with his hands. " We shall see," he said, " we shall see."

He locked the door and lit a couple of candles with ritualistic deliberation. " Turn out the lamp, amico mio, and let us sleep on all this. The best way of choosing between two loves is to say one's prayers and go to bed. These things decide themselves in dreams."

" In dreams," repeated the other, submissively following him upstairs, " in dreams. But I wish I knew why the Doctor's ankles look so thick when he sits down. He must wear extraordinary under-clothes."

VI

BRIDGE-HEAD AND WITHY-BED

PHILIPPA RENSHAW'S light-spoken words about Linda recurred more than once to the mind of the master of Oakguard as April gave place to May and May itself began to slip by. The wet fields and stunted woods of Rodmoor seemed at that time to be making a conscious and almost human effort to throw off the repressive influence of the sea and to respond to the kindlier weather. The grasses began to grow high and feathery by the roadside, and in the water-meadows, buttercups superseded marigolds.

As he went to and fro between his house and his office in Mundham, Brand — though he made as yet no attempt to see her — became more and more preoccupied with the *idea* of the young girl. That terror of the sea in the little unknown touched, as his sister well knew it would, something strangely deep-rooted in his nature. His ancestors had lived so long in this place that there had come to exist between the man's inmost being and the voracious tides which year by year devoured the land he owned, an obstinate reciprocity of mood and feeling. That a young and fragile intruder should have this morbid fear of the very element which half-consciously he assimilated to himself, gave him a subtle and sullen exultation. The thing promised to become a sort of perverted link between them, and he pleased himself by fancying, even while, in fear of disillusionment, he kept putting off their encounter, that the girl herself could not be quite free of some sort of premonition of what awaited her.

Thus it happened that Philippa Renshaw's stroke in her own defence worked precisely as she had anticipated. Brooding, in his slow tenacious way, as the weeks went by, upon this singular projection of his imagination, he let his sister do what she chose, feeling assured that in her pride of race, she would not seriously commit herself with a nameless foreigner, and promising himself to end the business with a drastic hand as soon as it suited him to do so.

It was about the middle of May when an event took place which gave the affair a decisive and fatal impulse. This was a chance encounter, upon the bridge crossing the Loon, between Brand and Rachel Doorm. He would have passed her even then without recognition, but she stopped him and held out her hand.

" Don't you remember me, Mr. Renshaw? " she said.

He removed his hat, displaying his closely cropped reddish head with its abnormal upward slope, and regarded her smilingly.

" You've changed, Miss Rachel," he remarked, " but your voice is the same. They told me you were here. I knew we should meet sooner or later."

" Put on your hat, Mr. Renshaw," she said, seating herself on a little stone bench below the parapet and making room for him at her side. " I knew, too, that we should meet. It's a long time from those days — isn't it? — a long time, and a dark one for some of us. Do you remember when you were a child, how you asked me once why they called this place the New

Bridge, when it's obviously so very old? Do you remember that, Mr. Renshaw?"

He looked at her curiously, screwing up his eyes and wrinkling his forehead. " My mother told me you'd come back," he muttered. " She was always fond of you. She used to hope — well, you know what I mean."

" That I'd marry Captain Herrick? " Miss Doorm threw in. " Don't be afraid to say it. The dead can't hear us and except the dead, there's none who cares. Yes, she hoped that, and schemed for it, too, dear soul. But it was not to be, Mr. Renshaw. Ellie Story was prettier. Ellie Story was cleverer. And so it happened. The bitter thing was that he swore an oath to Mary before she died, swore it on the head of my darling Nance, that if he did ever marry again, I should be the one. Mary died thinking that certain. Anything else would have hurt her to the heart. I know that well enough; for she and I, Mr. Renshaw, as your mother could tell you, were more than sisters."

" I thought you and Linda's mother were friends, too," observed Brand, looking with a certain dreamy absorption up the straight white road that led to the Doorm house. The mental fantasies the man had woven round the name he now uttered for the first time in his life had so vivid a meaning for him that he let pass unnoticed the spasm of vindictiveness that convulsed his companion's face.

Rachel Doorm folded her arms across her lean bosom and flung back her head.

" Ellie was *afraid* of me, Mr. Renshaw," she pronounced huskily, and then, looking at him sharply: " Yes," she said, " Mrs. Herrick and I were excellent friends, and so are Linda and I. She's a soft, nervous, impressionable little thing — our dear Linda — and very pretty, too, in her own way — don't you think so, Mr. Renshaw?"

It was the man's turn now to suffer a change of countenance. "Pretty?" he laughed. "I'm sure I don't know. I've never seen her!"

Rachel clasped her hands tightly on the lap of her black dress and fixed her eyes upon him. "You'd like to see her, wouldn't you?" she murmured eagerly. He answered her look, and a long, indescribable passage of unspoken thoughts flickered, wavered and took shape between them.

"I've seen Nance — in the distance — with my mother," he remarked, letting his glance wander to the opposite parapet and away beyond it where the swallows were skimming, "but I've never yet spoken to either of the girls. I keep to myself a good deal, as every one about here knows, Miss Rachel."

Rachel Doorm rose abruptly to her feet with such unexpected suddenness that the man started as if from a blow.

"Your sister," she jerked out with concentrated vehemence, "is doing my Nance a deadly injury. She's given her heart — sweet darling — absolutely and without stint to that foreigner down there." She waved her hand towards the village. "And if Miss Renshaw doesn't let him go, there'll be a tragedy."

Brand looked at her searchingly, his lips trembling with a smile of complicated significance.

"Do make her let him go!" the woman repeated, advancing as if she were ready to clasp his hand; "you can if you like. You always could. If she takes him away, my darling's heart will be broken. Mr. Renshaw — please — for the sake of old days, for the sake of old friends, do this for me, and make her give him up!"

He drew back a little, the same subtle and ambiguous smile on his lips. "No promises, Miss Rachel," he said, "no promises! I never promise any one anything. But we shall see; we shall see. There's plenty of time. I'm keeping my eye on Philippa; you may be sure of that."

He held out his hand as he spoke to the agitated woman. She took it in both of her own and quick as a flash raised it to her lips.

"I knew I should meet you, Mr. Renshaw," she said, turning away from him, "and you see it has happened! I won't ask why you didn't come to me before. I haven't asked *that* yet — have I? — and I won't ever ask it. We've met at last; that's the great thing. That's the only thing. Now we'll see what'll come of it all."

They separated, and Brand proceeded to cross the Bridge. He had hardly done so when he heard her voice calling upon him to stop. He turned impatiently.

"When you were a little boy, Mr. Renshaw,"— her words came in panting gasps —"you said once, down by the sea, that Rachel was the only person in the world who really loved you. Your mother heard you say it and looked — you know how she looks! You used always to call me 'Cousin' then. Far back, they say, the Renshaws and the Doorms *were* cousins. But you didn't know that. It was just your childish fancy. 'Cousin Rachel,' you said once — just like that — 'come and take me away from them.'"

Brand acquiesced in all this with an air of strained politeness. But his face changed when he heard her final words. "Listen," she said, "I've talked to Linda about you. She's got the idea of you in her mind."

At the very moment when this encounter at the New Bridge ended — which was about six in the afternoon — Nance Herrick was walking with a beating heart to a promised assignation with Sorio. This was to take place at the southern corner of a little withy-bed situated about half a mile from Dyke House in the direction of Mundham. It was Nance's own wish that her lover — if he could still be called so — should meet her here rather than in the house. She had discovered the spot herself and had grown fond of it. Sheltered from the wind by the clump of low-growing willows, and cut off by the line of the banked-up tow-path from the melancholy horizon of fens, the girl had got into the habit of taking refuge here as if from the pursuit of vague inimical presences. In the immediate neighbourhood of the withy-bed were several corn fields, the beginning of a long strip of arable land which divided the river from the marshes as far as Mundham.

The particular spot where she hoped to find Sorio awaiting her was a low grassy bank overshadowed by alders as well as willows, and bordered by a field of well-grown barley, a field which, though still green, showed already an experienced eye the kind of grain which a month or so of not too malicious weather would ripen and turn to gold. Already amid the blades of the young corn could be seen the stalks and leaves of newly grown poppies, and mingled with these, also at their early stage of growth, small, indistinguishable plants that would later show themselves as corn-flowers and succory.

The neighbourhood of this barley field, with its

friendly look and homely weeds, promising a revel of reassuring colour as the summer advanced, had come to be, to the agitated and troubled girl, a sort of symbol of hope. It was the one place in Rodmoor — for the Doorm garden shared the gloomy influences of the Doorm house — where she could feel something like her old enjoyment in the natural growths of the soil. Here, in the freshly sprouting corn and the friendly weeds that it protected, was the strong, unconquerable pressure of earth-life, refusing to be repressed, refusing to be thwarted, by the malign powers of wind and water.

Here, on the bank she had chosen as her retreat, little childish plants she knew by name — such as pimpernel and milkwort — were already in flower and from the alders and willows above her head sweet and consolatory odours, free from the tang of marsh mist or brackish stream, brought memories of old country excursions into places far removed from fen or sea.

She had never yet revealed this sanctuary of hers to Sorio and it was with throbbing pulses and quickened step that she approached it now, longing to associate its security with her master-feeling, and yet fearful lest, by finding her lover unkind or estranged, the place should lose its magic forever. She had dressed herself with care that afternoon, putting on — though the weather was hardly warm enough to make such airy attire quite suitable — a white print frock, covered with tiny roses. Several times in front of the mirror she had smoothed down her dress and unloosened and tied back again her shining masses of hair. She held her hat in her hand now, as she approached the spot, for he had told her once in London that he liked her better when she was bareheaded.

She had left her parasol behind, too, and as she hastened along the narrow path from the river to the withy-bed, she nervously switched the green stalks by her side with a dead stick she had unconsciously picked up.

Her print dress hung straight and tight over her softly moulded figure and her limbs, as she walked, swayed with a free and girlish grace.

Passionately, intently, she scanned the familiar outlines of the spot, hoping and yet fearing to see him. Not yet — not yet! Nothing visible yet, but the low-lying little copse and the stretch of arable land around it. She drew near. She was already within a few paces of the place. Nothing! He was not there — he had failed her!

She drew a deep breath and stood motionless, the dead stick fallen from her hand and her gloveless fingers clasping and unclasping one another mechanically.

" Oh, Adrian! Adrian! " she moaned. " You don't care any more — not any more."

Suddenly she heard a swish of leafy branches and a crackle of broken twigs. He was there, after all.

" Adrian! " she cried. " Is that you, Adrian? "

There was more rustling and swishing, and then with a discordant laugh he burst out from the undergrowth.

" You frightened me," she said, looking at him with quivering lips. " Why did you hide away like that, Adrian? "

He went straight up to her, seized her fiercely in his arms and covered her mouth, her throat and neck with hot, furious kisses. This was not what Nance's heart craved. She longed to sob out her suppressed feelings on his shoulder. She longed to be petted and caressed, gently, quietly, and with soft endearing words.

Instead of which, it seemed to her that he was seeking, as he embraced her body and clung to her flesh with his lips, to escape from his own thoughts, to suppress *her* thoughts, to sweep them both away — away from all rational consciousness — on the brutal impulse of mere animal passion.

Her tears which were on the point of flowing, in a tide of heart-easing abandonment, were driven inwards by his violence, and in her grey eyes, if he had cared to look, he would have seen a frightened appeal — pitiful and troubled — like the wild glance of a deer harried by dogs.

His violence brought its own reaction at last and, letting her go, he flung himself panting upon the ground. She stood above him for a while, flushed and silent, smoothing down her hair with her hands and looking into his face with a puzzled frown.

" Sit down," he gasped. " Why do you stare at me like that? "

Obediently she placed herself by his side, tucked her skirt around her ankles and let her hands fall on her lap.

" Adrian," she said, glancing shyly at him. " Why did you kiss me like that, just now? "

He propped himself up and gazed gloomily across the barley field. " Why — did — I — kiss you? " he muttered, as if speaking in a dream.

" Yes — why, like that, just then," she went on. " It wasn't like you and me at all. You were rough, Adrian. You weren't yourself. Oh, my dear, my dear! I don't believe you care for me half as you used to! "

He beat his fists irritably on the ground and an almost vindictive look came into his eyes.

"That's the way!" he flung out, "that's the way I knew you'd take it. You girls want to be loved but you must be loved just thus and so. A touch too near, a word too far — and you're all up in arms."

Nance felt as though an ice-cold wedge had been thrust between her breasts.

"Adrian," she cried, "how can you treat me in this way?' How can you say these things to me? Have I ever stopped you kissing me? Have I ever been unresponsive to you?"

He looked away from her and began pulling up a patch of moss by its roots. "What are you annoyed about, then?" he muttered.

She sighed bitterly. Then with a strong effort to give her voice a natural tone. "I didn't feel as though you were kissing me at all just now. I was simply a girl in your arms — any girl! It was a shame, Adrian. It hurt me. Surely, dear,"— her voice grew gentle and pleading —"you *must* know what I mean."

"I don't know in the least what you mean," he cried. "It's some silly, absurd scruple some one's been putting in your head. I can't always make love to you as if we were two children, can I — two babes in the wood?"

Nance's mouth quivered at this and she stretched out her arm towards him and then, letting it drop, fumbled with her fingers at a blade of grass. A curious line, rarely visible on her face, wrinkled her forehead and twitched a little as if it had been a nerve beneath the skin. This line had a pathos in it beyond a mere frown. It would have been well if the Italian had recalled, as he saw it, certain ancient tragic masks of his native country, but it is one of life's persistent ironies that the tokens of monumental sorrow, which serve so nobly the purposes of art, should only excite peevish irritation when seen near at hand. Sorio did not miss that line of suffering but instead of softening him it increased his bitterness.

" You're really not angry about my kissing you," he said. " That's what all you women do — you pitch upon something quite different and revenge yourself with it, when all the time you're thinking about — God knows what! — some mad grievance of your own that has no connection with what you say! "

She leapt up at this, as if bitten by an adder and looked at him with flashing eyes.

" Adrian! You've no right — I've never given you the right — to speak to me so. Come! We'd better go back to the house. I wish — oh, how I wish — I'd never asked you to meet me here."

She stooped to pick up her hat. " I liked it so here," she added with a wistful catch in her voice, " but it's all spoilt now." Sorio did not move. He looked at her gravely.

" You're a little fool, Nance," he said, " absolutely a little fool. But you look extraordinarily lovely at this moment, now you're in a fury. Come here, child, come back and sit down and let's talk sensibly. There are other things and much more important things in the world than our ridiculous quarrels."

The tone of his voice had its effect upon her but she did not yield at once.

" I think perhaps to-day," she murmured, " it would be better to go back." She continued to stand in front

of him, swaying a little — an unconscious trick of hers
— and smiling sadly.

"Come and sit down," he repeated in a low voice.
She obeyed him, for it was what her heart ached for,
and clinging tightly to him she let her suppressed emotions have full vent. With her head pressed awkwardly
against his coat she sobbed freely and without restraint.

Sorio gently buttoned up the fastening of one of her
long sleeves which had come unloosed. He did this
gravely and without a change of expression. That peculiar and tragic pathos which emanates from a girl's
forgetfulness of her personal appearance did not apparently cross his consciousness. Nance, as she leant
against him, had a pitiable and even a grotesque air.
One of her legs was thrust out from beneath her skirt.
Sorio noticed that her brown shoes were a little worn
and did not consort well with her white stockings. It
momentarily crossed his mind that he had fancied
Nancy's ankles to be slenderer than it seemed they were.

Her sobs died away at last in long shuddering gasps
which shook her whole frame. Sorio kept stroking her
head, but his eyes were fixed on the distant river bank
along which a heavily labouring horse was tugging at a
rope. Every now and then his face contracted a little
as if he were in physical pain. This was due to the fact
that from the girl's weight pressing against his knee
he began to suffer from cramp. Though her sobs had
died down, Nance still seemed unwilling to stir.

With one of her hands she made a tremulous movement in search of his, and he answered it by tightly
gripping her fingers. While he held her thus his gaze
wandered from the horse on the tow-path and fixed itself upon a large and beautifully spotted fly that was

moving slowly and tentatively up a green stalk. With
its long antennæ extended in front of it the fly felt
its way, every now and then opening and shutting its
gauzy wings.

Sorio hated the horse, hated the fly and hated himself. As for the girl who leant so heavily upon him,
he felt nothing for her just then but a dull, inert patience and a kind of objective pity such as one might
feel for a wounded animal. One deep, far-drawn channel of strength and hope remained open in the remote
depths of his mind — associated with his inmost identity
and with what in the fortress of his soul he loved to call
his " secret "— and far off, at the end of this vista,
visualized through clouds of complicated memories —
was the image of his boy, his boy left in America, from
whom, unknown even to Nance, he received letters week
by week, letters that were the only thing, so it seemed
to him at this moment, which gave sweetness to his life.

He had sought, in giving full scope to his attraction
to Nance, to cover up and smooth over certain jagged,
bleeding edges in his outraged mind, and in this, even
now, as he returned the pressure of her soft fingers, he
recognized that he had been successful.

It was, he knew well, only the appearance of this
other one — this insidious " rose au regard saphique "
— this furtive child of marsh and sea — who had spoilt
his delight in Nance — Nance had not changed, nor indeed had he, himself. It was only the discovery of
Philippa, the revelation of Philippa, which had altered
everything.

With his fingers entangled in the shining hair, beneath his hand, he found himself cursing the day he had
ever come to Rodmoor. And yet — as far as his " se-

cret " went — that " fleur hypocrite " of the salt-
marshes came nearer, nearer than mortal soul except
Baptiste — to understanding the heart of his mystery.
The sun sinking behind them, had for some while now
thrown long dark shadows across the field at their feet.

The flies which hovered over the girl's prostrate form
were no longer radiantly illuminated and from the vague
distances in every direction came those fitful sounds of
the closing day — murmurs and whispers and subtle
breathings, sweet and yet profoundly sad, which indicate the ebb of the life-impulse and approach of twilight.

The girl moved at last, and lifting up a tear-stained
face, looked timidly and shyly into his eyes. She appeared at that moment so submissive, so pitiful, and so
entirely dependent on him that Sorio would have been
hardly human if he had not thrown his arms reassur-
ingly round her neck and kissed her wet flushed cheek.

They rose together from the ground and both laughed
merrily to see how stained and crumpled her newly
starched frock had become.

" I'll meet you here again — to-morrow if you like,"
he said gently. She smiled but did not answer. Sim-
ple-hearted though she was, she was enough of a woman
to know well that her victory, if it could be called victory, over his morose mood was a mere temporary matter. The future of their love seemed to her more than
ever dubious and uncertain, and it was with a chilled
heart, in spite of her gallant attempts to make their
return pleasant to them both, that she re-entered the
forlorn garden of Dyke House and waved good-bye to
him from the door.

VII

VESPERS

NANCE continued to resort to her withy-bed, in spite of the spoiling of its charm, but she did not again ask Sorio to meet her there. She met him still, however,— sometimes in Rachel's desolate garden which seemed inspired by some occult influence antipathetic to every softening touch, and sometimes — and these latter encounters were the happier ones — in the little graveyard of Mr. Traherne's church. She found him affectionate enough in these ambiguous days and even tender, but she was constantly aware of a barrier between them which nothing she could say or do seemed able to surmount.

Her anxiety with regard to the relations between Rachel and Linda did not grow less as days went on. Sometimes the two seemed perfectly happy and Nance accused herself of having a morbid imagination, but then again something would occur — some quite slight and unimportant thing — which threw her back upon all her old misgivings.

Once she was certain she heard Linda crying in the night and uttering Rachel's name but the young girl, when roused from her sleep, only laughed gaily and vowed she had no recollection of anything she had dreamed.

As things thus went on and there seemed no outlet from the difficulties that surrounded her, Nance began making serious enquiries as to the possibility of finding work in the neighbourhood. She read the advertisements in the local papers and even answered some of them but the weeks slipped by and nothing tangible seemed to emerge.

Her greatest consolation at this time was a friendship she struck up with Hamish Traherne, the curate-in-charge of Rodmoor upon whose organ in the forlorn little Norman church, Linda was now daily practising.

Dr. Raughty, too, when she chanced to meet him, proved a soothing distraction. The man's evident admiration for her gratified her vanity, while her tender and playful way of expressing it put a healing ointment upon his wounded pride.

One late afternoon when the sun at last seemed to have got some degree of hold upon that sea-blighted country, she found herself seated with Mr. Traherne on a bench adjoining the churchyard, waiting there in part for the service — for Hamish was a rigorous ritualist in these things and rang his bell twice a day with devoted patience — and in part for the purpose of meeting Mrs. Renshaw, who, as she knew, came regularly to church, morning and evening.

Linda was playing inside the little stone edifice and the sound of her music came out to them as they talked, pleasantly softened by the intervening walls. Mr. Traherne's own dwelling, a battered, time-worn fragment of monastic masonry, clumsily adapted to modern use, lay behind them, its unpretentious garden passing by such imperceptible degrees into the sacred enclosure that the blossoms raised, in defiance of the winds that swept the marshes, in the priest's flower-beds, shed their petals upon the more recently dug of his parishioners' graves.

It may have been the extreme ugliness of Rodmoor's curate-in-charge that drew Nance so closely to him. Mr. Traherne was certainly in bodily appearance the least prepossessing person she had ever beheld. He resembled nothing so much as an over-driven and excessively patient horse, his long, receding chin, knobbed bulbous nose, and corrugated forehead not even being relieved by any particular quality in his small, deeply-set colourless eyes — eyes which lacked everything such as commonly redeems an otherwise insignificant face and which stared out of his head upon the world with a fixed expression of mild and dumb protest.

Whether it was his ugliness, or something indefinable in him that found no physical or even vocal expression — for his voice was harsh and husky — the girl herself would have been puzzled to say, but whatever it was, it drew her and held her and she experienced curious relief in talking with him.

This particular afternoon she had permitted herself to go further than usual in these relieving confidences and had treated the poor man as if he were actually and in very truth her father-confessor.

" I've had no luck so far," she said, speaking of her attempts to get work, " but I think I shall have before long. I'm right, am I not, in *that* at any rate? Whatever happens, it's better Linda and I should be independent."

The priest nodded vigorously and clasped his bony hands over his knees.

" I wish," he said, " that I knew Mr. Sorio as I know you. When I know people I like them, and as a rule —" he opened his large twisted mouth and smiled humorously at her —" as a rule they like me."

"Oh, don't misunderstand what I said just now," cried Nance anxiously. "I didn't mean that Adrian doesn't like you. I know he likes you very much. It's that he's afraid of your influence, of your religion, of your goodness. He's afraid of you. That's what it is."

"Of course we know," said Hamish Traherne, prodding the ground with his oak stick and tucking his long cassock round his legs, "of course we know that it's really Mr. Sorio who ought to find work. He ought to find it soon, too, and as soon as he's got it he ought to marry you! That's how I would see this affair settled." He smiled at her with humorous benignity.

Nance frowned a little. "I don't like it when you talk like that," she remarked, "it makes me feel as though I'd done wrong in saying anything about it. It makes me feel as though I had been disloyal to Adrian."

For so ugly and clumsy a man, there was a pathetic gentleness in the way he laid his hand, at that, upon his companion's arm. "The disloyalty," he said in a low voice, "would have been *not* to have spoken to me. Who else can help our friend? Who else is anxious to help him?"

"I know, I know," she cried, "you're as sweet to me as you can be. You're my most faithful friend. It's only that I feel — sometimes — as though Adrian wouldn't like it for me to talk about him at all — to any one. But that's silly, isn't it? And besides I must, mustn't I? Otherwise there'd be no way of helping him."

"I'll find a way," muttered the priest. "You needn't mention his name again. We'll take him for granted in future, little one, and we'll both work together in his interests."

" If he could only be made to understand," the girl went on, looking helplessly across the vast tract of fens, " what his real feelings are! I believe he loves me at the bottom of his heart. I know I can help him as no one else can. But how to make him understand that? "

They were interrupted at this point by the appearance of Mrs. Renshaw who, standing in the path leading to the church door, looked at them hesitatingly as if wondering whether she ought to approach them or not.

They rose at once and crossed the grass to meet her. At the same time Linda, emerging from the building, greeted them with excited ardour.

" I've done so well to-day, Mr. Traherne," she cried, " you'd be astonished. I can manage those pedals perfectly now, and the stops too. Oh, it's lovely! It's lovely! I feel I'm going really to be a player."

They all shook hands with Mrs. Renshaw, and then, while the priest went in to ring his bell, the three women strolled together to the low stone parapet built as a protection against floods, which separated the churchyard from the marshes.

Tiny, delicate mosses grew on this wall, interspersed with small pale-flowered weeds. On its further side was a wide tract of boggy ground, full of deep amber-coloured pools and clumps of rushes and terminated, some half mile away, by a raised dyke. There was a pleasant humming of insects in the air, and although a procession of large white clouds kept crossing the low, horizontal sun, and throwing their cold shadows over the landscape, the general aspect of the place was more friendly and less desolate than usual.

They sat down upon the parapet and began to talk. "Brand promised to come and fetch me to-night," said Mrs. Renshaw. "I begged him to come in time for the service but —" and she gave a sad, expressive little laugh, "he said he wouldn't be early enough for that. Why is it, do you think, that men in these days are so unwilling to do these things? It isn't that they're wiser than their ancestors. It isn't that they're cleverer. It isn't that they have less need of the Invisible. Something has come over the world, I think — something that blots out the sky. I've thought that often lately, particularly when I wake up in the mornings. It seems to me that the dawns used to be fresher and clearer than they are now. God has got tired of helping us, my dears," and she sighed wearily.

Linda extended her warm little hand with a caressing movement, and Nance said, gently, "I know well what you mean, but I feel sure — oh, I feel quite sure — it's only for a time. And I think, too, in some odd way, that it's our own fault — I mean the fault of women. I can't express clearly what's in my mind but I feel as though we'd all changed — changed, that is, from what we used to be in old days. Don't you think there's something in that, Mrs. Renshaw? But of course that only applies to Linda and me."

The elder woman's countenance assumed a pinched and withered look as the girl spoke, the lines in it deepening and the pallor of it growing so noticeable that Nance found herself recalling the ghastly whiteness of her father's face as she saw him at the last, laid out in his coffin. She shivered a little and let her fingers stray over the crumbling masonry and tangled weeds at her side, seeking there, in a fumbling, instinctive manner, to get into touch with something natural, earthy, and reassuring.

The procession of clouds suffered a brief interlude at that moment in their steady transit and the sinking sun shone out warm and mellow, full of odours of peat and moss and reedy mud. Swarms of tiny midges danced in the long level light and several drowsy butterflies rose out of nowhere and fluttered over the mounds.

" Oh, there's Brand coming ! " cried Mrs. Renshaw, suddenly, with a queer contraction of her pale forehead, " and the bell has stopped. How strange we none of us noticed that ! Listen ! Yes — he's begun the service. Can't you hear? Oh, what a pity ! I can't bear going in after he's begun."

Brand Renshaw, striding unceremoniously over the graves, approached the group. They rose to greet him. Nance felt herself surveyed from head to foot, weighed in the balances and found wanting. Linda hung back a little, shamefaced and blushing deeply. It was upon her that Brand kept his eyes fixed all the while he was being introduced. She — as Nance recognized in a flash — was *not* found wanting.

They stood talking together, easily and freely enough, for several minutes, but nothing that Nance heard or said prevented her mind from envisaging the fact that there had leapt into being, magnetically, mysteriously, irresistibly, one of those sudden attractions between a man and a girl that so often imply — as the world is now arranged — the emergence of tragedy upon the horizon.

" I think — if you don't mind, Brand," said Mrs. Renshaw when a pause arrived in their conversation, " we'll slip into the church now for a minute or two.

He's got to the Psalms. I can hear. And it hurts me, somehow, for the poor man to have to go through them alone."

Nance moved at once, but Linda pouted and looked shyly at Brand. "I'm tired of the church," she murmured. "I'll wait for you out here. Are you going in with them, Mr. Renshaw?"

Brand made no reply to this, but walked gravely with the two others as far as the porch.

"Don't be surprised if your sister's spirited away when you come out, Miss Herrick," he said smilingly as he left them at the door.

Returning with a quick step to where Linda stood gazing across the marshes, he made some casual remark about the quietness of the evening and led her forth from the churchyard. Neither of them uttered any definite reference to what they were doing. Indeed, a queer sort of nervous dumbness seemed to have seized them both, but there was a suppressed surge of excitement in the man's resolute movements and under the navy blue coat and skirt which hung so delicately and closely round her slender figure. The girl's pulses beat a wild excited tune.

He led her straight along the narrow, reed-bordered path, with a ditch on either side of it which ended in the bridge across the Loon. Before they reached the bridge, however, he swerved to the left and helped her over a low wooden railing. From this point, by following a rough track along the edge of one of the water meadows it was possible to reach the sand-dunes without entering the village.

"Not to the sea," pleaded Linda, holding back when she perceived the direction of their steps.

" Yes, to the sea! " he cried, pulling her forward with merciless determination. She made no further resistance. She did not even protest when, arrived at the end of their path, he lifted her bodily over the gate that barred their way. She let him help her across the heavily sinking sand, covered with pallid, coarse grass which yielded to every step they took. She let him, when at last they reached the summit of the dunes and saw the sea spread out before them, retain the hand she had given him and lead her down, hardly holding back at all now, to the very edge of the water.

They were both at that moment like persons under the power of some sort of drug. Their eyes were wild and bright and when they spoke their voices had an unnatural solemnity. In the absoluteness of the magnetic current which swept them together, they could do nothing, it seemed, but take all that happened to them for granted — take all — all — as if it could not be otherwise, as if it were *unthinkable* otherwise.

When they reached the place where the tide turned and the tremulous line of spindrift glimmered in the dying sunlight, the girl stopped at last. Her lips and cheeks were pale as the foam itself. She tried to tear her fingers from his grasp. Her feet, sinking in the wet sand, were splashed by the inflowing water.

" They told me you were afraid," he muttered, and his voice sounded to them both as if it came from far away, " but I didn't believe it. I thought it was some little girl's nonsense. But I see now they were right. You *are* afraid."

He rose to his full height, drawing into his lungs with a breath of ecstasy the sharp salt wind that blew across the water's surface.

"But out of your fear we'll make a bond between us," he went on, raising his voice, "a bond which none of them shall be able to break!"

He suddenly bent down and, scooping with his fingers in the water, lifted towards her a handful of sea-foam that gleamed ghostly white as he held it.

"There, child," he cried, "you can't escape from me now!"

As he spoke he flung, with a wild laugh, straight across her face, the foam-bubbles which he had caught. She started back with a little gasp, but recovering herself instantly lifted the hand which held her own and pressed it against her forehead. They stood for a moment, after this, staring at one another, with a hushed, dazed, bewildered stare, as though they felt the very wind of the wing of fate pass over their heads.

Brand broke the spell with a laugh. "I've christened you now," he said, "so I can call you what I like. Come up here, Linda, my little one, and let's talk of all this."

Hand in hand they moved away from the sea's edge and crouched down in the shadow of the sand-dunes. The rose-coloured light died out along the line of foam and the mass of the waters in front of them darkened steadily, as if obscured by the over-hovering of some colossal bird. Far off, on the edge of the horizon, a single fragment of drifting cloud took the shape of a bloody hand with outstretched forefinger but even that soon faded as the sun, sinking into the fens behind them, gave up the struggle with darkness.

With the passing of the light from the sea's surface, all that was left of the wind sank also into absolute immobility. An immense liberating silence intensified,

rather than interrupted by the monotonous splash of
the waves, seemed to stream forth from some planetary
reservoir and overflow the world.

Not a sea-gull screamed, not a sound came from the
harbour, not a plover cried from the marshes, not a
step, not a voice, not a whisper, approached their solitude or disturbed their strange communion.

Linda sat with her head sunk low upon her breast
and her hands clasped upon her knees. Brand, beside
her, caressed her whole figure with an intense gaze of
concentrated possession.

Neither of them spoke a word, but one of the man's
heavy hands lay upon hers like a leaden weight bruising
a fragile plant.

What he seemed attempting to achieve in that con-
spiring hour was some kind of magnetizing of the girl's
senses so that the first movement of overt passion should
come from her rather than from himself. In this it
would seem he was not unsuccessful, for after two or
three scarce audible sighs her body trembled a little and
leant towards his and a low whisper uttered in a tone
quite unlike her ordinary one, tore itself from her lips,
as if against her volition.

" What are you doing to me? " she murmured.

While the invisible destinies were thus inaugurating
their projected work upon Brand and Linda, Nance
and Mrs. Renshaw issued forth from the churchyard.

" If only life were clearer," the girl was thinking,
" it would be endurable. It's this uncertainty in everything — this dreadful uncertainty — which I can't
bear! "

" That was a beautiful psalm we had just now," said
Mrs. Renshaw, in her gentle penetrating voice as, after

some minutes' silent walking they emerged upon the bridge across the Loon. Nance looked down over the parapet and in her depressed fancy she saw the drowned figure of herself, drifting, face upward, upon the flowing water.

"Yes," she replied mechanically, "the psalms are always beautiful."

"I don't believe," the lady went on, glancing at her with eyes so hollow and sorrowful that it seemed as though the twilight of a world even sadder than the one they looked upon emanated from them, "I don't believe I understand that little sister of yours. She's very highly strung — she's very nervous. She requires a great deal of care. To tell the truth, I don't consider my son Brand at all a good companion for her. I wish they'd waited and not gone off like that. He doesn't always remember what a sensitive thing the heart of a young girl is."

They had now reached the southern side of the Loon and were on the main road between Rodmoor and Mundham. A few paces further brought them to the first houses of the village. Something in the helpless, apologetic, deprecatory way with which, just then, Mrs. Renshaw greeted an old woman who passed them, had a strangely irritating effect upon Nance's nerves.

"I don't see why young people should be considered more than any one else!" she burst out. "It's a purely conventional idea. We all have our troubles, and what I think is the older you get the more difficult life becomes."

Mrs. Renshaw's face assumed a mask of weary obstinacy and she walked more slowly, her head bent forward a little and her feet dragging.

" Women have to learn what duty means," she said,
" and the sooner they learn it the better. Those among
us who are privileged to make one good man happy have
the best that life can give. It's natural to be restless
till you have this. But we must try to overcome our
restlessness. We must ask for help."

She was silent. Her white face drooped and bowed
itself, while her tired fingers relaxed their hold on her
skirt which trailed in the dust of the road. Her profile,
as Nance glanced sideways at it, had a look of hopeless
and helpless passivity.

The girl withdrew into herself, irritated and yet remorseful. She felt an obscure longing to be of some
service to this unhappy one; yet as she watched her,
thus bowed and impenetrable, she felt shut out and ex-
cluded.

Before they reached the centre of the village — for
Nance felt unwilling to leave Mrs. Renshaw until she
had seen her safe within her park gates — they suddenly came upon Baltazar Stork returning from his
daily excursion to Mundham.

He was as elegantly dressed as usual and in one hand
carried a little black bag, in the other a bunch of
peonies. Nance, to her surprise, caught upon her companion's face a look of extraordinary illumination as
the man advanced towards them. In recalling the look
afterwards, she found herself thinking of the word
" vivacity " in regard to it.

" Oh, I'm always the same," Mr. Stork replied to the
elder lady's greeting. " I grow more annoyingly the
same every day. I say the same things, think the same
thoughts and meet the same people. It's — lovely ! "

" I'm glad you ended like that," observed Nance,

laughing. It was one of her peculiarities to laugh — a little foolishly — when she was embarrassed and though she had encountered Sorio's friend once or twice before, she felt for some reason or other ill at ease with him.

With exquisite deliberation Mr. Stork placed the black bag upon the ground and selecting two of the freshest blooms from his gorgeous bunch, handed one by the light of a little shop window to each of the women.

" How is your friend? " enquired Mrs. Renshaw with a touch of irony in her tone. " This young lady has not seen him to-day."

At that moment Nance realized that she hated this melancholy being whom a chance encounter with her husband's son seemed to throw into such malicious spirits. She felt that everything Mrs. Renshaw was destined to say from now till they separated, would be designed to humiliate and annoy her. This may have been a fantastic illusion, but she acted upon it with resolute abruptness.

" Good-bye," she exclaimed, turning to her companion, " I'll leave you in Mr. Stork's care. I promised Rachel not to be late to-night. Good-bye — and thank you," she bowed to the young man and held up the peony, " for this."

" She's jealous," remarked Baltazar as he led Mrs. Renshaw across the green under the darkening sycamores. " She is abominably jealous! She was in a furious temper — I saw it myself — when Adrian took her sister out the other day and now she's wild because he's friendly with Philippa. Oh, these girls, these girls! "

An amused smile flickered for a moment across the

lady's face but she suppressed it instantly. She sighed heavily. " You are all too much for me," she said, " too much for me. I'm getting old, Tassar. God be merciful! This world is not an easy place to live in."

She walked by his side after this in heavy silence till they reached the entrance of the park.

VIII

SUN AND SEA

AS the days began to grow warmer and in the more sheltered gardens the first roses appeared, Nance was not the only one who showed signs of uneasiness over Adrian Sorio's disturbed state of mind.

Baltazar was frequently at a loss to know where, in the long twilights, his friend wandered. Over and over again, after June commenced, the poor epicure was doomed to take his supper in solitude and sit companionless through the evening in the grassy enclosure at the back of his house.

As the longest day approached and the heavily scented hawthorn tree which was the chief ornament of his small garden had scattered nearly all its red blossoms, Stork's uneasiness reached such a pitch that he protested vigorously to the wanderer, using violent expressions and, while not precisely accusing him of ingratitude, making it quite plain that this was neither the mood nor the treatment he expected from so old a friend.

Sorio received this outburst meekly enough — indeed he professed himself entirely penitent and ready to amend his ways — but as the days went on, instead of any improvement in the matter, things became rapidly worse and worse.

Baltazar could learn nothing definitely of what he

did when he disappeared but the impression gradually emphasized itself that he spent these lonely hours in immense, solitary walks along the edge of the sea. He returned sometimes like a man absolutely exhausted and on these occasions his friend could not help observing that his shoes were full of sand and his face scorched.

One especially hot afternoon, when Stork had returned from Mundham by the midday train in the hope of finding Adrian ready to stroll with him under the trees in the park, there occurred quite a bitter and violent scene between them when the latter insisted, as soon as their meal was over, on setting off alone.

" Go to the devil! " Adrian finally flung back at his entertainer when — his accustomed urbanity quite broken down — the aggrieved Baltazar gave vent to the suppressed irritation of many days. " Go to the devil! " the unconscionable man repeated, putting down his hat over his head and striding across the green.

Once clear of the little town, he let his speed subside into a more ordinary pace and, crossing the bridge over the Loon, made his way to the sea shore. The blazing sunshine, pouring down from a sky that contained no trace of a cloud, seemed to have secured the power that day of reducing even the ocean itself to a kind of magnetised stupor. The waters rolled in, over the sparkling sands, with a long, somnolent, oily ripple that spent itself and drew back without so much as a flicker or flake of foam. The sea-gulls floated languidly on the unruffled tide, or quarrelled with little, short, petulant screams over the banks of bleached pungent-smelling seaweed where swarms of scavenging flies shared with them their noonday fretfulness.

On the wide expanse of the sea itself there lay a

kind of glittering haze, thin and metallic, as if hammered out of some marine substance less resistant but not less dazzling than copper or gold. This was in the mid-distance, so to speak, of the great plain of water. In the remote distance the almost savage glitter diminished and a dull livid glare took its place, streaked in certain parts of the horizon by heavy bars of silvery mist where the sea touched the sky. The broad reaches of hard sand smouldered and flickered under the sun's blaze and little vibrating heat waves danced like shapeless demons over the summit of the higher dunes.

Turning his face northward, Sorio began walking slowly now and with occasional glances at the dunes, along the level sand by the sea's edge. He reached in this way a spot nearly two miles from Rodmoor where for leagues and leagues in either direction no sign of human life was visible.

He was alone with the sun and the sea, the sun that was dominating the water and the water that was dominating the land.

He stood still and waited, his heart beating, his pulses feverish, his deep-sunken eyes full of a passionate, expectant light. He had not long to wait. Stepping down slowly from the grass-covered dunes, past a deserted fisherman's hut which had become their familiar rendezvous, came the desired figure. She walked deliberately, slowly, with a movement that, as Sorio hastened to meet her, had something almost defiant in its dramatic reserve.

They greeted one another with a certain awkwardness. Neither held out a hand — neither smiled. It might have been a meeting of two conspirators fearful of betrayal. It was only after they had walked in

silence, side by side and still northwards for several
minutes, that Sorio began speaking, but his words broke
from him then with a tempestuous vehemence.

" None of these people here know me," he cried, " not
one of them. They take me for a dawdler, an idler, an
idiotic fool. Well! That's nothing. Nance doesn't
know me. She doesn't care to know me. She — she
loves! As if love were what I wanted — as if love were
enough!"

He was silent and the girl looked at him curiously,
waiting for him to say more.

" They'd be a bit surprised, wouldn't they," he burst
out, " if they knew about the manuscripts *he* "— he uttered this last word with concentrated reverence,— " is
guarding for me over there? *He* understands me, Phil,
and not a living person except him. Listen, Phil!
Since I've known you I've been able to breathe — just
able to breathe — in this damned England. Before
that — God! I shudder to think of it — I was dumb,
strangled, suffocated, paralyzed, dead. Even now —
even with you, Phil,— I'm still fumbling and groping
after it — after what I have to say to the world, after
my secret, my idea!

" It hurts me, my idea. You know that feeling, Phil.
But I'm getting it into order — into shape. Look
here!"

He pulled out of his pocket a small thick notebook
closely written, blurred with erasures and insertions,
stained with salt-water.

" That's what I've done since I've known you — in
this last month — and it's better than anything I've
written before. It's clearer. It hits the mark more
crushingly. Phil, listen to me! I *know* I've got it in

me to give to the world something it's never dreamed of
— something with a real madness of truth in it — something with a bite that gets to the very bone of things.
I know I've got that in me."

He stooped down and picked up a stranded jelly-fish
that lay — a mass of quivering, helpless iridescence —
in the scorching sun. He stepped into the water till it
was over his shoes and flung the thing far out into the
oily sea. It sank at once to the bottom, leaving a small
circle of ripples.

" Go on, go on! " cried the girl, looking at him with
eyes that darkened and grew more insatiable as she
felt his soul stir and quiver and strip itself before her.

" Go on! Tell me more about Nance."

" I *have* told you," he muttered, " I've told you everything. She's good and faithful and kind. She gives
me love — oh, endless love! — but that's not what I
want. She no more understands me than *I* understand
— eternity! Little Linda reads me better."

" Tell me about Linda," murmured the girl.

Sorio threw a wild glance around them. " It's her
fear that taught her what she knew — what she guessed.
Fear reads deep and far. Fear breaks through many
barriers. But she's changed now since she's been with
Brand. She's become like the rest."

" Oh, Brand —! " Philippa shrugged her shoulders.
" So *he's* come into it? Well, let them go. Tell me
more about Nance. Does she cling to you and make a
fuss? Does she try the game of tears? "

Sorio looked at her sharply. A vague suspicion invaded the depths of his heart. They walked along in
silence for several minutes. The power of the sun
seemed to increase. A mass of seaweed, floating below

the water, caused in one place an amber-coloured shadow
to break the monotony of the glittering surface.

" Does your son believe in you — as I do? " she asked
gently.

As soon as the words had crossed her lips she knew
they were the very last she ought to have uttered. The
man withdrew into himself with a rigid tightening of
every nerve. No one — certainly not Nance — had
ever dared to touch this subject. Once to Nance, in
London, and twice recently to his present companion,
had he referred to Baptiste but this direct question
about the boy was too much; it outraged something in
him which was beyond articulation. The shock given
him was so intense and the reaction upon his feelings so
vivid that, hardly conscious of what he did, he thrust
his hand into his pocket and clutched tightly with his
fingers the book containing his work, as though to protect it from aggression. As he thus stood there before
her, stiff and speechless, she could only console herself
by the fact that he avoided her eyes.

Her mind moved rapidly. She must invent, at all
costs, some relief to this tension. She had trusted her
magnetism too far.

" Adriano," she said, imitating with feminine instinct
Baltazar's caressing intonation, " I want to bathe.
We're out of sight of every one. We know each other
well enough now. Shall we — together? "

He met her eyes now. There was a subtile appeal in
their depths which drew him to her and troubled his
senses. He nodded and uttered an embarrassed laugh.
" Why not? " he answered.

" Very well," she said quickly, clinching her suggestion before he had time to revoke his assent, " I'll just

run behind these sand hills and take off my things. You undress here and get into the water. And swim out, too, Adrian, with your back to me! I'll soon join you."

She left him and he obeyed her mechanically — only looking nervously round for a moment as he folded his coat containing the precious manuscript and laid a heavy stone upon it.

He plunged out into the waveless sea with fierce, impetuous strokes. The water yielded to his violent movements like a lake of quicksilver. Dazzling threads and flakes and rainbows flashed up, wavered, trembled, glittered and vanished as he swam forward. With his eyes fixed on the immense dome of sky above him, where, like the rim of a burnished shield, it cut down into the horizon, he struck out incessantly, persistently, seeking, in thus embracing a universe of white light, to find the escape he craved.

Strange thoughts poured through his brain as he swam on. The most novel, the most terrific of the points contained in those dithyrambic notes left behind under the stone surged up before him and, mingling with them in fierce exultant affection, the image of Baptiste beckoned to him out of a moulten furnace of white light.

Far away behind him at last he heard the voice of his companion. Whether she intended him to turn he did not know, for her words were inaudible, but when he did he perceived that she was standing, a slim white figure, at the water's edge. He watched her with feelings that were partly bitter and partly tender.

" Why does she stand there so long? " he muttered to himself. " Why doesn't she get in and start swimming? "

As if made aware of his thought by some telepathic instinct the girl at that moment slipped into the water and began walking slowly forward, her hands clasped behind her head. When the water reached above her knees she swung up her hands and with a swift spring of her white body, disappeared from view. She remained so long invisible that Sorio grew anxious and took several vigorous strokes towards her. She re-appeared at last, however, and was soon swimming vigorously to meet him.

When they met she insisted on advancing further and so, side by side, with easy, leisurely movements, they swam out to sea, their eyes on the far horizon and their breath coming and going in even reciprocity.

"Far enough!" cried Sorio at last, treading water and looking closely at her.

There was a strange wild light in the girl's face. "Why go back?" her look seemed to say —"Why not swim on and on together — until the waters cover us and all riddles are solved?" There was something in her expression at that moment — as, between sky and sea, the two gazed mutely at one another — which seemed to interpret some terrible and uttermost mystery. It was, however, too rare a moment to endure long, and they turned their heads landwards.

The return took longer than they had anticipated and the girl was swimming very slowly and displaying evident signs of exhaustion before they got near shore. As soon as she could touch the bottom with her feet she hurried out and staggered, with stiff limbs, across the sands to where she had left her clothes.

When she came back, dressed and in lively spirits, her unbound hair shimmering in the sunshine like wet silk, she found him pacing the sea's edge with an expression of gloomy resolution.

"I shall have to rewrite every word of these notes," he said, striking his hand against his pocket. "I had a new thought just now as I was in the water and it changes everything."

She threw herself down on the hot sand and spread out her hair to let it dry.

"Don't let's go yet, Adrian," she pleaded. "I feel so sleepy and happy."

He looked at her thoughtfully, hardly catching the drift of her words. "It changes everything," he repeated.

"Lie down here," she murmured softly, letting her gaze meet his with a wistful entreaty.

He placed himself beside her. "Don't get hurt by the sun," he said. She smiled at that — a long, slow, dreamy smile — and drawing him towards her with her eyes, "I believe you're afraid of me to-day, Adrian," she whispered.

Her boyish figure, outlined beneath the thin dress she wore, seemed to breathe a sort of classic voluptuousness as she languidly stretched her limbs. As she did this, she turned her head sideways, till her chin rested on her shoulder and a tress of brown hair, wet and clinging, fell across her slender neck.

A sudden impulse of malice seemed to seize the man who bent over her. "Your hair isn't half as long as Nance's," he said, turning abruptly away and hugging his knees with his arms.

The girl drew herself together, at that, like a snake from under a heavy foot and, propping herself up on her hands, threw a glance upon him which, had he caught it, might have produced a yet further change in the book of philosophic notes. Her eyes, for one passing second, held in them something that was like livid fire reflected through blue ice.

For several minutes after this they both contemplated the level mass of illuminated waters with absorbed concentration. At last Adrian broke the silence.

" What I'm aiming at in my book," he said, " is a revelation of how the essence of life is found in the instinct of destruction. I want to show — what is simply the truth — that the pleasure of destruction, destruction entered upon out of sheer joy and for its own sake, lies behind every living impulse that pushes life forward. Out of destruction alone — out of the rending and tearing of something — of something in the way — does new life spring to birth. It isn't destruction for cruelty's sake," he went on, his fingers closing and unclosing at his side over a handful of sand. " Cruelty is mere inverted sentiment. Cruelty implies attraction, passion, even — in some cases — love. Pure destruction — destruction for its own sake — such as I see it — is no thick, heavy, muddy, perverted impulse such as the cruel are obsessed by. It's a burning and devouring flame. It's a mad, splendid revel of glaring whiteness like this which hurts our eyes now. I'm going to show in my book how the ultimate essence of life, as we find it, purest and most purged in the ecstasies of the saints, is nothing but an insanity of destruction! That's really what lies at the bottom of all the asceticism and all the renunciation in the world. It's the instinct to destroy — to destroy what lies nearest to one's hand — in this case, of course, one's own body and the passions of the body. Ascetics fancy they do this for the sake of their souls. That's their illusion. They do it for its own sake — for the sake of the ecstasy of destruction! Man is the highest of all animals because he can destroy the most. The saints are the highest among men because they can destroy humanity."

He rose to his feet and, picking up a flat stone from the sea's edge, sent it skimming across the water.

" Five!" he cried, as the stone sank at last.

The girl rose and stood beside him. " I can play at ' Ducks and Drakes ' too," she said, imitating his action with another stone which, however, sank heavily after only three cuttings of the shiny surface.

" You can't play ' Ducks and Drakes ' with the universe," retorted Sorio. " No girl can — not even you, with your boy-arms and boy-legs! You can't even throw a stone out of pure innocence. You only threw that — just now — because I did and because you wanted me to see you swing your arm — and because you wanted to change the conversation."

He looked her up and down with an air of sullen mockery. " What the saints and the mystics seek," he went on, " is the destruction of everything within reach — of everything that sticks out, that obtrudes, that is simply *there*. That is why they throw their stones at every form of natural life. But the life they attack is doing the same thing itself in a cruder way. The sea is destroying the land; the grass is destroying the flowers; the flowers one another; the woods, the marshes, the fens, are all destroying something. The saints are only the maddest and wisest of all destroyers —"

" Sorio! There's a starfish out there — being washed in. Oh, let me try and reach it!"

She snatched his stick from him and catching up her skirt stepped into the water.

" Let it be ! " he muttered, " let it be ! "

She gave up her attempt with an impatient shrug but continued to watch the steady pressure of the incoming tide with absorbed interest.

" What the saints aim at," Sorio continued, " and the great poets too, is that absolute *white light*, which means the drowning, the blinding, the annihilating, of all these paltry-coloured things which assert themselves and try to make themselves immortal. The only godlike happiness is the happiness of seeing world after world tumbled into oblivion. That's the mad, sweet secret thought at the back of all the religions. God — as the great terrible minds of antiquity never forgot — is the supreme name for that ultimate destruction of all things which is the only goal. That's why God is always visualised as a blaze of blinding white light. That's why the Sun-God, greatest of destroyers, is pictured with burning arrows."

While Adrian continued in this wild strain, expounding his desperate philosophy, it was a pity there was no one to watch the various expressions which crossed in phantasmal sequence, like evil ghosts over a lovely mirror, the face of Philippa Renshaw.

The conflict between the man and woman was, indeed, at that moment, of curious and elaborate interest. While he flung out, in this passionate way, his metaphysical iconoclasm, her instinct — the shrewd feminine instinct to reduce everything to the personal touch — remained fretting, chafing, irritable, and unsatisfied. It was nothing to her that the formula he used was the formula of her own instincts. She loved destruction but in her subtle heart she despised, with infinite contempt, all philosophical theories — despised them as being simply irrelevant and off the track of actual life — off the track, in fact, of those primitive personal impulses which alone possess colour, perfume, salt and sweetness!

Vaguely, at the bottom of his soul, even while he was speaking, Sorio knew that the girl was irritated and piqued; but the consciousness of this, so far from being unpleasant, gave an added zest to his words. He revenged himself on her for the attraction he felt towards her by showing her that in the metaphysical world at any rate, he could reduce her to non-existence! Her annoyance at last gave her, in desperation, a flash of diabolic cunning. She tossed out to him as a bait for his ravening analysis, her own equivocal nature.

" I know well what you mean," she said, as they moved slowly back towards Rodmoor. " Poor dear, you must have been torn and rent, yourself, to have come to such a point of insight! I, too, in my way, have experienced something of the sort. My brain — you know *that*, by this time, don't you, Adriano? — is the brain of a man while my body is the body of a woman. Oh, I hate this woman's body of mine, Adrian! You can't know how I hate it! All that annoys you in me, and all that annoys myself too, comes from this," and she pressed her little hands savagely to her breast as she spoke, as though, there before him, she would tear out the very soul of her femininity.

" From earliest childhood," she went on, " I've loathed being a girl. Long nights, sometimes, I've lain awake, crying and crying and crying, because I wasn't born

different. I've hated my mother for it. I hate her
still, I hate her because she has a morbid, sentimental
mania for what she calls the sensitiveness of young
girls. The sensitiveness! As if they weren't the
toughest, stupidest, sleepiest things in the world!
They're not sensitive at all. They've neither sensitiveness nor fastidiousness nor modesty nor decency! It's
all put on — every bit of it. I *know*, for I'm like that
myself — or half of me is. I betray myself to myself
and lacerate myself for being myself. It's a curious
state of things — isn't it, Adriano? "

She had worked herself up into such a passion of emotional self-pity that great swimming tears blurred the
tragic supplication of her eyes. The weary swing of
her body as she walked by his side and the droop of her
neck as she let her head fall when his glance did not respond were obviously not assumed. The revelation of
herself, entered upon for an exterior purpose, had gone
further than she intended and this very stripping of
herself bare which was to have been her triumph became
her humiliation when witnessed so calmly, so indifferently.

After this they walked for a long while in silence,
he so possessed by the thrilling sense of having a new
vista of thought under his command that he was hardly
conscious of her presence, and she in obstinate bitter
resolution wrestling with the remorse of her mistake
and searching for some other means — any means —
of sapping the strength of his independence.

As they moved on and the afternoon advanced, a
large and striking change took place in the appearance
of the scene. A narrow, clear-cut line of shadow made
itself visible below the sand-dunes. The sky lost its

metallic glitter and became a deep hyacinthine blue, a blue which after a while communicated itself, with hardly any change in its tint, to the wide-spread volume of water beneath it. In those spots where masses of sea-weed floated beneath the surface, the omnipresent blue deepened to a rich indescribable purple, that amazing purple more frequent in southern than in northern seas, which we may suppose is indicated in the Homeric epithet " wine dark."

As the friends approached the familiar environs of Rodmoor they suddenly came upon a fisherman's boat pulled up upon the sand, with some heavy nets left lying beside it.

" Sorio! " cried the girl, stooping down and lifting the meshes of one of these, " Sorio! there's something alive left here. Look! "

He bent over the net beside her and began hastily disentangling several little silvery fish which were struggling and flapping feebly and opening their tiny gills in labouring gasps.

" All right — all right! " cried the man, addressing in his excitement the tiny prisoners, " I'll soon set you free."

" What are you doing, Adrian? " expostulated the girl. " No — no! You mustn't throw them back — you mustn't! The children always come round when school's over and search the nets. It's a Rodmoor custom."

" It's a custom I'm going to break, then! " he shouted, rushing towards the sea with a handful of gasping little lives. His fingers when he returned, were covered with glittering scales but they did not outshine the gleam in his face.

" You should have seen them dash away," he cried. " I'm glad those children won't find them ! "

" They'll find others," remarked Philippa Renshaw. " There'll always be some nets that have fish left in them."

IX

PRIEST AND DOCTOR

THERE are hours in every man's day when the main current of his destiny, rising up from some hidden channel, becomes a recognizable and palpable element in his consciousness. Such hours, if a man's profoundest life is — so to speak — in harmony with the greater gods, are hours of indescribable and tremulous happiness.

It was nothing less than an experience of this kind which flowed deliciously, like a wave of divine ether, over the consciousness of Hamish Traherne on the day following the one when Sorio and Philippa walked so far.

As he crossed his garden in the early morning and entered the church, the warm sun and clear-cut shadows filled him with that sense of indestructible joy to which one of the ancient thinkers has given the beautiful name of μονοχρονος ἡδονὴ — the Pleasure of the Ideal Now.

From the eastern window, flooding the floor of the little chancel, there poured into the cool, sweet-smelling place a stream of quivering light. He had opened wide the doors under the tower and left them open and he heard, as he sank on his knees, the sharp clear twittering of swallows outside and the chatter of a flock of starlings. Through every pulse and fibre of his being, as he knelt, vibrated an unutterable current of hap-

118

piness, of happiness so great that the words of his
prayer melted and dissolved and all definite thought
melted with them into that rare mood where prayer becomes ecstasy and ecstasy becomes eternal.

Returning to his house without spilling one golden
drop of what was being allowed him of the wine of the
Immortals, he brought his breakfast out into the garden
and ate it, lingeringly and dreamily, by the side of his
first roses. These were of the kind known as " the
seven sisters "— small and white-petaled with a faint
rose-flush — and the penetrating odour of them as he
bent a spray down towards his face was itself suggestive of old rich wine, " cooled a long age in the deep-
delved earth."

From the marshes below the parapet came exquisite
scents of water-mint and flowering-rush and, along with
these, the subtle fragrance, pungent and aromatic, of
miles and miles of sun-heated fens.

The grass of his own lawn and the leaves of the trees
that over-shadowed it breathed the peculiar sweetness
— a sweetness unlike anything else in the world — of
the first hot days of the year in certain old East Anglian
gardens. Whether it is the presence of the sea which
endows these places with so rare a quality or the mere
existence of reserve and austere withholding in the ways
of the seasons there, it were hard to say, but the fact
remains that there are gardens in Norfolk and Suffolk
— and to Hamish Traherne's flower-beds in spite of the
modesty of their appeal, may well be conceded something of this charm — which surpass all others in the
British Isles in the evocation of wistful and penetrating
beauty.

The priest had just lit his cigarette and was sipping

his tea when he was startled by the sudden appearance of Nance Herrick, white and desperate and panting for breath.

" I had to come to you," she gasped, refusing his proffered chair and sinking down on the grass. " I had to! I couldn't bear it. I couldn't sleep. I couldn't stop in that house. I saw him last night. He was walking with *her* near the harbour. I spoke to them. I was quiet — not angry or bitter at all and he let her insult me. He let her whip me with her tongue, wickedly, cruelly and yet so under cover, so sideways — you know the kind of thing, Hamish? — that I couldn't answer. If I'd been alone with her I could have, but his being there made me stupid, miserable, foolish! And she took advantage of it. She said — oh, such mean, biting things! I can't say them to you. I hate to think of them. They went right through me like a steel lash. And he stood there and did nothing. He was like a man in a trance. He stood there and let her do it. Hamish — Hamish — I wish I were at the bottom of the sea! "

She bowed her white, grief-distorted face until it was buried in the grass. The sun, playing on her bright hair, made it look like newly-minted gold. Mr. Traherne sank on his knees beside her. His ugliness, intensified by the agitation of his pity, reached a pitch that was almost sublime. He was like a gargoyle consoling a goddess.

" Child, child, listen to me! " he cried, his husky grating voice flinging itself upon the silence of her misery like a load of rubble upon a marble pavement.

" There are moments in our life when no words, however tender, however wise, can do any good. The only way — child, it is so — it is so! — the only way is to find in love itself the thing that can heal.   For love *can* do this, I know it, I have proved it."

He raised one of his arms with a queer, spasmodic gesture and let it drop as suddenly as he had raised it.

"Love rejoices to bear everything," he went on. "It forgives and forgives again.   It serves its beloved night and day, unseen and unfelt, it draws strength from suffering.   When the blows of fate strike it, it sinks into its own heart and rises stronger than fate. When the passing hour's cruel to it, it sinks away within, below the passing of every possible hour, beyond the hurt of every conceivable stroke.   Love does not ask anything.   It does not ask to be recognized.   It is its own return, its own recognition.   Listen to me, child!   If what I'm saying to you is not true, if love is not like this, then the whole world is dust and ashes and ' earth's base built on stubble ' ! "

His harsh voice died away on the air and for a little while there was no sound in that garden except the twitter of birds, the hum of insects, and the murmur of the sea.   Then she moved, raised herself from the ground and rubbed her face with her hands.

"Thank you, Hamish," she said.

He got up from his knees and she rose too and they walked slowly together up and down the little grass plot.   His harsh voice, harsher than ever when its pitch was modulated, rose and fell monotonously in the sunny air.

"I don't say to you, Nance, that you shouldn't expect the worst.   I think we always should expect that and prepare to meet it.   What I say is that in the very

power of the love you feel there is a strength capable of
sustaining you through your whole life, whatever happens. And it is out of this very strength — a strength
stronger than all the world, my dear — than all the
world! — that you'll be able to give your Adrian what
he needs. He needs your love, little one, not your
jealousy, nor your self-pity, nor your anger. God
knows how much he needs it! And if you sink down
into your heart and draw upon that and wait for him
and pray for him and endure for him you will see how,
in the end, he'll come back to you! No — I won't even
say that. For in this world he may never realize whose
devotion is sustaining him. I'll say, whether he comes
back or not, you'll have been his only true love and he'll
know it, child, in this world or another, he'll know you
for what you are!"

The sweet, impossible doctrine, older than the centuries, older than Plato, of the supremacy of spiritual
passion had never — certainly not in that monastic
garden — found a more eloquent apologist. As she
listened to his words and her glance lingered upon a certain deeply blue border of larkspurs, which, as they
paced up and down mingled with the impression he made
upon her, Nance felt that a crisis had indeed arrived in
her life — had arrived and gone — the effect of which
could never, whatever happened, altogether disappear.
She was still unutterably sad. Her new mood brought
no superficial comfort. But her sadness had nothing in
it now of bitterness or desperation. She entered, at
any rate for that hour, into the company of those who
resolutely put life's sweetness away from them and find
in the accepted pressure of its sharp sword-point a
pride which is its own reward.

This mood of hers still lasted on, when, some hours later, she found herself in the main street of the little town, staring with a half-humorous smile at the reflection of herself in the bow-window of the pastry-cook's. She had just emerged from the shop adjoining this one, a place where she had definitely committed herself to accept the post of " forewoman " in the superintendence of half a dozen young girls who worked in the leisurely establishment of Miss Pontifex, " the only official dress-maker," as the advertisement announced, " on that side of Mundham."

She felt unspeakably relieved at having made this plunge. She had begun to weary of idleness — idleness rendered more bitter by the misery of her relations with Sorio — and the independence guaranteed by the eighteen shillings a week which Miss Pontifex was to pay her seemed like an oasis of solid assurance in a desert of ambiguities. She cared nothing for social prestige. In that sense she was a true daughter of her father, the most " democratic " officer in the British Navy. What gave her a profound satisfaction in the midst of her unhappiness was the thought that now, without leaving Rodmoor, she could, if Rachel's jealousy or whatever it was, became intolerable, secure some small, separate lodging for herself and her sister.

Linda even, now her organ-playing had advanced so far, might possibly be able to earn something. There were perhaps churches in Mundham willing to pay for such assistance if the difficulty of getting over there on Sundays when the trains were few, could in some way be surmounted. At any rate, she felt, she had made a move in the right direction. For the present, living at Dyke House, she would be able to save every penny Miss

Pontifex gave her, and the sense of even this relative independence would strengthen her hand and afford her a sort of vantage-ground whatever happened in the future.

She was still standing in front of the confectioner's window when she heard a well-known voice behind her and, turning quickly round, found herself face to face with Fingal Raughty. The Doctor looked at her with tender solicitude.

" Feeling the heat? " he said, retaining her fingers in his own and stroking them as one might stroke the petals of a rare orchid.

She smiled affectionately into his eyes and thought how strange an irony it was that every one, except the person she cared most for, should treat her thus considerately.

" Come," the Doctor said, " now I've got you I'm not going to let you go. You must see my rooms! You promised you would, you know."

She hadn't the heart to refuse him and together they walked up the street till they came to the tiny red-brick house which the Doctor shared with the family of a Mundham bank-clerk. He opened the door and led her upstairs.

" All this floor is mine," he explained. " There's where I see my patients, and here," he led her into the room looking out on the street, " here's my study."

Nance was for the moment inclined to smile at the use of the word " study " as applied to any room in Rodmoor High Street, but when she looked round at walls literally lined with books and at tables and chairs covered with books, some of them obviously rare and valuable, she felt she had not quite done justice to the

Doctor's taste. He fluttered round her now with a hundred delicate attentions, made her remove her hat and gloves and finally placed her in a large comfortable armchair close to the open window. He pulled one of the green blinds down a little way to soften the stream of sunshine and, rushing to his book-case, snatched at a large thin volume which stood with others of the same kind on the lowest shelf. This he dusted carefully with his sleeve and laid gently upon her lap.

"I think you'll like it," he murmured. "It's of no value as an edition, but it's in his best style. I suppose Miss Doorm has all the old masters up at Dyke House bound in morocco and vellum? Or has she only county histories and maps?"

While his visitor turned over the pages of the work in question, her golden head bent low and her lips smiling, the doctor began piling up more books, one on the top of another, at her side.

"Apuleius! — he's a strange old fellow, not without interest, but you know him, of course? Petronius Arbiter! you had better not read the text but the illustrations may amuse you. William Blake! There are some drawings here which have a certain resemblance to — to one or two people we know! Bewick! Oh, you'll enjoy this, if you don't know it. I've got the other volume, too. You mustn't look at *all* the vignettes but some of them will please you."

"But — Fingal —" the girl protested, lifting her head from Pope's Rape of the Lock illustrated by Aubrey Beardsley —"what are *you* going to do? I feel as if you were preparing me for a voyage. I'd sooner talk to you than look at any books."

"I'll be back in a moment," he said, throwing at her

a nervous and rather harassed look, " I must wash my hands."

He hurried precipitously from the room and Nance, lifting her eyebrows and shrugging her shoulders, returned to the " Rape of the Lock."

The doctor's bathroom was situated, it appeared, in the immediate vicinity of the study. Nance was conscious of the turning of what sounded like innumerable taps and of a rush of mighty waters.

" Is the dear man going to have a bath? " she said to herself, glancing at the clock on the chimney-piece. If her conjecture was right, Dr. Raughty took a long while getting ready for his singularly timed ablution for she heard him running backwards and forwards in the bathroom like a mouse in a cage. She uttered a little sigh and, laying the " Rape of the Lock " on the top of " Bewick," looked wearily out of the window, her thoughts returning to Sorio and the event of the preceding evening.

Quite ten minutes elapsed before her host returned. He returned in radiant spirits but all that was visible to the eye as the result of his prolonged toilet was a certain smoothness in the lock of hair which fell across his forehead and a certain heightening of the colour of his cheeks. This latter change was obviously produced by vigorous rubbing, not by the application of any cosmetic.

He drew a chair close to her side and ignored with infinite kindness the fact that his pile of books lay untouched where he had placed them.

" Your neck is just like a column of white marble," he said. " Are your arms the same — I mean are they as white — under this? "

Very gently and using his hands as if they belonged to someone else, he began rolling up the sleeve of her summer frock. Nance was sufficiently young to be pleased at his admiration and sufficiently experienced not to be shocked at his audacity. She let him turn the sleeve quite far back and smiled sadly to herself as she saw how admirably its freshly starched material showed off the delicacy and softness of the arm thus displayed. She was not even surprised or annoyed when she found that the Doctor, having touched several times with the tips of his fingers the curve of her elbow, possessed himself of her hand and tenderly retained it. She continued to look wistfully and dreamily out of the window, her lips smiling but her heart weary, thinking once more what an ironic and bitter commentary it was on the little ways of the world that amorousness of this sort — gentle and delicate though it might be — was all that was offered her in place of what she was losing.

"You ought to be running barefooted and full of excellent joy," the voice of Dr. Raughty murmured, "along the sands to-day. You ought to be paddling in the sea with your skirts pinned round your waist! Why don't you let me take you down there?"

She shook her head, turning her face towards him and releasing her fingers.

"I must get back now," she remarked, looking him straight in the eyes, "so please give me my things."

He meekly obeyed her and she put on her hat and gloves. As they were going downstairs, she in front of him, Nance had a remote consciousness that Dr. Raughty murmured something in which she caught Adrian's name. She let this pass, however, and gave him her hand gratefully as he opened the door for her.

"Mayn't I even see you home?" he asked.

Once more she shook her head. She felt that her nerves, just then, had had enough of playful tenderness.

"Good-bye!" she cried, leaving him on his threshold.

She cast a wistful glance at Baltazar's cottage as she crossed the green.

"Oh, Adrian, Adrian," she moaned, "I'd sooner be beaten by you than loved by all the rest of the world!"

It was with a slow and heavy step that Dr. Raughty ascended his little staircase after he had watched her disappear. Entering his room he approached the pile of books left beside her chair and began transporting them, one by one, to their places in the shelves.

"A sweet creature," he murmured to himself as he did this, "a sweet creature! May ten thousand cartloads of hornified devils carry that damned Sorio into the pit of Hell!"

X

LOW TIDE

NANCE was so absorbed, for several days after this, in making her final arrangements with the dressmaker and getting into touch with the work required of her that she was able to keep her nerves in quite reasonable control. She met Sorio more than once during this time and was more successful than she had dared to hope in the effort of suppressing her jealous passion. Her feelings did not remain, she admitted that to herself sadly enough, on the sublime platonic level indicated by Mr. Traherne, but as long as she made no overt reference to Philippa nor allowed her intercourse with her friend to be poisoned by her wounded pride, she felt she had not departed far from the priest's high doctrine.

It was from Sorio himself, however, that she learned at last of a new and alarming turn of events, calculated to upset all her plans. This was nothing less than that her fatal presentiment in the churchyard had fulfilled itself and that Brand and Linda were secretly meeting. Sorio seemed surprised at the tragic way she received this news and she was equally indignant at his equanimity over it. The thing that made it worse to her was her deep-rooted suspicion that Rachel Doorm was implicated. Adrian laughed when she spoke of this.

"What did you expect?" he said. "Your charming friend's an old crony of the Renshaws and nothing would please her better than to see Linda in trouble.

She probably arranges their meetings for them. She has the look of a person who'd do that."

They were walking together along the Mundham road when this conversation took place. It was then about three o'clock and Nance remembered with a sudden sinking of her heart how cheerfully both of her companions had encouraged her to make this particular excursion. She was to walk with Sorio to Mundham and return late in the evening by train.

" I shall go back," she cried, standing still and looking at him with wild eyes. " This is too horrible! They must have plotted for me to be out of the way. How could Linda do it? But she's no more idea than a little bird in the hedge what danger she's in."

Sorio shrugged his shoulders.

" You can't go back now," he protested. " We're more than two miles away from the bridge. Besides, what's the use? You can't do anything. You can't stop it."

Nance looked at him with flashing eyes.

" I don't understand what you mean, Adrian. She's in danger. Linda's in danger. Of course I shall go. I'm not afraid of Brand."

She glanced across the wide expanse of fens. On the southern side of the road, as she looked back, the park trees of Oakguard stood out against the sky and nearer, on the northern side, the gables of Dyke House itself rose above the bank of the river.

" Oh, my dear, my dear," she cried distractedly, " I must get back to them! I must! I must! Look — there's our house! You can see its roof! There's some way — surely — without going right back to the bridge? There *must* be some way."

She dragged him to the side of the road. A deep black ditch, bordered by reeds, intersected the meadow and beyond this was the Loon. A small wooden enclosure, isolated and forlorn, lay just inside the field and from within its barrier an enormous drab-coloured sow surveyed them disconsolately, uttering a lamentable squeal and resting its front feet upon the lower bar of its prison, while its great, many-nippled belly swung under it, plain to their view. Their presence as they stood in a low gap of the hedge tantalized the sow and it uttered more and more discordant sounds. It was like an angry impersonation of fecundity, mocking Nance's agitation.

" Nothing short of wading up to your waist," said Sorio, surveying the scene, " would get you across that ditch, and nothing short of swimming would get you over the river."

Angry tears came into Nance's eyes. " I would do it," she gasped, " I would do it if I were a man."

Sorio made a humorous grimace and nodded in the direction of the sow.

" What's your opinion about it — eh, my beauty? "

At that moment there came the sound of a trotting horse.

" Here's something," he added, " that may help you if you're bent on going."

They returned to the road and the vehicle soon approached, showing itself, as it came near, to be the little pony-cart of Dr. Raughty. The Doctor proved, as may be imagined, more than willing to give Nance a lift. She declared she was tired but wouldn't ask him to take her further than the village.

" I'll take you wherever you wish," said Fingal

Raughty, giving a nervous little cough and scrambling down to help her in.

"Ah! I forgot! Excuse me one minute. Hold the pony, please. I promised to get some water-mint for Mrs. Sodderly."

He ran hurriedly into the field and Nance, sitting in the cart, looked helplessly at Sorio who, making a gesture as if all the world had gone mad, proceeded to stroke the pony's forehead. They waited patiently and the Doctor let them wait. They could see him through the gap in the hedge running hither and thither and every now and then stooping down and fumbling in the grass. He seemed entirely oblivious of their discomfort.

"This water-mint business," muttered Sorio, "is worse than the shrew-mouse hunt. I suppose he collects groundsel and feverfew for all the old women in Rodmoor."

Nance soon reached the limit of her patience. "Dr. Raughty!" she cried, and then in feminine desperation, "Fingal! Fingal!" she shouted.

The Doctor came hurrying back at that and to Sorio's astonishment it appeared he had secured his desired plants. As he clambered up into the little cart a delicious aromatic fragrance diffused itself around Nance.

"I've found them all right," he said. "They're under my hat. Sorry I've only got room for one of you. Get on, Elizabeth!"

They drove off, Sorio making a final, Pilate-like gesture of complete irresponsibility.

"A noble creature — that sow," the Doctor observed, glancing nervously at his companion, "a noble,

beautiful animal! I expect it likes to feed on water-
melons as well as any one. Did you observe its eye?
Like a small yellow daisy! A beautiful eye, but with
something wicked in it — didn't you think so? — something menacing and malicious."

Nance compelled herself to smile at this sally but her
hands itched to snatch the whip and hasten the pony's
speed. They arrived at last at the New Bridge and
Nance wondered whether the Doctor would be really
amenable to her wishes or whether he would press her
to visit his study again. But he drove on without
a word, over the Loon, and westward again on the
further side of it straight in the direction of Dyke
House.

As they drew near the place Nance's heart began to
beat furiously and she cast about in her mind for some
excuse to prevent her companion taking her any further. He seemed to read her thoughts for, with almost
supernatural tact, he drew up when they were within a
few hundred yards of the garden gate.

" I won't come in if you don't mind," he said. " I
have several patients to see before supper and I want
to take Mrs. Sodderly her water-mint."

Nance jumped quickly out of the cart and thanked
him profusely.

" You're looking dreadfully white," he remarked, as
he bade her good-bye. " Oh, wait a moment, I must
give you a few of these."

He carefully removed his hat and once more the aromatic odour spread itself on the air.

" There! " he said, handing her two or three damp-
rooted stems with purplish-green leaves. She took
them mechanically and was still holding them in her

hands when she arrived with pale lips and drawn, white face, at the entrance to the Doorm dwelling.

All was quiet in the garden and not a sound of any living thing issued from the house. With miserable uncertainty she advanced to the door, catching sight, as she did so, of her own garden tools left lying on the weedy border and some newly planted and now sadly drooping verbenas fading by their side. She blamed herself even at that moment for having, in her excitement at going to meet Sorio, forgotten to water these things. She resolved — at the back of her mind — that she would pull up every weed in the place before she had done with it.

Never before had she realized the peculiar desolation of Dyke House. With its closed windows and smokeless chimneys it looked as if it might have been deserted for a hundred years. She entered and standing in the empty hall listened intently. Not a sound! Except for a remote ticking and the buzzing of a blue bottle fly in the parlour windows, all was hushed as the inside of a tomb. There came over her as she stood there an indescribable sense of loneliness. She felt as though all the inhabitants of the earth had been annihilated and she only left — she and the brainless ticking of clocks in forsaken houses.

She ran hurriedly up the staircase and entered the room she shared with Linda. The child's neatly made little bed with the embroidered night-dress cover lying on the pillow, struck her with a passion of maternal feeling.

" My darling! My darling!" she cried aloud. " It's all my fault! It's all my fault!"

She moved to the window and looked out. In a moment her hands clasped tightly the wooden sash and she leaned forward with motionless intensity. The uninterrupted expanse of that level landscape lent itself to her quick vision. She made out, clearly and instantaneously, a situation that set her trembling from head to foot. In one rapid moment she took it in and in another moment she was prepared for swift action.

Moored on the further side of the river was a small boat and in the boat, sitting with his forehead bowed upon his hands, was Brand Renshaw. His head was bare and the afternoon sun shining upon it made it look red as blood. On the further side of the Mundham road — the very road she had so recently traversed — she could see the figure of a girl, unmistakably her sister — advancing quickly and furtively towards the shelter of a thin line of pine trees, the most western extremity of the Oakguard woods. The man in the boat could see nothing of this. Even if he rose to his feet he could see nothing. The river bank was too high. For the same reason the girl crossing the fields could see nothing of the man in the boat. Nance alone, from her position at the window, was in complete command of both of them. She drew back a little into the room lest by chance Brand should look up and catch sight of her. What a fortunate thing she had entered so quietly! They were taking every precaution, these two! The man was evidently intending to remain where he was till the girl was well concealed among the trees. Rachel Doorm, it seemed, had taken herself off to leave them to their own devices but it was clear that Brand preferred an assignation in his own park to risking an entrance to Dyke House in the absence of its mistress. For that, at any rate, Nance was devoutly thankful.

Watching Linda's movements until she saw her disappear beneath the pines, Nance hurried down the stairs and out into the garden. She realized clearly what she had to do. She had to make her way to her sister before Brand got wind she was there at all.

She knew enough of the Renshaw family to know that if she were to call out to him across the river he would simply laugh at her. On the other hand if he got the least idea she were so near he would anticipate events and hasten off at once to Linda.

But how on earth could she herself reach the girl? The Loon flowed mercilessly between them. One thing she had not failed to remark as she looked at Brand in his little sea boat and that was that the tide was now running very low. Sorio had been either mistaken or treacherous when he assured her it was at its height. It must have been falling even then.

She let herself noiselessly out of the gate and stood for a moment contemplating the river bank. No, Brand could not possibly see her. Without further hesitation she left the path and moved cautiously, ankle-deep in grass, to where the Loon made a sharp turn to the left. She had a momentary panic as she crawled on hands and knees up the embankment. No, even here, as long as she did not stand upright, she was invisible from the boat. Descending on the further side she slipped down to the brink of the river. The Loon was low indeed. Only a narrow strip of rapidly moving water flowed in the centre of the channel. On either side, glittering in the sun, sloped slimy banks of mud.

Her face was flushed now and through her parted lips the breath came heavily, in excited gasps.

" Linda — little Linda ! " she murmured, " it's my fault — all my fault ! "

With one nervous look at the river she sank down on the sun-baked mud and took off her shoes and stockings. Then, thrusting the stockings inside the shoes and tying the laces of these latter together, she pulled up her skirts and secured them round her waist. As she did this she peered apprehensively round her. But she was quite alone and with another shuddering glance at the tide she picked up her shoes and began advancing into the slippery mud. She staggered a little at first and her feet sank deep into the slime but as soon as she was actually in the water she walked more easily, feeling a surer footing. The Loon swirled by her, sending a chill of cold through her bare white limbs. The water was soon high above her knees and she was hardly a quarter of the way across ! Her heart beat miserably now and the flush died from her cheeks. It came across her mind like an ice-cold hand upon her throat, how dreadful it would be to be swept off her feet and carried down that tide — down to the Rodmoor harbour and out to sea — dead and tangled in weeds — with wide-open staring eyes and the water pouring in and out of her mouth. Nothing short of her desperate maternal instinct, intensified to frenzy by the thought that she was responsible for Linda's danger, could have impelled her to press on. The tide was up to her waist now and all her clothes were drenched but still she had not reached the middle of the current.

It was when, taking a step further, she sank as deep as her arm-pits, that she wavered in earnest and a terrible temptation took her to turn and give it up.

" Perhaps, after all," she thought, " Brand has no

evil intentions. Perhaps — who can tell? — he is genuinely in love with her."

But even as she hesitated, looking with white face up and down the swirling stream, she knew that this reasoning was treacherous. She had heard nothing but evil of Brand's ways with women ever since she came to Rodmoor. And why should he treat her sister better than the rest?

Suddenly, without any effort of her own, she seemed to visualize with extraordinary clearness a certain look with which, long ago, when she was quite a child, Linda had appealed to her for protection. A passion of maternal remorse made her heart suddenly strong and she plunged recklessly forward. For one moment she lost her footing and in the struggle to recover herself the tide swept over her shoulders. But that was the worst. After that she waded steadily forward till she reached the further side.

Dripping from head to foot she pulled on her shoes, wrung as much of the water as she could out of her drenched skirts and shook them down over her knees. Then she scrambled up the bank, glanced round to make certain she was still unseen and set off through the fields. She could not help smiling to herself when she reached the Mundham high-road and fled quickly across it to think how amazed Sorio would have been had he seen her just then! But neither Sorio nor any one else was in sight and leaving behind her the trail of wet shoes in the hot road dust, she ran, more rapidly than ever, towards the group of ancient and dark-stemmed pines, into the shadow of which she had seen her sister vanish.

XI

THE SISTERS

LINDA was so astounded that she could hardly repress a scream when, as she sat with her back against a tree on a carpet of pine-needles, Nance suddenly appeared before her breathless with running. It was some moments before the elder girl could recover her speech. She seized her sister by the shoulders and held her at arms' length, looking wildly into her face and panting as she struggled to find words. "I waded," she gasped, "across the Loon — to get to you. Oh, Linda! Oh, Linda!"

A deep flush appeared in the younger sister's cheeks and spread itself over her neck. She gazed at Nance with great terrified eyes.

"Across the river —" she began, and let the words die away on her lips as she realized what this meant.

"But you're wet through — wet through!" she cried. "Here! You must wear something of mine."

With trembling fingers she loosened her own dress, hurriedly slipped out of her skirt, flung it aside and began to fumble at Nance's garments. With little cries of horror as she found how completely drenched her sister was, she pulled her into the deeper shadow of the trees and forced her to take off everything.

"How beautiful you look, my dear," she cried, searching as a child might have done for any excuse to delay the impending judgment. Nance, even in the re-

action from her anxiety, could not be quite indifferent
to the naïveté of this appeal and she found herself actually laughing presently as with her arms stretched
high above her head and her fingers clinging to a
resinous pine branch, she let her sister chafe her body
back to warmth.

"Look! I'll finish you off with ferns!" cried the
younger girl, and plucking a handful of new-grown
bracken she began rubbing her vigorously with its sweet-
scented fronds.

"Oh, you do look lovely!" she cried once more, surveying her from head to foot. "*Do* let me take down
your hair! You'd look like — oh, I don't know what!"

"I wish Adrian could see you," she added. This
last remark was a most unlucky blunder on Linda's
part. It had two unfortunate effects. It brought
back to Nance's mind her own deep-rooted trouble and
it restored all her recent dread as to her sister's destiny.

"Give me something to put on," she said sharply.
"We must be getting away from here."

Linda promptly stripped herself of yet more garments and after a friendly contest as to which of them
should wear the dry skirt they were ready to emerge
from their hiding-place. Nance fancied that all her
difficulties for that day were over. She was never more
mistaken.

They had advanced about half a mile towards the
park, keeping tacitly within the shadow of the pines
when suddenly Linda, who was carrying her sister's
wet clothes, dropped the bundle with a quick cry and
stood, stone-still, gazing across the fields. Nance
looked in the direction of her gaze and understood in

a moment what was the matter. There, walking hastily towards the spot they had recently quitted — was the figure of a man.

Evidently this was the appointed hour and Brand was keeping his tryst. Nance seized her sister's hand and pulled her back into the shadow. Linda's eyes had grown large and bright. She struggled to release herself.

" What are you doing, Nance? " she cried. " Let me go! Don't you see he wants me? "

The elder sister's grasp tightened.

" My dear, my dear," she pleaded, " this is madness! Linda, Linda, my darling, listen to me. I can't let you go on with this. You've no idea what it means. You've no idea what sort of a man that is."

The young girl only struggled the more violently to free herself. She was like a thing possessed. Her eyes glittered and her lips trembled. A deep red spot appeared on each of her cheeks.

" Linda, child! My own Linda! " cried Nance, desperately snatching at the girl's other wrist and leaning back, panting against the trunk of a pine.

" What has come to you? I don't know you like this. I can't, I can't let you go."

" He wants me," the girl repeated, still making frantic efforts to release herself. " I tell you he wants me! He'll hate me if I don't go to him."

Her fragile arms seemed endowed with supernatural strength. She wrenched one wrist free and tore desperately at the hand that held the other.

" Linda! Linda! " her sister wailed, " are you out of your mind? "

The unhappy child actually succeeded at last in free-

ing herself and sprang away towards the open. Nance
flung herself after her and, seizing her in her arms, half-
dragged her, half-carried her, back to where the trees
grew thick. But even there the struggle continued.
The girl kept gasping out, " He loves me, I tell you!
He loves me! " and with every repetition of this cry
she fought fiercely to extricate herself from the other's
embrace. While this went on the wind, which had been
gusty all the afternoon, began to increase in violence,
blowing from the north and making the branches of the
pines creak and mutter over their heads. A heavy
bank of clouds covered the sun and the air grew colder.
Nance felt her strength weakening. Was fate indeed
going to compel her to give up, after all she had endured?

She twined her arms round her sister's body and the
two girls swayed back and forwards over the dry, sweet-
scented pine-needles. Their scantily-clothed limbs were
locked tightly together and, as they struggled, their
breasts heaved and their hearts beat in desperate reciprocity.

" Let me go! I hate you! I hate you! " gasped
Linda, and at that moment, stumbling over a moss-
covered root, they fell together on the ground.

The shock of the fall and the strain of the struggle
threw the younger girl into something like a fit of
hysteria. She began screaming and Nance, fearful
lest the sound should reach Brand's ears, put her hand
over the child's mouth. The precaution was unneces-
sary. The wind had increased now to such a pitch
that through the moaning branches and rustling foliage
nothing could be heard outside the limits of the wood.

" I hate you! I hate you! " shrieked Linda, biting

in her frenzy at the hand which was pressed against her mouth. Nance's nerves had reached the breaking point.

"Won't you help me, God?" she cried out.

Suddenly Linda's violence subsided. Two or three shuddering spasms passed through her body and her lips turned white. Nance released her hold and rose to her feet. The child's head fell back upon the ground and her eyes closed. Nance watched her with fearful apprehension. Had she hurt her heart in their struggle? Was she dying? But the girl did not even lose consciousness. She remained perfectly still for several minutes and then, opening her eyes, threw upon her sister a look of tragic reproach.

"You've won," she whispered faintly. "You're too strong for me. But I'll never forgive you for this — never — never — never!"

Once more she closed her eyes and lay still. Nance, kneeling by her side, tried to take one of her hands but the girl drew it away.

"Yes, you've won," she repeated, fixing upon her sister's face a look of helpless hatred. "And shall I tell you why you've done this? Shall I tell you why you've stopped my going to him?" she went on, in a low exhausted voice. "You've done it because you're jealous of me, because you can't make Adrian love you as you want, because Adrian's got so fond of Philippa! You can't bear the idea of Brand loving me as he does — so much more than Adrian loves you!"

Nance stared at her aghast. "Oh, Linda, my little Linda!" she whispered, "how can you say these terrible things? My only thought, all the time, is for you."

Linda struggled feebly to her feet, refusing her sister's help.

"I can walk," she said, and then, with a bitterness that seemed to poison the air between them, "you needn't be afraid of my escaping from you. He wouldn't like me now, you've hurt me and made me ugly."

Nance picked up her bundle of mud-stained clothes. The smell of the river which still clung to them gave her a sense of nausea.

"Come," she said, "we'll follow the park wall."

They moved off slowly together without further speech and never did any hour, in either of their lives, pass more miserably. As they came within sight of Oakguard, Linda looked so white and exhausted that Nance was on the point of taking her boldly in and begging Mrs. Renshaw's help, but somehow the thought of meeting Philippa just at that moment was more than she was able to endure, and they dragged on towards the village.

Emerging from the park gates and coming upon the entrance to the green, Nance became aware that it would be out of the question to make Linda walk any further and, after a second's hesitation, she led her across the grass and under the sycamores to Baltazar's cottage.

The door was opened by Mr. Stork himself. He started back in astonishment at the sight of their two figures pale and shivering in the wind. He led them into his sitting-room and at once proceeded to light the fire. He wrapped warm rugs round them both and made them some tea. All this he did without asking them any questions, treating the whole affair as if it were a thing of quite natural occurrence. The warmth of the fire and the pleasant taste of the epicure's tea restored Nance, at any rate, to some degree of comfort. She explained that they had walked too far and that she had tried to cross the river to get help for her sister. Linda said hardly anything but gazed despairingly at the picture of the Ambassador's secretary. The young Venetian seemed to answer her look and Baltazar, always avid of these occult sympathies, watched this spiritual encounter with sly amusement. He had wrapped an especially brilliant oriental rug round the younger girl and the contrast between its rich colours and the fragile beauty of the face above them struck him very pleasantly.

In his heart he shrewdly guessed that some trouble connected with Brand was at the bottom of this and the suspicion that she had been interfering with her sister's love affair did not diminish the prejudice he had already begun to cherish against Nance. Stork was constitutionally immune from susceptibility to feminine charm and the natural little jests and gaieties with which the poor girl tried to " carry off " a sufficiently embarrassing situation only irritated him the more.

" Why must they always play their tricks and be pretty and witty? " he thought. " Except when one wants to make love to them they ought to sit still." And with a malicious desire to annoy Nance he began making much of Linda, persuading her to lie down on the sofa and wrapping an exquisite cashmere shawl round her feet.

To test the truth of his surmise as to the cause of their predicament, he unexpectedly brought in Brand's name.

" Our friend Adrian," he remarked, " refuses to allow that Mr. Renshaw's a handsome man. What do you ladies think about that?"

His device met with instant success. Linda turned crimson and Nance made a gesture as if to stop him.

"Ha! Ha!" he laughed to himself, "so that's how the wind blows. Our little sister must be allowed no kind of fun, though we ourselves may flirt with the whole village."

He continued to pay innumerable attentions to Linda. Professing that he wished to tell her fortune he drew his chair to her side and began a long rigamarole about heart lines and life lines and dark men and fair men. Nance simply moved closer to the fire while this went on and warmed her hands at its blaze.

"I must ask him to fetch us a trap from the Inn," she thought. "I wish Adrian would come. I wonder if he will, before we go."

Partly by reason of the fact that he had himself arranged her drapery and partly because of a touch of something in the child's face which reminded him of certain pictures of Pinturicchio, Baltazar began to feel tenderer towards Linda than he had done for years towards any feminine creature. This amused him immensely and he gave the tenuous emotion full rein. But it irritated him that he couldn't really vex his little protégé's sister.

"I expect," he said, replacing Linda's white fingers upon the scarlet rug, "I expect, Miss Herrick, you're beginning to feel the effects of our peculiar society. Yes, that's my Venetian boy, Flambard"— this was addressed to Linda —"isn't he delicious? Wouldn't you like to have him for a lover? — for Rodmoor is a rather curious place. It's a disintegrating place, you know, a place where one loses one's identity and forgets the rules. Of course it suits *me* admirably because I never consider rules, but you — I should think — must find it somewhat disturbing? Fingal maintains there's a definite physiological cause for the way people behave here. For we all behave very badly, you know, Miss Herrick. He says it's the effect of the North Sea. He says all the old families that live by the North Sea get queer in time,— take to drink, I mean, or something of that sort. It's an interesting idea, isn't it? But I suppose that sort of thing doesn't appeal to you? You take — what do you call it? — a more serious view of life."

Nance turned round towards him wearily.

"If Adrian doesn't come in a minute or two," she thought, "I shall ask him to get a trap for us, or I shall go to Dr. Raughty."

"It's an odd thing," Baltazar continued, lighting a cigarette and walking up and down the room, "how quickly I know whether people are serious or not. It must be something in their faces. Linda, now "— he looked caressingly at the figure on the sofa —" is obviously never serious. She's like me. I saw that in her hand. She's destined to go through life as I do, playing on the surface like a dragon-fly on a pond."

The young girl answered his look with a soft but rather puzzled smile, and once more he sat down by her side and renewed his fortune-telling. His fingers, as he held her hand, looked almost as slender as her own and his face, as Nance saw it in profile, had a subtle delicacy of outline that made her think of Philippa. There was, to the mind of the elder girl, a refined inhumanity about every gesture he made and every word he spoke which filled her with aversion. The contours of his face were exquisitely moulded and his round small head covered with tight fair curls was supported on a neck as soft and white as a woman's; but his eyes, coloured like some glaucous sea plant, were to the girl's thinking extraordinarily sinister. She could not help a swift mental comparison between Baltazar's attitude as he leaned over Linda and that of Dr. Raughty when, on various occasions, that honest man had made playful love to herself. It was hard to define the difference but, as she watched Baltazar she came to the conclusion that there was a soul of genuine affectionateness in the doctor's amorous advances which made them harmless as compared with this other's.

Linda, however, was evidently very pleased and flattered. She lay with her head thrown back and a smile of languid contentment. She did not even make an attempt to draw away her hand when the fortune-telling was over. Nance resolved that she would wait five minutes more by their host's elegant French time-piece and then, if Adrian had not come, she would make Mr. Stork fetch them a conveyance. It came over her that there was something morbid and subtly unnatural about the way Baltazar was treating Linda and yet she could not put her finger upon what was wrong. She felt, however, by a profound instinct, an instinct which she could not analyse, that nothing that Brand Renshaw could possibly do — even were he the unscrupulous seducer she suspected him of being — could be as dangerous for the peace of her sister's mind as what she was now undergoing. With Brand there was quite simply a strong magnetic attraction, formidable and overpowering, and that was all, but she trembled to think what elements of complicated morbidity Baltazar's overtures were capable of arousing.

" Look," he said presently, " Flambard's watching us! I believe he's jealous of me because of you, or of you because of me. I don't believe he's ever seen any one so near being his rival as you are! I. think you must have something in you that he understands. Perhaps you're a re-incarnation of one of his Venetians! Don't you think, Miss Herrick," and he turned urbanely to Nance, " she's got something that suggests Venice in her as she lies there — with that smile? "

The languorous glance of secret triumph which Linda at that moment threw upon her sister was more than Nance could endure.

" Do you mind getting us a trap of some sort at the Admiral's Head? " she said brusquely, rising from her seat.

Baltazar assented at once with courteous and even effusive politeness and left the room. As soon as he was gone, Nance moved to Linda's side.

" Little one," she said, with trembling lips, " I seem not to know you to-day. You're not my Linda at all."

The child's face stiffened spasmodically and her whole expression hardened. She fixed her gaze on the ambiguous Flambard and made no answer.

" Linda, darling — I'm only thinking all the time of you," pleaded Nance, putting out her hand.

A gleam of positive hatred illuminated the child's eyes. She suddenly snatched at the proffered hand and surveyed it vindictively.

" I can see where I bit you just now. I'm glad I did! " she cried, and once more she set herself to stare at Flambard.

Nance went over to the fire-place and sat down. But something seemed to impel Linda to strike her again.

" You thought you were going to have every one in Rodmoor to yourself, didn't you? " she said. " You thought you'd have Adrian and Dr. Raughty and Mr. Traherne and everybody. You never thought any one would begin liking me! "

Nance looked at her in sheer terrified astonishment. Certainly the influence of Baltazar was making itself felt.

" You brought me here," Linda went on. " I didn't want to come and *you knew I didn't*. Now — as *he* says, we must make the best of it."

The phrase " and you knew I didn't " went through Nance's heart like a poisoned dagger. Yes, she had known! She had tried to put the thing far from her — to throw the responsibility for it upon her reluctance to hurt Rachel. But she had known. And now her punishment was beginning. She bowed her head upon her hands and covered her face.

" You came," the girl's voice went on, " because you hated leaving Adrian. But Adrian doesn't want you any more now. He wants Philippa. Do you know, Nance, I believe he'd marry Philippa, if he could — if Brand would let him! "

The hands that hid Nance's face trembled. She longed to run away and sob her heart out. She had thought she was at the bottom of all possible misery. She had never expected this. Linda, as if drawing inspiration for the suffering she inflicted, continued to look Flambard in the eyes.

" Brand told me Philippa meets Adrian every night in the park. He said he spied on them once and found them kissing each other. He said they were leaning against one of the oak trees and Adrian bent her head back against the trunk and kissed her like that. He showed me just how he did it. And he made me laugh like anything afterwards by something else he said. But I don't think I'll tell you that — unless you want to hear very much — Do you want to hear? "

Nance, at this moment, lifted up her head. She had a look in her eyes that nothing except the inexhaustible pitilessness of a woman thwarted in her passion could have endured without being melted.

" Are you trying to kill me, Linda? " she murmured.

Her sister gave her one quick glance and looked away again at Flambard. She remained silent after that, while the French clock ticked out the seconds with a jocular malignity.

The wind, rising steadily, swept large drops of rain against the window and the noise of the waves which it brought with it sounded louder and clearer than before as if the sea itself had advanced several leagues across the land since first they entered the house.

XII

HAMISH TRAHERNE

NANCE said nothing to Rachel Doorm on the night they returned, driven home by the landlord of the Admiral's Head. What Rachel feared, or what she imagined, as the sisters entered the house in their thin attire carrying the bundle of drenched clothes, it was impossible to surmise. She occupied herself with lighting a fire in their room and while they undressed she brought them up their supper with her own hands. It was a wretched night for both of the sisters and few were the words exchanged between them as they ate their meal. Once in bed and the light extinguished, it was Nance, in spite of all, who fell asleep first. "The pangs of despised love" have not the same corrosive poison as the sting of passion embittered by rancour.

Nance was up early and took her breakfast alone. She felt an irresistible need to see Mr. Traherne. She arrived at the priest's house almost as early as she had done on a former occasion, only this time, the day being overcast and the wind high, he received her within-doors. She found him reading "Don Quixote" and, without giving her time to speak, he made her listen to the gentle and magnanimous story of the poor knight's death.

"There's no book," he said, when he had finished, "which so recovers my spirits as this one. Cervantes

is the noblest soul of them all and the bravest. He's
the only author who never gives up his humility before
God or his pride before the Universe. He's the author
for me! He's the author for us poor priests!"

Mr. Traherne lit a cigarette and looked at Nance
through its smoke with a grotesque scowl of infinite
reassurance.

"Cheer up, little one!" he said, "the spirit of the
great Cervantes is not dead in the world. God has
not deserted us. Nothing can hurt us while we hold
to Christ and defy the Devil!"

Nance smiled at him. The conviction with which he
spoke was like a cup of refreshing water to her in a
dry desert.

"Mr. Traherne," she began, but he interrupted her
with a wave of his arm.

"My name's Hamish," he said.

"Hamish, then," she went on, smiling at the ghoul-
ish countenance before her, round which the cigarette
smoke ascended like incense about the head of an idol,
"I've more to tell you than I can say. So you must
listen and be very good to me!"

He settled himself in his deep horse-hair chair with
one leg over the other and his ancient, deplorably-
stained cassock over both. And she poured forth the
full history of her troubles, omitting nothing — except
one or two of Linda's cruel speeches. When she had
completed her tale she surveyed him anxiously. One
terrible fear made her heart beat — the fear lest he
should tell her she must carry Linda back to London.
He seemed to read her thoughts in her eyes. "One
thing," he began, "is quite clear. You must both of
you leave Dyke House. Don't look so scared, child.

I don't mean you must leave Rodmoor. You can't
kidnap your sister by force and nothing short of force
would get her, in her present mood, to go away with
you. But I think — I think," he added, "we could
persuade her to leave Miss Doorm."

He straightened out his legs, puckered his forehead
and pouted his thick lips.

"Have a strawberry," he said suddenly, reaching
with his hand for a plate lying amid a litter of books
and papers, and stretching it out towards her. "Oh,
there are ashes on it. I'm sorry! But the fruit's all
right. There! keep it by you — on the floor — anywhere — and help yourself!"

He once more subsided into his chair and frowned
thoughtfully. Nance, with a smile of infinite relief —
for had he not said that to leave Rodmoor was impossible? — kept the plate on her lap and began eating the fruit. She longed to blow the ashes away but
fear of hurting his feelings restrained her. She
brushed each strawberry surreptitiously with the tips
of her fingers before lifting it to her mouth.

"You're not cold, are you?" he said suddenly, "because I *could* light a fire."

Nance looked at the tiny grate filled with a heap of
bracken-leaves and wondered how this would be achieved.

"Oh, no!" she said, smiling again. "I'm perfectly
warm."

"Then, if you don't mind," he added, making the
most alarming grimace, "pull your skirt down. I can
see your ankles."

Nance hurriedly drew up her feet and tucked them
under her. "All right now?" she asked, with a faint
flush.

"Sorry, my dear," said Hamish Traherne, "but you must remember I'm a lonely monk and ankles as pretty as yours disturb my mind." He glared at her so humorously and benevolently that Nance could not be angry with him. There was something so boyish in his candour that it would have seemed inhuman to take offence.

"I believe I could think better if I had Ricoletto," he cried a moment later, jumping up and leaving the room. Nance took the opportunity of blowing every trace of cigarette-ash from her strawberry plate into the fender. She had hardly done this and demurely tucked herself up again in her chair when Mr. Traherne re-entered the room carrying in his hands a large white rat.

"Beautiful, isn't he?" he remarked, offering the animal for the girl to stroke. "I love him. He inspires me with all my sermons. He pities the human race, don't you, Ricoletto? And doesn't hate a living thing except cats. He has a seraphic temper and no wish to marry. Ankles are nothing to him — are they, Ricoletto? — but he likes potatoes."

As he spoke the priest brushed aside a heap of papers and laid bare the half-gnawed skin of one of these vegetables.

"Come, darling!" he said, reseating himself in his chair and placing rat and potato-skin together upon his shoulder, "enjoy yourself and give me wisdom to defeat the wiles of all the devils. Devils are cats, Ricoletto darling, great, fluffy, purring cats with eyes as big as saucers."

Nance quietly went on eating strawberries and thinking to herself how strange it was that with every con-

ceivable anxiety tugging at her heart she could feel
such a sense of peace.

"He's a papistical rat," remarked Mr. Traherne,
"he likes incense."

Once more he relapsed into profound thought and
Ricoletto's movements made the only sound in the room.

"What you want, my child," he began at last, while
the girl put her plate down on the table and hung upon
his words, "is lodgings for yourself and Linda in the
village. I know an excellent woman who'd take you in
— quite close to Miss Pontifex and not far from our
dear Raughty. In fact, she's the woman who cleans
Fingal's rooms. So that's all in her favour! Fingal
has a genius for getting nice people about him. You
like Fingal, Nance, eh? But I know you do, and I
know," and the priest made the most outrageous grimace, "I know he adores *you*. You're perfectly safe, let
me tell you, with Fingal, my dear; however, he may
tease you. He's a hopeless heathen but he has a heart
of gold."

Nance nodded complete assent to the priest's words.
She smiled, however, to herself to think what a little way
this "safety" he spoke of would go if by chance her
heart were not so entirely preoccupied. She couldn't
resist the thought of how pathetically like children all
these admirable men were, both in their frailties and in
their struggles against their frailties. Her sense of
peace and security grew upon her, and with this — for
she was human — a delicate feeling of feminine power.
Mr. Traherne continued —

"Yes, you must take lodgings in the village. Eighteen shillings a week — that was what that Pontifex
woman promised you, wasn't it? — won't be over much

for two of you. But it'll keep you alive. Wait,
though, wait! I don't see why Linda shouldn't play
for us, up here, on Sundays. I'm always having to go
round begging for some one. Often I have to be organist myself as well as priest. Yes — let her try — let
her try! It'll help me to keep an eye on her. It'll be
a distraction for her. Yes, let her try! I could give
her a little for doing it — not what she ought to have,
of course, but a little, enough to make her feel she was
helping you in your housekeeping. Yes," he clapped
his hands together so violently that Ricoletto scrambled up against his collar and clung there with his
paws. "Yes, that's what we'll do, my dear. We'll
turn your sister into a regular organist. Music's the
best charm in the world to drive away devils, isn't it,
Ricoletto? Better even than white rats."

Nance looked at him with immense gratitude and,
completely forgetting his instructions, altered her position to what it had been before. Mr. Traherne rose
and, turning his back to her, drummed with his fingers
on the mantelpiece while Ricoletto struggled desperately to retain his balance.

A queer thought came suddenly into Nance's head
and she asked the priest why it was that there were so
many unmarried men in Rodmoor. He swung round at
that and gave her a most goblinish look, rubbing the
rat's nose as he did so, against his cheek.

"You go far, Nance, you go far with your questions. As a matter of fact, I've sometimes asked myself that very thing. You're quite right, you know,
perfectly right. It applies to the work-people here
as much as to the gentry. We must see what Fingal
Raughty says. He'd laugh at my explanation."

"What's your explanation?" enquired the girl.

"A very simple one," returned the priest. "It's the effect of the sea. If you look at the plants which grow here you'll understand better what I mean. But you haven't seen the plant yet which is most of all characteristic of Rodmoor. It'll be out soon and I'll show it to you. The yellow horned poppy! When you see that, Nance,— and it's the devil's own flower, I can assure you!— you'll realize that there's something in this place that tends to the abnormal and the perverse. I don't say that the devil isn't active enough everywhere and I don't say that all married people are exempt from his attacks. But the fact remains that the Rodmoor air has something about it, something that makes it difficult for those who come under its influence to remain quite simple and natural. We should grow insane ourselves — shouldn't we, old rat? shouldn't we, my white beauty? — if it weren't that we had the church to pray in and 'Don Quixote' to read! I don't want to frighten you, Nance, and I pray earnestly that your Adrian will shake off, like King Saul, the devil that troubles him. But Rodmoor isn't the place to come to unless you have a double share of sound nerves, or a bottomless fund of natural goodness — like our friend Fingal Raughty. It's absurd not to recognize that human beings, like plants and animals, are subject to all manner of physical influences. Nature can be terribly malign in her tricks upon us. She can encourage our tendencies to morbid evil just as she can produce the horned yellow poppy. The only thing for us to do is to hold fast to a power completely beyond Nature which can come in from out-

side, Nance — from outside! — and change everything."

While Nance listened to Mr. Traherne's discourse
with a portion of her mind, another part of it reverted
to Linda and as soon as he paused she broke in.

" Can't we do anything, anything at all, to stop Mr.
Renshaw from seeing my sister? "

The priest sighed heavily and screwed his face into a
hundred grotesque wrinkles.

" I'll talk to him," he said. " It's what I dread doing more than anything on earth, for, to tell you the
honest truth, I'm a thorough coward in these things.
But I'll talk to him. I knew you were going to ask
me to do that. I knew it directly you came here. I
said to myself as soon as I saw you, ' Hamish, my friend,
you've got to face that man again,' but I'll do it, Nance.
I'll do it. Perhaps not to-day. Yes, I'll do it to-day.
He'll be up at Oakguard this evening. I'll go after
supper. It'll be precious little supper I'll eat, Nance,
but I'll see him, I'll see him! "

Nance showed her gratitude by giving him her hand
and looking tenderly into his eyes. It was Mr. Traherne who first broke the spell and unclasped their fingers.

" You're a good girl, my dear," he muttered, " a
good girl," and he led her gently to the door.

XIII

DEPARTURE

AFTER her talk with Mr. Traherne, Nance went straight to the village and visited the available lodging. She found the place quite reasonably adapted to her wishes and met with a genial, though a somewhat surprised reception from the woman of the house. It was arranged that the sisters should come to her that very evening, their more bulky possessions — and these were not, after all, very extensive — to follow them on the ensuing day, as suited the convenience of the local carrier. It remained for her to secure her sister's agreement to this sudden change and to announce their departure to Rachel Doorm. The first of these undertakings proved easier than Nance had dared to hope.

During these morning hours Miss Doorm gave Linda hardly a moment of peace. She persecuted her with questions about the events of the preceding day and betrayed such malignant curiosity as to the progress of the love affair with Brand that she reduced the child to a condition bordering upon hysterical prostration. Linda finally took refuge in her own room under the excuse of changing her dress but even here she was not left alone. Lying on her bed, with loosened hair and wide-open, troubled eyes fixed upon the ceiling, she heard Rachel moving uneasily from room to room below like a revengeful ghost disappointed of its prey.

The young girl put her fingers in her ears to keep this sound away. As she did so, her glance wandered to the window through which she could discern heavy dark clouds racing across the sky, pursued by a pitiless wind. She watched these clouds from where she lay and her agitated mind increased the strangeness of their ominous storm-blown shapes. Unable at last to endure the sight of them any longer she leapt to her feet and, with her long bare arms, pulled down the blind. To any one seeing her from outside as she did this she must have appeared like a hunted creature trying to shut out the world. Flinging herself upon her bed again she pressed her fingers once more into her ears. In crossing the room she had heard the heavy steps of her enemy ascending the staircase. Conscious of the vibration of these steps, even while she obliterated the sound they made, the young girl sat up and stared at the door. She could see it shake as the woman, trying the handle, found it locked against her.

Nothing is harder than to keep human ears closed by force when the faculty of human attention is strained to the uttermost. It was not long before she dropped her hands and then in a moment her whole soul concentrated itself upon listening. She heard Miss Doorm move away and walk heavily to the end of the passage. Then there was a long pause of deadly silence and then, tramp — tramp — tramp, she was back again.

"I won't unlock the door! I won't! I won't! I won't!" muttered the girl, and as if to make certain that her body obeyed her will she stretched herself out stiffly and clutched the iron bars above her head. She lay like this for some minutes, her lips parted, her eyes wildly alert and her breast rising and falling under her bodice.

Once more the door shook and she heard her name pronounced in a low clear-toned voice.

" Linda! Linda! " the voice repeated. " Linda! I must talk to you! "

Unable to endure the tension any longer and finding the dimness of the room more trying than the view of the sky, the girl ran to the window and pulled up the blind as hastily as she had pulled it down. She gazed out, pressing her face against the pane. The clouds, darker and more threatening than ever, followed one another across the heavens like a huge herd of monstrous beasts driven by invisible herdsmen. The Loon swirled and eddied between its banks, its waters a pale brownish colour and here and there, floating on its surface, pieces of seaweed drifted. The vast horizon of fens, stretching away towards Mundham, looked almost black under the sky and the tall pines of Oakguard seemed to bow their heads as if at the approach of some unknown menace.

The door continued to be shaken and the voice of Rachel Doorm never ceased its appeal. Linda went back to her bed and sat down upon it, propping her chin on her hands. There is something about the darkening of a house by day, under the weight of a threatened storm, that has more of what is ominous and evil in it than anything that can occur at night. The " demon that walketh by noonday " draws close to us at these times.

" Linda! Linda! Let me in! I want to speak to you," pleaded the woman. The girl rose to her feet and, rushing to the door, unlocked it quickly. Returning to her bed she threw herself down on her face and remained motionless. Rachel Doorm entered and, seating herself close to Linda's side, laid her hand upon the girl's shoulder.

"Why haven't you got on your frock?" she murmured. "Your arms must be cold as ice. Yes, so they are! Let me help you to dress as I used to in the old days."

Linda drew herself away from her touch and with a convulsive jerk of her body turned over towards the wall.

"It's a pity you didn't think over everything," Miss Doorm went on, "before you began this game with Mr. Renshaw. It's begun to hurt you now, hasn't it? Then why don't you stop? Tell me that, Linda Herrick. Why don't you stop and refuse to see him any more? What? You won't answer me? I'll answer for you then. You don't stop now, you don't draw back now, because you can't! He's got hold of you. You feel him even now — don't you — tugging at your heart? Yes, you're caught, my pretty bird, you're caught. No more tossing up of your little chin and throwing back your head! No more teasing this one and that with your dainty ways — while you whistle them all down the wind. It's you — you — that has to come now when some one else calls, and come quickly, too, wherever you may have run! How do you know he doesn't want you now? How do you know he's not waiting for you now over there by the pines? Take care, my girl! Mr. Renshaw isn't a man you can play with, as you played with those boys in London. It'll be you who'll do the whining and crying this time. The day's near when you'll be on your knees to him begging

and begging for what you'll never get! Did you think
that a chit of a child like you, just because you've got
soft hair and white skin, could keep and hold a man
like that?

" Don't say afterwards that Rachel Doorm hadn't
warned you. I say to you now, give him up, let him
go, hide yourself away from him! I say that — but I
know very well you won't do what I say. And you
won't do it because you can't do it, because he's got
your little heart and your little body and your little
soul in the palm of his hand! I can tell you what that
means. I know why you press your hands against
your breast and turn to the wall. I've done that in
my time and turned and tossed, long nights, and got no
comfort. And you'll turn and toss, too, and call and
call to the darkness and get no answer — just as I got
none. Why don't you leave him now, Linda, before it's
too late? Shall I tell you why you don't? Because
it's too late already! Because he's got you for good
and all — got you forever and a day — just as some
one, no matter who, got Rachel once upon a time!"

Her voice was interrupted by a sudden splashing of
rain against the window and the loud moaning gust of
a tremendous wind making all the casements of the
house rattle.

"Where's Nance?" cried the young girl, starting
up and leaping from the bed. "I want Nance! I
want to tell her something!"

At that moment there were voices below and the
sound of a vehicle driven to the rear of the house. Miss
Doorm left the room and ran down the stairs. Linda
flung on the first dress that offered itself and going to
the mirror began hastily tying up her hair. She had

hardly finished when her sister entered. Nance stood on the threshold for a moment hesitating, and looking anxiously at the other. It was Linda who made the first movement.

" Take me away from here," she gasped, flinging herself into her sister's arms and embracing her passionately, " take me away from here ! "

Nance returned the embrace with ardour but her thoughts whirled a mad dance through her brain. She had a momentary temptation to reveal at once her new plan and let her sister's cry have no other answer. But her nobler instinct conquered.

" At once, at once ! My darling," she murmured. " Yes, oh, yes, let's go at once ! I've got some money and Mr. Traherne will send me some more. We'll take the three o'clock train and be safe back in London before night. Oh, my darling, my darling ! I'm so glad ! We'll begin a new life together — a new life."

At the mention of the word " London " Linda's arms relaxed their hold and her whole body stiffened.

" No," she gasped, pushing her sister away and pressing her hand to her side, " no, Nance dear, I can't do it. It would kill me. I should run away from you and come back here if I had to walk the whole way. I won't see him. I won't ! I won't ! I won't talk to him — I won't let him love me — but I can't go away from here. I can't go back to London. I should get ill and die. I should want him so much that I should die. No, no, Nance darling, if you dragged me by force to London I should come back the next day somehow or another. I know I should — I feel it *here* — as she said."

She kept her hand still pressed against her side and

gazed into Nance's face with a look of helpless pleading.

" We can find somewhere to live, you and I, without going far away, somewhere where we shan't see *her* any more — can't we, Nance? "

It was then, and with a clear conscience now, that the elder girl, speaking hurriedly and softly, communicated the preparations she had made and the fact that they were free to leave Dyke House at any moment they chose.

" I've asked the man to put up the horse here for the afternoon," she said, " so that we shall have time to collect the things we want. They'll send for our trunks to-morrow."

Linda's relief at hearing this news was pathetic to see.

" Oh, you darling — you darling! " she cried, " I might have known you'd save me. I might have known it! Oh, Nance dear, it was horrid of me to say those things to you yesterday. I'll be good now and do whatever you tell me. As long as I'm not far away from *him* — not too far — I won't see him, or speak to him, or write to him! How sweet of Mr. Traherne to let me play the organ! And he'll pay me, too, you say? So that I shall be helping you and not only be a burden? Oh, my dear, what happiness, what happiness! "

Nance left her and descended to the kitchen to help Miss Doorm prepare their midday meal. The two women, as they busied themselves at their task, avoided any reference to the issue between them, and Nance wondered if the man from the Admiral's Head, who now sat watching their preparations and speculating whether they intended to give him beer as well as meat, had intimated to Rachel the object of his delayed departure. When the meal was ready, Linda was summoned to share it and the thirsty ostler, sipping lemonade with a wry countenance, at a side table, was given the privilege of hearing how three feminine persons, their heads full of agitation and antipathy, could talk and laugh and eat as if everything in the wide world was smooth, safe, harmless and uninteresting.

When the meal was over Nance and Linda once more retired to their room and busied themselves with selecting from their modest possessions such articles as they considered it advisable to take with them. The rest they carefully packed away in their two leather trunks — trunks which bore the initials " N. H." and " L. H." and still had glued to their sides railway labels with the word " Swanage " upon them, reminiscent of their last seaside excursion with their father.

The afternoon slipped rapidly away and still the threatened storm hung suspended, the rain coming and going in fitful gusts of wind and the clouds racing along the sky. By six o'clock it became so dark that Nance was compelled to light candles. Their packing had been interrupted by eager low-voiced consultation as to how they would arrange their days when these were, for the first time in their lives, completely at their own disposal. No further reference had been made between them, either to Adrian or to Mr. Renshaw. The candles, flickering in the gusty wind, threw intermittent spots of light upon the girls' figures as they stooped over their work or bent forward, on their knees, whispering and laughing. Not since either of them had arrived in Rodmoor had they been quite so happy. The relief at escaping from Dyke House lifted the atmos-

phere about them so materially that while they spoke of
their lodging in the High Street and of the virtues of
Mrs. Raps, Nance began to feel that Adrian would,
after all, soon grow weary of Philippa and Linda began to dream that, in spite of all appearances, Brand's
attitude towards her was worthy of a man of honour.

At six o'clock they were ready and Nance went down
to announce their departure to Rachel Doorm. She
found their driver asleep by the kitchen fire and, having roused him and told him to put his horse into the
trap, she went out to look for her mother's friend.

She found Rachel standing on the tow path gazing
gloomily at the river. She was bareheaded and the
wind, wailing round her, fluttered a wisp of her grey
hair against her forehead. Beneath this her sunken
eyes seemed devoid of all light. She turned when she
heard Nance's step, her heavy skirt flapping in the wind
as she did so, like a funereal flag.

" I see," she said, pointing at the light in the sisters'
room where the figure of Linda could be observed passing and re-passing, " I see you're taking her away. I
suppose it's because of Mr. Renshaw. May I ask —
if it's of any interest to you that I should care at all
— what you're going to do with her? She's been —
she and her mother — the curse of *my* life, and I fancy
she's now going to be the curse of yours."

Nance wrapped herself more tightly in a cloak she
had picked up as she came out and looked unflinchingly
into the woman's haggard face.

" Yes, we're going away — both of us," she said.
" We're going to the village."

" To live on air and sea-water? " enquired the other
bitterly.

" No," rejoined Nance gently, " to live in lodgings
and to work for our living. I've got a place already
at the Pontifex shop and Mr. Traherne's going to pay
Linda for playing the organ. It'll be better like that.
I couldn't let her go on here after what happened yesterday."

Her voice trembled but she continued to look Miss
Doorm straight in the face.

" You were away on purpose yesterday, Rachel," she
said gravely, " so that those two might be together.
It was only some scruple, or fear, on Mr. Renshaw's
part that stopped him meeting her in the house. How
often this has happened before — his seeing her like
this — I don't know, and I don't want to know — I only
pray to God that no harm's been done. If it *has* been
done, the child's ruin's on *our* head. I cannot understand you, Rachel, I cannot understand you."

Miss Doorm's haggard mouth opened as if to utter
a cry but she breathed deeply and restrained it. Her
gaunt fingers twined and untwined themselves and the
wind, blowing at her skirt, displayed the tops of her
old-fashioned boots with their worn, elastic sides.

" So she's separated us, has she? " she hissed. " I
thought she would. She was born for that. And it's
nothing to you that I've nursed you and cared for you
and planned for you since you were a baby? Nothing! Nothing at all! She comes between us now as
her mother came before. I knew it would happen so!
I knew it would! She's just like her mother — soft and
clinging — soft and white — and this is the end of it."

Her voice changed to a low, almost frightened tone.

" Do you realize that her mother comes to me every
night and sits looking at me with her great eyes just

as she used to do when Linda had been rude to me in the old days? Do you realize that she walks backwards and forwards outside my door when I've driven her away? Do you realize that when I go to bed I find her there, waiting for me, white and soft and clinging?"

Her voice rose to a kind of moan and the wind carried it across the empty road and tossed it over the fields.

"And she speaks, too, Nance. She says things to me, soft, clinging, crying things that drive me distracted. One day, she told me *that* only last night, one day she's going to kiss me and never let me go — going to kiss me with soft, pleading, terrified lips through all eternity, kiss me just as she did once when Linda lost my beads. You remember my beads, Nance? Real jade, they were, with funny red streaks. I often see them round her neck. They'll be round her neck when she kisses me, jade, you know, my dear, with red streaks. I shall see nothing else then, nothing else while we lie buried together!"

She lowered her voice to a whisper.

"It was the Captain who brought them. He brought them over far seas. He brought them for me, do you hear — for me! But they're always round her neck now, after that day."

Nance listened to this wild outburst with a set stern face. She had always suspected that there was something desperate and morbid about Rachel's attachment to her father but never, until this moment, had she dreamed how far the thing went. She looked at the woman's face now and sighed and with that sigh she flung to the blowing wind the covenant between herself and her own mother. All the girl's natural sanity and sense of proportion were awake now and she stiffened her nerves and hardened her heart for what she had to do.

" Between a vow to the dead," she thought, " and the safety of the living, there can be only one choice for me."

" So you're going away," began Miss Doorm again. " Well, go, my dear, go and leave me! I shan't trouble the earth much longer after you're gone."

She turned her face to the river and remained motionless, watching the flowing water. The heavy weight of the threatening storm, the storm that seemed as though some powerful earth-god, with uplifted hand, were holding back its descent, had destroyed all natural and normal daylight without actually plunging the world into darkness. A strange greenish-coloured shadow, like the shadow of water seen through water, hung over the trees of the park and the opposite bank of the river. The same greenish shadow, only touched there with something darker and more mysterious, brooded over the far fens out of which, in the remote distance, a sort of reddish exhalation indicated the locality of the Mundham factories. The waters of the Loon — as Rachel and Nance looked at them now — had a dull whitish gleam, like the gleam of a dead fish's eye. The sense of thunder in the air, though no sound of it had yet been heard, seemed to evoke a kind of frightened expectancy. The smaller birds had been reduced to absolute stillness, their twitterings hushed as if under the weight of a pall. Only a solitary plover's scream, at rare intervals, went whirling by on the wind.

" Come back, come in, will you? " said Nance at last,
" and say good-bye to us, Rachel. I shall come and
see you, of course. We shall not be far away."

She stretched out her hand to help her down the
slope of the embankment. Rachel made no response
to this overture but followed her in silence. No sooner,
however, had they entered the garden and closed the
little gate behind them, than the woman fell on her
knees on the ground and caught the girl round the
waist.

" Nance, my treasure! " she cried pitifully, " Nance,
my heart's baby! Nance, oh, Nance, you won't leave
me like this after all these years? No, I won't let
you go! Nance, you can't mean it? You can't really
mean it? "

The wind, blowing in gusts about them, made the gate
behind them swing open on its hinges. Rachel's di-
shevelled tress of grey hair flapped like a tattered piece
of rag against the girl's side.

" Look," the woman wailed, " I pray you on my
knees not to desert me! You don't know what you're
doing to me. You don't, Nance, you don't! It's all
my life you're taking. Oh, my darling, won't you have
pity? You're the only thing I've got — the only thing
I love. Nance, Nance, have pity on me! "

Nance, with tears in her eyes but her face still firm
and hard-set, tried to free herself from the hands that
held her. She tried gently and tenderly at first but
Rachel's despair made the attempt difficult. Then she
realized that this appalling tension must be brought
at all costs to an end. With a sudden, relentless jerk,
she tore herself away and rushed towards the house.
Rachel fell forward on her face, her hands clutching

the damp mould. Then she staggered up and raised her
hand towards the lighted window above at which Linda's
figure was clearly visible.

" It's you — it's you," she called aloud, " it's you
who've done this — who've turned my heart's darling
against me, and may you be cursed for it! May your
love turn to poison and eat your white flesh! May
your soul pray and pray for comfort and find none!
Never — never — never — find any! Oh, you may
well hide yourself! But *he* will find you. Brand will
find you and make you pay for this! Brand and the
sea will find you. Listen! Do you hear me? Listen!
It's crying out for you now!"

Whether it was the sudden cessation of her voice,
intensifying the stillness, or a slight veering of the wind
to the eastward, it is certain that at that moment,
above the noise of the creaking gate and the rustling
bushes, came the sound which, of all others, seemed the
expression of Rodmoor's troubled soul. Linda herself may not have heard it for at that moment she was
feverishly helping Nance to pile up their belongings
in the cart. But the driver of their vehicle heard
it.

" The wind's changing," he remarked. " Can you
hear that? That's the darned sea!"

The trap carrying the two sisters was already some
distance along the road when Nance turned her head
and looked back. They had blown out their candles
before leaving and the kitchen fire had died down so
that there was no reason to be surprised that no light
shone from any of the windows. Yet it was with a
cold sinking of the heart that the girl leaned forward
once more by the driver's side. She could not help

seeing in imagination a broken figure stumbling round the walls of that dark house, or perhaps even now standing in their dismantled room alone amid emptiness and silence, alone amid the ghosts of the past.

XIV

BRAND RENSHAW

WHILE the sisters were taking possession of
their new abode and trying to eat — though
neither had much appetite — the supper
provided for them by Mrs. Raps, Hamish Traherne, his
cassock protected from the threatening storm by a
heavy ulster, was making his promised effort to " talk "
with the master of Oakguard. Impelled by an instinct
he could not resist, perhaps with a vague notion that
the `creature's presence would sustain his courage, he
carried, curled up in an inside pocket of his cloak,
his darling Ricoletto. The rat's appetite had been unusually good that evening and it now slept peacefully
in its warm nest, oblivious of the beating heart of its
master. Carrying his familiar oak stick in his hand
and looking to all appearance quite as formidable as
any highwayman the priest made his way through the
sombre avenue of gnarled and weather-beaten trees that
led to the Renshaw mansion. He rang the bell with an
impetuous violence, the violence of a visitor whose in-
ternal trepidation mocks his exterior resolution. To
his annoyance and surprise he learnt that Mr. Renshaw was spending the evening with Mr. Stork down
in the village. He asked to be allowed to see Mrs. Renshaw, feeling in some obscure way suspicious of the
servant's statement and unwilling to give up his enterprise at the first rebuff. The lady came out at once
into the hall.

"Come in, come in, Mr. Traherne," she said, quite eagerly. "I suppose you've already dined but you can have dessert with us. Philippa always sits long over dessert. She likes eating fruit better than anything else. She's eating gooseberries to-night."

Mrs. Renshaw always had a way of detaching herself from her daughter and speaking of her as if she were a strange and somewhat menacing animal with whom destiny had compelled her to live. But the priest refused to remove his ulster. The interest of seeing Philippa eat gooseberries was not strong enough to interrupt his purpose.

"Your son won't be home till late, I'm afraid?" he said. "I particularly — yes, particularly — wanted to see him to-night. I understand he's at the cottage."

"Wait a minute," cried the lady in her hurried, low-voiced tone. "Sit down here, won't you? I'll just — I'll just see Philippa."

She returned to the dining-room and the priest sat down and waited. Presently she came hurrying back carrying in her hands a plate upon which was a bunch of grapes.

"These are for you," she said. "Philippa won't touch them. There! Let me choose you out some nice ones."

The servant had followed her and now stood like a pompous and embarrassed policeman uncertain of his duty. It seemed to give Mrs. Renshaw some kind of inscrutable satisfaction to cause this embarrassment. She sat down beside the priest and handed him the grapes, one by one, as if he were a child.

"Brand orders these from London," she remarked,

" that's why we get them now. I call it extravagance,
but he *will* do it." She sighed heavily. " Philippa,"
she repeated, " prefers garden fruit so you mustn't
mind eating them. They'll get bad if they're not
eaten."

The servant hastened on tip-toe to the dining-room
door, peered in, and returned to his post. He looked
for all the world, thought Mr. Traherne, like a ruffled
and disconsolate heron. "He'll stand on one leg
soon," he said to himself.

" When do you expect your son home? " he enquired
again. " Perhaps I might call at the cottage and walk
back with him."

" Yes, do! " Mrs. Renshaw cried with unexpected
eagerness. " Do call at the cottage. It'll be nice for
you to join them. They'll all be there — Mr. Sorio
and the Doctor and Brand. Yes, do go in! It'll be
a relief to me to think of you with them. I'm sometimes
afraid that cousin Tassar encourages dear Brand to
drink too much of that stuff he likes to make. They
will put spirits into it. I'm always telling them that
lime juice would be just as nice. Yes, do go, Mr. Traherne, and insist on having lime juice! "

The priest looked at the lady, looked at the servant
and looked at the hall door. He felt a faint scratching going on inside his cloak. Ricoletto was beginning
to wake up.

" Well, I'll go! " he exclaimed, rising to his feet.

At that moment the figure of Philippa, exquisitely
dressed in a dark crimson gown, emerged from the dining-room. She advanced slowly towards them with
more than her usual air of dramatic reserve. Mr. Traherne noticed that her lips were even redder than her

dress. Her eyes looked dark and tired but they shone with a mischievous menace. She held out her hand sedately and as he took it, fumbling with his ulster, " I hope you enjoyed your grapes," she said.

" You ought to apologize to Mr. Traherne for appearing before him at all in that wild costume," remarked Mrs. Renshaw. " You wouldn't think she'd been at the dentist's all day, would you? She looks as if she were in a grand London house, doesn't she, just waiting to go to a ball?

" Yes, at the dentist's," Mrs. Renshaw went on, speaking quite loudly, " at the dentist's in Mundham. She's got an abscess under one of her teeth. It kept her awake in the night. I think your face is still a little swollen, dear, isn't it? She oughtn't to stand in this cold hall, ought she, Mr. Traherne? And with so much of her neck exposed. It was quite a large abscess. Let me look, dear." She moved towards her daughter, who drew hastily back.

" She won't let me look at it," she added plaintively. " She never would, not even when she was a child."

Hamish, fumbling with his fingers inside his ulster, made a grotesque grimace of sympathy and once more intimated his desire to say good-night. He discerned in the look the girl had now fixed upon her mother an expression which indicated how little sympathy there was between them. It was nearly half past nine when he reached Rodmoor and knocked at Baltazar's door. There was some sort of village revel going on inside the tavern and the sound of this blended, in intermittent bursts of uproar, with the voices from Stork's little sitting-room. Both wind and rain had subsided and the thunder-feeling in the air had grown less oppressive.

Traherne found himself, as he had been warned, in the presence of Raughty, Sorio and Brand. Ushered in by the urbane Baltazar he greeted them all with a humorous and benignant smile and took, willingly enough, a cup of the admirable wine which they were drinking. They all seemed, except their host himself, a little excited by what they had imbibed and the priest observed that several other bottles waited the moment of uncorking. Dr. Raughty alone appeared seriously troubled at the new-comer's entrance. He coughed several times, as was his habit when disconcerted, and glanced anxiously at the others.

Sorio, it seemed, was in the midst of some sort of diatribe, and as soon as they had resumed their seats he made no scruple about continuing it.

" It's all an illusion," he exclaimed, looking at Mr. Traherne as if he defied him to contradict his words, " it's all an absolute illusion that women are more subtle than men. The idea of their being so is simply due to the fact that they act on impulse instead of by reason. Any one who acts on impulse appears subtle if his impulses vary sufficiently! Women are extraordinarily simple. What gives them the appearance of subtlety is that they never know what particular impulse they're going to have next. So they just lie back on themselves and wait till it comes. They're eminently *physiological*, too, in their reactions. Am I not right there, Doctor? They're more entirely material than we are," he went on, draining his glass with a vicious gulp, " they're simply soaked and drenched in matter. They're not really completely or humanly *conscious*. Matter still holds them, still clings to them, still drowns them. That is why the poets represent Nature as a woman. The sentimental writers always speak of women as so responsive, so porous, to the power of Nature. They put it down to their superior sensitiveness. It isn't their sensitiveness at all! It's their element. Of course they're porous to it. They're part of it! They've never emerged from it. It flows round them like waves round seaweed. Take this question of drink — of this delicious wine we're drinking! No woman who ever lived could understand the pleasure we're enjoying now — a pleasure almost purely intellectual. They think, in their absurd little heads, that all we get out of it is the mere sensation of putting hot stuff or sweet stuff or intoxicating stuff into our mouths. They haven't the remotest idea that, as we sit in this way together, we enter the company of all great and noble souls, philosophizing upon the nature of the gods and sharing their quintessential happiness! They think we're simply sensual beasts — as they are themselves, the greedy little devils! — when they eat pastry and suck sugar-candy at the confectioner's. No woman yet understood, or ever will, the sublime detachment from life, the victory over life, which an honest company of sensible and self-respecting friends enjoy when they drink, serenely and quietly, a wine as rare, as well chosen, as harmless as this! Women hate to think of the happiness we're enjoying now. I know perfectly well that every one of the women who are connected with us at this moment — and that only applies," he added with a smile, " to Mr. Renshaw and myself — would suffer real misery to see us at this mo-

ment. It's an instinct and from *their* point of view
they're justified fully enough.

"Wine separates us from Nature. It frees us from
sex. It sets us among the gods. It destroys — yes!
— that's what it does, it destroys our physiological fatality. With wine like this," he raised his glass above
his head, "we are no longer the slaves of our senses and
consequently the slaves of matter. We have freed ourselves from matter. We have *destroyed* matter!"

"I'm not quite sure," said Doctor Raughty, going
carefully to the fireplace where, on the fender, he had
deposited for later consumption, a saucer of brandied
cherries, "I am not sure whether you're right about
wine obliterating sex. I've seen quite plain females, in
my time, appear like so many Ninons and Thaises when
one's a bit shaky. Of course I know they may appear
so," he went on patiently and assiduously letting every
drop of juice evaporate from the skin of the cherry
he held between his fingers before placing it in his
mouth, "appear desirable wenches, I mean, without our
having any inclination to meddle with them but the impulse is the same. At least," he added modestly, "their
being there does not detract from the pleasure."

He paused and, with his head bent down over his
cherries, became absolutely oblivious to everything else
in the world. What he was trying now was the delicate experiment of dipping the fruit, dried by being
waved to and fro in the air, in the wine-glass at his
side. As he achieved this end, his cheeks flushed and
nervous spasmodic quiverings twitched his expressive
nostrils.

"I am inclined to agree with the Doctor," said Brand
Renshaw. "It seems mere monkish nonsense to me to

separate things that were so obviously meant to go together. I like drinking while girls dance for me. I like them to dance on and on, and on and on till they're tired out and then —" He was interrupted by a sudden crash which made all the glasses ring and ting. Mr. Traherne had brought down his fist heavily upon the rosewood table.

" What you people are forgetting," shouted the priest, " is that God is not dead. No! He's not dead, even in Rodmoor. Nature, girls, wine, rats,— are all shadows in flickering water. Only one thing's eternal and that is a pure and loving heart! "

There was a general and embarrassed hush after this and the priest looked round at the four men with a sort of wistful bewilderment. Then an expression of indescribable sweetness came into his face.

" Forgive me, children," he muttered, pressing his hand to his forehead. " I didn't mean to be violent. Baltazar, you must have filled my glass too quickly. No, no! I mustn't touch a drop more."

Stork leaned forward towards him.

" We understand," he said. " We understand perfectly. You felt we were going a little too far. And so we were! These discourses about the mystery of wine and the secret of women always betray one into absurdity. Adrian ought to have known better than to begin such a thing."

" It was my fault," repeated Mr. Traherne humbly. " If you'll excuse me I'll get something out of my pocket."

He rose and went into the passage. Brand Renshaw shrugged his shoulders and lifted his glass to his lips.

"I believe it's his rat," whispered Dr. Raughty softly. "He lives too much alone."

The priest returned with Ricoletto in his hand and resuming his seat stroked the animal dreamily. Baltazar looked from one to another of his guests and his delicate features assumed a curious expression, an expression as though he isolated himself from them all and washed his hands of them all.

"Traherne refers to God," he began in a flutelike tone, "and it's no more than what he has a right to do. But I should be in a sorry position myself if my only escape from the nuisance of women was to drag in Eternity. Our dear Adrian, whose head is always full of some girl or another, fancies he can get out of it by drink. Brand here doesn't want to get out of it. He wants to play the Sultan. Raughty — we know what an amorous fellow *you* are, Doctor! — has his own fantastic way of drifting in and out of the dangerous waters. I alone, of all of you, have the true key to escape. For, between ourselves, my dears, we know well enough that God and Eternity are just Hamish's innocent illusion."

The priest seemed quite deaf to this last remark but Brand turned his hatchet-shaped head towards the speaker.

"Shut up, Tassar," he muttered harshly, "you'll start him again."

"What do you mean?" cried Sorio. "Go on! Go on and tell us what you mean."

"Wait one moment," intervened Dr. Raughty, "talk of something else for one moment. I must cool my head."

He put down his pipe by the side of his saucer of

cherries, arranging it with exquisite care so that its
stem was higher than its bowl. Lifting his chair, he
placed it at a precise angle to the table, returning
twice to add further little touches to it before he was
half-way to the door. Finally, laying down his tobacco
pouch, lightly as a feather upon the seat of the chair,
he rushed out of the room and up the stairs.

"When the Doctor gets into the bathroom," remarked Brand, "we may as well put him out of our
minds. The last time he dined with me at Oakguard
he nearly flooded the house."

Mr. Traherne pressed his rat to his cheek and
grinned like a satyr.

"None of you people understand Fingal," he burst
out, "it's his way of praying. Yes, I mean it! It's
his way of saying his prayers. He does it just as
Ricoletto does. It's ritual with him. I understand
it perfectly."

The conversation at this point seemed to have a
peculiarly irritating effect upon Sorio. He fidgeted
and looked about him uneasily. Presently he made an
extraordinary gesture with one of his hands, opening
it, extending the fingers stiffly back and then closing it
again. Baltazar, watching him closely, remarked at
last,

"What's on your mind now, Adriano? Any new
obsession?"

They all looked at the Italian. His heavy "Roman-
Emperor" face quivered through all its muscles.

"It's not ritual," he muttered gloomily, "you'd better not ask me what it is for I *know!*"

Brand Renshaw smiled a cruel smile.

"He means that it's *madness*," he remarked carelessly, "and I dare say he's quite right."

"Fingal Raughty's not mad," protested Mr. Traherne, "I tell you he bathes himself just as my rat does — to praise God and purge his sins!"

"I wasn't thinking about the Doctor," said Brand quietly, the same cruel gleam in his eyes. "Mr. Sorio knows what I meant."

The Italian made a movement as if he were about to leap upon him and strike him, but the reappearance of Fingal, his cheeks shining and his face softly irradiated, distracted the general attention.

"You'd begun to tell us, Stork," said the Doctor, "what *your* escape is from the sting of sensuality. You wipe out, altogether, you say, God and Eternity?"

Baltazar's feminine features hardened as if under a thin mask of enamel. Brand shot a malignant glance at him.

"I can answer that," he said, with venomous bitterness. "Tassar thinks himself an artist, you know. He despises the whole lot of us as numbskulls and Philistines. He'll tell you that art's the great thing and that critics of art know much more about it than the damned fools who do it, all there is to be known, in fact."

Baltazar's expression as he listened to his half-brother's speech was a palimpsest of conflicting emotions. The look that predominated, however, was the look of a woman under the lash, waiting her hour. He smiled lightly enough and gesticulated with his delicate hand.

"We all have our secret," he declared gaily.
"Brand thinks he knows mine but he's as far from
knowing it as that new moon over there is from knowing
the secret of the tide."

His words caused them to glance at the window.
The clouds had vanished and the thin ghostly crescent
peered at them from between the curtains.

"The tide obeys it," he added significantly, "but it
keeps its own counsel."

"And it has," put in Sorio fiercely, "depths below
depths which it were better for no corpse-world to interfere with!"

Dr. Raughty, who had cleared his throat uneasily
several times during the last few moments, now called
the attention of the company to a scorched moth which,
hurt by one of the candles, lay shuddering upon the
edge of the table.

"Hasn't it exquisite markings?" he said, touching
the creature with the tip of his forefinger, and bending forward over it like a lover. "It's a puss-moth!
I wish I had my killing-bottle here. I'd keep it for
Horace Pod."

Sorio suddenly leapt from his seat and made a snatch
at the moth.

"Shame!" he cried, addressing indiscriminately the
Doctor, Horace Pod and the universe. "Poor little
thing!" he added, seizing it in his fist and carrying it
to the window. When, with some difficulty and many
muttered imprecations he had flung it out, "it tickled
me," he remarked gravely. "Moths flutter so in your
hand."

"Most things flutter," remarked Brand, "when you
try to get rid of them. Some of them," he added in a

significant tone, " don't confine themselves to flutter-
ing."

The incident of the moth seemed to break up, more
than any of the preceding interruptions, the harmony
of the evening. Dr. Raughty, looking nervously at
Sorio and replacing his pipe in his pocket, announced
that he intended to depart. Brand Renshaw rose too
and with him, Mr. Traherne.

" May I walk with you a little way? " said the
priest.

The master of Oakguard stared at him blankly.

" Of course, of course," he replied, " but I'm afraid
it'll take you out of your road."

It was some time before they got clear of the house
as Baltazar with a thousand delicate attentions to each
of them and all manner of lively speeches, did his best,
in the stir of their separation, to smooth over and
obliterate from their minds the various little shocks
that had ruffled his entertainment. They got away,
however, at last and Brand and the priest, bidding the
rest good night, took the road to the park. The sky
as they entered the park gates was clear and starry
and the dark trees of the avenue up which they walked,
rose beside them in immovable stillness.

Mr. Traherne, putting his hand into the pocket of
his ulster to derive courage from contact with his pet,
plunged without preamble into the heart of the perilous
subject.

" You may not know, Renshaw," he said, " that Miss
Herrick and her sister are leaving Dyke House and
are going to live in the village. Nance has got work
at Miss Pontifex' and Linda is going to play the organ
regularly for me. I believe there's been something

— lately "— he hesitated and his voice shook a little but, recovering himself with a tremendous effort, " something," he went on, " between Linda and yourself. Now, of course, in any other case I should be very reluctant to say anything. Interference in these things is usually both impertinent and useless. But this case is quite different. The girl is a young girl. She has no parents. Her sister is herself quite young and they are both, in a sense, dependent on me as the priest of this place for all the protection I can give. I feel responsible for these girls, Renshaw, responsible for them, and no feelings of a personal kind with regard to any one," here he squeezed Ricoletto so tightly that the rat emitted a frightened little squeal, " shall interfere with what I feel is my duty. No, hear me out, hear me out, Renshaw!" he continued hurriedly, as his companion began to speak. " The matter is one about which we need not mind being quite open. I want you, in fact, to promise me — to promise me on your word of honour — that you'll leave this child alone. I don't know how far things have gone between you. I can't imagine, it would be shameful to imagine, that it has gone beyond a flirtation. But whatever it has been, it must stop now. It's only your word of honour I want, nothing but your word of honour, and I can't believe you'll hesitate, as a gentleman, to give me that. You'll give me that, won't you, Renshaw? Just say yes and the matter's closed."

He removed his hand from his pocket and laid it on his companion's wrist. Brand was sufficiently cool at that moment to remark as an interesting fact that the priest was trembling. Not only was he trembling but as he removed his hat to give further solemnity to his

appeal, large drops of perspiration, known only to
himself, for darkness dimmed his face, trickled down
into his eyes. Brand quietly freed himself and moved
back a step.

"I'm not in the least surprised," he said, "at your
speaking to me like this, and strange as it may seem it
does not annoy me. In fact it pleases me. I like it.
It raises the value of the girl — of Linda, I mean —
and it makes me respect you. But if you imagine, my
good Mr. Traherne, that I'm going to make any such
promise as you describe, you can have no more notion
of what I'm like than you have of what Linda's like.
Talk to *her*, Hamish Traherne, talk to her, and see
what she says!"

The priest clenched his fingers round the handle of
his oak stick. He felt rising in him a tide of natural
human anger. Mentally he prayed to his God that
he might retain his self-control and not make matters
worse by violence.

"If it interests you to know," Brand continued, "I
may tell you that it's quite possible I shall marry Linda.
She attracts me, I confess it freely, more than I could
possibly explain to you or to any one. I presume you
wouldn't carry your responsibility so far as to make
trouble about my marrying her, eh? But that's nothing. That's neither here nor there. Married or unmarried, I do what I please. Do I convey my meaning sufficiently clearly? I — do — what — I — please.
Let that be your clue henceforth, Mr. Hamish Traherne, and the clue of everybody else in Rodmoor, in
dealing with me. Listen to me, sir. I do you the honour of talking more openly to you to-night than I'm
ever likely to talk again. Perhaps you have the idea

that I'm a mere commonplace sensualist, snatching at every animal pleasure that comes my way? Perhaps you fancy I've a vicious — what do you call it? — 'penchant'— for the seduction of young girls? Let me tell you this, Mr. Hamish, a thing that may somewhat surprise you. I've walked these woods till I know every scent in them by night and day — do you catch that fungus-smell now? That's one of the smells I love best of all! — and in these walks, absolutely alone, — I love being alone! — I've faced possibilities of evil — faced them and resisted them, mind you! — compared with which these mere normal sexual lapses we're talking about are silly child's play! Linda does me good. Do you hear? She does me good. She saves me from things that never in your wildest dreams you'd suppose any one capable of. Oh, you priests! You priests! You shut yourselves up among your crucifixes and your little books, and meanwhile — beyond your furthest imagination — the great tides of evil sweep backwards and forwards! Listen! I needn't tell you what that sound is? Yes — you can hear it. In every part of this place you can hear it! I was born to that tune, Traherne, and I shall die to that tune. It's better than rustling leaves, isn't it? It's deeper. It's the kind of music a man might have in his head when doing something compared with which such little sins as you're blaming me for are virtues! Did you see that bat? I've watched them under these trees from midnight to morning. A bat in the light of dawn is a curious thing to see. Do you like bats, Mr. Traherne, or do you confine yourself to rats?

"Bah! I'm talking like an idiot. But what I want you to understand is this. When you're dealing with

me, you are dealing with some one who's lost the power
of being frightened by words, some one who's broken
the world's crust and peeped behind it, some one who's
seen the black pools — did you guess there were black
pools in this world? — and has seen the red stains in
them and who knows what caused those stains! Damn
it all — Hamish Traherne — what did you take me for
when you talked to me like that? A common, sensual
pig? A vulgar seducer of children? A fellow to be
frightened back into the fold by talk of honour and
the manners of gentlemen? I tell you *I've seen bats in
the dawn* — and seen them too, with images in my memory that only *that sound* — do you hear it still? —
could equal for horror.

"It's because Linda knows the horror of the sea
that I love her. I love to lead her to it, to feel her
draw back and not to let her draw back! And she
loves me *for the same reason!* That's a fact, Mr.
Hamish, that may be hard for you to realize. Linda
and I understand each other. Do you hear that, you
lover of rats? We understand each other. She does
me good. She distracts me. She keeps those black
pools out of my mind. She keeps Philippa's eyes from
following me about. She takes the taste of funguses
out of my mouth. She suits me, I tell you! She's
what I need. She's what I need and must have!

"Bah! I'm chattering like an idiot. I must be
drunk. I *am* drunk. But that's nothing. That's one
of the vices that are *my* virtues. I'll tell you another
thing, while I'm about it, Hamish Traherne. You've
wondered sometimes, I expect, why I'm so good to
Baltazar. Quite Christian of me, you've thought it,
eh? Quite noble and Christian — considering what he

is and what I am? That just shows how little you
know us, how little you know either of us! Tassar can
no more get away from me than I can get away from
him. We're bound together for life, my boy, bound
together by what those black pools mean and what
that sound — you wouldn't think you could hear it
here, would you? — never stops meaning.

"Bah! I'm drunk as a pig to-night! I've not
talked like this to any one, not for years. Listen, Traherne! You have an ugly face but you're not a fool.
Wasn't it Saint Augustine who said once that evil was
a mere rent in the cloak of goodness? The simple innocent! I tell you, evil goes down to the bottom of
life and out beyond! I know that, for I've gone with
it. *I've seen the bats in the dawn.*

"Yes, Tassar's gone far, Hamish Traherne, farther
than you guess. Sometimes I think he's gone farther
than *I* guess. *He* never talks, you know. You'll never
catch *him* drunk. Tassar could look the devil in the
face, and worse, and keep his pretty head cool! — Oh,
damn it all, Traherne, it's not easy for a person never
to open his mouth! But Tassar's got the secret of
that. He must get it from my father. There was a
man for you! You wouldn't have dared to talk to him
like this."

Several times during this long outburst, Mr. Traherne's fingers had caused pain to Ricoletto. But now
he flung out his long arms and clutched Brand fiercely by
the shoulders.

"Pray — you poor lost soul," he shouted, "pray
the great God above us to have mercy upon you and
have mercy upon us all!"

His arms trembled as he uttered these words and,

hardly conscious of what he was doing, he shook the heavy frame of the man before him backwards and forwards as if he had been a child in his hands. There was dead silence for several seconds and, unheeded by either of them, a weasel ran furtively across the path and disappeared among the trees. The damp odours of moss and leaf-mould rose up around them and, between the motionless branches above, the stars shone like pinpricks through black parchment. Suddenly Brand broke away with a harsh laugh.

"Enough of this!" he cried. "We've had enough melodramatic nonsense for one night. You'd better go back to bed, Traherne, or you'll be oversleeping yourself to-morrow and my mother will miss her matins."

He held out his hand.

"Good night!—and sleep soundly!" he added, in his accustomed dull, sarcastic tone.

The priest sighed heavily and groped about on the ground for the hat he had dropped. Just as he had secured it and was moving off, Brand called out to him laughingly,

"Don't you believe a word of what I said just now. I'm not drunk at all. I was only fooling. I'm just a common ruffian who knows a pretty face when he sees it. Talk to Linda about me and see what she says!" He strode off up the avenue and the priest turned heavily on his heel.

XV

BROKEN VOICES

NANCE and Linda were not long in growing accustomed to their new mode of life. Nance, after her London experiences, found Miss Pontifex' little work-room, looking out on a pleasant garden, a place of refuge rather than of irksome labour. The young girls under her charge were good-tempered and docile; and Miss Pontifex herself — an excitable little woman with extravagantly genteel manners, and a large Wedgewood brooch under her chin — seemed to think that the girl's presence in the establishment would redound immensely to its reputation and distinction.

"I'm a conservative born and bred," she remarked to Nance, "and I can tell a lady out of a thousand. I won't say what I might say about the people here. But we know — we know what we think."

Nance's intimate knowledge of the more recondite aspects of the trade took an immense load off the little dressmaker's mind. She had more time to devote to her garden, which was her deepest passion, and it filled her with pride to be able to say to her friends, "Miss Herrick from Dyke House works with me now. Her father was a Captain in the Royal Navy."

The month of July went by without any further agitating incidents. As far as Nance knew, Brand left Linda in peace, and the young girl, though looking

weary and spiritless, seemed to be reconciling herself
fairly well to the loss of him and to be deriving definite
distraction and satisfaction from her progress in organ-
playing. Day by day in the early afternoon, she
would cross the bridge, under all changes of the weather,
and make her way to the church. Her mornings were
spent in household duties, so that her sister might be
free to give her whole time to the work in the shop,
and in the evenings, when it was pleasant to be out of
doors, they both helped Miss Pontifex watering her
phloxes and delphiniums.

Nance herself — as July drew to its close and the
wheat fields turned yellow — was at once happier and
less happy in her relations with Sorio. Her happiness
came from the fact that he treated her now more gently
and considerately than he had ever done before; her
unhappiness from the fact that he had grown more reserved and a queer sort of nervous depression seemed
hanging over him. She knew he still saw Philippa, but
what the relations between the two were, or how far any
lasting friendship had arisen between them, it was impossible to discover. They certainly never met now,
under conditions open to the intrusion of Rodmoor
scandal.

Nance went more than once, before July was over,
to see Rachel Doorm, and the days when these visits occurred were the darkest and saddest of all she passed
through during that time. The mistress of Dyke
House seemed to be rapidly degenerating. Nance was
horrified to find how inert and indifferent to everything
she had come to be. The interior of the house was now
as dusty and untidy as the garden was desolate, and
judging from her manner on the last visit she paid, the

girl began to fear she had found the same solace in her
loneliness as that which consoled her father.

Nance made one desperate attempt to improve matters. Without saying anything to Miss Doorm, she
carried with her to the house one of Mrs. Raps' own
buxom daughters, who was quite prepared, for an in-
finitesimal compensation, to go every day to help her.
But this arrangement collapsed hopelessly. On the
third day after her first appearance, the young woman
returned to her home, and with indignant tears declared
she had been " thrown out of the nasty place."

One evening at the end of the month, just as the
sisters were preparing to go out for a stroll together,
their landlady, with much effusion and agitation,
ushered in Mrs. Renshaw. Tired with walking, and
looking thinner and whiter than usual, she seemed extremely glad to sit down on their little sofa and sip the
raspberry vinegar which Nance hastened to prepare.
She ate some biscuits, too, as if she were faint for want
of food, but all the time she ate there was in her air an
apologetic, deprecatory manner, as though eating had
been a gross vice or as though never in her life before
had she eaten in public. She kept imploring Nance to
share the refreshment, and it was not until the girl made
at least a pretence of doing so that she seemed to recover her peace of mind.

Her great, hollow, brown eyes kept surveying the little apartment with nervous admiration. " I like it
here," she remarked at last. " I like little rooms much
better than large ones." She picked up from the table
a well-worn copy of Palgrave's " Golden Treasury " and
Nance had never seen her face light up so suddenly as
when, turning the pages at random, she chanced upon

Keats' "Ode to Autumn." "I know that by heart,"
she said, "every word of it. I used to teach it to
Philippa. You've no idea how nicely she used to say
it. But she doesn't care for poetry any more. She
reads more learned books, more clever books now. She's
got beyond me. Both my children have got beyond
me." She sighed heavily and Nance, with a sense of
horrible pity, seemed to visualize her — happy in little
rooms and with little anthologies of old-world verse —
condemned to the devastating isolation of Oakguard.

"I see you've got 'The Bride of Lammermoor' up
there," she remarked presently, and rising impetuously
from her seat on the sofa, she took the book in her
hands. Nance never forgot the way she touched it, or
the infinite softness that came into her eyes as she murmured, "Poor Lucy! Poor Lucy!" and began turning the pages.

Suddenly another book caught her attention and she
took down "Humphrey Clinker" from the shelf.
"Oh!" she cried, a faint flush coming into her sunken
cheeks, "I haven't seen that book for years and years.
I used to read it before I was married. I think Smollett was a very great writer, don't you? But I suppose young people nowadays find him too simple for
their taste. That poor dear Mr. Bramble! And all
that part about Tabitha, too! I seem to remember it
all. I believe Dickens used to like Smollett. At least,
I think I read somewhere that he did. I expect he liked
that wonderful mixture of humour and pathos, though
of course, when it comes to that, I suppose none of
them can equal Dickens himself."

As Mrs. Renshaw uttered these words and caressed
the tattered volume she held as if it had been made of

pure gold, her face became irradiated with a look of such innocent and guileless spirituality, that Nance, in a hurried act of mental contrition, wiped out of her memory every moment when she had not loved her. " What she must suffer!" the girl said to herself as she watched her. " What she must *have* suffered — with those people in that great house."

Mrs. Renshaw sighed as she replaced the book in the shelf. " Writers seem to have got so clever in these last years," she said plaintively. " They use so many long words. I wonder where they get them from — out of dictionaries, do you think? — and they hurt me, they hurt me, by the way they speak of our beloved religion. They can't *all* of them be great philosophers like Spinoza and Schopenhauer, can they? They can't all of them be going to give the world new and comforting thoughts? I don't like their sharp, snappy, sarcastic tone. And oh, Nance dear!"— she returned to her seat on the sofa —" I can't bear their slang! Why is it that they feel they must use so much slang, do you think? I suppose they want to make their books seem real, but *I* don't hear real people talking like that. But perhaps it comes from America. American writers seem extraordinarily clever, and American dictionaries — for Dr. Raughty showed me one — seem much bigger than ours."

She was silent for a while and then, looking gently at Linda, " I think it's wonderful, dear, how well you play now. I thought last Sunday evening you played the hymns better than I've ever heard them! But they were beautiful hymns, weren't they? That last one was my favourite of all."

Once more she was silent, and Nance seemed to catch

her lips moving, as she fixed her great sorrowful eyes upon the book-shelf, and began slowly pulling on her gloves.

"I must be going now," she said, with a little sigh. "I thank you for the raspberry vinegar and the biscuits. I think I was tired. I didn't sleep very well last night. Good-bye, dears. No, don't, please, come down. I can let myself out. It's a lovely evening, isn't it, and the poppies in the cornfields are quite red now. I can see a big patch of them from our terrace, just across the river. Poppies always make me think of the days when I was a young girl. We used to think a lot of them then. We used to make fairies out of them."

Nance insisted on seeing her into the street. When she entered the room again, she was not altogether surprised to find Linda convulsed with sobs. "I can't — I can't help it," gasped the young girl. "She's too pitiful. She's too sad. You feel you want to hug her and hug her, but you're afraid even to touch her hand!" She made an effort to recover herself, and then, with the tears still on her cheeks, "Nance dear," she said solemnly, "I don't believe she'll live to the end of this year. I believe, one of these days, when the Autumn comes, we shall hear she's been found dead in her bed. Nance, listen!"— and the young girl's voice became awe-struck and very solemn —"won't it be dreadful for *those two*, over there, when they find her like that, and feel how little they've done to make her happy? Can't you imagine it, Nance? The wind wailing and wailing round that house, and she lying there all white and dreadful — and Philippa with a candle standing over her —"

"Why do you say 'with a candle'?" said Nance brusquely. "You're talking wildly and exaggerating everything. If they found her in the morning, like that, Philippa wouldn't come with a candle."

Linda stared dreamily out of the window. "No, I suppose not," she said, "and yet I can't see it without Philippa holding a candle. And there's something else I see, too," she added in a lower voice.

"I don't want —" Nance began and then, more gently, "*What* else, you silly child?"

"Philippa's red lips," she murmured softly, "red as if she'd put rouge on them. Do you think she ever does put rouge on them? That's, I suppose, what made me think of the candle. I seemed to see it flickering against her mouth. Oh, I'm silly — I'm silly, I know, but I couldn't help seeing it like that — her lips, I mean."

"You're morbid to-day, Linda," said Nance abruptly. "Well? Shall we go to the garden? I feel as though carrying watering-pots and doing weeding will be good for both of us."

While this conversation was going on between the sisters in their High Street lodging, Sorio and Baltazar were seated together on a bench by the harbour's side. The tide was flowing in and cool sea-breaths, mixed with the odour of tar and paint and fisherman's tobacco, floated in upon them as they talked.

"It's absurd to have any secrets between you and me," Sorio was saying, his face reflecting the light of the sunset as it poured down the river's surface to where they sat. "When I become quite impossible to you as a companion, I suppose you'll tell me so and turn me out. But until then I'm going to assume that I interest you and don't bore you."

"It isn't a question of boring any one," replied the other. "You annoyed me just now because I thought you were making no effort to control yourself. You seemed trying to rake up every repulsive sensation you've ever had and thrust it down my throat. Bored? Certainly I wasn't bored! On the contrary, I was much more what you might call *bitten*. You go so far, my dear, you go so far!"

"I don't call that going far at all," said Sorio sulkily. "What's the use of living together if we can't talk of everything? Besides, you didn't let me finish. What I wanted to say was that for some reason or other, I've lately got to a point when every one I meet — every mortal person, and especially every stranger — strikes me as odious and disgusting. I've had the feeling before but never quite like this. It's not a pleasant feeling, my dear, I can assure you of that!"

"But what do you mean — what do you mean by odious and disgusting?" threw in the other. "I suppose they're made in the same way we are. Flesh and blood is flesh and blood, after all."

As Baltazar said this, what he thought in his mind was much as follows: "Adriano is evidently going mad again. This kind of thing is one of the symptoms. I like having him here with me. I like looking at his face when he's excited. He has a beautiful face — it's more purely antique in its moulding than half the ancient cameos. I especially like looking at him when he's harassed and outraged. He has a dilapidated wistfulness at those times which exactly suits my taste.

I should miss Adriano frightfully if he went away. No one I've ever lived with suits me better. I can annoy him when I like and I can appease him when I like. He fills me with a delicious sense of power. If only Philippa would leave him alone, and that Herrick girl would stop persecuting him, he'd suit me perfectly. I like him when his nerves are quivering and twitching. I like the ' wounded-animal look ' he has then. But it's these accursed girls who spoil it all. Of course it's their work, this new mania. They carry everything so far! I like him to get wild and desperate but I don't want him mad. These girls stick at nothing. They'd drive him into an asylum if they could, poor helpless devil! "

While these thoughts slid gently through Stork's head, his friend was already answering his question about " flesh and blood." " It's just that which gets on my nerves," he said. " I can stand it when I'm talking to you because I forget everything except your mind, and I can stand it when I'm making love to a girl, because I forget everything but —"

" Don't say her body! " threw in Baltazar.

" I wasn't going to," snarled the other. " I know it isn't their bodies one thinks of. It's — it's — what the devil is it? It's something much deeper than that. Well, never mind! What I want to say is this. With you and Raughty, and a few others who really interest me, I forget the whole thing. *You* are individuals to me. I'm interested in you, and I forget what you're like, or that you have flesh at all.

" It's when I come upon people I'm neither in love with nor interested in, that I have this sensation, and of course," and he surveyed a group of women who at

that moment were raising angry voices from an arch-
way on the further side of the harbour, " and of course
I have it every day."

Stork looked at him with absorbed attention, holding between his fingers an unlit cigarette. "What
exactly *is* the feeling you have? " he enquired gently.

The light on Sorio's face had faded with the fading
of the glow on the water. There began to fall upon the
place where they sat, upon the cobble-stones of the little quay, upon the wharf steps, slimy with green seaweed, upon the harbour mud and the tarred gunwales
of the gently rocking barges, upon the pallid tide flowing inland with gurglings and suckings and lappings
and long-drawn sighs, that indescribable sense of the
coming on of night at a river's mouth, which is like
nothing else in the world. It is, as it were, the meeting of two infinite vistas of imaginative suggestion —
the sense of the mystery of the boundless horizons sea-
ward, and the more human mystery of the unknown
distance inland, its vague fields and marshes and woods
and silent gardens —blending there together in a suspended breath of ineffable possibility, sad and tender,
and touching the margin of what cannot be uttered.

" What is it? " repeated Sorio dreamily, and in a
low melancholy voice. " How can I tell you what it
is? It's a knowledge of the inner truth, I suppose.
It's the fact that I've come to know, at last, what
human beings are really like. I've come to see them
stripped and naked — no! worse than that — I've come
to see them *flayed*. I've got to the point, Tassar, my
friend, when I see the world *as it is*, and I can tell you
it's not a pleasant sight! "

Baltazar Stork regarded him with a look of the most

exquisite pity, a pity which was not the less genuine because the emotion that accompanied it was one of indescribable pleasure. In the presence of his friend's massive face and powerful figure he felt deliciously delicate and frail, but with this sense of fragility came a feeling of indescribable power — the power of a mind that is capable of contemplating with equanimity a view of things at which another staggers and shivers and grows insane. It was allotted to Baltazar by the secret forces of the universe to know during that hour, one of the most thrilling moments of his life.

" To get to the point I've reached," continued Sorio gently, watching the colour die out from the water's surface and a whitish glimmer, silvery and phantom-like, take its place, " means to sharpen one's senses to a point of terrible receptivity. In fact, until you can hear the hearts of people beating — until you can hear their contemptible lusts hissing and writhing in their veins, like evil snakes — you haven't reached the point. You haven't reached it until you can smell the grave-yard — yes! the graveyard of all mortality — in the cleanest flesh you approach. You haven't reached it till every movement people make, every word they speak, betrays them for what they are, betrays the vulture on the wing, and the hyena on the prowl. You haven't reached it till you feel ready to cry out, like a child in a nightmare, and beat the air with your hands, so suffocating is the pressure of loathsome living bodies — bodies marked and sealed and printed with the signs of death and decomposition ! "

Baltazar Stork struck a match and lit his cigarette.

" Well? " he remarked, stretching out his legs and leaning back on the wooden bench. " Well? The

world is like that, then. You've found it out. You
know it. You've made the wonderful discovery. Why
can't you smoke cigarettes, then, and make love to your
lovely friends, and let the whole thing go? You'll be
dead yourself in a year or two in any case.

" Adriano dear," he lowered his voice to an impres-
sive whisper, " shall I tell you something? You are
making all this fuss and driving yourself desperate
about a thing which doesn't really concern you in the
least. It's not your business if the world does reek
like a carcass. It's not your business if people's brains
are full of poisonous snakes and their bellies of greedy
lecheries. It's not your business — do you understand — if human flesh smells of the graveyard. Your
affair, my boy, is to get what amusement you can out
of it and make yourself as comfortable as you can in it.
It might be worse, it might be better. It doesn't really
make much difference either way.

" Listen to me, Adriano! I say to you now, as we
sit at this moment watching this water, unless you get
rid of this new mania of yours, you'll end as you did
in America. You'll simply go mad again, my dear,
and that would be uncomfortable for you and extremely
inconvenient for me. The world is not *meant* to be
taken seriously. It's meant to be handled as you'd
handle a troublesome girl. Take what amuses you and
let the rest go to the devil! Anything else — and I
know what I'm talking about — tends to simple misery.

" Heigh ho! But it's a most delicious evening!
What nonsense all this talk of ours is! Look at that
boy over there. He's not worrying himself about
grave-yards. Here, Harry! Tommy! Whatever you
call yourself — come here! I want to speak to you."

The child addressed was a ragged barelegged urchin, of about eleven, who had been for some while slowly gravitating around the two men. He came at once, at Baltazar's call, and looked at them both, wonderingly and quizzically.

"Got any pictures?" he asked. Stork nodded and, opening a new box of cigarettes, handed the boy a little oblong card stamped with the arms of some royal European dynasty. "I likes the Honey-Dew ones best," remarked the boy, "them as has the sport cards in 'em."

"We can't always have sport cards, Tommy," said Baltazar. "Little boys, as the world moves round, must learn to put up with the arms of European princes. Let me feel your muscle, Tommy. I've an idea that you're suffering from deficient nourishment." The child extended his arm, and then bent it, with an air of extreme and anxious gravity. "Pretty good," said Stork, smiling. "Yes, I may say you're decidedly powerful for your size. What's your opinion, Tommy, about things in general? This gentleman here thinks we're all in a pretty miserable way. He thinks life's a hell of a bad job. What do you think about it?"

The boy looked at him suspiciously. "Ben Porter, what cleans the knives up at the Admiral's, tried that game on with me. But I let him know, soon enough, who he were talking to." He moved off hastily after this, but a moment later ran back, pointing excitedly at a couple of sea-gulls which were circling near them.

"A man shot one of them birds last night," he said, "and it fell into the water. Lordy! But it did splash! 'Tweren't properly killed, I reckon — just knocked over."

"What's that?" said Sorio sharply. "What became of it then? Who picked it up?"

The boy looked at him with a puzzled stare. "*They* ain't no good to eat," he rejoined, "they be what you call cannibal-birds. They feeds on muck. Cats'll eat 'em, though," he added.

"What became of it?" shouted Sorio, in a threatening voice.

"Went out with the tide, Mister, most like," answered the child, moving apprehensively away from him. "I saw some fellows in a boat knock at it with their oars, but they couldn't get it. It sort o' flapped and swimmed away."

Sorio rose from his seat and strode to the edge of the quay. He looked eastward, past the long line of half-submerged wooden stakes which marked the approach to the harbour. "When did that devil shoot it, do you say?" he asked, turning to the boy. But the youngster had taken to his heels. Angry-looking bronze-faced gentlemen who interested themselves in wounded sea-gulls were something new in his experience.

"Let's get a boat and row out to those stakes," said Adrian suddenly. "I seem to see something white over there. Look! Don't you think so?"

Baltazar moved to his side. "Heavens! my dear," he remarked languidly, "you don't suppose the thing would be there now, after all this time? However," he added, shrugging his shoulders, "if it'll put you into a better mood, by all means let's do it."

It was, when it came to the point, Baltazar who untied an available boat from its moorings, and Baltazar who appropriated a pair of oars that were leaning against a fish shed. In details of this kind the passionate Sorio was always seized with a paralysis of nervous incompetence. Once in the boat, however, the younger man refused to do anything but steer. "I'm not going to pull against this current, for all the seagulls in the world," he remarked.

Sorio rowed with desperate impetuosity, but it was a slow and laborious task. Several fishermen, loitering on the quay after their supper, surveyed the scene with interest. "The gentleman wants to exercise 'isself afore dinner-time," observed one. "'Tis a wonder if he moves 'er," rejoined another, "but 'e's rowin' like 'twas a royal regatta."

With the sweat pouring down his face and the muscles of his whole body taut and quivering, Sorio tugged and strained at the oars. At first it seemed as though the boat hardly moved at all. Then, little by little, it forged ahead, the tide's pressure diminishing as the mouth of the harbour widened. After several minutes' exhausting effort, they reached the place where the first of the wooden piles rose out of the water. It was tangled with seaweed and bleached with sun and wind. The tide gurgled and foamed round it. Baltazar yawned.

"They're all like this one," he said. "You see what they're like. Nothing could possibly cling to them, unless it had hands to cling with."

Sorio, resting on his oars, glared at the darkening waters. "Let's get to the last of them anyway," he muttered. He pulled on, the effort becoming easier and easier as they escaped from the in-flow of the river-mouth and reached the open sea. When at last the

boat rubbed its side against the last of the stakes,
they were nearly a quarter of a mile from land. No,
there was certainly no sea-gull here, alive or dead!

A buoy, with a bell attached to it, sent at intervals,
over the water, a profoundly melancholy cry — a cry
subdued and yet tragic, not absolutely devoid of hope
and yet full of heart-breaking wistfulness. The air was
hot and windless; the sky heavy with clouds; the horizon concealed by the rapidly falling night. Sorio
seized the stake with his hand to keep the boat steady.
There were already lights in the town, and some of
these twinkled out towards them, in long, radiating,
quivering lines.

"Tassar!" whispered Sorio suddenly, in a tone
strangely and tenderly modulated.

"Well, my child, what is it?" returned the other.

"I only want to tell you," Adrian went on, "that
whatever I may say or do in the future, I recognize
that you're the best friend I've got, except one." As
he said the words "except one," his voice had a vibrant
softness in it.

"Thank you, my dear," replied his friend calmly.
"I should certainly be extremely distressed if you made
a fool of yourself in any way. But who is my rival,
tell me that! Who is this one who's a better friend
than I? Not Philippa, I hope — or Nance Herrick?"

Sorio sighed heavily. "I vowed to myself," he muttered, "I would never talk to any one again about him;
but the sound of that bell — isn't it weird, Tassar?
Isn't it ghostly? — makes me long to talk about him."

"Ah! I understand," and Baltazar Stork drew in
his breath with a low whistle, "I understand! You're
talking about your boy over there. Well, my dear, I

don't blame you if you're homesick for him. I have
a feeling that he's an extraordinarily beautiful youth.
I always picture him to myself like my Venetian. Is he
like Flambard, Adrian?"

Sorio sighed again, the sigh of one who sins against
his secret soul and misses the reward of his sacrilege.
"No — no," he muttered, "it isn't that! It isn't anything to do with his being beautiful. God knows if
Baptiste *is* beautiful! It's that I want him. It's that
he understands what I'm trying to do in the darkness.
It's simply that I want him, Tassar."

"What do you mean by that 'trying in the darkness,' Adriano? What 'darkness' are you talking
about?"

Sorio made no immediate answer. His hand, as he
clung to the stake amid the rocking of the boat, encountered a piece of seaweed of that kind which possesses slippery, bubble-like excrescences, and he dug his
nails into one of these leathery globes, with a vague
dreamy idea that if he could burst it he would burst
some swollen trouble in his brain.

"Do you remember," he said at last, "what I showed
you the other night, or have you forgotten?"

Baltazar looked at his mistily outlined features and
experienced, what was extremely unusual with him, a
faint sense of apprehensive remorse. "Of course I
remember," he replied. "You mean those notes of
yours — that book you're writing?"

But Sorio did not hear him. All his attention was
concentrated just then upon the attempt to burst another seaweed bubble. The bell from the unseen buoy
rang out brokenly over the water; and between the side
of their boat and the stake to which the man was

clinging there came gurglings and lappings and whispers, as if below them, far down under the humming
tide, some sad sea-creature, without hope or memory
or rest, were tossing and moaning, turning a drowned
inhuman face towards the darkened sky.

XVI

THE FENS

NANCE was able, in a sort of lethargic obstinacy, to endure the strain of her feelings for Sorio, now that she had the influence of her familiar work to dull her nerves. She tried hard to make things cheerful for her not less heart-weary sister, devising one little scheme after another to divert and distract the child, and never permitting her own trouble to interfere with her sympathy.

But behind all this her soul ached miserably, and her whole nature thirsted and throbbed for the satisfaction of her love. Her work played its part as a kind of numbing opiate and the evenings spent among Letitia Pontifex' flower-beds were not devoid of moments of restorative hope, but day and night the pain of her passion hurt her and the tooth of jealousy bit into her flesh.

It was worst of all in the nights. The sisters slept in two small couches in the same room and Nance found herself dreading more and more, as July drew to its close, that hour when they came in from their neighbour's garden and undressing in silence, lay down so near to one another. They both tried hard, Linda no less than her sister, to put the thoughts that vexed them out of their minds and behave as if they were fancy-free and at peace, but the struggle was a difficult one. If they only hadn't known, so cruelly well, just what the

other was feeling, as they turned alternately from side
to side, and like little feverish animals gasped and
fretted, it would have been easier to bear. "Aren't
you asleep yet?" one of them would whisper plaintively, and the submissive, "I'm so sorry, dear; but oh!
I wish the morning would come," that she received in
answer, met with only too deep a response.

One unusually hot night — it happened to be the
first Sunday in August and the eve of the Bank Holiday — Nance felt as though she would scream out aloud
if her sister moved in her bed again.

There was something that humiliated and degraded
in this mutual misery. It was hard to be patient, hard
not to feel that her own aching heart was in some subtle
way mocked and insulted by the presence of the same
hurt in the heart of another. It reduced the private
sorrow of each to a sort of universal sex pain, to suffer
from which was a kind of outrage to what was sacred
and secret in their individual souls.

There were two windows in their room, one opening
on the street and one upon an enclosed yard at the back
of the house. Nance, as she now lay, with the bed-
clothes tossed aside from her, and her hands clasped
behind her head, was horribly conscious not only of the
fact that her sister was just as wide awake as she herself, but that they were listening *together* to the same
sounds. These sounds were two-fold, and they came
sometimes separately and sometimes simultaneously.
They consisted of the wailing of an infant in a room on
the other side of the street, and the whining of a dog
in a yard adjoining their own.

The girl felt as though every species of desolation
known in the world were concentrated in these two

sounds. She kept her eyes tightly shut so as not to see the darkness, but this proceeding only intensified the acute receptivity of her other senses. She visualized the infant and she visualized the dog. The one she imagined with a puckered, wrinkled face — a face such as Mr. Traherne might have had in his babyhood — and plague-spots of a loathsome colour; she saw the colour against her burning eyeballs as if she were touching it with her fingers and it was of a reddish brown. The dog had a long smooth body, without hair, and as it whined she saw it feebly scratching itself, but while it scratched, she knew, with evil certainty, that it was unable to reach the place where the itching maddened it.

There was hardly any air in the room, in spite of the open windows, and Nance fancied that she discerned an odour proceeding from the wainscoting that resembled the dust that had once greeted her from a cupboard in one of the unused bedrooms in Dyke House, dust that seemed to be composed of the moth-eaten garments of generations of dead humanity.

She felt that she could have borne these things — the whining dog, and the wailing infant — if only Linda, lying with her face to the wall, were not listening to them also, listening with feverish intentness. Yes, she could have borne it if the whole night were not listening — if the whole night were not listening to the turnings and tossings of humanity, trying to ease the itch of its desire and never able to reach, toss and turn as it might, the place where the plague-spot troubled it.

With a cry she leapt from her bed and, fumbling on the dressing-table, struck a match and lit a candle.

The flickering flame showed Linda sitting bolt-upright with lamentable wide-open eyes.

Nance went to the window which looked out on the yard. Here she turned and threw back from her forehead her masses of heavy hair. "God help us, Linda!" she whispered. "It's no use. Nothing is any use."

The young girl slowly and wearily left her bed and, advancing across the room, nestled up against her sister and caressed her in silence.

"What shall we do?" Nance repeated, hardly knowing what she said. "What shall we do? I can't bear this. I can't bear it, little one, I can't bear it!"

As if in response to her appeal, the dog and the infant together sent forth a pitiful wail upon the night.

"What misery there is in the world — what horrible misery!" Nance murmured. "I'm sure we're all better off dead, than like this. Better off dead, my darling."

Linda answered by slipping her arms round her waist and hugging her tightly. Then suddenly, "Why don't we dress ourselves and go out?" she cried. "It's too hot to sleep. Yes, do let's do that, Nance! Let's dress and go out."

Nance looked at her with a faint smile. There was a childish ardour about her tone that reminded her of the Linda of many years ago. "Very well," she said, "I don't mind."

They dressed hurriedly. The very boldness of the idea helped them to recover their spirits. Bareheaded and in their house-shoes they let themselves out into the street. It was between two and three o'clock. The little town was absolutely silent. The infant in the house opposite made no sound. " Perhaps it's dead now," Nance thought.

They walked across the green, and Nance gave a long wistful look at the windows of Baltazar's cottage. The heavy clouds had lifted a little, and from various points in the sky the stars threw down a faint, uncertain glimmer. It remained, however, still so dark that when they reached the centre of the bridge, neither bank was visible, and the waters of the Loon flowing beneath were hidden in profound obscurity. They leant upon the parapet and inhaled the darkness. What wind there was blew from the west so that the air was heavy with the scent of peat and marsh mud, and the sound of the sea seemed to come from far away, as if it belonged to a different world.

They crossed the bridge and began following the footpath that led to the church. Coming suddenly on an open gate, however, they were tempted, by a curious instinct of unconscious self-cruelty, to deviate from the path they knew and to pursue a strange and unfamiliar track heading straight for the darkened fens. It was on the side of the path removed from the sea that this track began, and it led them, along the edge of a reedy ditch, into a great shadowy maze of silent water-meadows.

Fortunately for the two girls, the particular ditch they followed had a high and clearly marked embankment, an embankment used by the owners of cattle in that district as a convenient way of getting their herds from one feeding-ground to another. No one who has never experienced the sensation of following one of these raised banks, or dyke-tracks, across the fens, can conceive the curious feelings it has the power of evok-

ing. Even by day these impressions are unique and
strange. By night they assume a quality which may
easily pass into something bordering upon panic-terror.
The palpable and immediate cause of this emotion is the
sense of being isolated, separated, and cut-off, from all
communication with the ordinary world.

On the sea-shore one is indeed in contact with the
unknown mass of waters, but there is always, close at
hand, the familiar inland landscape, friendly and reassuring. On the slope of a mountain one may look
with apprehension at the austere heights above, but
there is always behind one the rocks and woods, the
terraces and ledges, past which one has ascended, and
to which at any moment one can return.

In the midst of the fens there is no such reassurance.
The path one has followed becomes merged in the il-
limitable space around; merged, lost and annihilated.
No mark, no token, no sign indicates its difference from
other similar tracks. No mark nor token separates
north from south or east from west. On all sides the
same reeds, the same meadows, the same gates, the same
stunted willow-trees, the same desolate marsh pools,
the same vast and receding horizons. The mind has
nothing to rest itself upon except the general expanse,
and the general expanse seems as boundless as infinity.

Nance and her sister were not, of course, far enough
away from their familiar haunts to get the complete
" fen-terror," but, aided by the darkness, the power of
the thing was by no means unfelt. The instinct to escape from the burden of their thoughts which drove
the girls on, became indeed more and more definitely
mingled, as they advanced, with a growing sense of
alarm. But into this very alarm they plunged for-

ward with a species of exultant desperation. They both experienced, as they went hand in hand, a morbid kind of delight in being cruel to themselves, in forcing themselves to do the very thing — and to do it in the dead of night — which, of all, they had most avoided, even in the full light of day.

Before they had gone much more than a mile from their starting-point they were permitted to witness a curious trick of the elemental powers. Without any warning, there suddenly arose from the west a much more powerful current of wind. Every cloud was driven sea-ward and with the clouds every trace of sea-mist. The vast dome of sky above them showed itself clear and unstained; and across the innumerable constellations — manifest to their eyes in its full length — stretched the Milky Way. Not only did the stars thus make themselves visible. In their visibility they threw a weird and phantom-like light over the whole landscape. Objects that had been mere misty blurs became distinct identities and things that had been absolutely out of sight were now unmistakably recognizable.

The girls stood still and looked around them. They could see the church tower rising squat and square against the line of the distant sand-dunes. They could see the roofs of the village, huddled greyly and obscurely together, beyond the dark curve of the bridge. They could make out the sombre shape of Dyke House itself, just distinguishable against the high tow-path of the river. And Nance, turning westward, could even discern her favourite withy-copse, surrounded by shadowy cornfields.

There was a pitiable pathos in the way each of the girls, now that the scene of their present trouble was

thus bared to their view, turned instinctively to the
object most associated with the thoughts they were
seeking to escape. Nance looked long and wistfully at
the little wood of willows and alders, now a mere misty
exhalation of thicker shadow above the long reaches of
the fens. She thought of how mercilessly her feelings
had been outraged there; of how violent and strange
and untender Sorio had been. Yet even at that moment, her heart aching with the recollection of what
she had suffered, the old fierce passionate cry went up
from her soul —" better be beaten by Adrian than
loved by all the rest of the world! "

It was perhaps because of her preoccupation with
her own thoughts and her long dreamy gaze at the spot
which recalled them, that she did not remark a certain
sight which set her companion trembling with intolerable excitement. This was nothing less than the sudden appearance, between the trees that almost hid the
house from view, of a red light in a window of Oakguard. It was an unsteady light and it seemed to
waver and flicker. Sometimes it grew deeply red, like
a threatening star, and at other times it paled in colour and diminished in size. All at once, after flickering and quivering for several seconds, it died out altogether.

Only when it had finally disappeared did Linda
hastily glance round to see if Nance had discerned it.
But her sister had seen nothing.

It was, as a matter of fact, small wonder that this
particular light observed in a window of Oakguard,
thrilled the young girl with uncontrollable agitation.
It had been this very signal, arranged between them
during their few weeks of passionate love-making, which

had several times flickered across the river to Dyke
House and had been answered, unknown to Nance,
from the sisters' room. Linda shivered through every
nerve and fibre of her being, and in the darkness her
cheeks grew hot as fire. She suddenly felt convinced
that by some strange link between her heart and his,
Brand knew that she was out in the fens, and was telling her that he knew it, in the old exciting way.

"He is calling me," she said to herself, "he is calling me!" And as she formed the words, there came
over her, with a sick beating of her heart and a dizzy
pain in her breast, the certainty that Brand had left
the house and was waiting for her, somewhere in the
long avenue of limes and cedars, where they had met
once before in the early evening.

"He is waiting for me!" she repeated, and the dizzi-
ness grew so strong upon her that she staggered and
caught at her sister's arm. "Nance," she whispered,
"I feel sick. My head hurts me. Shall we go back
now?"

Nance, full of concern and anxiety, passed her fingers across her sister's forehead. "Oh, my dear, my
dear," she cried, "you're in a fever! How silly of me
to let you come out on this mad prank!"

Supporting her on her arm she led her slowly back,
along the embankment. As they walked, Nance felt
more strongly than she had done since she crossed the
Loon, that deep maternal pity, infinite in its emotion
of protection, which was the basic quality in her nature.
For the very reason, perhaps, that Linda now clung to
her like a child, she felt happier than she had done for
many days. A mysterious detachment from her own
fate, a sort of resigned indifference to what happened,

seemed to liberate her at that moment from the worst
pang of her loss. The immense shadowy spaces about
her, the silence of the fens, broken only by the rustling
of the reeds and an occasional splash in the stream by
their side as a fish rose, the vast arch of starlit sky
above her, full of a strange and infinite reassurance —
all these things thrilled the girl's heart, as they moved,
with an emotion beyond expression.

At that hour there came to her, with a vividness unfelt until then, the real meaning of Mr. Traherne's
high platonic mystery. She told herself that whatever henceforth happened to her or did not happen,
it was not an illusion, it was not a dream — this strange
spiritual secret. It was something palpable and real.
She had felt it — at least she had touched the fringe
of it — and even if the thing never quite returned or
the power of it revived as it thrilled her now, it remained that it *had been*, that she had known it, that it
was there, somewhere in the depths, however darkly hidden.

Very different were the thoughts that during that
walk back agitated the mind of the younger girl. Her
whole nature was obsessed by one fierce resolve, the
resolve to escape at once to the arms of her lover. He
was waiting for her; he was expecting her; she felt
absolutely convinced of that. An indefinable pain in
her breast and a throbbing in her heart assured her that
he was watching, waiting, drawing her towards him.
The same large influences of the night, the same silent
spaces, the same starlit dome, which brought to Nance
her spiritual reassurance, brought to the frailer figure
she supported only a desperate craving.

She could feel through every nerve of her feverish

body the touch of her love's fingers. She ached and shivered with pent-up longing, with longing to yield herself to him, to surrender herself absolutely into his power. She was no longer a thing of body, soul, and senses. The normal complexity of our mortal frame was annihilated in her. She was one trembling, quivering, vibrant chord, a chord of feverish desire, only waiting to break into one wild burst of ecstatic music, when struck by the hand she loved.

Her desire at that moment was of the kind which tears at the root of every sort of scruple. It did not only endow her with the courage of madness, it inspired her with the cunning of the insane. All the way along the embankment she was devising desperate plans of escape, and by the time they reached the church path these plans had shaped themselves into a definite resolution.

They emerged upon the familiar way and turned southward towards the bridge. Nance, thankful that she had got her sister so near home without any serious mishap, could not resist, in the impulse of her relief, the pleasure of stopping for a moment to pick a bunch of flowers from the path's reedy edge. The coolness of the earth as she stooped, the waving grasses, the strongly blowing, marsh-scented wind, the silence and the darkness, all blent harmoniously together to strengthen her in her new-found comfort.

She pulled up impetuously, almost by their roots, great heavy-flowered stalks of loose-strife and willow-herb. She scrambled down into the wet mud of a shallow ditch to add to her bunch a tall spray of hemp-agrimony and some wild valerian. All these things, ghostly and vague and colourless in the faint

starlight, had a strange and mystic beauty, and as she
gathered them Nance promised herself that they should
be a covenant between her senses and her spirit; a
sign and a token, offered up in the stillness of that hour,
to whatever great invisible powers still made it possible
on earth to renounce and be not all unhappy. She
returned with her flowers to her sister's side and together they reached the bridge.

When they were at the very centre of this, Linda
suddenly staggered and swayed. She tore herself from
her sister's support and sank down on the little stone
seat beneath the parapet — the same stone seat upon
which, some months before, that passage of sinister
complicity had occurred between Rachel Doorm and
Brand. Falling helplessly back now in this place, the
young girl pressed her hands to her head and moaned
pitifully.

Nance dropped her flowers and flung herself on her
knees beside her. "What is it, darling?" she whispered in a low frightened voice. "Oh, Linda, what is
it?" But Linda's only reply was to close her eyes
and let her head fall heavily back against the stone-
work of the parapet. Nance rose to her feet and stood
looking at her in mute despair. "Linda! Linda!"
she cried. "Linda! What is it?"

But the shadowy white form lay hushed and motionless, the soft hair across her forehead stirring in the
wind, but all else about her, horribly, deadly still.

Nance rushed across the bridge and down to the
river's brink. She came back, her hands held cup-wise,
and dashed the water over her sister's face. The
child's eyelids flickered a little, but that was all. She
remained as motionless and seemingly unconscious as

before. With a desperate effort, Nance tried to lift her up bodily in her arms, but stiff and limp as the girl was, this seemed an attempt beyond her strength.

Once more she stood, helpless and silent, regarding the other as she lay. Then it dawned upon her mind that the only possible thing to do was to leave her where she was and run to the village for help. She would arouse her own landlady. She would get the assistance of Dr. Raughty.

With one last glance at her sister's motionless form and a quick look up and down the river on the chance of there being some barge or boat at hand with people — as sometimes happened — sleeping in it, she set off running as fast as she could in the direction of the silent town.

As soon as the sound of her retreating steps died away in the distance, the hitherto helpless Linda leapt quickly and lightly to her feet. Standing motionless for awhile till she had given her sister time to reach the high-street, she set off herself with firm and rapid steps in the same direction. She resolved that she would not risk crossing the green, but would reach the park wall by a little side alley which skirted the backs of the houses. She felt certain that when she did reach this wall it would be easy enough to climb over it. She remembered its loose uneven stones and its clinging ivy. And once in the park — ah! she knew well enough what way to take then!

Deserted by its human invaders, the old New Bridge relapsed into its accustomed mood of silent expectancy. It had witnessed many passionate loves and many passionate hatreds. It had felt the feet of generations of Rodmoor's children, light as gossamer seeds, upon its shoulders, and it had felt the creaking of the death-wagon carrying the same persons, heavy as lead then, to the oblong holes dug for them in the churchyard. All this it had felt, but it still waited, still waited in patient expectancy, while the tides went up and down beneath it, and sea airs swept over it and night by night the stars looked down on it; still waited, with the dreadful patience of the eternal gods and the eternal elements, something that, after all, would perhaps never come.

Nance's flowers, meanwhile, lay where she had dropped them, upon the ground by the stone seat. They were there when, some ten minutes after her departure, the girl returned with Dr. Raughty and Mrs. Raps to find Linda gone; and they were there through all the hours of the dawn, until a farm boy, catching sight of them as he went to his work, threw them into the river in order that he might observe the precise rapidity with which they would be carried by the tide under the central arch. They were carried very swiftly under the central arch; but linger as the boy might, he did not see them reappear on the other side.

XVII

THE DAWN

THE dawn was just faintly making itself felt among the trees of Oakguard when Philippa Renshaw, restless as she often was on these summer nights, perceived, as she leaned from her open window, a figure almost as slender as herself standing motionless at the edge of one of the terraces and looking up at the house. There was no light in Philippa's room, so that she was able to watch this figure without risk of being herself observed. She was certain at once in her own mind of its identity, and she took it immediately for granted that Brand was even now on his way to meet the young girl at the spot where she now saw her standing.

She experienced, therefore, a certain surprise and even annoyance — for she would have liked to have witnessed this encounter — when, instead of remaining where she stood, the girl suddenly slipped away like a ghostly shadow and merged herself among the park-trees. Philippa remained for some minutes longer at the window peering intently into the grey obscurity and wondering whether after all she had been mistaken and it was one of the servants of the house. There *was* one of the Oakguard maids addicted to walking in her sleep, and she confessed to herself that it was quite possible she had been misled by her own morbid fancy into supposing that the nocturnal wanderer was Linda Herrick.

She returned to her bed after a while and tried to sleep, but the idea that it was really Linda she had seen and that the young girl was even now roaming about the grounds like a disconsolate phantom, took possession of her mind. She rose once more and cautiously pulling down the blind and drawing the curtains began hurriedly to dress herself, taking the precaution to place the solitary candle which she used behind a screen so that no warning of her wakefulness should reach the person she suspected.

Opening the door and moving stealthily down the passage, she paused for a moment at the threshold of her brother's room. All was silent within. Smiling faintly to herself, she turned the handle with exquisite precaution and glided into the room. No! She was right in her conjecture. The place was without an occupant, and the bed, it appeared, had not been slept in. She went out, closing the door silently behind her.

Her mother's room was opposite Brand's and the fancy seized her to enter that also. She entered it, and stepped, softly as a wandering spirit, to her mother's side. Mrs. Renshaw was lying in an uneasy posture with one arm stretched across the counterpane and her head close to the edge of the bed. She was breathing heavily but was not in a deep sleep. Every now and then her fingers spasmodically closed and unclosed, and from her lips came broken inarticulate words. The pallid light of the early dawn made her face seem older than Philippa had ever seen it. By her side on a little table lay an open book, but it was still too dark for the intruder to discern what this book was.

The daughter stood for some minutes in absolute rigidity, gazing upon the sleeper. Her face as she gazed wore an expression so complicated, so subtle, that the shrewdest observer seeking to interpret its meaning would have been baffled. It was not malignant. It certainly was not tender. It might have been compared to the look one could conceive some heathen courtesan in the days of early Christianity casting upon a converted slave.

Uneasily conscious, as people in their sleep often are, without actually waking, of the alien presence so near her, Mrs. Renshaw suddenly moved round in her bed and with a low moaning utterance, settled herself to sleep with her face to the window. It was a human name she had uttered then. Philippa was sure of that, but it was a name completely strange to the watcher of her mother's unconsciousness.

Passing from the room as silently as she had entered, the girl ran lightly down the staircase, picked up a cloak in the hall, and let herself out of the front door.

Meanwhile, through the gradually lifting shadows, Linda with rapid and resolute steps was hastening across the park to the portion of the avenue where grew the great cedar-trees. This was the place to which her first instinct had called her. It was only an after-thought, due to cooler reason that had caused her to deviate from this and approach the house itself.

As she advanced through the dew-drenched grass, silvery now in the faint light, she felt that vague indescribable sensation which all living creatures, even those scourged by passion, are bound to feel, at the first palpable touch of dawn. Perfumes and odours that could not be expressed in words, and that seemed to have no natural origin, came to the girl on the wind which went sighing past her. This — so at least Linda vaguely felt — was not the west wind any more. It was not any ordinary wind of day or night. It was the dawn wind, the breath of the earth herself, indrawn with sweet sharp ecstasy at the delicate terror of the coming of the sun-god.

As she approached the avenue where the trunks of the cedars rose dark against the misty white light, she was suddenly startled by the flapping wings of an enormous heron which, mounting up in front of her out of the shadow of the trees, went sailing away across the park, its extended neck and outstretched legs outlined against the eastern sky. She passed in among the shadows from which the heron had emerged, and there, as though he had been waiting for her only a few moments, was Brand Renshaw.

With one swift cry she flung herself into his arms and they clung together as if from an eternity of separation. In her flimsy dress wet with mist she seemed like a creature evoked by some desperate prayer of earth-passion. Her cheeks and breast were cold to his touch, but the lips that answered his kisses were hot as if with burning fever. She clung to him as though some abysmal gulf might any moment open beneath their feet. She nestled against him, she twined herself around him. She took his head between her hands and with her cold fingers she caressed his face. So thinly was she clad that he could feel her heart beating as if it were his own.

"I knew you were calling me," she gasped at last. "I felt it — I felt it in my flesh. Oh, my only love, I'm all yours — all, all yours! Take me, hold me, save me from every one! Hold me, hold me, my only love, hold me tight from all of them!"

They swayed together as she clung to him and, lifting her up from the ground he carried her, still wildly kissing him, into the deeper shadow of the great cedars. Exhausted at last by the extremity of her passion, she hung limp in his arms, her face white as the white light which now flooded the eastern horizon. He laid her down then at the foot of one of the largest trees and bending over her pushed back the hair from her forehead as if she had been a tired child.

By some powerful law of his strange nature, the very intensity of her passion for him and her absolute yielding to his will calmed and quieted his own desire. She was his now, at a touch, at a movement; but he would as soon have hurt an infant as have embraced her then. His emotion at that moment was such as never again in his life he was destined to experience. He felt as though, untouched as she was, she belonged to him, body and soul. He felt as though they two together were isolated, separated, divided, from the whole living world. Beneath the trunks of those black-foliaged cedars they seemed to be floating in a mystic ship over a great sea of filmy white waves.

He bent down and kissed her forehead, and under his kiss, chaste as the kiss a father might give to a little girl, she closed her eyes and lay motionless and still, a faint-flickering smile of infinite contentment playing upon her lips.

They were in this position — the girl's hand resting passively in his — and he bending over her, when through an eastward gap between the trees the sun rose above the mist. It sent towards them a long blood-coloured finger that stained the cedar trunks and caused the strangely shaped head of the stooping man to look as if it had been dipped in blood. It made the girl's mouth scarlet-red and threw an indescribable flush over her face, a flush delicate and diaphanous as that which tinges the petals of wild hedge roses.

Linda opened her eyes and Brand leapt to his feet with a cry. "The sun!" he shouted, and then, in a lower voice, "what an omen for us, little one — what an omen! Out of the sea, out of *our* sea! Come, get up, and let's watch the morning in! There won't be a trace of mist left, or dew either, in an hour or so."

He gave her his hand and hurriedly pulled her to her feet. "Quick!" he cried. "You can see it across the sea from over there. I've often seen it, but never like this, never with you!"

Hand in hand they left the shade of the trees and hastening up the slope of a little grassy mound — perhaps the grave of some viking-ancestor of his own — they stood side by side surveying the wonder of the sunrise.

As they stood there and the sun, mounting rapidly higher and higher, dispersed the mists and flooded everything with golden light, Brand's mood began to change towards his companion. The situation was reversed now and it was his arms that twined themselves round the girl's figure, while she, though only resisting gently and tenderly, seemed to have recovered the normal instincts of her sex, the instincts of self-protection and aloofness.

The warmer the sun became and the more clearly the familiar landscape defined itself before them, the more swiftly did the relations between the two change and reverse. No longer did Brand feel as though some mystic spiritual union had annihilated the difference between their sex. The girl was once more an evasive object of pursuit. He desired her and his desire irritated and angered him.

"We shan't have the place to ourselves much longer," he said. "Come — let's say good-bye where we were before — where we weren't so much in sight."

He sought to lead her back to the shade of the cedars; but she — looking timidly at his face — felt for the first time a vague reaction against him and an indefinable shrinking.

"I think I'll say good-bye to you here," she said, with a faint smile. "Nance will be looking for me everywhere and I mustn't frighten her any further."

She was astonished and alarmed at the change in his face produced by her words.

"As you please," he said harshly, "here, as well as anywhere else, if that's your line! You'd better go back the way you came, but the gates aren't locked if you prefer the avenue." He actually left her when he said this, and without touching her hand or giving her another look, strode down the slope and away towards the house.

This was more than Linda could bear. She ran after him and caught him by the arm. "Brand," she whispered, "Brand, my dearest one, you're not really angry with me, are you? Of course, I'll say good-bye wherever you wish! Only — only —" and she gave an agitated little sigh, "I don't want to frighten Nance more than I can help."

He led her back to the spot where, under the dark wide-spreading branches, the red finger of the sun had first touched them. She loved him too well to resist long, and she loved him too well not to taste, in the

passionate tears that followed her abandonment to his
will, a wild desperate sweetness, even in the midst of
all her troubled apprehensions as to the calamitous
issues of their love.

It was in the same place, finally, and under the same
dark branches, that they bade one another good-bye.
Brand looked at his watch before they parted and they
both smiled when he announced that it was nearly six,
and that at any moment the milk-cart might pass them
coming up from the village. As he moved away, Linda
saw him stoop and pick up something from the ground.
He turned with a laugh and flung the thing towards
her so that it rolled to her feet. It was a fir-cone and
she knew well why he threw it to her as their farewell
signal. They had wondered, only a little while ago,
how it drifted beneath their cedar-tree, and Brand had
amused himself by twining it in her hair.

She picked it up. The hair was twisted about it
still — of a colour not dissimilar from the cone, but of
a lighter shade. She slipped the thing into her dress
and let it slide down between her breasts. It scratched
and pricked her as soon as she began to walk, but this
discomfort gave her a singular satisfaction. She felt
like a nun, wearing for the first time her symbol of
separation from the world — of dedication to her lord's
service. " I am certainly no nun now," she thought,
smiling sadly to herself, " but I am dedicated — dedicated forever and a day. Oh, my dear, dear Love, I
would willingly die to give you pleasure ! "

She moved away, down the avenue towards the village. She had not gone very far when she was startled
by a rustle in the undergrowth and the sound of a
mocking laugh. She stopped in terror. The laugh

was repeated, and a moment later, from a well-chosen hiding-place in a thicket of hazel-bushes, Philippa Renshaw, with malignant shining eyes, rushed out upon her.

"Ah!" she cried joyously, "I thought it was you. I thought it was one or other of you! And where is our dear Brand? Has he deserted you so quickly? Does he prefer to have his little pleasures before the sun is *quite* so high? Does he leave her to go back all alone and by herself? Does he sneak off like a thief as soon as daylight begins?"

Linda was too panic-stricken to make any reply to this torrent of taunts. With drawn white face and wide-open terrified eyes, she stared at Philippa as a bird might stare at a snake. Philippa seemed delighted with the effect she produced and stepping in front of the young girl, barred her way of escape.

"You mustn't leave us now," she cried. "It's impossible. It would never do. What will they say in the village when they see you like that, crossing the green, at this hour? What you have to do, Linda Herrick, is to come back and have breakfast with us up at the house. My mother will be delighted to see you. She always gets up early, and she's very, very fond of you, as you know. You *do* know my mother's fond of you, don't you?

"Listen, you silly white-faced thing! Listen, you young innocent, who must needs come wandering round people's houses in the middle of the night! Listen — you Linda Herrick! I don't know whether you're stupid enough to imagine that Brand's going to marry you? Are you stupid enough for that? Are you, you dumb staring thing? Because, if you are, I can tell you a little about Brand that may surprise you. Perhaps you think you're the first one he's ever made love to in this precious park of ours. No, no, my beauty, you're not the first — and you won't be the last. We Renshaws are a curious family, as you'll find out, you baby, before you've done with us. And Brand's the most curious of us all!

"Well, are you coming back with me? Are you coming back to have a nice pleasant breakfast with my mother? You'd better come, Linda Herrick, you'd better come! In fact, you *are* coming, so that ends it. People who spend the night wandering about other people's grounds must at least have the decency to show themselves and acknowledge the hospitality! Besides, how glad Brand will be to see you again! Can't you imagine how glad he'll be? Can't you see his look?

"Oh, no, Linda Herrick, I can't possibly let you go like this. You see, I'm just like my dear mother. I love gentle, sensitive, pure-minded young girls. I love their shyness and their bashfulness. I love the unfortunate little accidents that lead them into parks and gardens. Come, you dumb big-eyed thing! What's the matter with you? Can't you speak? Come! Back with you to the house! We'll find my mother stirring — and Brand too, unless he's sick of girls' society and has gone off to Mundham. Come, white-face; there's nothing else for it. You must do what I tell you."

She laid her hand on Linda's shoulder, and, such was the terror she excited, the unhappy girl might actually have been magnetized into obeying her, if a timely and unexpected interruption had not changed the entire situation. This was the appearance upon the scene of Adrian Sorio. Sorio had recently acquired an almost daily habit of strolling a little way up the Oakguard avenue before his breakfast with Baltazar. On two or three of these occasions he had met Philippa, and he had always sufficient hope of meeting her to give these walks a tang of delicate excitement. He had evidently heard nothing of Linda's disappearance. Nance in her distress had, it seemed, resisted the instinct to appeal to him. He was consequently considerably surprised to see the two girls standing together in the middle of the sunlit path.

Linda, flinging Philippa aside, rushed to meet him. "Adrian! Adrian!" she cried piteously, "take me home to Nance." She clung to his arm and in the misery of her outraged feelings, began sobbing like a child who has been lost in the dark. Sorio, soothing and petting her as well as he could, looked enquiringly at Philippa as she came up.

"Oh, it's nothing. It's nothing, Adrian. It's only that I wanted her to come up to the house. She seems to have misunderstood me and got silly and frightened. She's not a very sensible little girl."

Sorio looked at Philippa searchingly. In his heart he suspected her of every possible perversity and maliciousness. He realized at that moment how entirely his attraction to her was an attraction to what is dangerous and furtive. He did not even respect her intelligence. He had caught her more than once playing up to his ideas in a manner that indicated a secret contempt for them. At those moments he had hated her, and — with her — had hated, as he fancied, the whole feminine tribe — that tribe which refuses to be impressed even by world-crushing logic. But how at-

tractive she was to him! How attractive, even at this
moment, as he looked into her defiant, inscrutable eyes,
and at her scornfully curved lips!

" You needn't pity her, Adrian," she went on, casting
a bitter smile at Linda's bowed head as the young girl
hid her face against his shoulder. " There's no need to
pity her. She's just like all the rest of us, only she
doesn't play the game frankly and honestly as I do.
Send her home to her sister, as she says, and come with
me across the park. I'll show you that oak tree if
you'll come — the one I told you about, the one that's
haunted."

She threw at him a long deep look, full of a subtle
challenge, and stretched out her hand as if to separate
him from the clinging child. Sorio returned her look
and a mute struggle took place between them. Then
his face hardened.

" I must go back with her," he said. " I must take
her to Nance."

" Nonsense!" she rejoined, her eyes darkening and
changing in colour. " Nonsense, my dear! She'll find
her way all right. Come! I really want you. Yes, I
mean what I say, Adrian. I really want you this
time!"

The expression with which she challenged him now
would have delighted the great antique painters of the
feminine mystery. The gates of her soul seemed to
open inwards, on magical softly-moving hinges, and an
incalculable power of voluptuous witchcraft emanated
from her whole body.

It is doubtful whether a spell so provocative could
have been resisted by any one of an origin different
from Sorio's. But he had in him — capable of being

roused at moments — the blood of that race in which of all others women have met their match. To this witchcraft of the north he opposed the marble-like disdain of the south — the disdain which has subtlety and knowledge in it — the disdain which is like petrified hatred.

His face darkened and hardened until it resembled a mask of bronze.

" Good-bye," he said, " for the present. We shall meet again — perhaps to-morrow. But anyway, good-bye! Come, Linda, my child."

" Perhaps to-morrow — and perhaps *not!* " returned Philippa bitterly. " Good-bye, Linda. I'll give your love to Brand! "

Sorio said little to his companion as he escorted her back to her lodging in the High Street. He asked her no questions and seemed to take it as quite a natural thing that she should have been out at that early hour. They discovered Dr. Raughty in the house when they arrived, doing his best to dissuade Nance from any further desperate hunt after the wanderer, and it was in accordance with the doctor's advice, as well as their own weariness that the two sisters spent the later morning hours of their August Bank-holiday in a profound and exhausted sleep.

XVIII

BANK-HOLIDAY

IT was nearly two o'clock in the afternoon when Nance woke out of a heavy dreamless sleep. She went to the window. The shops in the little street were all closed and several languid fishermen and young tradesmen's apprentices were loitering about at the house doors, chaffing lazily and with loud bursts of that peculiarly empty laughter which seems the prerogative of rural idleness, the stray groups of gaily dressed young women who, in the voluptuous contentment of after-dinner repletion, were setting forth to take the train for Mundham or to walk with their sweethearts along the sea-shore. She turned and looked closely at her still sleeping sister.

Linda lay breathing softly. On her lips was a child-like smile of serene happiness. She had tossed the bed-clothes away and one of her arms, bare to the elbow, hung over the edge of the bed. It seemed she was holding fast, in the hand thus pathetically extended, some small object round which her fingers were tightly closed. Nance moved to her side and took this hand in her own. The girl turned her head uneasily but continued to sleep. Nance opened the fingers which lay helplessly in her own and found that what they held so passionately was a small fir-cone. The bright August sunshine pouring down upon the room enabled her to catch sight of several strands of light brown hair woven round the thing's rough scales.   She let the unconscious fingers close once more round the fir-cone and glanced anxiously at the sleeping girl.   She guessed in a moment the meaning of that red scratch across the girl's bosom.   She must have been carrying this token pressed close against her flesh and its rough prickly edges had drawn blood.

Nance sighed heavily and remained for a moment buried in gloomy thought.   Then, stepping softly to the door, she ran downstairs to see if Mrs. Raps were still in her kitchen or had left any preparations for their belated dinner.   Their habit was to make their own breakfast and tea, but to have their midday meal brought up to them from their landlady's table.   She found an admirable collation carefully prepared for them on a tray and a little note on the dresser telling her that the family had gone to Mundham for the afternoon.

"Bless your poor, dear heart," the note ended, "the old man and I thought best not to disappoint the children."

Nance felt faint with hunger.   She put the kettle on the fire and made tea and with this and Mrs. Raps' tray she returned to her sister's side and roused her from her sleep.

Linda seemed dazed and confused when she first woke.   For the moment it was difficult not to feel as though all the events of the night and morning were a troubled and evil dream.   Nance noticed the nervous and bewildered way in which she put her hand to the mark upon her breast as if wondering why it hurt her and the hasty disconcerted movement with which she concealed the fir-cone beneath her pillow.   In spite of everything,

however, their meal was not by any means an unhappy
one. The sun shone warm and bright upon the floor.
Pleasant scents, in which garden-roses, salt-sea freshness and the vague smell of peat and tar mingled together, came in through the window, blent with the lazy,
cheerful sounds of the people's holiday. After all they
were both young and neither the unsatisfied ache in the
soul of the one nor the vague new dread, bitter-sweet and
full of strange forebodings, in the mind of the other
could altogether prevent the natural life-impulse with
which, like two wind-shaken plants in an intermission of
quiet, they raised their heads to the sky and the sunshine. They were young. They were alive. They
knew — too well, perhaps! — but still they knew what
it was to love, and the immense future, with all its infinite possibilities, lay before them. " Sursum Corda! "
the August airs whispered to them. " Sursum Corda! "
" Lift up your hearts! " their own young flesh and
blood answered.

Linda did not hesitate as she ate and drank to confess to Nance how she had betrayed her and how she
had seen Brand in the park. Of the cedar trees and
their more ominous story she said nothing, but she told
how Philippa had sprung upon her in the avenue and of
wild, cruel taunts.

" She frightened me," the girl murmured. " She always frightens me. Do you think she would really
have made me go back with her to the house — to meet
Brand and Mrs. Renshaw and all? I couldn't have
done it," she put her hands to her cheeks and trembled
as she spoke, " I couldn't — I couldn't! It would
have been too shameful! And yet I believe she was
really going to make me. Do you think she was,

Nance? Do you think she *could* have done such a thing? "

Nance gripped the arms of her chair savagely.

" Why didn't you leave her, dear? " she exclaimed. " Why didn't you simply leave her and run off? She isn't a witch. She's simply a girl like ourselves."

Linda smiled. " How fierce you look, darling! I believe if it had been you you'd have slapped her face or pushed her down or something."

Nance gazed out of the window, frowning. She wondered to herself by what spiritual magic Mr. Traherne and his white rat proposed to obliterate the poisonous rage of jealousy. She wondered what he would say, the devoted priest, to this uncalled for and cruel attack upon her sister. She had never heard him mention Philippa at any time in their talks. Was he as much afraid of *her* beauty as he pretended to be of her own? Did he make Philippa hide her ankles in her skirt when she visited him? But she supposed she never did visit him. It was somehow very difficult to imagine the sister of Brand Renshaw in the priest's little study.

From Traherne, Nance's mind wandered to Dr. Raughty. How kind he had been to her when she was in despair about Linda! She had never seen him half so serious or troubled. She could hardly help smiling as she remembered the peculiar expression he wore and the way he pulled on his coat and laced up his boots. She had let him give her a little glass of *crême de menthe* and she could see now, with wonderful distinctness, the gravity with which he had watched her drink it. She felt certain his hand had shaken with nervousness when he took the glass from her. She could hear him clearing his throat and muttering some fantastic invocation to what sounded like an Egyptian divinity. Surely the effect of extreme anxiety could produce upon no one else in the world but Dr. Raughty a tendency to allude to the great god Ra! And what extraordinary things he had put into his little black bag as he sallied forth with her to the bridge! Linda might have been in need of several kinds of surgical operations from the preparations he made.

He had promised to spend that day on a fishing trip, out to sea, with Adrian and Baltazar. She wondered whether their boat was still in sight or whether they had got beyond the view of Rodmoor harbour.

" Linda, dear," she said presently, catching her sister's hand feeling about under her pillows for the fir-cone she had hidden, " Linda, dear, if I'm to forgive you for what you did last night, for running away from me, I mean, and pretending things, will you do something that I want now? Will you come down to the shore and see if we can see anything of Adrian's boat? He's fishing with Dr. Raughty and Mr. Stork, and I'd love to get a sight of their sail. I know it's a sailing boat they've gone in because Dr. Raughty said he was going to take his mackintosh so that when they went fast and the water splashed over the side he might be protected. I think he was a little scared of the expedition. Poor dear man, between us all, I'm afraid we give him a lot of shocks ! "

Linda jumped up quite eagerly. She felt prepared at that moment to do anything to please her sister. Besides, there were certain agitating thoughts in her brain which cried aloud for any kind of distraction. They dressed and went out, choosing, as suited the holiday occasion, brighter frocks and gayer hats than they

had worn for many weeks. Nance's position in the
Pontifex shop was a favourable one as far as their ward-
robe was concerned.

They made their way down to the harbour. They
were surprised, and in Linda's case at any rate not very
pleasantly surprised, to find tied to a post where the
wharf widened and the grass grew between the cobble-
stones the little grey pony and brown pony-cart which
Mrs. Renshaw was in the habit of using when the hot
weather made it tiring for her to walk.

"Let's go back! Oh, Nance, let's go back!" whispered Linda in a panic-stricken voice. "I don't feel I
can face her to-day."

They stood still, hesitating.

"There she is," cried Nance suddenly, "look —
who's she got there with her?"

"Oh, Nance, it's Rachel, yes, it's Rachel!"

"She must have gone to Dyke House to fetch her,"
murmured the other. "Quick! Let's go back."

But it was already too late. Rising from the seat
where they were talking together at the harbour's edge,
the two women moved towards the girls, calling them by
name. There was no escape now and the sisters advanced to meet them.

They made a strange foreground to the holiday
aspect of the little harbour, those two black-gowned figures. Mrs. Renshaw was a little in front and her less
erect and less rigid form had a certain drooping pathos
in its advance as though she deprecated her appearance
in the midst of so cheerful a scene. Both the women
wore old-fashioned bonnets of a kind that had been discarded for several years; but the dress and the bonnet
of Rachel Doorm presented the appearance of having

been dragged out of some ancient chest and thrust upon her in disregard of the neglected condition of her other clothes. Contrasted with the brightly rocking waters of the river mouth and the gay attire of the boat-load of noisy lads and girls that was drifting sea-ward on the out-flowing tide, the look of the two women, as they crossed the little quay, might have suggested the sort of scene that, raised to a poetic height by the genius of the ancient poets, has so often in classical drama symbolized the approach of messengers of ill-omen.

Mrs. Renshaw greeted the two sisters very nervously. Nance caught her glancing with an air of ascetic dis-approval at their bright-coloured frocks and hats. Rachel, avoiding their eyes, extended a cold limp hand to each in turn. They exchanged a few conventional and embarrassed sentences, Nance as usual under such circumstances, giving vent to little uncalled for bursts of rather disconcerting laughter. She had a trick of opening her mouth very wide when she laughed like this, and her grey eyes even wider still, which gave her an air of rather foolish childishness quite inexpressive of what might be going on in her mind.

After a while they all moved off, as if by an in-stinctive impulse, away from the harbour mouth and towards the sea-shore. To do this they had to pass a piece of peculiarly desolate ground littered with dead fish, discarded pieces of nets and dried heaps of sun-bleached seaweed. Nance had a moment's quaint and morbid intimation that the peculiar forlornness of this particular spot gratified in some way the taste of Mrs. Renshaw, for her expression brightened a little and she moved more cheerfully than when under the eyes of the loiterers on the wharf. There were some young women

paddling in the sea just at that place and some young
men watching them so that Mrs. Renshaw, who with
Nance kept in advance of the other two, led the way
along the path immediately under the sand-dunes. This
was the very spot where, on the day of their first ex-
ploration of the Rodmoor coast, they had seen the
flowerless leaves of the little plant called the rock-rose.
The flowers of this plant, as Nance observed them now,
were already faded and withered, but other sea growths
met her eye which were not unfamiliar. There were
several tufts of grey-leaved sea-pinks and still greyer
sea-lavender. There were also some flaccid-stalked,
glaucous weeds which she had never noticed before and
which seemed in the moist sappy texture of their foliage
as though their natural place was rather beneath than
above the salt water whose propinquity shaped their
form. But what made her pause and stoop down with
sudden startled attention, was her first sight of that
plant described to her by Mr. Traherne as peculiarly
characteristic of the Rodmoor coast. Yes, there it was
— the yellow horned poppy! As she bent over it
Nance realized how completely right the priest had been
in what he said. The thing's oozy, clammy leaves were
of a wonderful bluish tint, a tint that nothing in the
world short of the sea itself, could have possibly called
into existence. They were spiked and prickly, these
leaves, and their shape was clear-edged and threatening,
as if modelled in sinister caprice, by some Da Vinci-
like Providence, willing enough to startle and shock
humanity. But what struck the girl more vividly than
either the bluish tint or the threatening spikes were the
large, limply-drooping flowers of a pallid sulphurous
yellow which the plant displayed. They were flowers

that bore but small resemblance to the flowers of other poppies. They had a peculiarly melancholy air, even before they began to fade, an air as though the taste of their petals would produce a sleep of a deeper, more obliterating kind than any "drowsy syrups" or "mandragora" which the sick soul might crave, to "rase out" its troubles.

Mrs. Renshaw smiled as Nance rose from her long scrutiny of this weird plant, a plant that might be imagined "rooting itself at ease on Lethe's wharf" while the ghost-troops swept by, whimpering and wailing.

"I always like the horned poppy," she remarked, "it's different from other flowers. You can't imagine it growing in a garden, can you? I like that. I like things that are wild — things no one can imprison."

She sighed heavily when she had said this and, turning her head away as they walked on, looked wearily across the water.

"Bank-holidays are days for the young," she went on, after a pause. "The poor people look forward to them and I'm glad they do for they have a hard life. But you must have a young heart, Nance, a young heart to enjoy these things. I feel sometimes that we don't live enough in other people's happiness but it's hard to do it when one gets older."

She was silent again and then, as Nance glanced at her sympathetically, "I like Rodmoor because there are no grand people here and no motor-cars or noisy festivities. It's a pleasure to see the poor enjoying themselves but the others, they make my head ache! They trouble me. I always think of Sodom and Gomorrah when I see them."

" I suppose," murmured the girl, " that they're human beings and have their feelings, like the rest of us."

A shadow of almost malignant bitterness crossed Mrs. Renshaw's face.

" I can't bear them! I can't bear them! " she cried fiercely. " Those that laugh shall weep," she added, looking at her companion's prettily designed dress.

" Yes, I'm afraid happy people are often hard-hearted," remarked Nance, anxious if possible to fall in with the other's mood, but feeling decidedly uneasy. Mrs. Renshaw suddenly changed the conversation.

" I went over to see Rachel," she said, " because I heard you had left her and were working in the shop."

She took a deep breath and her voice trembled.

" I think it was wrong of you to leave her," she went on, " I think it was cruel of you. I know what you will say. I know what all you young people nowadays say about being independent and so forth. But it was wrong all the same, wrong and cruel! Your duty was clearly to your mother's friend. I suppose," she added bitterly, " you didn't like her sadness and loneliness. You wanted more cheerful companionship."

Nance wondered in her heart whether Mrs. Renshaw's hostility to the complacent and contented ones of the earth was directed, in this case, against the hard-worked sewing girls or against poor Miss Pontifex and her little garden.

" I did it," she replied, " for Linda's sake. She and Miss Doorm didn't seem happy together."

As she spoke, she glanced apprehensively round to ascertain how near the others were, but it seemed as though Rachel had resumed her ascendency over the young girl. They appeared to be engaged in absorbing conversation and had stopped side by side, looking at the sea. Mrs. Renshaw turned upon her resentfully, a smouldering fire of anger in her brown eyes.

"Rachel has spoken to me about that," she said. "She told me you were displeased with her because she encouraged Linda to meet my son. I don't like this interference with the feelings of people! My son is of an age to choose for himself and so is your sister. Why should you set yourself to come between them? I don't like such meddling. It's interfering with Nature!"

Nance stared at her blankly, watching mechanically the feverish way her fingers closed and unclosed, plucking at a stalk of sea-lavender which she had picked.

"But you said — you said — " she protested feebly, "that Mr. Renshaw was not a suitable companion for young girls."

"I've changed my mind since then," continued the other, "at any rate in this case."

"Why?" asked Nance hurriedly. "Why have you?"

"Because," and the lady raised her voice quite loudly, "because he told me himself the other day that it was possible that he would marry before long."

She glanced triumphantly at Nance. "So you see what you've been doing! You've been trying to interfere with the one thing I've been praying for for years!"

Nance positively gasped at this. Had Brand really said such a thing? Or if he had, was it possible that it was anything but a blind to cover the tracks of his selfishness? But whatever was the reason of the son's remark it was clear that Nance could not, especially in the woman's present mood, justify her dark suspicions of him to his mother. So she did nothing but continue to stare, nervously and helplessly, at the stalk which Mrs. Renshaw's excited fingers were pulling to pieces.

" I know why you're so opposed to my son," continued Mrs. Renshaw in a lower and somewhat gentler tone. " It's because he's so much older than your sister. But you're wrong there, Nance. It's always better for the man to be older than the woman. Tennyson says that very thing, in one of his poems, I think in ' The Princess.' He puts it poetically of course, but he must have felt the truth of it very strongly or he wouldn't have brought it in. Nance, you've no idea how I have been praying and longing for Brand to see some one he felt he could marry! I know it's what he needs 'to make him happy. That is to say, of course, if the girl is good and gentle and obedient."

The use of the word " obedient " in this connection was too much for Nance's nerves. Her feelings towards Mrs. Renshaw were always undergoing rapid and contradictory changes. When she had talked of Smollett and Dickens in their little sitting room the girl felt she could do anything for her, so exquisitely guileless her soul seemed, so spiritual and, as it were, transparent. But at this moment, as she observed her, there was an obstinate, pinched look about her face and a rigid tightening of all its lines. It was an expression that harmonized only too well with her next remark.

" Your setting yourself against my son," she said, " is only what I expected. Philippa would be just like you if I said anything to her. All you young people are too much for me. You are too much for me. But I hear what you say and go on just the same."

The look of dogged and inflexible resolution with which she uttered this last sentence contrasted strangely with her frail aspect and her weary drooping frame.

But that phrase about " obedience " still rankled in Nance's mind, and she could not help saying,

" Why is it, Mrs. Renshaw, that you always speak as though all the duty and burden of marriage rested upon the woman? I don't see why it's more necessary for her to be good and gentle than it is for the man!"

Her companion's pallid lips quivered at this into a smile of complicated irony and a strange light came into her hollow eyes.

" Ah, my dear, my dear!" she exclaimed, " you are indeed young yet. When you're a few years older and have come to know better what the world is like, you will understand the truth of what I say. God has ordered, in his inscrutable wisdom, that there should be a different right and wrong for us women, from what there is for men. It may seem unjust. It may *be* unjust. We can no more alter it or change it than we can alter or change the shape of our bodies. A woman is *made* to obey. She finds her happiness in obeying. You young people may say what you please, but any deviation from this rule is contrary to Nature. Even the cleverest people," she added with a smile, " can't interfere with Nature without suffering for it."

Nance felt absolutely nonplussed. The woman's words fell from her with such force and were uttered with such a melancholy air of finality, that her indignation died down within her like a flame beneath the weight of a rain-soaked garment. Mrs. Renshaw looked sadly over the brightly-rocking expanse of sunlit water, dotted with white sails.

" It may appear to us unjust," she went on. " It may *be* unjust. God does not seem in his infinite pleasure to have considered our ideas of justice in making the world. Perhaps if he had there would be no women in the world at all! Ah, Nance, my dear, it's no use kicking against the pricks. We were made to bear, to endure, to submit, to suffer. Any attempt to escape this great law necessarily ends in misery. Suffering is not the worst evil in the world. Yielding to brutal force is not the worst, either. I sometimes think, from what I've observed in my life, that there are depths of horror known to men, depths of horror through which men are driven, compared with which all that *we* suffer at their hands is paradise!"

Her eyes had so strange and illumined an expression as she uttered these words that Nance could not help shuddering.

"We, too," she murmured, "fall into depths of horror sometimes and it is men who drive us into them."

Mrs. Renshaw did not seem to hear her. She went on dreamily.

"We can console ourselves. We have our duties. We have our little things which must be done. God has given to these little things a peculiar consecration. He has touched them with his breath so that they are full of unexpected consolations. There are horizons and vistas in them such as no one who hasn't experienced what I mean can possibly imagine. They are like tiny ferns or flowers — our 'little things,' Nance, growing at the bottom of a precipice."

The girl could restrain herself no longer.

"I don't agree with you! I don't, I don't!" she cried. "Life is large and infinite and splendid and there are possibilities in it for all of us — for women just as much as men; just, just as much!"

Mrs. Renshaw smiled at her with a look in her face that was half pitiful and half ironical. "You don't like my talk of 'little things.' You want great things. You want Abana and Pharpar, rivers of Damascus! Even your sacrifice — if you *do* sacrifice yourself — must be striking, stirring, wonderful! Ah, my dear, my dear, wait a little, wait a little. A time will come when you'll learn what the secret is of a woman's life on this earth."

Nance made a desperate gesture of protest. Something treacherous in her own heart seemed to yield to her companion's words but she struggled vigorously against it.

"What we women have to do," Mrs. Renshaw continued pitilessly, " is to make some one need us — need us with his whole nature. That is what is meant by loving a man. Everything else is mere passion and tends to misery. The more submissive we are, the more they need us. I tell you, Nance, the deepest instinct in our blood is the instinct to be needed. When a person needs us we love him. Everything else is mere animal instinct and burns itself out."

Nance fumbled vaguely and helplessly in her mind, as she listened, to get back something of the high, inspiring tone of Mr. Traherne's mystical doctrine. *That* had thrilled her and strengthened her, while *this* flung her into the lowest depths of despondency. Yet, in a certain sense, as she was compelled to admit to herself, there was very little practical difference between the two points of view. It was only that, with Mrs. Renshaw, the whole thing took on a certain desolate and disastrous colour as if high spirits and gaiety and adventurousness were wrong in themselves and as if nothing but what was pitched in a low unhappy key could possibly be the truth of the universe. The girl had a curious feeling, all the while she was speaking, that in some subtle way the unfortunate woman was deriving a morbid pleasure from putting thrilling and exalted things upon a ground that annihilated the emotion of heroism.

" Shall we go down to the sea now, dear? " said Mrs. Renshaw suddenly. " The others will see us and follow."

.They moved together across the clinging sand. When they approached the water's edge, now deserted of holiday-makers, Nance searched the skyline for any sail that might be the one carrying Sorio and his friends. She made out two or three against the blue distance but it was quite impossible to tell which of these, if any, was the one that bore the man who, according to her companion's words, would only " need " her if she served him like a slave.

Mrs. Renshaw began picking up shells from the debris-scattered windrow at the edge of the wet tide-mark. As she did this and showed them one by one to Nance, her face once more assumed that clear, transparent look, spiritual beyond description and touched with a childish happiness, which the girl had noticed upon it when she spoke of the books she loved. Could it be that only where religion or the opposite sex were concerned this strange being was diseased and perverted? If so, how dreadful, how cruel, that the two things which were to most people the very mainspring of life were to this unhappy one the deepest causes of wretchedness! Yet Nance was far from satisfied with her reading of the mystery of Mrs. Renshaw. There was something in the woman, in spite of her almost savage outbursts of self-revelation, so aloof, so proud, so reserved that the girl felt only vaguely assured she was on the right track with regard to her. Perhaps, after all, below that tone of self-humiliating sentiment with which she habitually spoke of both God and man, there was some deep and passionate current of feeling, hidden from all the world? Or was she, essentially and in secret truth, cold and hard and pagan and only forcing herself to drink the cup of what she conceived to be Christianity out of a species of half-insane pride? In all her utterances with regard to religion and sex there was, Nance felt, a kind of heavy materiality, as if she got an evil satisfaction in rendering what is usually called " goodness " as colourless and contemptible as possible. But now as she picked up a trumpet-shaped shell from the line of debris and held it up, her eyes liquid with pleasure, to the girl's view, Nance could not resist the impression that she was in some strange way a creature forced and driven out of her natural element into these obscure perversities.

" I used to paint these shells when I was a girl," Mrs. Renshaw remarked.

" What colour? " Nance answered, still thinking more of the woman than of her words. Her companion looked at her and burst into quite a merry laugh.

" I don't mean paint the shell itself," she said. " You're not listening to me, Nance. I mean copy it, of course, and paint the drawing. I used to collect seaweeds too, in those days, and dry them in a book. I have that book somewhere still," she added, wistfully, " but I don't know where."

She had won the girl's attention completely now.

Nance seemed to visualize with a sudden sting of infinite pity the various little relics so entirely dissociated from Rodmoor and its inhabitants which this reserved woman must keep stored up in that gloomy house.

" It's a funny thing," Mrs. Renshaw went on, " but I can smell at this moment quite distinctly (I suppose it's being down here by the sea that makes it come to me) the very scent of that book! The pages used to get stuck together and when I pulled them apart there was always the imprint of the seaweed on the paper. I used to like to see that. It was as though Nature had drawn it."

" It's lovely, collecting things," Nance remarked sympathetically. " I used to collect butterflies when I was a child. Dad used to say I was more like a boy than a girl."

Mrs. Renshaw glanced at her with a curious look.

" Nance, dear," she said in a low, trembling voice, " don't ever get into the habit of trying to be boyish and that sort of thing. Don't ever do that! The only good women are the women who accept God's will and bow to his pleasure. Anything else leads to untold wretchedness."

Nance made no reply to this and they both began searching for more shells among the stranded sea-drift.

Over their heads the sea-gulls whirled with wild disturbed screams. There was only one sail on the horizon now and Nance fixed her thoughts upon it and an immense longing for Adrian surged up in her heart.

Meanwhile, between Linda and Miss Doorm a conversation much more sinister was proceeding. Rachel seemed from their first encounter and as soon as the girl came into contact with her to reassert all her old mastery. She deliberately overcame the frightened child's instinctive movement to keep pace with the others and held her closely to her side as if by the power of some ancient link between them, too strong to be overcome.

"Let me look at you," she said as soon as their friends were out of hearing. "Let me look into your eyes, my pretty one!"

She laid one of her gaunt hands on the girl's shoulder and with the other held up her chin.

"Yes," she remarked after a long scrutiny during which Linda seemed petrified into a sort of dumb submission, "yes, I can see you've struggled against him. I can see you've not given up without an effort. That means that you *have* given up! If you hadn't fought against him he wouldn't have followed you. He's like that. He always *was* like that." She removed her hands but kept her eyes fixed gloomily on the girl's face. "I expect you're wishing now you'd never seen this place, eh? Aren't you wishing that? So this is the end of all your selfishness and your vanity? Yes, it's the end, Linda Herrick. It's the end."

She dragged the girl slowly forward along the path. On their right as they advanced, the sun flickered upon the rank grasses which grew intermittently in the soft sand and on their left the glittering sea lay calm and serene under the spacious sky.

Linda felt her feet grow heavy beneath her and her heart sank with a sick misgiving as she saw how far they had permitted the others to outstrip them. Beyond anything else it was the power of cruel memories which held the young girl now so docile, so helpless, in the other's hands. The old panic-stricken terror which

Rachel had the power of exciting in her when a child seemed ineluctable in its endurance. Faintly and feebly in her heart Linda struggled against this spell. She longed to shake herself free and rush desperately in pursuit of the others but her limbs seemed turned to lead and her will seemed paralyzed.

Rachel's face was white and haggard. She seemed animated by some frenzied impulse — some inward, demoniac force which drove her on. Drops of perspiration stood out upon her forehead and made the grey hair that fell across it moist and clammy under the rim of her dusty black hat. Her clothes, as she held the girl close to her side, threw upon the air a musty, fetid odour.

" Where are your soft ways now? " she went on, " your little clinging ways, your touching little babyish ways? Where are your whims and your fancies? Your caprices and your blushes? Where are your white-faced pretences, and your sham terrors, only put on to make you look sweet? "

She had her hand upon the girl's arm as she spoke and she tightened her grasp, almost shaking her in her mad malignity.

" Before you were born your mother was afraid of me," she went on. " Oh, she gained little by cutting me out with her pretty looks! She gained little, Linda Herrick! She dared scarcely look me in the face in those days. She was afraid even to hate me. That is why *you* are what you are. You're the child of her terror, Linda Herrick, the child of her terror! "

She paused for a moment while the girl's breath came in gasps through her white lips as if under the burden of an incubus.

"Listen!" the woman hissed at last, staggering a little and actually leaning against the girl as though the frenzy of her malignity deprived her of her strength. "Listen, Linda. Do you remember what I used to tell you about your father? How in his heart all the time he loved only me? How he would sooner have got rid of your mother than have got rid of me? Do you remember that? Listen, then! There's something else I must say to you — something that you've never guessed, something that you couldn't guess. When you were —" she stopped, panting heavily and if Linda had not mechanically assisted her she would have fallen. "When you were — when I was —" Her breath seemed to fail her then completely. She put her hand to her side and in spite of the girl's feeble effort to support her she sank, moaning, to the ground.

Linda looked helplessly round. Nance and Mrs. Renshaw had passed beyond a little promontory of sand-hills and were concealed from view. She knelt down by Rachel's side. Even then — even when those vindictive dark eyes looked at her without a sign of consciousness, they seemed to hold her with their power. As they remained mute and motionless in this manner, the prostrate woman and the kneeling girl, a faint gust of wind, blowing the sand in a little cloud before it and rustling the leaves of the horned poppies, brought to Linda's senses an odour of inland fields. She felt a dim return, under this air, of her normal faculties and taking one of the woman's hands in her own she began gently chafing it. Rachel answered to the touch and a shiver passed through her frame. Then, in a flash, intelligence came back into her eyes and her lips moved. Linda bent lower so as to catch her words. They came brokenly, and in feeble gasps.

"I loved him so, I loved him more than my life. He took my life and killed it. He killed my heart. He brought me those beads from far across the sea. They were for me — not for her. He brought them for me, I tell you. I gave him my heart for them and he killed it. He killed it and buried it. This isn't Rachel's heart any more. No! No! It isn't Rachel's. Rachel's heart has gone with him — with the Captain — over great wide seas. He got it — out of me — when — he — kissed my mouth."

Her voice died away in inarticulate mutterings. Then once more her words grew human and clear.

"My heart went with him long ago, after that, over the sea. It was in all his ships. It was in every ship he sailed in — over far-off seas. And in place of my heart — something else — something else — came and lived in Rachel. It is this that — that —" The intelligence once more faded out of her eyes and she lay stiff and motionless. Linda had a sudden thought that she was dead and, with the thought, her fear of her rolled away. Looking at her now, lying there, in her black dress and crumpled bonnet, she seemed to see her as she was, a mad, wretched, passion-scorched human being. It crossed the young girl's mind how inconceivable it was that this haggard image of desolation had once been young and soft-limbed, had once danced out on summer mornings to meet the sun as any other child! But even as this thought came to her, Rachel stirred and moved again. Her eyes had a dazed expression now — a clouded, sullen, hopeless expression. Slowly and with laborious effort, refusing Linda's assistance, she rose to her feet.

" Go and call them," she said in a low voice. " Go and call them. Tell Mrs. Renshaw that I'm ill — that she must take me home. You won't be troubled with me much longer — not much longer! But you won't forget me. Brand will see to that! No, you won't forget me, Linda Herrick."

The girl ran off without looking back. When the three of them returned, Rachel Doorm seemed to have quite resumed her normal taciturnity.

They walked back, all four together, to the harbour mouth. The sisters helped the two women into the little cart and untied the pony. As they clattered away over the cobble-stones, Nance received from Mrs. Renshaw a smile of gratitude, a smile of such illumined and spiritual gaiety that it rendered the pale face which it lit up beautiful with the beauty of some ancient picture.

When the pony-cart had disappeared, Nance and Linda sat down together on the wooden bench watching the white sail upon the horizon and talking of Rachel Doorm.

Most of the holiday-makers had now retired to their tea and a fresh breeze, coming in with the turn of the tide, blew pleasantly upon the girls' foreheads and ruffled the soft hair under their daintily beribboned hats. Nance, holding in her fingers the trumpet-shaped shell, found herself suddenly wondering — perhaps because the shape of the shell reminded her of it — whether Linda had left that ominous fir-cone behind her in her room or whether at the last moment she had again slipped it into her dress. She glanced sideways at her sister's girlish bosom, scarcely stirring now as with her head turned she looked at the full-brimmed tide, and she wondered if, under that white and pink frock so coquettishly open at the throat, there were any newly created blood-stains from the rasping impact of that rough-edged trophy of the satyr-haunted woods of Oakguard.

The afternoon light was so beautiful upon the water at that moment and the cries of the circling sea-gulls so full of an elemental callousness that the elder girl experienced a sort of fierce reaction against the whole weight of this intolerable sex-passion that was spoiling both their lives. Something hard, free and reckless seemed to rise up within her, in defiance of every sort of feminine sentiment and, hardly thinking what she did or of the effect of her words, " Quick, my dear," she cried suddenly, " give me that fir-cone you've got under your dress! "

Linda's hands rose at once and she clutched at her bosom, but her sister was too quick for her and too strong. Nance's feeling at that moment was as if she were plucking a snake away. Rising to her feet when she had secured the trophy, she lifted up her arm and, with a fierce swing of her whole body, flung both it and the shell she had herself been holding far into the centre-current of the inflowing tide.

" So much for Love! " she cried fiercely.

The shell sank at once to the bottom but the fir-cone floated. For a moment, when she saw Linda's dismay, she felt a pang of remorse. But she crushed it fiercely down. Behind her whole mood at that moment was a savage reaction from Mrs. Renshaw's emotional perversity.

"Come!" she cried, snatching at her sister's hand as Linda wavered on the wharf-brink and watched the fir-cone drift behind an anchored barge and disappear. "Come! Let's go back and help Miss Pontifex water her garden. Then we'll have tea and then we'll go for a row if it isn't too dark! Perhaps Dr. Raughty will be home by then and we'll make him take us."

She was so resolute and so dominant that Linda could do nothing but meekly submit to her. Strangely enough she, too, felt a certain rebound of youthful vivacity now she was conscious no longer of the rough wood-token pressing against her flesh. She also, after what she had heard from the lips of Rachel, experienced a reaction against the sorrow of "what men call love." Their mood continued unaltered until they reached the gate of the dressmaker's garden.

"Then it's Dr. Raughty — not Adrian," the younger girl remarked with a smile, "that we're to have to row us to-night?"

Nance looked quickly back at her and made an effort to smile too. But the sight of the flower-beds and the carefully tended box-hedges of the little garden, had been associated too long and too deeply with the pain at her heart. Her smile died away from her face and it was in silence after all and still bowed, for all their brave revolt under the burden of their humanity, that the two girls set themselves to water, as the August sun went down into the fens, the heavily-scented phloxes and sweet lavender of the admirable Miss Pontifex. That little lady was herself at that moment staring demurely, under the escort of a broad-shouldered nephew from London, at a stirring representation of "East Lynne" in a picture show in Mundham!

XIX

LISTENERS

AUGUST, now it had once come, proved hotter than was usual in that windy East Anglian district Before the month was half over the harvest had begun and the wheat fields by the river bank stood bare and stubbly round their shocks of corn. Twined with the wheat stalks and fading now, since their support had been cut away, were all those bright and brilliant field flowers which Nance had watched with so tender an emotion in their yet unbudded state from her haunt by the willow bed.   Fumitory and persicaria, succory and corn cockles, blent together in those fragrant holocausts with bindweed and hawkweed.   At the edges of the fields the second brood of scarlet poppies still lingered on like thin streaks of spilt red blood round the scalps of closely cropped heads.   In the marshy places and by the dykes and ditches the newly grown rush spears were now feathery and high, overtopping their own dead of the year before and gradually hiding them from sight.   The last of all the season's flowers, the lavender-coloured Michaelmas daisies alone refused to anticipate their normal flowering.   But even these, in several portions of the salt marshes, were already high-grown and only waiting the hot month's departure to put forth their autumnal blossoms.   In the dusty corners of Rodmoor yards and in the littered outskirts of Mundham, where there were several gravel-

quarries, camomile and feverfew — those pungent children of the late summer, lovers of rubbish heaps and deserted cow sheds — trailed their delicate foliage and
friendly flowers. In the wayside hedges, wound-wort
was giving place to the yellow spikes of the flower
called "archangel," while those "buds of marjoram,"
appealed to in so wistful and so bitter a strain by the
poet of the *Sonnets*, were superseding the wild basil.
The hot white dust of the road between Rodmoor and
Mundham rose in clouds under the wheels of every kind
of vehicle and, as it rose, it swept in spiral columns
across that grassy expanse which, in accordance with
the old liberal custom of East Anglian road-makers, separated the highway on both sides from the enclosing
hedges. With the sound of the corn-cutting machine
humming drowsily all day and, in the twilight, with the
shouts and cries of the children as their spirits rose with
the appearance of the moths and bats, there mingled
steadily, day in and day out, the monotonous splash of
the waves on Rodmoor beach.

To those in the vicinity, whom Nature or some ill-
usage of destiny had made morbidly sensitive to that
particular sound, there was perhaps something harder
to bear in its placid reiterated rhythm under these
halcyon influences than when, in rougher weather, it
broke into fury. The sound grew in intensity as it
diminished in volume and with the *beat, beat, beat,* of its
eternal refrain, sharpened and brought nearer in the
silence of the hot August noons there came to such nervously sensitive ears as were on the alert to receive it,
an increasingly disturbing resemblance to the sistole
and diastole, the inbreathing and outbreathing of some
huge, half-human heart.

Among the various persons in Rodmoor from whom the greater and more beneficent gods seemed turning away their faces and leaving them a prey to the lesser and more vindictive powers, it is probable that not one felt so conscious of this note of insane repetition, almost bestial in its blind persistence, as did Philippa Renshaw. Philippa, in those early August weeks, became more and more aloof from both her mother and Brand. She met Sorio once or twice but that was rather by chance than by design and the encounters were not happy for either of them. Insomnia grew upon her and her practise of roaming at night beneath the trees of the park grew with it. Brand often followed her on these nocturnal wanderings but only once was he successful in persuading her to return with him to the house. In proportion as she drew away from him he seemed to crave her society.

One night, after Mrs. Renshaw had retired to bed, the brother and sister lingered on in the darkened library. It was a peculiarly sultry evening and a heavy veil of mist obscured the young crescent moon. Through the open windows came hot gusts of air, ruffling the curtains and making the candle flames flicker. Brand rose and blew out all the lights except one which he placed on a remote table below the staring dark-visaged portrait, painted some fifty years before, of Herman Renshaw, their father. The other pictures that hung in the spaces between the book-shelves were now reduced to a shadowy and ghostly obscurity, an obscurity well adapted to the faded and melancholy lineaments of these older, but apparently no happier, Renshaws of Oakguard. Round the candle he had left alight a little group of agitated moths hovered and at

intervals as one or other of them got singed it would
dash itself with wild blind flutterings, into the remotest
corners of the room. From the darkness outside came
an occasional rustle of leaves and sighing of branches
as the gusts of hot air rose and died away. The oppressive heat was like the burden of a huge, palpable
hand laid upon the roof of the house. Now and again
some startled creature pursued by owl or weasel uttered
a panic-stricken cry, but whether its enemy seized upon
it, or whether it escaped, the eyes of the darkness alone
knew. Its cry came suddenly and stopped suddenly
and the steady beat of the rhythm of the night went
on as before.

Brand flung himself down in a low chair and his sister
balanced herself on the arm of it, a lighted cigarette
between her mocking lips. Hovering thus in the shadow
above him, her flexible form swaying like a phantom
created out of mist, she might have been taken for the
embodiment of some perverse vision, some dream avatar
from the vices of the dead past.

" After all," Brand murmured in a low voice, a voice
that sounded as though his thoughts were taking shape
independently of his conscious will, " after all, what do
I want with Linda or any of them since I've got you? "

She made a mocking inclination of her head at this
but kept silence, only letting her eyes cling, with a
strange light in them, to his disturbed face. After a
pause he spoke again.

" And yet she suits me better than any one — better than I expected it was possible for a girl like that
to suit me. She'll never get over her fear of me and
that means she'll never get over her love. I ought to be
contented with that, oughtn't I? "

He paused again and still Philippa uttered no word.
" I don't think you quite understand," he went on, " all
that there is between her and me. We touch one another *in the depths,* there's no doubt about that, and
our boat takes us where there are no soundings, none at
least that I've ever made! We touch one another where
that noise — oh, damn the wind! I don't mean the
wind! — is absolutely still. Have *you* ever reached a
point when you've got that noise out of your ears? No
— you know very well you haven't! You were born
hearing it — just as I was — and you'll die hearing it.
But with her, just because she's so afraid, so madly
afraid — do you understand? — I *have* reached that
point. I reached it the other night when we were together. Yes! You may smile — you little devil —
but it's quite true. She put it clear out of my head
just as if she'd driven the tide back! "

He stared at the cloud of faint blue smoke that
floated up round his sister's white face and then he met
her eyes again.

" Bah! " he flung out angrily. " What absurd nonsense it all is! We've been living too long in this place,
we Renshaws, that's what's the matter with us! We
ought to sell the confounded house and clear out altogether! I will too, when mother dies. Yes, I will —
brewery or no brewery — and go off with Tassar to one
of his foreign places. I'll sell the whole thing, the land
and the business! It's begun to get on my nerves. It
must have got on my nerves, mustn't it, when that simple
break, break, break, as mother's absurd poem says of
this damned sea, sounds to me like the beating heart of
something, of something whose heart ought to be
stopped from beating! "

His voice which had risen to a loud pitch of excitement died away in a sort of apologetic murmur.

" Sorry," he muttered, " only don't look at me like
that, you girl. There, clear off and sit further away!
It's that look of yours that makes me talk in this silly
fashion. God help us! I don't blame that foreign fellow for getting queer in his head. You've got something in those eyes of yours, Philippa, that no living
girl ought to be allowed to have! Bah! You've made
me talk like an absolute fool."

Instead of moving away as she had been bidden,
Philippa touched her brother with a light caress.
Never had she looked so entirely a creature of the old
perverse civilizations as she looked at that moment.

" Mother thinks you're going to marry that girl,"
she whispered, " but I know better than that, and I'm
always right in these things, am I not, Brand darling? "

He fell back under her touch and the shadowy lines
of his face contracted. He presented the appearance
of something withered and crumpled. Her mocking
smile still divided her curved lips, curved in the subtle,
archaic way as in the marbles of ancient Greece. Whatever may have been the secret of her power over him, it
manifested itself now in the form of a spiritual cruelty
which he found very difficult to bear. He made a
movement that was almost an appeal.

" Say I'm right, say I'm always right in these
things! " she persisted.

But at that moment a diversion occurred, caused by
the sudden entrance of a large bat. The creature uttered a weird querulous cry, like the cry of a newborn
babe and went wheeling over their heads in desperate
rapid circles, beating against the bookcase and the pic-

ture frames. Presently, attracted by the light, it swooped down upon the flame of the candle and in a moment had extinguished it, plunging the room into complete darkness.

Philippa, with a low taunting laugh, ran across the room and wrapped herself in one of the window curtains.

" Open the door and drive it out," she cried. " Drive it out, I say! Are you afraid of a thing like that? "

But Brand seemed either to have sunk into a kind of trance or to be too absorbed in his thoughts to make any movement. He remained reclining in his chair, silent and motionless.

The girl cautiously withdrew from her shelter and, fumbling about for matches, at last found a box and struck a light. The bat flew past her as she did so and whirled away into the night. She lit several candles and held one of them close to her brother's face. Thus illuminated, Brand's sinister countenance had the look of a mediæval wood-carving. He might have been the protagonist of one of those old fantastic prints representing Doctor Faustus after some hopeless struggle with his master-slave.

" Take it away, you! Let me alone. I've talked too much to you already. This is a hot night, eh? A hot night and the kind that sets a person thinking. Bah! I've thought too much. It's thinking that causes all the devilries in the world. Thinking, and hearing hearts beating, that ought to be stopped! "

He pushed her aside and rose, stretching himself and yawning.

" What's the time? What? Only ten o'clock? How early mother must have gone to bed! This is the kind of night in which people kill their mothers. Yes,

they do, Philippa. You needn't peer at me like that!
And they do it when their mothers have daughters that
look like you — just like you at this very moment."

He leaned against the back of a chair and watched
her as she stood negligently by the mantelpiece, her
arm extended along its marble surface.

"Why does mother always say these things to you
about my marrying?" he continued in a broken thick
voice. "You lead her on to think of these things and
then when she comes out with them you bring them to
me, to make me angry with her. Tell me this, Philippa,
why do you hate mother so? Why did you have that
look in your face just now when I talked of killing her?
What — would — you — Hang it all, girl, stop staring and smiling at me like that or it'll be you I'll kill!
Oh, Heaven above, help us! This hot night will send
us all into Bedlam!"

He suddenly stopped and began intently listening,
his eyes on his sister's face. "Did you hear that?" he
whispered huskily. "She's walking up and down the
passage — walking in her slippers, that's why you can
hardly hear her. Hush! Listen! She'll go presently
into father's room. She always does that in the end.
What do you think she does there, Philippa? Rum-
mages about, I suppose, and opens and shuts drawers
and changes the pictures! What people we are! God
— what people we are! I suppose the sound of her doing all that irritates you till your brain nearly bursts.
It's a strange thing, isn't it, this family life! Human
beings like us weren't meant to be stuck in a hole together like wasps in a bottle. Listen! Do you hear
that? She's doing something to his window now. A
lot he cares, six feet under the clay! But it shows how

he holds her still, doesn't it?" He made a gesture in the direction of his father's picture upon which the candle-light shone clearly now, animating its heavy features.

"Do you know," he continued solemnly, looking closely at his sister again, "I believe one of these nights, when she walks up and down like that, in her soft slippers, you'll go straight up and kill her yourself. Yes, I believe you listen like this every night till you could put your fingers in your ears and scream."

He moved across the room and, approaching his sister, shook her roughly by the arm. Some psychic change in the atmosphere about them seemed to have completely altered their relations.

"Confess — confess — you girl!" he muttered harshly. "Confess now — when you go rushing off like that into the park it isn't to see that foreign fellow at all? It isn't even to lie, as I know you love to do, touching the stalks of the poison funguses with the tip of your tongue under the oak trunks? It's to escape from hearing her, that's what it is! Confess now. It's to escape from hearing her!"

He suddenly relaxed his grasp and stood erect, listening intently. The sweet heavy scent of magnolia petals floated in through the window and somewhere — far off among the trees — a screech-owl uttered a broken wail, followed by the flapping of wings. The clock in the hall outside began striking the hour. Before each stroke a ponderous metallic vibration trembled through the silent house.

"It's only ten now," he said. "The clock in here is fast."

As he spoke there was a loud ring at the entrance

door. The brother and sister stared blankly at one another and then Philippa gave a low unnatural laugh. "We might be criminals," she whispered. They instinctively assumed more easy and less dramatic positions and waited in silence, while from the distant servants' quarters some one came to answer the summons. They heard the door opened and the sound of suppressed voices in the hall. There was a moment's pause, during which Philippa looked mockingly and enquiringly at Brand.

"It's our dear priest," she whispered, "and some one else, too."

"Surely the fool's not going to try —" began Brand.

"Mr. Traherne and Dr. Raughty!" announced the servant, opening the library door and holding it open while the visitors entered.

The clergyman advanced first. He shook hands with Brand and bowed with old-fashioned courtesy to Philippa. Dr. Raughty, following him, shook hands with Philippa and nodded nervously at her brother. The two men sank into the seats offered them and accepted an invitation to smoke. Brand moved to a side table and mixed for them, with an air of resigned politeness, cool and appropriate drinks. He drank nothing himself, however, but his sister, with a mocking apology to Mr. Traherne, lit herself a cigarette.

"How's the rat?" she began, throwing a teasing and provocative smile upon the priest's perturbed countenance.

"Out there," he replied, emptying his glass at one gulp.

"What? In your coat pocket on such a night as this?"

Mr. Traherne put down his glass and inserted his huge workman's fingers into the bosom of his cassock.

"Nothing under this but a shirt," he said. "Cassocks have no pockets."

"Haven't they?" laughed Brand. "They have something then where you can put money. That is, unless you parsons are like kangaroos and have some natural little orifice in which to hide the offerings of the faithful."

"Is he happy always in your pocket?" enquired Philippa.

"Do you want me to see?" replied the priest, rising with a movement that almost upset the table. "I'll bring him in and I'll make him go scimble-scamble all about the room."

The tone in which he uttered these words said, as plainly as words could say, "You're a pretty, silly, flirtatious piece of femininity! You only talk about my rat for the sake of fooling me. You don't really care whether he's happy in my pocket or not. It's only out of consideration for your silly nerves that I don't play with him now. And if you tease me an inch more I will, and make him run up your petticoats, too!"

"Sit down again, Traherne," said Brand, "and let me fill up your glass. We'll all visit the rat presently and find him some supper. Just at present I'm anxious to know how things are in the village. I haven't been down that way for weeks."

This was a direct challenge to the priest to come, without further delay, to the matter of his visit. Hamish Traherne accepted it.

"We came really," he said, "to see *you*, Renshaw. A little later, perhaps before we go, we must have our conversation. We hardly expected to have the pleasure of finding Miss Philippa sitting up so late."

Dr. Raughty, who all this while had been watching with the most intense delight the beauty of the girl's white skin and scarlet lips and the indescribable charm of her sinuous figure, now broke in impetuously.

" But it can wait! It can wait! Oh, please don't go to bed yet, Miss Renshaw. Look, your cigarette's out! Throw it away and try one of these. They're French, they're the yellow packets, I know you like them. They're what you smoked once when we were on the river — when you caught that great perch."

Philippa, who had risen to her feet at Traherne's somewhat brusque remark, came at once to the Doctor's side.

" Oh, the perch," she cried, " yes, I should think I do remember! You insisted on killing it at once so that it shouldn't jump back into the water. You put your thumb into its mouth and bent back its head. Oh, yes! That yellow packet brings it all back to me. I can smell the sticky dough we tried to catch dace with afterwards and I can see the look of your hands all smeared with blood and silver scales. Oh, that was a lovely day, Doctor! Do you remember how you twisted those things, bryony leaves they were, round my head when the others had gone? Do you remember how you said you'd like to treat me as you treated the perch? Do you remember how you ran after a dragon-fly or something? "

She stopped breathlessly and, balancing herself on the arm of the Doctor's chair, blew a great cloud of smoke over his head, filling the room in a moment with the pungent odour of French tobacco.

Both Traherne and Brand regarded her with astonishment. She seemed to have transformed herself and to have become a completely different person. Her eyes shone with childish gaiety and when she laughed, as she did a moment afterwards at some sally of the Doctor's, there was a ring of unforced, spontaneous merriment in the sound such as her brother had not heard for many years. She continued to bend over Dr. Raughty's chair, covering them both in a thick cloud of cigarette smoke, and the two of them soon became absorbed in some intricate discussion concerning, as far as the others could make out, the question of the best bait to be used for pike.

The priest took the opportunity of delivering himself of what was on his mind.

" I'm afraid, Renshaw," he said, " you've gone your own way in that matter of Linda Herrick. No! Don't deny it. You may not have seen her as often as before our last conversation, but you've seen her. She's confessed as much to me herself. Now look here, Renshaw, you and I have known one another for some good few years. How long is it, man? Fifteen, twenty? It can't be less. Long enough, anyway, for me to have earned the right to speak quite plainly and I tell you this, you must stop the whole business!"

His voice sank as he spoke to a formidable whisper. Brand glanced round at the others but apparently they were quite preoccupied. Mr. Traherne continued.

" The whole business, Renshaw! After this you must leave that child absolutely alone. If you don't — if you insist on going on seeing her — I shall take strong measures with you. I shall — but I needn't say any more! I think you can make a pretty shrewd guess what I shall do."

Brand received this solemn ultimatum in a way calculated to cause the agitated man who addressed it to him a shock of complete bewilderment. He yawned carelessly and stretched out his long arms.

"As you please, Hamish," he said, "I'm perfectly ready not to see her. In fact, I probably shouldn't have seen her in any case. To tell you the truth, I've got a bit sick of the whole thing. These young girls are silly little feather-weights at best. It's first one mood and then another! You can't be sure of them for two hours at a stretch. So it's all right, Hamish Traherne! I won't interfere with her. You can make a nun of her if you like — or whatever else you fancy. All I beg of you is, don't go round talking about me to your parishioners. Don't talk about me to Raughty! I don't want my affairs discussed by any one — not even by my friends. All right, my boy — you needn't look at me like that. You've known me, as you say, long enough to know what I am. So there you are! You've had your answer and you've got my word. I don't mind even your calling it 'the word of a gentleman' as you did the other night. You can call it what you like. I'm not going to see Linda for a reason quite personal and private but if you like to make it a favour to yourself that I don't — well! throw that in, too!"

Hamish Traherne thrust his hand into his cassock thinking, for the moment, that it was his well-worn ulster and that he would feel the familiar form of Ricoletto.

It may be noted from this futile and unconscious gesture, how much hangs in this world upon insignificant threads. Had the priest's fingers touched at that moment the silky coat of his little friend he would have derived sufficient courage to ask his formidable host point-blank whether, in leaving Linda in this way, he left her as innocent and unharmed as when he crossed her path at the beginning. Not having Ricoletto with him, however, and his fingers encountering nothing but his own woolen shirt, he lacked the inspiration to carry the matter to this conclusion. Thus, upon the trifling accident of a tame rodent having been left outside a library or, if you will, upon an eccentric parson having no pocket, depended the whole future of Linda Herrick. For, had he put that question and had Brand confessed the truth, the priest would undoubtedly, under every threat in his power, have commanded him to marry her and it is possible, considering the mood the man was in at that moment and considering also the nature of the threat held over him, he would have bowed to the inevitable and undertaken to do it.

The intricate and baffling complications of human life found further illustration in the very nature of this mysterious threat hinted at so darkly by Mr. Traherne. It was in reality — and Brand knew well that it was — nothing more or less than the making clear to Mrs. Renshaw beyond all question or doubt, of the actual character of the son she tried so conscientiously to idealize. For some basic and profound reason, inherent in his inmost nature, it was horrible to Brand to think of his mother knowing him. She might suspect and *she might know that he knew she suspected*, but to have the thing laid quite bare between them

would be to send a rending and shattering crack
through the unconscious hypocrisy of twenty years.
For certain natures any drastic cleavage of slowly
built-up moral relations is worse than death. Brand
would have felt less remorse in being the cause of his
mother's death than of being the cause of her knowing
him as he really was. The matter of Linda being thus
settled between the two men, if the understanding so
reached could be regarded as settling it, they both
turned round, anxious for some distraction, to the quarter of the room where their friends had been conversing.
But Philippa and the Doctor were no longer with them.
Brand looked whimsically at the priest who, shrugging
his shoulders, poured himself out a third glass from
the decanter on the table. They then moved to the
window which reached almost to the ground. Stepping
over its low ledge, they passed out upon the terrace.
They were at once aware of a change in the at-
mospheric conditions. The veil of mist had entirely
been swept away from the sky. The vast expanse
twinkled with bright stars and, far down among the
trees, they could discern the cresent form of the new
moon.

Brand pulled towards him a spray of damask roses
and inhaled their sweetness. Then he turned to his
companion and gave him an evil leer.

" The Doctor and Philippa have taken advantage of
our absorbing conversation," he remarked.

" Nonsense, man, nonsense! " exclaimed the priest.
" Raughty's only showing her some sort of moth or
beetle. Can't you stop your sneering for once and
look at things humanly and naturally? "

His words found their immediate justification.

Turning the corner of the house they discovered the two escaped ones on their knees by the edge of the dew-drenched lawn watching the movements of a toad. The Doctor was gently directing its advance with the stalk of a dead geranium and Philippa was laughing as merrily as a little girl.

They now realized the cause of the disappearance of the sultriness and the heat. From over the wide-stretching fens came, with strong steady breath, the northwest wind. It came with a full deep coolness in it which the plants and the trees seemed to drink from as out of some immortal cistern. It brought with it the odour of immense marsh-lands and fresh inland waters and as it bowed the trees and rustled over the flower-beds, it seemed to obliterate and drive back all indications of their nearness to the sea.

Raughty and Philippa rose to their feet at the approach of their friends.

"Doctor," said Brand, "what's the name of that great star over there — or planet — or whatever it is?"

They all surveyed the portion of the sky he indicated and contemplated the unknown luminary.

"I wish they'd taught me astronomy instead of Greek verses when I was at school," sighed Mr. Traherne.

"It's Venus, I suppose," remarked Dr. Raughty. "Isn't it Venus, Philippa?"

The girl looked from the men to the sky, and from the sky to the men.

"Well, you *are* a set of wise fellows," she cried, "not to know the star which rules us all! And that's *not* Venus, Doctor! Don't any of you really know?

Brand — you surely do?   Well, I'll tell you then, that's
Jupiter, that's the lord-star Jupiter!"

And she burst into a peal of ringing boyish laughter.   Brand turned to the Doctor, who had moved away
to cast a final glance at the toad.

"What have you done to her, Fingal?" he called
out.   "She hasn't laughed like that for years."

The only answer he received to this was an embarrassed cough, but when they returned to the library
and began looking at some of the more interesting of
the volumes in its shelves it was noticed by both Brand
and Mr. Traherne that the Doctor treated the young
girl with a frank, direct, simple and humorous friendliness as if completely oblivious of her sex.

XX

RAVELSTON GRANGE

THE hot weather continued with the intermission of only a few wet and windy days all through the harvest. One Saturday afternoon Sorio, who had arranged to take Nance by train to Mundham, loitered with Baltazar at the head of the High Street waiting the girl's appearance. She had told him to meet her there rather than at her lodging because since the occasion when they took refuge in the cottage it had been agitating to her to see Linda and Baltazar together. She knew without any question asked that for several weeks her sister had seen nothing of Brand and she was extremely unwilling, now that the one danger seemed removed, that the child should risk falling into another.

Nance herself had lately been seeing more of her friend's friend than she liked. It was difficult to avoid this, however, now that they lived so near, especially as Mr. Stork's leisure times between his journeys to Mundham, coincided so exactly with her own hours of freedom from work at the dressmaker's. But the more she saw of Baltazar, the more difficult she found it to tolerate him. With Brand, whenever chance threw him across her path, she was always able to preserve a dignified and conventional reserve. She saw that he knew how deep her indignation on behalf of her sister went and she could not help respecting him for the

tact and discretion with which he accepted her tacit
antagonism and made any embarrassing clash between
them easy to avoid. At the bottom of her heart she
had never felt any personal dislike of Brand Renshaw,
nor did that peculiar fear which he seemed to inspire
in the majority of those who knew him affect her in
the least. She would have experienced not the slightest
trepidation in confronting him on her sister's behalf
if circumstances demanded it and meanwhile she only
asked that they should be left in peace.

But with Baltazar it was different. She disliked
him cordially and, with her dislike, there mingled a
considerable element of quite definite fear. The precise nature of this fear she was unable to gauge. In a
measure it sprang from his unfailing urbanity and the
almost effusive manner in which he talked to her and
rallied her with little witticisms whenever they met.
Nance's own turn of mind was singularly direct and
simple and she could not avoid a perpetual suspicion in
dealing with Mr. Stork that the man was covertly
mocking at her and seeking to make her betray herself
in some way. There was something about his whole
personality which baffled and perplexed her. His languid and effeminate manner seemed to conceal some
hard and inflexible attitude towards life which, like a
steel blade in a velvet scabbard, was continually on
the point of revealing its true nature and yet never
actually did. She completely distrusted his influence
over Sorio and indeed carried her suspicion of him to
the extreme point of even doubting his affection for his
old-time friend. Nothing about him seemed to her genuine or natural. When he spoke of art, as he often
did, or uttered vague, cynical commentaries upon life

in general, she felt towards him just as a girl feels
towards another girl whose devices to attract attention
seem to be infringing the legitimate limit of recognized
rivalry. It was not only that she suspected him of
every sort of hypocritical diplomacy or that every attitude he adopted seemed a deliberate pose; it was that
in some indescribably subtle way he seemed to make her
feel as if her own gestures and speeches were false. He
troubled and agitated her to such an extent that she
was driven sometimes into a mood of such desperate
self-consciousness that she did actually become in-
sincere or at any rate felt herself saying and doing
things which failed to express what she really had in
her mind. This was especially the case when he was
present at her encounters with Sorio. She found herself on such occasions uttering sometimes the wildest
speeches, speeches quite far from her natural character, and even when she tried passionately to be herself
she was half-conscious all the while that Baltazar was
watching her and, so to speak, clapping his hands en-
couragingly and urging her on. It was just as if she
heard him whispering in her ear and saying, " That's
a pretty speech, that's an effective turn of the head,
that's a happily timed smile, that's an appealing little
silence! "

His presence seemed to perplex and bewilder the
very basis and foundation of her confidence in herself.
What was natural he made unnatural and what was
spontaneous he made premeditated. He seemed to dive
down into the very depths of her soul and stir up and
make muddy and clouded what was clearest and simplest
there. The little childish impulses and all the impetuous girlish movements of her mind became silly and

forced when he was present, became something that might have been different had she willed them to be different, something that she was deliberately using to bewitch Adrian.

The misery of it was that she *couldn't* be otherwise, that she couldn't look and talk and laugh and be silent, in any other manner. And yet he made her feel as if this were not only possible but easy. He was diabolically and mercilessly clever in his malign clairvoyance. Nance was not so simple as not to recognize that there are a hundred occasions when a girl quite legitimately and naturally " makes the best " of her passing moods and feelings. She was not so stupid as not to know that the very diffusion of a woman's emotions, through every fibre and nerve of her being, lends itself to innumerable little exaggerations and impulsive underscorings, so to speak, of the precise truth. But it was just these very basic or, if the phrase may be permitted, these " organic " characteristics of her self-expression, that Baltazar's unnatural watchfulness was continually pouncing on. In some curious way he succeeded, though himself a man, in betraying the very essence of her sex-dignity. He threw her, in fact, into a position of embarrassed self-defence over what were really the inevitable accompaniments of her being a woman at all.

The unfairness of the thing was constantly being accentuated and made worse by the fact of her having so often to listen to bitter and sarcastic diatribes from both Adrian and his friend, directed towards her sex in general. A sort of motiveless jibing against women seemed indeed one of the favourite pastimes of the two men and Nance's presence, when this topic came forward, appeared rather to enhance than mitigate their hostility.

On one or two occasions of this kind, Dr. Raughty had happened to be present and Nance felt she would never forget her gratitude to this excellent man for the genial and ironical way he reduced them to silence.

" I'm glad you have invented," he would say to them, " so free and inexpensive a way of getting born. You've only to give us a little more independence and death will be equally satisfactory."

On this particular afternoon, however, Baltazar was not encouraging Sorio in any misogynistic railings. On the contrary he was endeavouring to soothe his friend who at that moment was in one of his worst moods.

" Why doesn't she come? " he kept jerking out. " She knows perfectly how I hate waiting in the street."

" Come and sit down under the trees," suggested Baltazar. " She's sure to come out on the green to look for you and we can see her from there."

They moved off accordingly and sat down, side by side, with a group of village people under the ancient sycamores. Above them the nameless Admiral looked steadily seawards and in the shadow thrown by the trees several ragged little girls were playing sleepily on the burnt-up grass.

" It's extraordinary," Sorio remarked, " what a lot of human beings there are in the world who would be best out of it! They get on my nerves, these people. I think I hear them more clearly and feel them nearer me here than ever before in my life. Every person in a place like this becomes more important and asserts himself more, and the same is true of every sound. If

you want really to escape from humanity there are only
two things to do, either go right away into the desert
where there's not a living soul or go into some large
city where you're absolutely lost in the crowd. This
half-and-half existence is terrible."

"My dear, my dear," protested his companion, "you
keep complaining and grumbling but for the life of me
I can't make out what it is that actually annoys you.
By the way, don't utter your sentiments too loudly!
These honest people will not understand."

"What annoys me — you don't understand what annoys me?" muttered the other peevishly. "It annoys
me to be stared at. It annoys me to be called out
after. It annoys me to be recognized. I can't move
from your door without seeing some face I know and
what's still worse, seeing that face put on a sort of silly,
inquisitive, jeering look, as much as to say, 'Ho! Ho!
here is that idiot again. Here is that fool who sponges
upon Mr. Stork! Here is that spying foreign devil!'"

"Adrian — Adrian," protested his companion, "you
really are becoming impossible. I assure you these
people don't say or think anything of the kind! They
just see you and greet you and wish you well and pass
on upon their own concerns."

"Oh, don't they, don't they," cried the other, forgetting in his agitation to modulate his voice and causing a sudden pause in the conversation that was going
on at their side. "Don't they think these things! I
know humanity better. Every single person who meets
another person and knows anything at all about him
wants to show that he's a match for his little tricks,
that he's not deceived by his little ways, that he knows
where he gets his money or doesn't get it and what

woman he wants or doesn't want and which of his parents he wishes dead and buried! I tell you you've no idea what human beings are really like! You haven't any such idea, for the simple reason that you're absolutely hard and self-centred yourself. You go your own way. You think your own thoughts. You create your own fancy-world. And the rest of humanity are nothing — mere pawns and puppets and dream-figures — nothing — simply nothing! I'm a completely different nature from you, Tassar. I've got my idea — my secret — but I'd rather not talk about that and you'd rather not hear. But apart from that, I'm simply helpless. I mean I'm helplessly conscious of everything round me! I'm porous to things. It's really quite funny. It's just as if I hadn't any skin, as if my soul hadn't any skin. Everything that I see, or hear, Tassar — and the hearing is worse, oh, ever so much worse — passes straight through me, straight through the very nerves of my inmost being. I feel sometimes as though my mind were like a piece of parchment, stretched out taut and tight and every single thing that comes near me taps against it, tip-tap, tip-tap, tip-tap, as if it were a drum! That wouldn't be so bad if it wasn't that I know so horribly clearly what people are thinking. For instance, when I go down that alley to the station, as I shall soon with Nance, and pass the workmen at their doors, I know perfectly well that they'll look at me and say to themselves, 'There goes that fool again,' or, 'There goes that slouching idiot from the cottage,' but that's not all, Tassar. They soon have the sense to see that I'm the kind of person who shrinks from being noticed and that pleases them. They nudge one another then and look more closely at me. They do their best to make me understand that they know their power over me and intend to use it, intend to nudge one another and look at me every time I pass. I can read exactly what their thoughts are. They say to themselves, ' He may slink off now but he'll have to come this way again and then we'll see! Then we'll look at him more closely. Then we'll find out what he's after in these parts and why that pretty girl puts up with him so long!' "

He was interrupted at that moment by a roar of laughter from the group beside them and Baltazar rose and pulled him away. "Upon my soul, Adrian," he whispered, as he led him back across the green, " you must behave better! You've given those honest fellows something to gossip about for a week. They'll think you really are up to something, you can't shout like that without being listened to and you can't quarrel with the whole of humanity."

Adrian turned fiercely round on him. "Can't I?" he exclaimed. "Can't I quarrel with humanity? You wait, my friend, till I've got my book published. Then you'll see! I tell you I'll strike this cursed human race of yours such a blow that they'll wish they'd treated a poor wanderer on the face of the earth a little better and spared him something of their prying and peering!"

"Your book!" laughed Baltazar. "A lot they'll care for your book! That's always the way with you touchy philosophers. You stir up the devil of a row with your bad temper and make the most harmless people into enemies and then you think you can settle it all and prove yourselves right and everybody else wrong by writing a book. Upon my soul, Adrian, if I didn't love you very much indeed I'd be inclined to let you loose on life just to see whether you or it could strike the hardest blows!"

Sorio looked at him with a curiously bewildered look. He seemed puzzled. His swarthy Roman face wore a clouded, weary, crushed expression. His brow contracted into an anxious frown and his mouth quivered. His air at that moment was the air of a very young child that suddenly finds the world much harder to deal with than it expected.

Baltazar watched him with secret pleasure. These were the occasions when he always felt strangely drawn towards him. That look of irresolute and bewildered weakness upon a countenance so powerfully moulded filled him with a most delicate sense of protective pity. He could have embraced the man as he watched him, blinking there in the afternoon sunshine, and fumbling with the handle of his stick.

But at that moment Nance appeared, walking rapidly with bent head, up the narrow street. Baltazar looked at her with a gleam of hatred in his sea-coloured eyes. She came to rob him of one of the most exquisite pleasures of his life, the pleasure of reducing this strong creature to humiliated submissiveness and then petting and cajoling him back into self-respect. The knowledge that he left Sorio in her hands in this particular mood of deprecatory helplessness, remorseful and gentle and like a wild beast beaten into docility, caused him the most acute pain. With poisonous antagonism under his urbane greeting he watched furtively the quick glance she threw at Adrian and the way her eyes lingered upon his, feeling her way into his mood. He cast about for some element of discord

that he could evoke and leave behind with them to spoil
the girl's triumph for he knew well that Adrian was
now, after what had just occurred, in the frame of mind
most adapted of all to the influence of feminine sympathy. Nance, however, did not give him an opportunity for this.

" Come on," she said, " we've only just time to catch
the three o'clock train. Come on! Good-bye for a
while, Mr. Stork. I'll bring him back safe to you,
sooner or later. Come on, Adrian, we really must be
quick ! "

They went off together and Baltazar wandered
slowly back across the green. He felt for the moment
so lonely that even his hatred drifted away and sank
to nothingness under the inflowing wave of bitter universal isolation. As he approached his cottage he
stopped stone-still with his eyes on the ground and his
hands behind his back. Elegantly dressed in pleasant
summer clothes, his slight graceful figure, easy bearing,
and delicate features, gave without doubt to the casual
bystanders who observed him, an impression of un-
mitigated well-being. As a matter of fact, had that
discerning historic personage who is reported to have
exclaimed after an interview with Jonathan Swift,
" there goes the unhappiest man who ever lived," exer-
cised his insight now, he might have modified his conclusion in favour of Baltazar Stork.

It would certainly have required more than ordinary
discernment to touch the tip of the iron wedge that was
being driven just then into this graceful person's brain.
Looking casually into the man's face one would have
seen nothing perhaps but a dreamy, pensive smile —
a smile a little bitter maybe, and self-mocking but with

no particularly sinister import. A deeper glance, however, would have disclosed a curious compression of the
lines about the mouth and a sort of indrawing of the
lips as if Mr. Stork were about to emit the sound of
whistling. Below the smiling surface of the eyes, too,
there might have been seen a sort of under-flicker of
shuddering pain as if, without any kind of anæsthetic,
Mr. Stork were undergoing some serious operation.
The colour had deserted his cheeks as if whatever it was
he was enduring the endurance of it had already exhausted his physical energies. Passing him by, as we
have remarked, casually and hastily, one might have
said to oneself —" Ah! a handsome fellow chuckling
there over some pleasant matter!" but coming close up
to him one would have instinctively stretched out a
hand, so definitely would it then have appeared that,
whatever his expression meant, he was on the point of
fainting. It was perhaps a fortunate accident that,
at this particular moment as he stood motionless, a
small boy of his acquaintance, the son of one of the
Rodmoor fishermen, came up to him and asked whether
he had heard of the great catch there had been that
day.

"There's a sight o' fish still there, Mister," the boy
remarked, " some of them monstrous great flounders
and a heap of Satans such as squirts ink out of their
bellies!"

Baltazar's twisted lips gave a genuine smile now.
A look of extraordinary tenderness came into his face.

"Ah, Tony, my boy," he said, " so there are fish
down there, are there? Well, let's go and see! You
take me, will you? And I'll make those fellows give
you some for supper."

They walked together across the green and down the street. Baltazar's hand remained upon the child's shoulder and he listened as he walked, to his chatter; but all the while his mind visualized an immense, empty plain — a plain of steely-blue ice under a grey sky — and in the center of this plain a bottomless crevasse, also of steely-blue ice, and on the edge of this crevasse, gradually relinquishing their hold from exhaustion, two human hands. This image kept blending itself as they walked with all the little things which his eyes fell upon. It blent with the cakes in the confectioner's window. It blent with the satiny blouses, far too expensive for any local purchaser, in Miss Pontifex's shop. It blent with the criss-cross lines of the brick-work varied with flint of the house where Dr. Raughty lived. It blent with their first glimpse of the waters of the harbour, seen between two ramshackle houses with gable roofs. Nor when they finally found themselves standing with a little crowd of men and boys round a circle of fish-baskets upon the shore did it fail to associate itself both with the blue expanse of waveless sea stretched before them and with the tangled mass of sea shells, seaweed and sea creatures which lay exposed to the sunlight, many-coloured and glistening as the deeper folds of the nets which had drawn them from the deep were explored and dragged forward.

Meanwhile Adrian and Nance, having safely caught their train, were being carried with the leisurely steadiness of a local line, from Rodmoor to Mundham. Jammed tightly into a crowded compartment full of Saturday marketers, they had little opportunity during the short journey to do more than look helplessly across their perspiring neighbours at the rising and falling of the telegraph wires against a background of blue sky. The peculiar manner in which, as a train carries one forward, these wires sink slowly downwards as if they were going to touch the earth and then leap up with an unexpected jerk as the next pole comes by, was a phenomenon that always had a singular fascination for Sorio. He associated it with his most childish recollections of railway travelling. Would the wires ever succeed in sinking out of sight before the next pole jerked them high up across the window again? That was the speculation that fascinated him even at this moment as he watched them across the brim of his companion's brightly trimmed hat. There was something human in the attempts the things made to sink down, down, down and escape their allotted burden and there was certainly something very like the ways of Providence in the manner in which they were pulled up with a remorseless jolt to perform their duties once more.

Emerging with their fellow-passengers upon the Mundham platform both Sorio and Nance experienced a sense of happiness and relief. They had both been so long confined to the immediate surroundings of Rodmoor that this little excursion to the larger town assumed the proportions of a release from imprisonment. It is true that it was a release that Adrian might easily have procured for himself on any day; but more and more recently, in the abnormal tension of his nerves, he had lost initiative in these things. They wandered leisurely together into the town and Sorio amused himself by watching the demure and practical way in which his companion managed her various economic transactions in the shops which she entered. He could not help feeling a sense of envy as he observed the manner in which, without effort or strain, she achieved the precise objects she had in mind and arranged for the transportation of her purchases by the carrier's cart that same evening.

He wondered vaguely whether all women.were like this and whether, with their dearest and best-loved dead at home, or their own peace of mind permanently shattered by some passage of fatal emotion only some few hours before, they could always throw everything aside and bargain so keenly and shrewdly with the alert tradesmen. He supposed it was the working of some blind atavistic power in them, the mechanical result of ages of mental concentration. He was amused, too, to observe how, when in a time incredibly short she had done all she wanted, instead of rushing off blindly for the walk they had promised themselves past the old Abbey church and along the river's bank, she shrewdly interpreted their physical necessities and carried him off to a little dairy shop to have tea and half-penny buns. Had *he* been the cicerone of their day's outing he would have plunged off straight for the Abbey church and the river fields, leaving their shopping to the end and dooming them to bad temper and irritable nerves from sheer bodily exhaustion. Never had Nance looked more desirable or attractive as, with heightened colour and little girlish jests, she poured out his tea for him in the small shop-parlour and swallowed half-penny buns with the avidity of a child.

Baltazar Stork was not wrong in his conjecture. Not since their early encounters in the streets and parks of South London had Sorio been in a gentler mood or one more amenable to the girl's charm. As he looked at her now and listened to her happy laughter, he felt that he had been a fool as well as a scoundrel in his treatment of her. Why hadn't he cut loose long since from his philandering with Philippa which led nowhere and *could* lead nowhere? Why hadn't he cast about for some definite employment and risked, without further delay, persuading her to marry him? With her to look after him and smooth his path for him, he might have been quite free from this throbbing pain behind his eyeballs and this nervous tension of his brain. He hurriedly made up his mind that he *would* ask her to marry him — not to-day, perhaps, or to-morrow — for it would be absurd to commit himself till he could support her, but very soon, as soon as he had found any mortal kind of an occupation! What that occupation would be he did not know. It was difficult to think of such things all in a moment. It required time. Besides, whatever it was it must be something that left him free scope for his book. After all, his book came first — his book and Baptiste. What would Baptiste think if he were to marry again? Would he be indignant and hurt? No! No! It was inconceivable that Baptiste should be hurt. Besides, he would love Nance when he knew her! Of that he was quite sure. Yes, Baptiste and Nance were made to understand one another. It would be different were it Philippa he was thinking of marrying. Somehow it distressed and troubled him to imagine Baptiste and Philippa together. That, at all costs, must never come about. His boy must never meet Philippa. All of this whirled at immense speed through Sorio's head as he smiled back at Nance across the little marble table and stared at the large blue-china cow which, with udders coloured a yet deeper ultramarine than its striped back, placidly, like an animal sacred to Jupiter, contemplated the universe. There must have been a wave of telepathic sympathy between them at that moment, for Nance suddenly swallowing the last of her bun, hazarded a question she had never dared to ask before.

" Adrian, dear, tell me this. Why did you leave your boy behind you in America when you came to England? "

Sorio was himself surprised at the unruffled manner in which he received this question. At any other moment it would have fatally disturbed him. He smiled back at her, quite easily and naturally.

" How could I bring him? " he said. " He's got a good place in New York and I have nothing. I *had* to get away, somewhere. In fact, they sent me away, ' deported ' me, as they call it. But I couldn't drag the boy with me. How could I? Though he was ready enough to come. Oh, no! It's much better as it is — much, much better! "

He became grave and silent and began fumbling in one of his inner pockets. Nance watched him breathlessly. Was he really softening towards her? Was Philippa losing her hold on him? He suddenly produced a letter — a letter written on thin paper and bearing an American stamp — and taking it with careful hands from its envelope, stretched it across the table towards her. The action was suggestive of such intimacy, suggestive of such a new and happy change in their relations, that the girl looked at the thing with moist and dazed eyes. She obtained a general sense of the firm clear handwriting. She caught the opening

sentence, written in caressing Italian and, for some reason or other, the address — perhaps because of its
strangeness to a European eye — fifteen West Eleventh
Street — remained engraved in her memory. More
than this she was unable to take in for the moment out
of the sheer rush of bewildering happiness which swept
over her and made her long to cry.

A moment later two other Rodmoor people, known to
them both by sight, entered the shop, and Sorio hurriedly took the letter back and replaced it in his pocket.
He paid their bill, which came to exactly a shilling,
and together they walked out from the dairy. The
ultramarine cow contemplated the universe as the new-
comers took their vacated table with precisely the same
placidity. Its own end — some fifty years after, amid
the debris of a local fire, with the consequent departure
of its shattered pieces to the Mundham dumping ground
— did not enter into its contemplation. Many lovers,
happier and less happy than Sorio and Nance, would
sit at that marble table during that epoch and the
blue cow would listen in silence. Perhaps in its ultimate resting-place its scorched fragments would become more voluble as the rains dripped upon the tins
and shards around them or perhaps, even in ruins —
like an animal sacred to Jupiter — it would hold its
peace and let the rains fall.

The two friends, still in a mood of delicate and
delicious harmony, threaded the quieter streets of the
town and emerged into the dreamy cathedral-like square,
spacious with lawns and trees, that surrounded the
abbey-church. A broad gravel-path, overtopped by
wide-spreading lime trees, separated the grey south
wall of the ancient edifice from the most secluded of

these lawns. The grass was divided from the path by
a low hanging chain-rail of that easy and friendly kind
that seems to call upon the casual loiterer to step over
its unreluctant barrier and take his pleasure under the
welcoming trees. They sat down on an empty bench
and looked up at the flying buttresses and weather-
stained gargoyles and richly traceried windows. The
sun fell in long mellow streams across the gravel beside them, broken into cool deep patches of velvet
shadow where the branches of the lime trees intercepted
it. From somewhere behind them came the sound of
murmuring pigeons and from further off still, from one
of the high-walled, old-fashioned gardens of the houses
on the remote side of the square, came the voices of
children playing. Sorio sat with one arm stretched
out along the top of the bench behind Nance's head and
with the other resting upon the handle of his stick.
His face had a look of deep, withdrawn contentment —
a contentment so absolute that it merged into a sort
of animal apathy. Any one familiar with the expression so often seen upon the faces both of street-
beggars and prince-cardinals in the city on the Tiber,
would have recognized something indigenous and racial
in the lethargy which then possessed him. Nance, on
the other hand, gave herself up to a sweet and passionate happiness such as she had not known since they
left London. While they waited thus together, reluctant by even a word to break the spell of that favoured hour, there came from within the church the
sound of an organ. Nance got up at once.

"Let's go in for just a minute, Adrian! Do you
mind — only just a minute?"

The slightest flicker of a frown crossed Sorio's face

but it vanished before she could repeat her request.

"Of course," he said, rising in his turn, "of course! Let's go round and find the door."

They had no difficulty in doing this. The west entrance of the church was wide open and they entered and sat down at the back of the nave. Above them the spacious vaulted roof, rich with elaborate fan-tracery, seemed to spread abroad and deepen the echoes of the music as if it were an immense inverted chalice spilling the odour of immortal wine. The coolness and dim shadowiness of the place fell gently upon them both and the mysterious rising and sinking of the music, with no sight of any human presence as its cause, thrilled Nance from head to foot as she had never been thrilled in her life. Oh, it was worth it — this moment — all she had suffered before — all she could possibly suffer! If only it might never stop, that heavenly sound, but go on and on and on until all the world came to know what the power of love was! She felt at that moment as if she were on the verge of attaining some clue, some signal, some sign, which should make all things clear to her — clear and ineffably sweet!

The deep crimsons and purples in the coloured windows, the damp chilly smell of the centuries-old masonry, the large dark recesses of the shadowy transepts, all blended together to transport her out of herself into a world kindlier, calmer, quieter, than the world she knew.

"And — he — shall — feed —" rang out, as they listened, the clear flutelike voice of some boy-singer, practising for the morrow's services, "shall — feed — his — flock."

The words of the famous antiphony, "staled and rung upon" as they might be, by the pathetic stammerings of so old a human repetition, were, coming just at this particular moment, more than Nance could bear. She flung herself on her knees and, pressing her hands to her face, burst into convulsive sobs. Sorio stood up and laid his hand on her shoulder. With the other hand — mindful of early associations — he crossed himself two or three times and then remained motionless. Slowly, by the action of that law which is perhaps the deepest in the universe, the law of *ebb and flow*, there began in him a reaction. Had the words the unseen boy singer was uttering been in Latin, had they possessed that reserve, that passionate aloofness in emotion, which the instinct of worship in the southern races protects from sentiment, such a reaction might have been spared him; but the thing was too facile, too easy. It might have been the climax of a common melodrama. It fell too pat upon the occasion. And it was insidiously, treacherously, horribly human. It was too human. It lacked the ring of style, the reserve of the grand manner. It wailed and sobbed. It whimpered upon the Almighty's shoulder. It wanted the tragic abandonment of the "Dies Irae," as it missed the calmer dignity of the "Tantum ergo." It appealed to what was below the level of the highest in religious pathos. It humiliated while it comforted. The boy's voice died away and the organ stopped. There was a sound of shuffling in the choir and the mutter of voices and even a suppressed laugh.

Sorio removed his hand from Nance's shoulder and stooping down picked up his hat and stick. He looked round him. A fashionably dressed lady, carrying a bunch of carnations, moved past them up the aisle and presently two younger women followed. Then a neatly attired dapper young clergyman strolled in, adjusting his eye-glasses. It was evidently approaching the hour of the afternoon service. The spell was broken.

But the kneeling girl knew nothing, felt nothing, of all this. She, at all events, was in the church of her fathers — the church that her most childish memories rendered sacred. Had she been able to understand Sorio's feeling, she would have swept it aside. The music was beautiful, she would have said, and the words were true. From the heart of the universe they came straight to her heart. Were they rendered unbeautiful and untrue because so many simple souls had found comfort in them?

"Ah! Adrian," she would have said had she argued it out with him. "Ah, Adrian, it *is* common. It is the common cry of humanity, set to the music of the common heart of the world, and is not that more essential than 'Latin,' more important than 'style'?"

As a matter of fact, the only controversy that arose between them when they left the building was brief and final.

"I fancy," remarked Sorio, "from what you tell me of her, that that's the sort of thing that would please Mrs. Renshaw — I mean the music we heard just now!"

Nance flushed as she answered him. "Yes, it would! It would! And it pleases *me* too. It makes me more certain than ever that Jesus Christ was really God." Sorio bowed his head at this and held his peace and together they made their way to the bank of the Loon.

What they were particularly anxious to see was an old house by the river-side about a mile east of the

town which had been, some hundred years before, the
abode of one of the famous East Anglian painters of
the celebrated Norwich school — a painter whose humorous aplomb and rich earth-steeped colouring ri-
valled some of the most notable of the artists of Amster-
dam and The Hague.

Their train back to Rodmoor did not leave till half-
past seven and as it was now hardly five they had ample
time to make this little pilgrimage as deliberately as
they pleased. They had no difficulty in reaching the
river, and once at its edge, it was only a question of
following its windings till they arrived at Ravelston
Grange. Their way was somewhat impeded at first by
a line of warehouses, between which and a long row of
barges fastened to a series of littered dusty wharves,
lay all manner of bales and casks and bundles of hay
and vegetable. There were coal-yards there too, and
timber-yards, and in other places great piles of beer-
barrels, all bearing the name " Keith Radipole " which
had been for half a century the business title of Brand
Renshaw's brewery. These obstacles surmounted, there
were no further interruptions to their advance along the
river path.

The aspect of the day, however, had grown less promising. A somewhat threatening bank of clouds with
dark jagged edges, which the efforts of the sun to
scatter only rendered more lurid, had appeared in the
west and when, for a moment, they turned to look back
at the town, they saw its chimneys and houses massed
gloomily together against a huge sombre bastion whose
topmost fringe was illuminated by fiery indentations.
Nance expressed some hesitation as to the wisdom of going further with this phalanx of storm threatenings fol-

lowing them from behind, but Sorio laughed at her fears and assured her that in a very short time they would arrive at the great painter's house.

It appeared, however, that the " mile " referred to in the little local history in which they had read about this place did not begin till the limits of Mundham were reached and Mundham seemed to extend itself interminably. They were passing through peculiarly dreary outskirts now. Little half-finished rows of wretchedly built houses trailed disconsolately towards the river's edge and mingled with small deserted factories whose walls, blackened with smoke, were now slowly crumbling to pieces. Desolate patches of half-cultivated ground where the stalks of potatoes, yellowing with damp, alternated with thickly growing weeds, gave the place that peculiar expression of sordid melancholy which seems the especial prerogative of such fringes of human habitation. Old decaying barges, some of them half-drowned in water and others with gaunt, protruding ribs and rotting planks, lay staring at the sky while the river, swirling past them, gurgled and muttered round their submerged keels. It was impossible for the two friends to retain long, under these depressing surroundings, their former mood of magical harmony. Little shreds and fragments of their happiness seemed to fall from them at every step and remain, bleakly flapping among the mouldering walls and weedy river-piles, like the bits of old paper and torn rag which fluttered feebly or fell into immobility as the wind rose or sank. The bank of clouds behind them had now completely obscured every vestige of the sun and a sort of premature twilight lay upon the surface of the river and on the fields on its further side.

"What's that?" asked Nance suddenly, putting her hand on his arm and pointing to a large square building which suddenly appeared on their left. They had been vaguely aware of this building for some while but one little thing or another in their more immediate neighbourhood had confined it to the remoter verge of their consciousness. As soon as she had asked the question Nance felt an unaccountable unwillingness to carry the investigation further. Sorio, too, seemed ready enough to let her enquiry remain unanswered. He shrugged his shoulders as much as to say "how can I tell?" and suggested that they should rest for a moment on a littered pile of wood which lay close to the water's edge.

They stepped down the bank where they were, out of sight of the building above, and seated themselves. With their arms around their knees they contemplated the flowing tide and the dull-coloured mud of the opposite bank. A coil of decaying rope, tossed aside from some passing barge, lay at Sorio's feet and, as he sat in gloomy silence, he thought how like the thing was to something he had once seen at an inquest in a house in New York. As for Nance, she found it difficult to remove her eyes from a shapeless bundle of sacking which the tide was carrying. Sometimes it would get completely submerged and then again it would reappear.

"Why is it," she thought, "that there is always something horrible about tidal rivers? Is it because of the way they have of carrying things backward and forward, backward and forward, without ever allowing them either to get far inland or clear out to sea? Is a tidal river," she said to herself, "the one thing in all the world in which nothing can be lost or hidden or forgotten?"

It was curious how difficult they both felt it just then either to move from where they were or to address a single word to one another. They seemed hypnotized by something — hypnotized by some thought which remained unspoken at the back of their minds. They felt an extreme reluctance to envisage again that large square building surrounded by weather-stained wall, a wall from which the ivy had been carefully scraped.

Slowly, little by little, the bank of clouds mounted up to the meridian, casting over everything as it did so a more and more ominous twilight. The silence between them became after a while, a thing with a palpable presence. It seemed to float upon the water to their feet and, rising about them like a wraith, like a mist, like the ghost of a dead child, it fumbled with clammy fingers upon their hearts.

"I'm sure," Sorio cried at last, with an obvious struggle to break the mysterious sorcery which weighed on them, "I'm perfectly sure that Ravelston Grange must be round that second bend of the river — do you see? — where those trees are! I'm sure it must! At any rate we *must* come to it at last if we only go on."

He looked at his watch.

"Heavens! We've taken an hour already getting here! It's nearly six. How on earth have we been so long?"

"Do you know, Adrian," Nance remarked — and she couldn't help noticing as she did so that though he spoke so resolutely of going forward he made not the least movement to leave his seat —"do you know I feel as if we were in a dream. I have the oddest feeling

that any moment we might wake up and find ourselves
back in Rodmoor. Adrian, dear, let's go back! Let's
go back to the town. There's something that depresses
me beyond words about all this."

" Nonsense! " cried Sorio in a loud and angry voice,
leaping to his feet and snatching up his stick. " Come
on, my girl, come, child! We'll see that Ravelston
place before the rain gets to us! "

They clambered up the bank and walked swiftly forward. Nance noticed that Sorio looked steadily at
the river, looked at the river without intermission and
with hardly a word, till they were well beyond the very
last houses of Mundham. It was an unspeakable relief to her when, at last, crossing a little footbridge
over a weir, they found themselves surrounded by the
open fens.

" Behind those trees, Nance," Sorio kept repeating,
" behind those trees! I'm absolutely sure I'm right
and that Ravelston Grange is there. By the way, girl,
which of your poets wrote the verses —

> ' She makes her immemorial moan,
> She keeps her shadowy kine,
> O, Keith of Ravelston,
> The sorrows of thy line! '

They've been running in my head all the afternoon
ever since I saw ' Keith Radipole,' on those beer-
barrels."

Nance, however, was too eager to reach the real
Ravelston to pay much heed to his poetic allusion.

" Oh, it sounds like — oh, I don't know — Tennyson, perhaps! " and she pulled him forward towards the
trees.

These proved to be a group of tall French poplars which, just then, were muttering volubly in the rain-smelling wind. They hurried past them and paused before a gate in a very high wall.

"What's this?" exclaimed Sorio. "*This* can't be Ravelston. It looks more like a prison."

For a moment his eyes encountered Nance's and the girl glanced quickly away from what she read in his face. She called out to an old man who was hoeing potatoes behind some iron railings where the wall ended.

"Could you tell me where Ravelston Grange is?" she enquired.

The old man removed his hat and regarded her with a whimsical smile.

" 'Tis across the river, lady, and there isn't no bridge for some many miles. Maybe with any luck ye may meet a cattle-boat to take ye over but there's little surety about them things."

"What's this place, then?" asked Sorio abruptly, approaching the iron railings.

"This, mister? Why this be the doctor's house of the County Asylum. This be where they keep the superior cases, as you might say, them what pays summat, ye understand, and be only what you might call half daft. You must a' seed the County Asylum as you came along. 'Tis a wonderful large place, one of the grandest, so they say, on this side of the kingdom."

"Thank you," said Sorio curtly. "That's just what we wanted to know. Yes, we saw the house you speak of. It certainly looks big enough. Have there been many new cases lately? Is this what you might call a good year for mental collapses?"

As he spoke he peered curiously between the iron bars as if anxious to get some sight of the " half daft," who could afford to pay for their keep.

" I don't know what you mean by ' a good year,' mister," answered the man, watching him with little twinkling eyes, " but I reckon folk have been as liable to go shaky this year as most other years. 'Tisn't in the season, I take it, 'tis in the man or for the matter of that," and he cast an apologetic leer in Nance's direction, " in the woman."

" Come on, Adrian," interposed his companion, " you see that guide-book told us all wrong. We'd better get back to the station."

But Sorio held tightly to the railings with both his hands.

" Don't tease me, Nance," he said irritably. " I want to talk to this excellent man."

" You'd better do what your missus says, mister," observed the gardener, returning to his work. " The authorities don't like no loitering in these places."

But Sorio disregarded the hint.

" I should think," he remarked, " it wouldn't be so very difficult to escape out of here." He received no reply to this and Nance pulled him by the sleeve.

" Please, Adrian, please come away," she pleaded, with tears in her voice. The old man lifted up his head.

" You go back where you be come from," he observed, " and thank the good Lord you've got such a pretty lady to look after you. There be many what envies you and many what 'ud like to stand in your shoes, and that's God's truth."

Sorio sighed heavily, and letting go his hold upon the railings, turned to his companion.

"Let's find another way to the town," he said. "There must be some road over there, or at worst, we can walk along the line."

They moved off hastily in the direction opposite from the river and the old man, after making an enigmatic gesture behind their backs, spat upon his hands and returned to his work. The sky was now entirely overclouded but still no rain fell.

XXI

THE WINDMILL

WITH the coming of September there was a noticeable change in the weather. The air got perceptibly colder, the sea rougher and there were dark days when the sun was hardly seen at all. Sometimes the prevailing west wind brought showers, but so far, in spite of the cooler atmosphere, there was little heavy rain. The rain seemed to be gathering and massing on every horizon, but though its presence was felt, its actual coming was delayed and the fields and gardens remained scorched and dry. The ditches in the fens were low that season — lower than they had been for many years. Some of them were actually empty and in others there was so little water that the children could catch eels and minnows with their naked hands. In many portions of the salt marshes it was possible to walk dry-shod where, in the early Spring, one would have sunk up to the waist, or even up to the neck.

Driven by the hot weather from their usual feeding-grounds several rare and curious birds visited the fens that year. The immediate environs of Rodmoor were especially safe for these, as few among the fishermen carried guns and none of the wealthier inhabitants cared greatly for shooting. Brand Renshaw, for instance, like his father before him, refused to preserve any sort of game and indeed it was one of the chief causes of his unpopularity with the neighbouring gentry that he was so little of a sportsman.

One species of visitor brought by that unusually hot August was less fortunate than the birds. This was a swallow-tail butterfly, one of the rarer of the two kinds known to collectors in that part of the country. Dr. Raughty was like a man out of his senses with delight when he perceived this beautiful wanderer. He bribed a small boy who was with him at the moment to follow it wherever it flew while he hurried back to his rooms for his net. Unluckily for the swift-flying nomad, instead of making for the open fens it persisted in hovering about the sand-dunes where grew a certain little glaucous plant and it was upon the sand dunes, finally, that the Doctor secured it, after a breathless and exhausting chase.

It seemed to cause Fingal Raughty real distress when he found that neither Nance nor Linda was pleased at what he had done. He met, indeed, with scanty congratulations from any of his friends. With Sorio he almost quarreled over the incident, so vituperative did the Italian become when reference was made to it in his presence. Mrs. Renshaw was gently sympathetic, evidently regarding it as one of the privileges of masculine vigour to catch and kill whatever was beautiful and endowed with wings, but even she spoilt the savour of her congratulations with a faint tinge of irony.

Two weeks of September had already passed when Sorio, in obedience to a little pencilled note he had received the night before, set off in the early afternoon to meet Philippa at one of their more recently discovered haunts. In spite of his resolution in the little dairy shop in Mundham he had made no drastic change

in his life, either in the direction of finding work to do
or of breaking off his relations with the girl from Oakguard. That excursion with Nance in which they tried
so ineffectively to find the great painter's house left,
in its final impression, a certain cruel embarrassment
between them. It became difficult for him not to feel
that she was watching him apprehensively now and with
a ghastly anxiety at the back of her mind and this
consciousness poisoned his ease and freedom with her.
He felt that her tenderness was no longer a natural,
unqualified affection but a sort of terrified pity, and
this impression set his nerves all the more on edge when
they were together.

With Philippa, on the other hand, he felt absolutely
free. The girl lived herself so abnormal and isolated a
life, for Mrs. Renshaw disliked visitors and Brand dis-
couraged any association with their neighbours, that
she displayed nothing of that practical and human
sense of proportion which was the basis of Nance's
character. For the very reason, perhaps, that she
cared less what happened to him, she was able to humour him more completely. She piqued and stimu-
lated his intelligence too, in a way Nance never did.
She had flashes of diabolical insight which could always
rouse and astonish him. Something radically cold and
aloof in her made it possible for her to risk alienating
him by savage and malicious blows at his pride. But
the more poisonous her taunts became, the more closely
he clung to her, deriving, it might almost seem, an
actual pleasure from what he suffered at her hands.
Anxious for both their sakes to avoid as much as possible the gossip of the village, he had continued his
habit of meeting her in all manner of out-of-the-way

places, and the spot she had designated as their rendezvous for this particular afternoon was one of the
remotest and least accessible of all these sanctuaries
of refuge. It was, in fact, an old disused windmill,
standing by itself in the fens about two miles north of
that willow copse where he had on one fatal occasion
caused Nance Herrick such distress.

Philippa was an abnormally good walker. From a
child she had been accustomed to roam long distances
by herself, so that it did not strike him as anything
unusual that she should have chosen a place so far off
from Oakguard as the scene of their encounter.
One of her most marked peculiarities was a certain imaginative fastidiousness in regard to the *milieu* of
her interviews with him. That was, indeed, one of the
ways by which she held him. It amounted to a genius
for the elimination of the commonplace or the "familiar" in the relations between them. She kept a
clear space, as it were, around her personality, only
approaching him when the dramatic accessories were
harmonious, and vanishing again before he had time to
sound the bottom of her evasive mood.

On this occasion Sorio walked with a firm and even
gay bearing towards their rendezvous. He followed
at first the same path as that taken by Nance and her
sister on the eve of their eventful bank-holiday but when
he reached Nance's withy-bed he debouched to his left
and plunged straight across the fens. The track he
now followed was one used rarely, even by the owners
of cattle upon the marshes and in front of him, as far
as his eye could reach, nothing except isolated poplars
and a few solitary gates, marking the bridges across
the dykes, broke the grey expanse of the horizon. The

deserted windmill towards which he made his way was larger than any of the others but while, in the gently-blowing wind the sails of the rest kept their slow and rhythmic revolution, this particular one stretched out its enormous arms in motionless repose as if issuing some solemn command to the elements or, like the biblical leader, threatening the overthrow of a hostile army.

As he walked, Sorio noticed that at last the Michael-mas daisies were really in bloom, their grey leaves and sad autumnal flowers blending congruously enough with the dark water and blackened reed-stems of the stagnant ditches. The sky above him was covered with a thin veil of leaden-coloured clouds, against which, flying so high as to make it difficult to distinguish their identity, an attenuated line of large birds — Sorio wondered if they were wild swans — moved swiftly towards the west. He arrived at last at the windmill and entered its cavernous interior. She rose to meet him, shaking the dust from her clothes. In the semi-darkness of the place, her eyes gleamed with a dangerous lustre like the eyes of an animal.

" Do you want to stay where we are? " he said when he had relinquished the hand she gave him, after lifting it in an exaggerated foreign manner, to his lips. She laughed a low mocking laugh.

" What's the alternative, Adriano mio? Even *I* can't walk indefinitely and it isn't nice sitting over a half-empty dyke."

" Well," he remarked, " let's stay here then ! Where were you sitting before I came? "

She pointed to a heap of straw in the furthest corner of the place beneath the shadow of the half-ruined flight of steps leading to the floor above. Adrian surveyed this spot without animation.

"It would be much more interesting," he said, "if we could get up that ladder. I believe we could. I tried it clumsily the other day when I broke that step."

"But how do we know the floor above will bear us if we do get up there?"

"Oh, it'll bear us all right. Look! You can see. The middle boards aren't rotted at all and that hole there is a rat-hole. There aren't any dangerous cracks."

"It would be so horrid to tumble through, Adrian."

"Oh, we shan't tumble through. I swear to you it's all right, Phil. We're not going to dance up there, are we?"

The girl put her hand on the dilapidated balustrade and shook it. The whole ladder trembled from top to bottom and a cloud of ancient flour-dust, grey and mouldy, descended on their heads.

"You see, Adrian?" she remarked. "It really isn't safe!"

"I don't care," he said stubbornly. "What's it matter? It's dull and stuffy down here. I'm going to try anyway."

He began cautiously ascending what remained intact of the forlorn ladder. The thing creaked ominously under his weight. He managed, however, to get sufficiently high to secure a hold upon the threshold-beam of the floor above when, with the aid of a projecting plank from the side-wall of the building, he managed to retain his position and after a brief struggle, disappeared from his companion's view.

His voice came down to her from above, muffled a little by the intervening wood-work.

"It's lovely up here, Phil! There are two little windows and you can see all over the fens. Wait a minute, we'll soon have you up."

There was a pause and she heard him moving about over her head.

"You'd much better come down," she shouted. "I'm not going up there. There's no possible way."

He made no answer to this and there was dead silence for several minutes. She went to the entrance and emerged into the open air. The wide horizon around her seemed void and empty. Upon the surface of the immense plain only a few visible objects broke the brooding monotony. To the south and east she could discern just one or two familiar landmarks but to the west there was nothing — nothing but an eternal level of desolation losing itself in the sky. She gave an involuntary shudder and moved away from the windmill to the edge of a reed-bordered ditch. There was a pool of gloomy water in the middle of the reeds and across this pool and round and round it whirled, at an incredible speed, a score or so of tiny water-beetles, never leaving the surface and never pausing for a moment in their mad dance. A wretched little moth, its wings rendered useless by contact with the water, struggled feebly in the centre of this pool, but the shiny-coated beetles whirled on round it in their dizzy circles as if it had no more significance than the shadow of a leaf. Philippa smiled and walked back to the building.

"Adrian," she called out, entering its dusty gloom

and looking up at the square hole in the ceiling, from which still hung a remnant of broken wood-work.

"Well? What is it?" her friend's voice answered. "It's all right; we'll soon have you up here!"

"I don't want to go up there," she shouted back. "I want you to come down. Please come down, Adrian! You're spoiling all our afternoon."

Once more there was dead silence. Then she called out again.

"Adrian," she said, "there's a moth being drowned in the ditch out here."

"What? Where? What do you say?" came the man's reply, accompanied by several violent movements. Presently a rope descended from the hole and swung suspended in the air.

"Look out, my dear," Sorio's voice ejaculated and a moment later he came swinging down, hand over hand, and landed at her side. "What's that?" he gasped breathlessly, "what did you say? A moth in the water? Show me, show me!"

"Oh, it's nothing, Adrian," she answered petulantly. "I only wanted you to come down."

But he had rushed out of the door and down to the stream's edge.

"I see it! I see it!" he called back at her. "Here, give me my stick!" He came rushing back, pushed roughly past her, seized his stick from the ground and returned to the ditch. It was easy enough to effect the moth's rescue. The same fluffy stickiness in the thing's wet wings that made it helpless in the water, made it adhere to the stick's point. He wiped it off upon the grass and pulled Philippa back into the building.

" I'm glad I came down," he remarked. " I know it'll hold now. You won't mind my tying it round you, will you? I'll have both the ends down here presently. It's round a strong hook. It's all right. And then I'll pull you up."

Philippa looked at him with angry dismay. All this agitating fuss over so childish an adventure irritated her beyond endurance. His proposal had, as a matter of fact, a most subtle and curious effect upon her. It changed the relations between them. It reduced her to the position of a girl playing with an elder brother. It outraged, with an element of the comic, her sense of dramatic fastidiousness. It humiliated her pride and broke the twisted threads of all kinds of delicate spiritual nets she had in her mind to cast over him. It placed her by his side as a weak and timid woman by the side of a willful and strong-limbed man. Her ascendency over him, as she well knew, depended upon the retaining, on her part, of a certain psychic evasiveness — a certain mysterious and tantalizing reserve. It depended — at any rate that is what she imagined — upon the inscrutable look she could throw into her eyes and upon the tragic glamour of her ambiguous red lips and white cheeks. How could she possibly retain all these characteristics when swinging to and fro at the end of a rope?

Sorio's suggestion outraged something in her that went down to the very root of her personality. Walking with him, swimming with him, rowing in a boat with him — all those things were harmonious to her mind and congruous with her personal charm. None of these things interfered with the play of her intelligence, with the poise, the reserve, the aloofness of her spiritual challenge. She was exceptionally devoid of fear in these boyish sports and could feel herself when she engaged in them with him, free of the limitations of her sex. She could retain completely, as she indulged herself in them, all the equilibrium of her being — the rhythm of her identity. But this proposal of Sorio's not only introduced a discordant element that had a shrewd vein of the ludicrous in it, it threw her into a physical panic. It pulled and tugged at the inmost fibres of her self-restraint. It made her long to sit down on the ground and cry like a child. She wondered vaguely whether it was that Adrian was revenging himself upon her at that moment for some accumulated series of half-physical outrages that he had himself in his neurotic state been subjected to lately. As to his actual sanity, it never occured to her to question *that*. She herself was too wayward and whimsical in the reactions of her nerves and the processes of her mind to find anything startling, in *that* sense, in what he was now suggesting. It was simply that it changed their relations — it destroyed her ascendency, it brought things down to brute force, it turned her into a woman.

Her mind, as she stood hesitating, reviewed the moth incident. That sort of situation — Adrian's fantastic mania for rescuing things — had just the opposite effect on her. He might poke his stick into half the ditches of Rodmoor and save innumerable drowning moths; the only effect *that* had on her was to make her feel superior to him, better adapted than he to face the essential facts of life, its inherent and integral cruelty for instance. But now — to see that horrible rope-end dangling from that gaping hole and to see the eager, violent, masculine look in her friend's eyes — it was un-

endurable; it drove her, so to speak, against the jagged
edge of the world's brute wall.

> "To dance to flutes, to dance to lutes,
>   Is delicate and rare —"

she found herself quoting, with a horrible sense that the
humour of the parody only sharpened the sting of her
dilemma.

"I won't do it," she said resolutely at last, trying
to brave it out with a smile. "It's a ridiculous idea.
Besides, I'm much too heavy. You couldn't pull me up
if you tried till nightfall! No, no, Adriano, don't be
so absurd. Don't spoil our time together with these
mad ideas. Let's sit down here and talk. Or why not
light a fire? That would be exciting enough, wouldn't
it?"

His face as he listened to her darkened to a kind of
savage fury. Its despotic and imperious lines emphasized themselves to a degree that was really terrifying.

"You won't?" he cried, "you won't, you won't?"
And seizing her roughly by the shoulder he actually began twisting the rope round her body.

She resisted desperately, pushing him away with all
the strength of her arms. In the struggle between
them, which soon became a dangerous one, her hand
thrusting back his head unintentionally drew blood with
its delicate finger-nails from his upper lip. The blood
trickled into his mouth and, maddened by the taste of
it, he let her go and seizing the end of the rope, struck
her with it across the breast. This blow seemed to bewilder her. She ceased all resistance. She became
docile and passive in his hands.

Mechanically he went on with the task he had set

himself, of fastening the rope round her beneath her
arm-pits and tying it into a knot. But her absolute
submissiveness seemed presently to paralyze him as
much as his previous violence had disarmed and paralyzed her. He unloosed the knot he was making and
with a sudden jerk pulled the rope away from her.
The rope swung back to its former position and dangled
in the air, swaying gently from side to side. They
stood looking at each other in startled silence and then,
quite suddenly, the girl moved forward and flung her
arms round his neck.

" I love you! " she murmured in a voice unlike any
he had heard her use before. " I love you! I love
you! " and her lips clung to his with a long and passionate kiss.

Sorio's emotions at that moment would have caused
her, had she been conscious of them, a reaction even less
endurable than that which she had just been through.
To confess the truth he had no emotion at all. He mechanically returned her kisses; he mechanically embraced her. But all the while he was thinking of those
water-beetles with shiny metallic coats that were gyrat-
ing even now so swiftly round that reedy pool.

" Water-beetles! " he thought, as the girl's convulsive
kisses, salt with her passionate tears, hurt his wounded
lip. " Water-beetles! We are all like that. The
world is like that! Water-beetles upon a dark stream."

She let him go at last and they moved out together
hand in hand into the open air. Above them the enormous windmill still upheld its motionless arms while
from somewhere in the fens behind it came a strange
whistling cry, the cry of one of those winged intruders
from foreign shores, which even now was perhaps bid-

ding farewell to regions of exile and calling out for
some companion for its flight over the North Sea.

With his hand still held tightly in hers, Philippa
walked silently by his side all that long way across the
meadows and dykes. Sorio took advantage of her unusually gentle mood and began plaintively telling her
about the nervous sufferings he endured in Rodmoor
and about his hatred for the people there and his conviction that they took delight in annoying him. Then
little by little, as the girl's sympathetic silence led him
on, he fell to flinging out — in short, jerky, broken
sentences — as if each word were torn up by the roots
from the very soil of his soul, stammered references to
Baptiste. He spoke as if he were talking to himself
rather than to her. He kept repeating over and over
again some muttered phrase about the bond of abnormal
affection which existed between them. And then he
suddenly burst out into a description of Baptiste. He
rambled on for a long while upon this topic, leaving in
the end only a very blurred impression upon his hearer's
mind. All, in fact, the girl was able to definitely arrive at from what he said was that Baptiste resembled
his mother — a Frenchwoman of the coast of Brittany
— and that he was tall and had dark blue eyes.

"With the longest lashes," Sorio kept repeating,
as if he were describing to her some one it was important she should remember, "that you, or any one else,
has ever seen! They lie on his cheek when he's asleep
like — like —"

He fumbled with the feathery head of a reed he had
picked as they were walking but seemed unable to find
any suitable comparison. It was curious to see the
shamefaced, embarrassed way he threw forth, one by

one, and as if each word caused him definite pain in the uttering, these allusions to his boy.

Philippa let him ramble on as he pleased, hardly interrupting him by a gesture, listening to him, in fact, as if she were listening to a person talking in his sleep. She learnt that it was only with the greatest difficulty that he had persuaded Baptiste to keep his position in New York and not fling everything up and follow him to London. She learnt that Baptiste had copied out with his own hand the larger portion of Sorio's book and that now, as he completed each new chapter, he sent it by registered mail straight to the boy in " Eleventh Street."

" It will explain my life, my whole life, that book," Adrian muttered. " You've only heard a few of its ideas, Phil, only a few. The secret of things being found, not in the instinct of creation but in the instinct of destruction, is only the beginning of it. I go further — much further than that. Don't laugh at me, Phil, if I just say this — only just this : I show in my book how what every living thing really aims at is to escape from itself, to escape from itself by the destruction of itself. Do you get the idea in that, Phil? Everything in the world is — how shall I put it? — these ideas are not easy, they tear at a person's brain before they become clear ! — everything in the world is on the edge, on the verge, of dissolving away into what people call nothingness. That is what Shakespeare had in his mind when he said, ' the great globe itself, yea ! all which it inherits, shall dissolve and — and —' I forget exactly how it runs but it ends with ' leave not a rack behind.' But the point I make in my book is this. This ' nothingness,' this ' death,' if you like, to which everything struggles is only a name for *what lies beyond life* — for what lies, I mean, beyond the extreme limit of the life of every individual thing. We shrink back from it, everything shrinks back from it, because it is the annihilation of all one's familiar associations, the destruction of the impulse to go on being oneself! But though we shrink back from it, something in us, something that is deeper than ourselves pushes us on to this destruction. This is why, when people have been outraged in the very roots of their being, when they have been lacerated and flayed more than they can bear, when they have been, so to speak, raked through and combed out, they often fall back upon a soft delicious tide of deep large happiness, indescribable, beyond words."

He was too absorbed in what he was saying to notice that as he made this remark his companion murmured a passionate assent.

" They do! They do! They do!" the girl repeated, with unrestrained emotion.

" That is why," he continued without heeding her, " there is always a fierce pleasure in what fools call ' cynicism.' Cynicism is really the only philosophy worth calling a philosophy because it alone recognizes ' that everything which exists ought to be destroyed.' Those are the very words used by the devil in Faust, do you remember? And Goethe himself knew in his heart the truth of cynicism, only he loved life so well,— the great child that he was! — that he *couldn't* endure the thought of destruction. He understood it though, and confessed it, too. Spinoza helped him to see it. Ah, Phil, my girl, *there* was a philosopher! The only one — the only one! And see how the rabble are afraid of Spinoza! See how they turn to the contemptible Hegel,

the grocer of philosophy, with his precious ' self-asser-
tion ' and ' self-realization '! And there are some idiots
who fail to see that Spinoza was a cynic, that he hated
life and wished to destroy life. They pretend that he
worshipped Nature. Nature! He denied the existence
of it. He wished to annihilate it, and he did annihilate
it, in his terrible logic. He worshipped only one thing,
that which is beyond the limit, beyond the extremest
verge, beyond the point where every living thing ceases
to exist and *becomes nothing!* That's what Spinoza
worshipped and that's what I worship, Phil. I worship
the blinding white light which puts out all the candles
and all the shadows in the world. It blinds you and
ends you and so you call it darkness. But it only begins where darkness is destroyed with everything else!
Darkness is like cruelty. It's the opposite of love.
But what I worship is as far beyond love as it is beyond the sun and all the shadows thrown by the sun!"

He paused and contemplated a nervous water-rat that
was running along close to the water of the ditch they
walked by, desperately searching for its hole.

" I call it white light," he continued, " but really it's
not light at all, any more than it's darkness. It's something you can't name, something unutterable, but it's
large and cool and deep and empty. Yes, it's empty
of everything that lives or makes a sound! It stops all
aching in one's head, Phil. It stops all the persecution
of people who stare at you! It stops all the sickening
tiredness of having to hate things. It'll stop all my
longing for Baptiste, for Baptiste is *there.* Baptiste
is the angel of that large, cool, quiet place. Let me
once destroy everything in the way and I get to Baptiste — and nothing can ever separate us again!"

He looked round at the grey monotony about them, streaked here and there by patches of autumnal yellow where the stubble fields intersected the fens.

"I prove that I'm right about this principle of destruction, Phil," he went on, "by bringing up instances of the way all human beings instinctively delight to overthrow one another's illusions and to fling doubt upon one another's sincerity. We all do that. You do, Phil, more than any one. You do it to me. And you're right in doing it. We're all right in doing it! That accounts for the secret satisfaction we all feel when something or other breaks up the complacency of another person's life. It accounts for the mad desire we have to destroy the complacency of our own life. What we're seeking is *the line of escape* — that's the phrase I use in my book. The line of escape from ourselves. That's why we turn and turn and turn, like fish gasping on the land or like those beetles we saw just now, or like that water-rat!"

They had now reached the outskirts of Nance's withy-bed. The path Sorio had come by deviated here sharply to the east, heading sea-wards, while another path, wider and more frequented, led on across the meadows to the bank of the Loon where the roof and chimneys of Dyke House were vaguely visible. The September twilight had already begun to fall and objects at any considerable distance showed dim and wraith-like. Damp mists, smelling of stagnant water, rose in long clammy waves out of the fens and moved in white ghostly procession along the bank of the river. Sorio stood at this parting of the ways and surveyed the shadowy outline of the distant tow-path and the yet more obscure form of Dyke House. He looked at the stubble field and then at the little wood where the alder trees differentiated themselves from the willows by their darker and more melancholy foliage.

" How frightening Dyke House looks from here," remarked Philippa, " it looks like a haunted house."

A sudden idea struck Sorio's mind.

" Phil," he said, letting go his companion's hand and pointing with his stick to the house by the river, " you often tell me you're afraid of nothing weird or supernatural. You often tell me you're more like a boy in those things than a girl. Look here, now! You just run over to Dyke House and see how Rachel Doorm is getting on. I often think of her — alone in that place, now Nance and Linda have gone. I've been thinking of her especially to-day as we've come so near here. It's impossible for me to go. It's impossible for me to see any one. My nerves won't stand it. But I must say I should be rather glad to know she hadn't quite gone off her head. It isn't very nice to think of her in that large house by herself, the house where her father died. Nance told me she feared she'd take to drink just as the old man did. Nance says it's in the Doorm family, that sort of thing, drink or insanity, I mean — or both together, perhaps! " and he broke into a bitter laugh.

Philippa drew in her breath and looked at the white mist covering the river and at the ghostly outlines of the Doorm inheritance.

" You always say you're like a boy," repeated Sorio, throwing himself down where four months ago he had sat with Nance, " well, prove it then! Run over to Dyke House and give Rachel Doorm my love. I'll wait for you here. I promise faithfully. You needn't do more than just greet the old thing and wish her well.

She loves all you Renshaws. She idealizes you." And
he laughed again.

Philippa regarded him silently. For one moment the
old wicked flicker of subtle mockery seemed on the point
of crossing her face. But it died instantly away and
her eyes grew childish and wistful.

"I'm not a boy, I'm a woman," she murmured in a
low voice.

Sorio frowned. "Well, go, whatever you are," he
cried roughly. "You're not tired, are you?" he added
a little more gently.

She smiled at this. "All right, Adrian," she said,
"I'll go. Give me one kiss first."

She knelt down hurriedly and put her arms round his
neck. Lying with his back against the trunk of an
alder, he returned her caress in a perfunctory, absent-
minded manner, precisely as if she were an importunate
child.

"I love you! I love you!" she whispered and then
leaping to her feet, "Good-bye!" she cried, "I'll never
forgive you if you desert me."

She ran off, her slender figure moving through the
growing twilight like a swaying birch tree half seen
through mist. Sorio's mind left her altogether. An
immense yearning for his son took possession of him and
he set himself to recall every precise incident of their
separation. He saw himself standing at the side of the
crowded liner. He saw the people waving and shouting from the wooden jetty of the great dock. He saw
Baptiste, standing a little apart from the rest, motionless, not raising even a hand, paralyzed by the misery
of his departure. He too was sick with misery then.
He remembered the exact sensation of it and how he en-

vied the sea-gulls who never knew these human sufferings
and the gay people on the ship who seemed to have all
they loved with them at their side.

" Oh, God," he muttered to himself, " give me back my
son and you may take everything — my book, my pride,
my brain — everything! everything!"

Meanwhile Philippa was rapidly approaching Dyke
House. A cold damp air met her as she drew near,
rising·with the white mists from off the surface of the
river. She walked round the house and pushed open the
little wooden gate. The face of desolation itself looked
at her from that neglected garden. A few forlorn
dahlias raised their troubled wine-dark heads from
among strangling nettles and sickly plants of pallid-
leaved spurge. Tangled raspberry canes and over-
grown patches of garden-mint mingled with wild cranes-
bill and darnel. Grass was growing thickly on the
gravel path and clumps of green damp moss clung to the
stone-work of the entrance. The windows, as she approached the house, stared at her like eyes — eyes that
have lost the power to close their lids. There were no
blinds down and no curtains drawn but all the windows
were dark. No smoke issued from the chimney and not
a flicker of light came from any portion of the place.
Silent and cold and hushed, it might have been only
waiting for her appearance to sink like an apparition
into the misty earth. With a beating heart the girl
ascended the steps and rang the bell. The sound
clanged horribly through the empty passages. There
was a faint hardly perceptible stir, such as one might
imagine being made by the fall of disturbed dust or the
rustle of loose paper, but that was all. Dead unbroken
silence flowed back upon everything like the flow of

water round a submerged wreck. There was not even
the ticking of a clock to break the stillness. It was
more than the mere absence of any sound, that silence
which held the Doorm house. It was silence such as
possesses an individuality of its own. It took on, as
Philippa waited there, the shadowy and wavering outlines of a palpable shape. The silence greeted the girl
and welcomed her and begged her to enter and let it
embrace her. In a kind of panic Philippa seized the
handle of the door and shook it violently. More to
her terror than reassurance it opened and a cold wave
of air, colder even than the mist of the river, struck her
in the face. She advanced slowly, her hand pressed
against her heart and a sense as if something was drum-
ming in her ears.

The parlour door was wide open. She entered the
room. A handful of dead flowers — wild flowers of
some kind but they were too withered to be distinguishable — hung dry and sapless over the edge of a vase of
rank-smelling water. Otherwise the table was bare and
the room in order. She came out again and went into
the kitchen. Here the presence of more homely and un-
sentimental objects relieved a little the tension of her
nerves. But the place was absolutely empty — save for
an imprisoned tortoise-shell butterfly that was beating
itself languidly, as if it had done the same thing for
days, against the pane.

Mindful of Sorio's habit and with even the faint ghost
of a smile, she opened the window and set the thing free.
It was a relief to smell the river-smell that came in as
she did this. She moved out of the kitchen and once
more stood breathless, listening intently in the silent
hall-way. It was growing rapidly darker; she longed

to rush from the place and return to Sorio but some indescribable power, stronger than her own will, retained her. Suddenly she uttered a little involuntary cry. Struck by a light gust of wind, the front door which she had left open, swung slowly towards her and closed with a vibrating shock. She ran to the back and opened the door which led to the yard. Here she was genuinely relieved to catch the sound of a sleepy rustling in the little wood-shed and to see through its dusty window a white blur of feathers. There were fowls alive anyway about Dyke House. That, at least, was some satisfaction. Propping the door open by means of an iron scraper she returned to the hall-way and looked apprehensively at the staircase. Dared she ascend to the rooms above? Dared she enter Rachel Doorm's bedroom? She moved to the foot of the stair-case and laid her hand upon the balustrade. A dim flicker of waning light came in through the door she had propped open and fell upon the heavy chairs which stood in the hall and upon a fantastic picture representing the eruption of Vesuvius. The old-fashioned colouring of this print was now darkened, but she could see the outlines of the mountain and its rolling smoke. Once again she listened. Not a sound! She took a few steps up the stairs and paused. Then a few more and paused again. Then with her hands tightly clenched and a cold shivering sensation making her feel sick and dizzy, she ran up the remainder and stood weak and exhausted, leaning against the pillar of the balustrade and gazing with startled eyes at a half-open door.

It is extraordinary the power of the dead over the living! Philippa knew that in that room, behind that door, was the thing that had once called itself a woman and had talked and laughed and eaten and drunk with other women. When Rachel Doorm was about the age she herself had now reached and she was a little child, she could remember how she had built sand-castles for her by the sea-shore and sang to her old Rodmoor songs about drowned sailors and sea-kings and lost children. And now she knew — as surely as if her hand was laid upon her cold forehead — that behind that door, probably in some ghastly attitude of eternal listening, the corpse of all that, of all those memories and many more that she knew nothing of, was waiting to be found, to be found and have her eyes shut and her jaw bandaged — and be prepared for her coffin. The girl gripped tight hold of the balustrade. The terror that took possession of her then was not that Rachel Doorm should be dead — dead and so close to her, but that she should *not* be dead!

At that moment, could she have brought herself to push that door wide open and pass in, it would have been much more awful, much more shocking, to find Rachel Doorm alive and see her rise to meet her and hear her speak! After all, what did it matter if the body of the woman was twisted and contorted in some frightful manner — or *standing* perhaps — Rachel Doorm was just the one to die standing! — or if her face were staring up from the floor? What did it matter, supposing she *did* go straight in and feel about in the darkness and perhaps lay her hand upon the dead woman's mouth? What did it matter even if she *did* see her hanging, in the faint light of the window, from a hook above the curtain with her head bent queerly to one side and a lock of her hair falling loose? None of these things mattered. None of them prevented her going straight into that room! What did prevent her and what sent her fleeing down the stairs and out of the house with a sudden scream of intolerable terror was the fact that at that moment, quite definitely, there came the sound of *breathing* from the room she was looking at. A simple thing, a natural thing, for an old woman to retire to her bedroom early and to lie, perhaps with all her clothes on, upon her bed, to rest for a while before undressing. A simple and a natural thing! But the fact remains as has just been stated, when the sound of breathing came from that room Philippa screamed and ran panic-stricken out into the night. She hardly stopped running, indeed, till she reached the willow copse and found Sorio where she had left him. He did not resist now when breathlessly she implored him to accompany her back to the house. They walked hurriedly there together, Adrian in spite of a certain apprehension smiling in the darkness at his companion's certainty that Rachel Doorm was dead and her equal certainty that she had heard her breathing.

"But I understand your feeling, Phil," he said. "I understand it perfectly. I used to have the same sensation at night in a certain great garden in the Campagna — the fear of meeting the boy I used to play with before I *expected* to meet him! I used to call out to him and beg him to answer me so as to make sure."

Philippa refused to enter the house again and waited for him outside by the garden gate. He was long in coming, so long that she was seized with the strangest thoughts. But he came at last, carrying a lantern in his hand.

"You're right, Phil," he said, "the gods have taken

her. She's stone-dead. And what's more, she's been dead a long time, several weeks, I should think."

" But the breathing, Adrian, the breathing? I heard it distinctly."

Sorio put down his lantern and leant against the gate. In spite of his calm demeanor she could see that he also had experienced something over and above the finding of Rachel's body.

" Yes," he said, " and you were right about that, too. Guess, child, what it was ! "

And as he spoke he put his hand against the front of his coat which was tightly buttoned up. Philippa was immediately conscious of the same stertorous noise that she had heard in the room of death.

" An animal ! " she cried.

" An owl," he answered, " a young owl. It must have fallen from a nest in the roof. I won't show it to you now, as it might escape and a cat might get it. I'm going to try and rear it if Tassar will let me. Baptiste will be so amused when he finds me with a pet owl ! He has quite a mania for things like that. He can make the birds in the park come to him by whistling. Well ! I suppose what we must do now is to get back to Rodmoor as quick as we can and report this business to the police. She must have been dead a week or more ! I'm afraid this will be a great shock to Nance."

" How did you find her ? " enquired the girl as they .walked along the road towards the New Bridge.

" Don't ask me, Phil — don't ask me," he replied, " She's out of her troubles anyway and had an owl to look after her."

" Should I have been —" began his companion.

" Don't ask me, girl ! " he reiterated. " I tell you it's

all past and over. Rachel Doorm will be buried in the
Rodmoor churchyard and I shall have her owl. An old
woman stops breathing and an owl begins breathing.
It's all natural enough."

XXII

THE NORTHWEST WIND

THE funeral of Rachel Doorm was a dark and troubled day for both Nance and Linda. Even the sympathy of Mr. Traherne seemed unable to console them or lift the settled gloom from their minds. Nance especially was struck dumb with comfortless depression. She felt doubly guilty in the matter. Guilty in her original acquiescence in the woman's desire to have them with her in Rodmoor and guilty in her neglect of her during the last weeks of her life. For the immediate cause of her death, or of the desperation that led to it, their leaving Dyke House for the village, she did not feel any remorse. That was inevitable after what had occurred. But this did not lessen her responsibility in the other two cases. Had she resolutely refused to leave London the probability was that Rachel would have been persuaded to go on living with them as she had formerly done. She might even have sold Dyke House and with the proceeds bought some cottage in the city suburbs for them all. It was her own ill-fated passion for Sorio, she recognized that clearly enough, that was the cause of all the disasters that had befallen them.

Linda's feeling with regard to Rachel's death was quite different. She had to confess in the depths of her heart that she was glad of it, glad to be relieved of the constant presence of something menacing and vindic-

tive on the outskirts of her life. Her trouble was of a
more morbid and abnormal kind, was, indeed, the fact
that in spite of the woman's death, she *hadn't* really got
rid of Rachel Doorm. The night before the funeral
she dreamed of her almost continually, dreamed that
she herself was a child again and that Rachel had
threatened her with some unknown and mysterious punishment. The night after the funeral it was still worse.
She woke Nance by a fit of wild and desperate crying
and when the elder girl tried to discover the nature of
her trouble she grew taciturn and reserved and refused
to say anything in explanation. All the following week
she went about her occupations with an air of abstraction and remoteness as if her real life were being lived
on another plane. Nance learnt from Mr. Traherne,
who was doing all he could think of to keep her attention fixed on her organ-playing, that as a matter of fact
she frequently came out of the church after a few minutes' practise and went and stood, for long periods together, by Rachel's grave. The priest confessed that
on one of the occasions when he had surprised her in
this posture, she had turned upon him quite savagely
and had addressed him in a tone completely different
from her ordinary one.

It was especially dreadful to Nance to feel she was
thrust out and alienated in some mysterious way from
her sister's confidence.

One morning towards the end of September, when
they were dressing together in the hazy autumnal light
and listening to the cries of sea-gulls coming up from
the harbour, Nance caught upon her sister's face, as
the girl's eyes met one another in their common mirror,
that same inscrutable look that she had seen upon it

five months before when, in their room at Dyke House they had first become acquainted with the eternal iteration of the North Sea's waves. Nance tried in vain all the remainder of that day to think out some clue to what that look implied. It haunted her and tantalized her. Linda had always possessed something a little pleading and sad in her eyes. It was no doubt the presence of that clinging wistfulness in them which had from the first attracted Brand. But this look contained in it something different. It suggested to Nance, though she dismissed the comparison as quite inadequate almost as soon as she had made it, the cry of a soul that was being *pulled backwards* into some interior darkness yet uttering all the while a desperate prayer to be let alone as if the least interference with what destiny was doing would be the cause of yet greater peril.

The following night as she lay awake watching a filmy trail of vaporous clouds sail across a wasted haggard moon, a moon that seemed to betray as that bright orb seldom does the fact that it was a corpse-world hung there with almost sacrilegious and indecent exposure, under the watchful stars, she noticed with dismay the white-robed figure of her sister rise from her bed and step lightly across the room to the open window. Nance watched her with breathless alarm. Was she awake or asleep? She leant out of the window, her long hair falling heavily to one side. Nance fancied she heard her muttering something but the noise of the sea, for the tide was high then in the early morning hours, prevented her catching the words. Nance threw off the bed-clothes and stole noiselessly towards her. Yes, certainly she was speaking. The words came in a low, plaintive murmur as if she were pleading with

some one out there in the misty night. Nance crept
gently up to her and listened, afraid to touch her lest
she should cause her some dangerous nervous shock but
anxious to be as close to her as she could.

" I am good now," she heard her say, " I am good
now, Rachel. You can let me out now! I will say
those words, I am good now. I won't disobey you
again."

There was a long silence, broken only by the sound
of the Sea and the beating of Nance's heart. Then
once more, the voice rose.

" It's down too deep, Rachel, you can't reach it with
that. But I'll go in. I'm not afraid any more! If
only you'll let me out. I'll go in deep — deep — and
get it for you. She can't hold it tight. The water is
too strong. Oh, I'll be good, Rachel. I'll get it for
you if only you'll let me out! "

Nance, unable to endure any more of this, put her
arms gently round her sister's body and drew her back
into the room. The young girl did not resist. With
wide-open but utterly unconscious eyes she let herself be
led across the room. Only when she was close to her
bed she held back and her body became rigid.

" Don't put me in there again, Rachel. Anything
but that! "

" Darling! " cried Nance desperately, " don't you
know me? I'm with you, dear. This is Nance with
you. No one shall hurt you! "

The young girl shuddered and looked at her with a
bewildered and troubled gaze as if everything were
vague and obscure. At that moment there came over
Nance that appalling terror of the unconscious, of the
sub-human which is one of the especial dangers of those

who have to look after the insane or follow the movements of somnambulists. But the shudder passed and the bewildered look was superseded by one of gradual obliviousness. The girl's body relaxed and she swayed as she stood. Nance, with a violent effort, lifted her in her arms and laid her down on the bed. The girl muttered something and turned over on her side. Nance watched her anxiously but she was soon relieved to catch the sound of her quiet breathing. She was asleep peacefully now. She looked so pathetically lovely, lying there in a childish position of absolute abandonment that Nance could not resist bending over her and lightly kissing her cheek.

" Poor darling!" she said to herself, " how blind I've been! How wickedly blind I've been!" She pulled the blanket from her own bed and threw it over her sister so as not to disturb her by altering the bed-clothes. Then, wrapping herself in her dressing-gown she lay back upon her pillows resigned for the rest of the night to remaining wakeful.

The next day she noticed no difference in Linda's mood. There was the same abstraction, the same listless lack of interest in anything about her and worst of all that same inscrutable look which filled Nance with every sort of wild imagination. She cast about in despair for some way of breaking the evil spell under which the girl was pining. She went again and again to see Mr. Traherne and the good man devoted hours of his time to discussing the matter with her but nothing either of them could think of seemed a possible solution.

At last one morning, some days after that terrifying night, she met Dr. Raughty in the street. She walked

with him as far as the bridge explaining to him as best
she could her apprehensions about her sister and asking
him for his advice. Dr. Raughty was quite definite and
unhesitating.

"What Linda wants is a mother," he said laconically.
Nance stared at him.

"Yes, I know," she said. "I know well enough, poor
darling! But that's the worst of it, Fingal. Her
mother's been dead years and years and years."

"There are other mothers in Rodmoor, aren't
there?" he remarked.

Nance frowned. "You think I don't look after her
properly," she murmured. "No, I suppose I haven't.
And yet I've tried to — I've tried my very best."

"You're as hopeless as your Adrian with his owl,"
cried the Doctor. "He was feeding it with cake the
other day. Cake! He'd better not bring his owl and
our friend's rat together. There won't be much of the
rat left. Cake!" And the Doctor put back his head
and uttered an immense gargantuan laugh. Nance
looked a little disturbed and even a little indignant at
his merriment.

"What do you mean by *other* mothers?" she asked.
They had just reached the bridge and Dr. Raughty bade
her look over the parapet.

"What exquisite bellies those dace have!" he remarked, snuffing the air as he spoke. "There'll be rain
before night. Do you feel it? I know from the way
those fish rise. The sea too, it has a different voice —
has that ever caught your attention? — when there's
rain on the wind. Those dace are shrewd fellows.
They're after the bits of garbage the sea-gulls drop on
their way up the river. You might think they were

after flies, but they're not. I suppose George Crabbe
or George Borrow would switch 'em out with some bait
such as was never dreamed of — the droppings of rab-
bits perhaps or ladybird grubs. I suppose old Doctor Johnson would wade in up to his knees and try and
scoop 'em up in his hands. There's a big one! Do
you see? The one waving his tail and turning sideways. I expect he weighs half a pound or more. Fish
are beautiful things, especially dace. Isn't it wonderful to think that if you pulled any of those things backwards through the water they would be drowned, simply
by the rush of water through their gills? Look, Nance,
at that one! What a silver belly! What a delicate,
exquisite tail! A plague on these fellows who philander
with owls and rats! Give me fish — if you want to
make a cult of something." He lowered his voice to a
whisper, " I should think Lubric de Lauziere must have
kept a pet fish in his round pond! "

" Good-bye, Fingal," said Nance, holding out her
hand.

" What! Well! Where! God help us! What's
wrong, Nance? You're not annoyed with me, are you?
Do you think I'm talking through my hat? Not at
all! I'm leading up to it. A mother — that's what
she wants. She wants it just as those dace want the
water to flow in their faces and not backwards through
their gills. She's being dragged backwards — that's
what's the matter with her. She wants her natural element and it must flow in the right direction. *You*
won't do. Traherne won't do. A mother is the thing!
A woman, Nance, who has borne children has certain
instincts in dealing with young girls which make the
wisest physicians in the world look small! "

Nance smiled helplessly at him.

" But, Fingal, dear," she said, " what can I do? I can't appeal to Mrs. Raps, can I — or your friend Mrs. Sodderley? When you come to think, there are very few mothers in Rodmoor ! "

The Doctor sighed. " I know it," he observed mournfully, " I know it. The place will die out altogether in fifty years. It's as bad as the sand-dunes with their sterile flora. Women who bear children are the only really sane people in the world."

He ran his thumb, as he spoke, backwards and forwards over a little patch of vividly green moss that grew between the stones of the parapet. The air, crisp and autumnal with that vague scent of burning weeds in it which more than anything else suggests the outskirts of a small town at the end of the summer, flowed round them both with a mute appeal to her, so it seemed to Nance, to let all things drift as they might and submit to destiny. She looked at the Doctor dreamily in one of those queer intermissions of human consciousness in which we stand apart, as it were, from our own fate and listen to the flowing of the eternal tide.

A small poplar tree growing at the village end of the bridge had already lost some of its leaves and a few of these came drifting, one by one, along the raised stone pathway to the girl's feet. Over the misty marsh lands in the other direction, she could see the low tower of the church. The gilded weather-vane on the top of it shimmered and glittered in a vaporous stream of sunlight that seemed to touch nothing else.

Dreamily she looked at the Doctor, too weary of the struggle of life to make an effort to leave him and yet quite hopeless as to his power to help her. Fingal

Raughty continued to discourse upon the instinctive wisdom of maternity.

"Women who've had children," he went on, "are the only people in the world who possess the open secret. They know what it is to find the ultimate virtue in exquisite resignation. They do not only submit to fate — they joyfully embrace it. I suppose we might maintain that they even 'love it'— though I confess that that idea of 'loving' fate has always seemed to me weird and fantastic. But I laugh, and so do you, I expect, when our friends Sorio and Tassar talk in their absurd way about women. What do they know of women? They've only met, in all their lives (forgive me, Nance!) a parcel of silly young girls. They've no right to speak of life at all, the depraved children that they are! They are outside life, they're ignorant of the essential mystery. Goethe was the fellow to understand these things, and you know the name *he* gives to the unutterable secret? *The Mothers.* That's a good name, isn't it? The Mothers! Listen, Nance! All the people in this place suffer from astigmatism and asymmetry. Those are the outward signs of their mental departure from the normal. And the clever ones among them are proud of it. You know the way they talk! They think abnormality is the only kind of beauty. Nance, my dear, to tell you the truth, I'm sick of them all. *My* idea of beauty is the perfect masculine type, such as you see it in that figure they call 'the Theseus '— in the Elgin marbles — or the perfect feminine type as you see it in the great Demeter. Do you suppose they can, any of them, get round that? Do you suppose they can fight against the rhythm of Nature?"

He pulled out his tobacco pouch and gravely lit his pipe, swinging his head backwards and forwards as he did so. Nance could not help noticing the shrewd, humorous *animalism* of his look as he performed this function.

"But what can be done? Oh, Fingal, what *can* be done about Linda?" she asked with a heavy sigh.

He settled his pipe in his mouth and blew violently down its stem, causing a cloud of smoke to go up into the September air.

"Take her to Mrs. Renshaw," he said solemnly. "That's what I've been thinking all this time. That's my conclusion. Take her to Mrs. Renshaw."

Nance stared at him. "Really?" she murmured, "you really think *she* could help?"

"Try it — try it — try it!" cried Dr. Raughty, flinging a bit of moss at the fish in the water below them.

"It's extraordinary," he added, "that these dace should come down so far as this! The water here must be almost entirely salt."

That afternoon Nance went to Mr. Traherne's vesper service. She found Mrs. Renshaw in the church and invited both her and the priest to come back with them to their lodgings. She did this under the pretense of showing them some new designs of a startling and fascinating kind that she had received from Paris. The circean witcheries of French costumery were not perhaps precisely the right attraction either for Mrs. Renshaw or Hamish Traherne, but the thing served well enough as an excuse and they both took it as such. She was careful to hurry on in advance with Mr. Traherne so as to make it inevitable that Linda should walk with Mrs. Renshaw. The mistress of Oakguard seemed unusually pale and tired that afternoon. She held Linda back in the churchyard until the others had got quite far and then she led her straight to Rachel Doorm's grave. They had buried the unhappy woman quite close to the outermost border of the priest's garden. Nothing but a few paces of level grass separated her from a row of tall crimson hollyhocks. The grave at present lacked any headstone. Only a bunch of Michaelmas daisies, placed there by Linda herself, stood at its foot in a glass jar. Several wasps were buzzing round this jar, probably conscious of some faint odour clinging still about it from what it had formerly contained. Mrs. Renshaw stood with her hand leaning heavily on Linda's shoulder. She seemed to know, from the depths of her own fathomless morbidity, precisely what the young girl was feeling.

"Shall we kneel down?" she said. Linda began trembling a little but with simple and girlish docility, free from any kind of embarrassment, she knelt at the other's side.

"We mustn't pray for the dead," whispered Mrs. Renshaw. "*He*," she meant Mr. Traherne, "tells us to in his sermons, but it hurts me when he does for we've been taught that all that is wrong — wrong and contrary to our simple faith! We mustn't forget the Martyrs — must we, Linda?"

But Linda's mind was far from the martyrs. It was occupied entirely with the thing that lay buried before them, under that newly disturbed earth.

"But we can pray to God that His will be done, on earth, even as it is in Heaven," murmured Mrs. Renshaw.

She was silent after that and the younger and the elder woman knelt side by side with bowed heads. Then in a low whisper Mrs. Renshaw spoke again.

"There are some lines I should like to say to you, dear, if you'll let me. I copied them out last week. They were at the end of a book of poetry that I found in Philippa's room. She must have just bought it or had it given to her. I didn't think she cared any more for poetry. The pages weren't cut and I didn't like to cut them without her leave but I copied this out from the end. It was the last in the book."

She hesitated a moment while Linda remained motionless at her side, trembling still a little and watching the movements of a Peacock butterfly which was then sharing with the wasps their interest in the ancient honey-jar.

Mrs. Renshaw then repeated the following lines in a clear exquisitely modulated voice which went drifting away over the surrounding marshes.

> "For even the purest delight may pall,
> And power must fail and the pride must fall,
> And the love of the dearest friends grow small,
> But the glory of the Lord is all in all."

Her voice sank. A slight gust of wind made the trees above them sigh softly as though the words of the kneeling woman were in harmony with the inarticulate heart of the earth.

Linda stopped trembling. A sweet indescribable calm began slowly to pervade her. Gently, like a child, she slipped her hand into her companion's.

"Do you remember the Forty-third Psalm, Linda?" Mrs. Renshaw continued and her clear dramatic voice,

with a power of feeling equal to that of any great
actress, once more rose upon the air.

" Our heart is not turned back, neither have our steps declined
    from thy way.
Though thou hast sore broken us, in the place of dragons, and
    covered us with the shadow of death."

Once more she was silent but with a slight veering of
the wind, the sound of the waves beyond the sand-dunes
came to them with pitiless distinctness. It seemed to
mock — this voice of the earth's antagonist — mock,
in triumphant derision, the forlorn hope which that
solemn invocation had roused in the girl's heart. But
in contending against Mrs. Renshaw's knowledge of
the Psalms even the North Sea had met its match.
With her pale face uplifted and a wild light in her eyes,
she continued to utter the old melodious incantations
with their constant references to a Power more formidable than " all thy waves and storms." She might have
been one of the early converts to the faith that came
from the sacred Desert, wrestling in spiritual ecstasy
with the gods and powers of those heathen waters.

Either by one of the fortunate coincidences which
sometimes interrupt even the irony of nature or, as Mrs.
Renshaw would herself have maintained, by a direct answer to her prayer, the weathercock on the church
tower swung round again. North-east it swung, then
north-north-east, then due north. And finally, even
while she was uttering her last antiphony, it pointed to
north-west, the quarter most alien and antagonistic to
the Rodmoor sea, the portion of the horizon from which
blew the wind of the great fens.

In a country like East Anglia so peculiarly at the

mercy of the elements, every one of the winds has its
own peculiar burden and brings with it something healing and restorative or baleful and malefic. The east
wind here is, in a paramount sense, the evil wind, the
accomplice and confederate of the salt deep, the blighter
of hopes, the herald of disaster. The north-west wind,
on the contrary, is the wind that brings the sense of inland spaces, the smell of warm, wet earth and the fragrance of leaf mould in sweet breathing woods. It is the
wind that fills the rivers and the wells and brings the
fresh purifying rain. It is a wind full of memories and
its heart is strong with the power of ancient love, revived even out of graves and sepulchres. To those
sensitive to finer and rarer earth influences among the
dwellers by the east coast there may be caught sometimes upon the north-west wind the feeling of pine woods
and moorland heather. For it comes from the opposite side of the great plain, from Brandon Heath and
even beyond and it finds nothing in the wide fen country
to intercept it or break the rush of its sea-ward passage.

Thus, when the two women rose finally to their feet it
was to be met by a cool, healing breath which, as it
bowed the ranks of the hollyhocks and rustled through
the trees, had in it a delicious odour of inland brooks
and the coming of pure rain.

"Listen to me, child," said Mrs. Renshaw as they
passed out of the churchyard, "I want to say this to
you. You mustn't think that God allows any intercourse between the living and the dead. That is a
wicked invention of our own sinful hearts. It is a
temptation, darling — a temptation of the devil — and
we must struggle against it. Whenever we feel it we

must struggle against it and pray. It is perfectly right for you to think gently and forgivingly of poor Miss Doorm. It were wrong to think otherwise. But you mustn't think of her as anywhere near us or about us now. She's in the hands of God and in the mercy of God and we must leave her there. Do you hear what I'm saying, Linda? Do you understand me? Anything else is wrong and evil. We are all sinners together and we are all in the same merciful hands."

Never was the exorcising of powers hurtful to humanity more effective. Linda bowed her head at her words and then raising it freely, walked with a lighter step than for seven long days. She wished in her heart that she had the courage to talk to Mrs. Renshaw about an anxiety much more earthly, much less easy to be healed, than the influence of Rachel Doorm, alive or dead, but so immense was her relief at that moment to be free from the haunting phantom that had been pulling her towards that mound in the churchyard that she found it in her heart to be hopeful and reckless even though she knew that, whatever happened, there was bound to be pain and trouble in store for her in the not far distant future.

XXIII

WARDEN OF THE FISHES

IT will be found not altogether devoid of a strange
substratum of truth, though fantastic enough
in the superficial utterance, the statement that
there are certain climacteric seasons in the history
of places when, if events of importance are looming
upon the horizon, they are especially liable to fall.
Such a season with regard to Rodmoor, or at least with
regard to the persons we are most concerned with there,
may be said to have arrived with the beginning of
Autumn and with the month of October.

The first weeks of this month were at any rate full of
exciting and fatal interest to Nance. Something in the
change of the weather, for the rains had come in earnest
now, affected Sorio in a marked degree. His whole being seemed to undergo some curious disintegrating process as difficult to analyze as the actual force in Nature
which was at that very time causing the fall of the
leaves. We may be allowed to draw at least this much
from Sorio's own theory of the universal impulse to
self-destruction — the possible presence, that is to say,
of something positive and active, if not personal and
conscious, in the processes of natural decadence. Life,
when it corrupts and disintegrates; life when it finally
falls away and becomes what we call death, does so
sometimes, or seems to do so, with a vehemence and impetuosity which makes it difficult not to feel the pres-

sure of some half-conscious "will to perish" in the thing thus plunging towards dissolution. The brilliant colour which many flowers assume when they approach decease bears out this theory. It is what the poet calls a "lightning before death" and the rich tints of the autumn foliage as well as the phosphorescent glories — only repulsive to our human senses in fatal association — of physical mortality itself, are symbols, if not more than symbols, of the same splendid rushing upon nothingness.

This change in Sorio was not at all to Nance's disadvantage in the external aspect of the relations between them; indeed, she was carried forward by it to the point of coming to anticipate with trembling excitement what had begun to seem an almost impossible happiness. For Sorio definitely and in an outburst of impatient pleading, implored her to marry him. In the deeper, more spiritual association between them, however, the change which took place in him now was less satisfactory. Nance could not help feeling that there was something blind, childish, selfish, unchivalrous,— something even reckless and sinister — about this proposal and the passionate eagerness with which he pressed it upon her, considering that he made no more attempt than before to secure any employment and seemed to take it for granted that either she or Baltazar Stork or his own son in America, or some vague providential windfall would provide the money for this startling adventure. Side by side with her surprise at his careless disregard for all practical considerations, Nance could not help feeling a profound apprehension which she herself was unwilling to bring to the surface of her mind with regard to his mood and manner during these days. He seemed to throw himself passively and helplessly upon her hands. He clung to her as a sick child might cling to its parent. His old savage outbursts of cynical humour seemed to have vanished and in their place was a constant querulousness and peevishness which rendered their hours together much less peaceful and happy than they ought to have been. All sorts of little things irritated him — irritated him even in her. He clung to her, she could not help fancying, more out of a strange instinct of self-preservation than out of natural love. She couldn't help wondering sometimes how it would be when they were actually married. He seemed to find it at once difficult to endure her society and impossible to do without it. The bitter saying of the old Latin poet might have been his motto at that time. " *Nec sine te nec tecum vivere possum.*"

And yet, in spite of all this, these early October days were days of exquisite happiness for Nance. The long probation through which her love had passed had purged and winnowed it. The maternal instinct in her, always the dominant note in her emotions, was satisfied now as it had never been satisfied before, as perhaps unless she had children of her own it would never be satisfied again.

In these days of new hope and new life her youth seemed to revive and put forth exquisite blossoms of gaiety and tenderness. In a physical sense she actually did revive, though this may have been partly due to the cool crisp air that now blew constantly across the fens, and Linda, watching the change with affectionate sympathy, declared she was growing twice as beautiful.

She offered no objection when Sorio insisted upon having their " bans " read out in church, a duty that

was most willingly performed without further delay by
Hamish Traherne.   She did not even protest when he
announced that they would be married before October
was over, announced it without any indication of how
or where they would live, upon whose money or under
whose roof!

She felt a natural reluctance to press these practical
details upon his notice.   The bond that united them
was too delicate, too tenuous and precarious, for her to
dare to lean heavily upon it, nor did the few hesitating
and tentative hints she threw out meet with any response
from him.   He waved them aside.   He threw them from
him with a jest or a childish groan of disgust or a vague
" Oh, *that* will work itself out.   *That* will be all right.
Don't worry about *that!*   I'm writing to Baptiste."

But, as we have said, in spite of all these difficulties
and in spite of the deep-hidden dismay which his nervous, querulous mood excited in her, Nance was full of a
thrilling and inexpressible happiness during these
Autumn days.   She loved the roar of the great wind —
the northwest wind — in chimneys and house-tops at
night.   She loved the drifting of the dead leaves along
the muddy roads.   She loved the long swishing murmur
of the rushes growing by the dyke paths as they bent
their feathery heads over the wet banks or bowed in
melancholy rhythm across the rain-filled ditches.

Autumn was assuredly and without doubt the climacteric season of the Rodmoor fens.   They reluctantly
yielded to the Spring; they endured the Summer, and
the Winter froze them into dead and stoical inertness.
But something in the Autumn called out the essential
and native qualities of the place's soul.   The fens rose
to meet the Autumn in happy and stormy nuptials.

The brown, full-brimmed streams mounted up joyously to the highest level of their muddy banks. The faded mallow-plants by the river's side and the tarnished St. John's wort in the drenched hedges assumed a pathetic and noble beauty — a beauty full of vague, far-drawn associations for sensitive humanity. The sea-gulls and marsh-birds, the fish, the eels, the water-rats of the replenished streams seemed to share in the general expansion of life with the black and white hornless cattle, the cattle of the fens, who now began to yield their richest milk. Long, chilly, rainy days ended in magnificent and sumptuous sunsets — sunsets in which the whole sky from zenith to nadir became one immense rose of celestial fire. Out of a hundred Rodmoor chimneys rose the smell of burning peat, that smell of all others characteristic of the country whose very soil was formed of the vegetation of forgotten centuries.

In the large dark barns the yellow grain lay piled roof-high, while in every little shed and outhouse in the country, damsons, pears and potatoes lay spread out as if for the enjoyment of some Dionysian gathering of the propitiated earth-gods.

The fishermen, above all, shared in the season's fortune, going out early and late to their buoy-marked spots on the horizon, where the presence of certain year-old wrecks lying on the sand at the bottom drew the migratory fish and held them for weeks as if by a marine spell.

But if the days had their especial quality, the nights during that October were more significant still. The sky seemed to draw back, back and away, to some purer, clearer, more ethereal level while with a radiance tender and solemn the greater and lesser stars shed down their

magical influence. The planets, especially Venus and
Jupiter, grew so luminous and large that they seemed
to rival the moon; while the Moon, herself, the mystic
red moon of the finished harvest, the moon of the equi-
nox, drew the tides after her, higher and fuller and with
a deeper note in their ebb and flow than at any other
season of the year.

Everywhere swallows were gathering for their long
flight, everywhere the wild geese and the herons were
rising to incredible heights in the sky and moving northward and westward; and all this while Nance was able,
at last really able, to give herself up to her passion
for the man she loved.

It was a passion winnowed by waiting and suffering,
purged to a pure flame by all she had gone through,
but it was a passion none the less — a long exclusive
passion — the love of a lifetime. It made her sometimes, this great love of hers, dizzy and faint with fear
lest something even now should at the last moment come
between them. Sometimes it made her strangely shy
of him too, shy and withdrawn as if it were not easy,
though so triumphantly sweet, to give herself up body
and soul into hands that after all were the hands of
a stranger!

Sorio did not understand all this. Sometimes when
she thrust him away as if the emotion produced by his
caresses were more than she could bear or as if some
incalculable pride in her, some inalienable chastity beyond the power of her senses, reluctcd to yield further,
he grew angry and morose and accused her of jealousy
or of coldness. This would have been harder to endure
from him if there had not existed all the while at the
bottom of her heart a strange, maternal pity, a pity

not untouched with a sort of humorous irony — the eternal irony of the woman as she submits to the eternal misunderstanding of the man, embracing her without knowing what he does. He seemed to her sometimes in the mere physical stress of his love-making almost like an amorous and vicious boy. She could not resist the consciousness that her knowledge of the mystery of sex — its depth and subtlety not less than its flame and intensity — was something that went much further and was much more complicated and involved with her whole being than anything he experienced. Especially did she smile in her heart at the queer way he had of taking it for granted that he was " seducing " her, of deriving, it seemed, sometimes a satyrish pleasure from that idea, and sometimes a fit of violent remorse. When he was in either of these moods she felt towards him precisely as a mother might feel towards a son whose egoism and ignorance gave him a disproportioned view of the whole world. And yet, in actual age, Sorio was some twenty years her senior.

In her own mind, as the weeks slipped by and their names had already been coupled twice in the Sunday services, Nance was taking thought as to what, in solid reality, she intended to do with this child-man of hers when the great moment came. She must move from their present lodging. *That* seemed certain. It also seemed certain that Linda would have still to go on living with her. Any other arrangement than that was obviously unthinkable. But where should they live? And could she, with the money at present at her disposal, support three people?

A solution was found to both these problems by Mr. Traherne. There happened to exist in Rodmoor, as in many other old decaying boroughs on the east coast, certain official positions the practical service of which was almost extinct but whose local prestige and financial emoluments, such as they were, lingered on unaffected by the change of conditions. The relentless encroachments of the sea upon the land were mainly responsible for this. In certain almost uninhabited villages there existed official persons whose real raison d'être lay with the submerged foundations of former human habitations, deep at the bottom of the waters.

It was, indeed, one of the essential peculiarities of life upon those strange sea-banks this sense of living on the edge, as it were, of the wave-drowned graves of one's fathers. It may have been the half-conscious knowledge of this, bred in their flesh and blood from infancy, that gave to the natives of those places so many unusual and unattractive qualities. Other abodes of men rest securely upon the immemorial roots of the past, roots that lie, layer beneath layer, in rich historic continuity endowing present usages and customs with the consecration of unbroken tradition. But in the villages of that coast all this is different. Tradition remains, handed down from generation to generation, but the physical continuity is broken. The east-coast dwellers resemble certain of the stellar bodies in the celestial spaces, they retain their identity and their names but they are driven, in slow perpetual movement, to change their physical position. In scriptural phrase, they have no " abiding-place " nor can they continue " in one stay."

The fishing boats of the present generation set their brown sails to cross the water where, some hundreds of years before, an earlier generation walked their cobbled streets. The storm-buoys rock and ring and the boat lanterns burn their wavering signals over the drowned foundations that once supported Town-Hall and church tower, Market place and Village Tavern. It is this slow, century-delayed flight from the invading tide which so often produces in East Anglian coast towns the phenomenal existence of two parish churches, both it may be still in use, but the later and newer one following the heart of the community in its enforced retreat. Thus it is brought about in these singular localities that the very law of the gods, the law which utters to the elements the solemn "thus far and no further" is as a matter of fact, daily and momently, though with infinite slowness, broken and defied.

It is perhaps small wonder that among the counties of England these particular districts should have won for themselves a sinister reputation for impiety and perversity. Nothing so guards and establishes the virtue of a community than its sense of the presence in its midst of the ashes of its generations. Consciously and in a thousand pious usages it "worships its dead." But East-Anglian coast-dwellers are not permitted this privilege. Their "Lares and Penates" have been invaded and submerged. The fires upon their altars have been drowned and over the graves of their fathers the godless tides ebb and flow without reverence. Fishes swim where once children were led to the font and where lovers were wedded the wild cormorant mocks the sea-horses with its disconsolate cry. It is easy to be believed that the remote descendants of human beings who actually walked and bartered and loved and philosophized on spots of ground now tangled with seaweed and sea-drift, and

with fathoms of moaning and whispering water above
them, should come in their hour to depart in a measure
from the stable and kindly laws of human integrity!
With the ground thus literally *moving* — though in
age-long process — *under their feet*, how should they
be as faithful as other tribes of men to what is per-
manent in human institution?

There was perhaps a certain congruity in the fact
that now, after all these ages of tidal malice, it was in
the interests of so singular an alien as Sorio — one
whose very philosophy was the philosophy of " destruction "— that this lingering on of offices, whose service
had been sea-drowned, remained as characteristic of
the place. But this is precisely what did occur.

There was in Rodmoor a local official, appointed by
the local town council, whose title, " The Warden of
the Fishes," carried the mind back to a time when the
borough, much larger then, had been a considerable
centre of the fishing industry. This office, tenable for
life, carried with it very few actual duties now but it
ensured a secure though small emolument and, what
was more important, the occupancy, free of rent, of
one of the most picturesque houses in the place, an old
pre-Elizabethan dwelling of incommodious size but of
romantic appearance, standing at the edge of the harbour.

The last incumbent of this quaint and historic office,
whose duties were so little onerous that they could be
performed by a very old and very feeble man, was a
notable character of the village called John Peewit
Swinebitter, whose chief glory was not attained until
the close of his mortal days, which ended under the
table in the Admiral's Head after a surfeit of the very

fish of which he was " warden " washed down by too
copious libations of Keith-Radipole ale.

Since Mr. Swinebitter's decease in June, there had
gone on all through July and August, a desperate rivalry between two town factions as to the choosing
of his successor and it was Mr. Traherne's inspired
notion to take advantage of this division to secure the
post for Nance's prospective husband.

Sorio, though of foreign blood, was by birth and
nationality English and moreover he had picked up,
during his stay in Rodmoor, quite as much familiarity
with the ways and habits of fish as were necessary for
that easy post. If, at any unforeseen crisis, more
scientific and intimate knowledge was required than was
at his disposal, there was always Dr. Raughty, a past
master in all such matters, to whom he could apply.
It was Mr. Traherne's business to wheedle the local
rivals into relinquishing their struggle in favour of
one who was outside the contention and when this was
accomplished the remaining obstacles in the way of the
appointment were not hard to surmount. Luckily for
the conspirators, Brand Renshaw, though the largest
local landowner and a Justice of the Peace, was not
on the Rodmoor council.

So skillfully did Mr. Traherne handle the matter and
so cautious and reserved was Nance that it was not till
after the final reading of their bans in the church on
the marshes and the completion of the arrangements
for their marriage at the end of the following week,
that even Baltazar Stork became aware of what was
in the wind.

Sorio himself had been extremely surprised at this
unexpected favour shown him by the local tradesmen.

He had brooded so long upon his morbid delusion of universal persecution that it seemed incredible to him, in the few interviews which he had with these people, that they should treat him in so courteous and kind a manner. As a matter of fact, so fierce and obstinate were their private dissensions, it was a genuine relief to them to deal with a person from outside; nor must it be forgotten that in the appointment of Nance's husband to the coveted post they were doing honour to the memory of the bride's father, Captain Herrick having been by far the most popular of all the visitors to Rodmoor in former times. Most of the older members of the council could well remember the affable sailor. Many of them had frequently gone out fishing with him in the days when there were more fish and rarer fish to be caught than there were at present — those " old days " in fact which, in most remote villages, are associated with stuffed wonders in tavern parlours and with the quips and quirks of half-legendary heroes of Sport and Drink.

It was a reversion to such " old days " to have a gentleman " Warden of the Fishes." Besides it was a blow at the Renshaws between whom and the town-council there was an old established feud. For it was not hidden from the gossips of Rodmoor that the relations between Nance and the family at Oakguard were more than a little strained, nor did the shrewder ones among them hesitate to whisper dark and ominous hints as to the nature of this estrangement.

Baltazar Stork received the news of his friend's approaching marriage with something like mute fury. The morning when Sorio announced it to him was one of concentrated gloom. The sea was high and rough.

The wind wailed through the now almost leafless sycamores and made the sign which bore the Admiral's head
creak and groan in its iron frame. It had rained
steadily all through the night and though the rain
had now ceased there was no sun to dry the little pools
of water which lay in all the trodden places in the
green or the puddles, choked up with dead leaves,
which stared desolately from the edges of the road
upon the sombre heaven. Sorio, having made his mo-
mentous announcement in a negligent, off-hand way,
as though it were a matter of small importance, rushed
off to meet Nance at the station and go with her to
Mundham.

As it was Saturday the girl had no scruple about
leaving her work. In any case she would have been
free, with the rest of Miss Pontifex's employees, in the
early afternoon. She was anxious to spend as long
a time as was possible making her final purchases pre-
paratory to their taking possession of Ferry Lodge.
The mere name of this relic of Rodmoor's faded glory
was indicative of how times had changed. What was
once an inland crossing — several miles from the shore
— had now become the river's mouth and where farmers
formerly watered their cattle the fishing boats spread
their sails to meet the sea.

Nance had made a clean sweep of the furniture of
their predecessor, something about the reputation of
Mr. Peewit Swinebitter prejudicing her, in perhaps an
exaggerated manner, against the buying of any of his
things. This fastidiousness on her part did not, however, lessen the material difficulties of the situation,
Sorio being of singularly little assistance in the rôle
of a house-furnisher.

Meanwhile, with hat pulled low down over his forehead and his cane switching the rain-drenched grass,
Baltazar Stork walked up and down in front of his
cottage.   He walked thus until he was tired and then
he came and stood at the edge of the green and looked
at his empty house and at the puddles in the road.
Into the largest of these puddles he idly poked his stick,
stirring the edge of a half-submerged leaf and making
it float across the muddy water.   Children passed him
unheeded, carrying cans and bottles to be filled at the
tavern.   Little boys came up to him, acquaintances of
his, full of gaiety and mischief, but something in his
face made them draw back and leave him.   Never, in
all his relations with his friend, had Baltazar derived
more pleasure from being with him than he had done
during the recent weeks.   That condition of helpless
and wistful incompetence which Nance found so trying
in Sorio was to Baltazar Stork the cause of the most
delicate and exquisite sensations.   Never had he loved
the man so well — never had he found him so fascinating.   And now, just at the moment when he, the initi-
ated adept in the art of friendship, was reaping the
reward of his long patience with his friend's wayward-
ness and really succeeding in making him depend on
him exactly in the way he loved best, there came this
accursed girl and carried him off!

The hatred which he felt at that moment towards
Nance was so extreme that it overpowered and swamped
every other emotion.   Baltazar Stork was of that peculiarly constituted disposition which is able to hate
the more savagely and vindicatively because of the
very fact that its normal mood is one of urbane and
tolerant indifference.   The patient courtesy of a life-

time, the propitiatory arts of a long suppression, had
their revenge just then for all they had made him endure. In a certain sense it was well for him that he
could hate. It was, indeed in a measure, an instinct of
self-preservation that led him to indulge such a feeling. For below his hatred, down in the deeper levels
of his soul, there yawned a gulf, the desolating emptiness of which was worse than death. He did not visualize this gulf in the same concrete manner as he had
done on a previous occasion, but he was conscious of
it none the less. It was as a matter of fact a thing
that had been for long years hidden obscurely under
the hard, gay surface of his days. He covered it over
by one distraction or the other. Its remote presence
had given an added intensity to his zest for the various
little pleasures, æsthetic or otherwise, which it was his
habit to enjoy. It had done more. It had reduced
to comparative insignificance the morbid vexations and
imaginative reactions from which his friend suffered.
He could afford to appear hard and crystal-cold, capable of facing with equanimity every kind of ultimate
horror. And he *was* capable of facing such. Under
the shadow of a thing like that — a thing beyond the
worst of insane obsessions, for his mind was cruelly
clear as he turned his eyes inward — he was able to
look contemptuously into the Gorgon face of any kind
of terror. When he chose he could always see the
thing as it was, see it as the desolation of emptiness,
as a deep, frozen space, void of sound or movement or
life or hope or end. There was not the least tinge of
insanity in the vision.

What he was permitted to see, by reason of some
malign clarity of intellect denied to the majority of

his fellows, was simply the real truth of life, its frozen
chemistry and deadly purposelessness. Most men visualize existence through a blurring cloud of personal
passion, either erotic or imaginative. They suffer,
but they suffer from illusion. What separated Baltazar from the majority was his power of seeing things
in absolute colourlessness — unconfused by any sort of
distorting mirage. Thus what he saw with his soul
was the ghastly loneliness of his soul. He saw this
frozen, empty, hollow space and he saw it as the natural country in which his soul dwelt, its unutterable
reality, its appalling truth. That was why no thought
of suicide ever came to him. The thing was too deep.
He might kill himself, but in so doing he would only
destroy the few superficial distractions that afforded
him a temporary freedom. For suicide would only
fling him — that at least is what, with horrible clarity,
he had come to feel about it — into the depths of his
soul, into the very abyss, that is to say, which he
escaped by living on the surface. It was a kind of
death-in-life that he was conscious of, below his crystal-
line amenities, but one does not fly to death to escape
from death.

It will be seen from this how laughable to him were
all Sorio's neurotic reactions from people and things.
People and things were precisely what Baltazar clung
to, to avoid that " frozen sea " lying there at the back
of everything. It will be easily imagined too, how absurd to him — how fantastic and unreal — were the
various hints and glimpses which Sorio had permitted
him into what his friend called his " philosophy of destruction." To make a " philosophy " out of a struggle to reach the ultimate horror of that " frozen sea,"

how lamentably pathetic it was, and how childish!
No sane person would contemplate such a thing and
the attempt proved that Sorio was not sane. As for
the Italian's vague and prophetic suggestions with regard to the possibility of something — philosophers
always spoke of " something " when they approached
nothing! — beyond " what we call life " that seemed
to Baltazar's mind mere poetic balderdash and moon-
struck mysticism. But he had always listened patiently to Sorio's incoherences. The man would not
have been himself without his mad philosophy! It was
part of that charming weakness in him that appealed
to Baltazar so. It was absurd, of course — this whole
business of writing philosophic books — but he was
ready to pardon it, ready to listen all night and day
to his friend's dithyrambic diatribes, as long as they
brought that particular look of exultation which he
found so touching into his classic face!

This " look of exultation " in Sorio's features had
indeed been accompanied during the last month by an
expression of wistful and bewildered helplessness and
it was just the union of these two things that Baltazar
found so irresistibly appealing. He was drawn closer
to Adrian, in fact, during these Autumn days, than he
had ever been drawn to any one. And it was just at
this moment, just when he was happiest in their life
together, that Nance Herrick must needs obtrude her
accursed feminine influence and with this result! So
he gave himself up without let or hindrance to his
hatred of this girl. His hatred was a cold, calculated, deliberate thing, clear of all volcanic disturb-
ances but, such as it was, it possessed him at that mo-

ment to the exclusion of everything else. He imagined
to himself now, as with the end of his stick he guided
that sycamore leaf across the puddle, how Nance would
buy those things in the Mundham shops and what
pleasure there would be in her grey eyes, that peculiar
pleasure unlike anything else in the world which a
woman has when she is indulging, at the same moment,
her passion for domestic detail and her passion for her
lover!

He saw the serene *possessive* look in her face, the
look of one who at last, after long waiting, arrives
within sight of the desired end. He saw the little outbursts of girlish humour — oh, he knew them so well,
those outbursts! — and he saw the fits of half-assumed,
half-natural shyness that would come over her and
the soft, dreamy tenderness in her eyes, as together
with Adrian, she bought this thing or the other, full
of delicate association, for their new dwelling-place.
His imagination went even further. He seemed to
hear her voice as she spoke sympathetically, pityingly,
of himself. She would be sure to do that! It would
come so prettily from her just then and would appeal
so much to Adrian! She would whisper to him over
their lunch in some little shop — he saw all that too —
of how sad she felt to be taking him away from his old
friend and leaving that friend alone. And he could see
the odd bewildered smile, half-remorseful and half-joy-
ful with which Sorio would note that disinterested
sympathy and think to himself what a noble affectionate
creature she was and how lucky he was to win her.
He saw how careful she would be not to tire him or
tease him with her purchases, how she would probably

vary the tedium of the day with some pleasant little
strolls together round the Abbey grounds or perhaps
down by the wharves and the barges.

Yes, she had won her victory. She was gathering
up her spoils. She was storing up her possessions!
Could any human feeling, he asked himself with a
deadly smile upon his lips, be more sickeningly, more
achingly, intense than the hatred he felt for this normal, natural, loving woman?

He swept his stick through the muddy water, splashing it vindictively on all sides and then, moving into
the middle of the road, looked at his empty cottage.
Here, then, he would have to live again alone! Alone
with himself, alone with his soul, alone with the truth
of life!

No, it was too much. He never would submit to
it. Better swallow at once and without more nonsense the little carefully concocted draught which he
had long kept under lock and key! After all he would
have to come to that, sooner or later. He had long
since made up his mind that if things and persons —
the "things and persons" he used as his daily drug,
failed him or lost their savour he would take the ir-
revocable step and close the whole farce. Everything
was the same. Everything was equal. He would only
move one degree nearer the central horror — the great
ice field of eternity — the plain without end or beginning, frozen and empty, empty and frozen! He stared
at his cottage windows. No, it was unthinkable, beginning life over again without Adrian. A hundred
little things plucked at random from the sweet monotony
of their days together came drifting through his mind.
The peculiar look Adrian had when he first woke in

the morning — the savage greediness with which he
would devour honey and brown bread — the pleading,
broken, childlike tones in his voice when, after some
quarrel between them he begged his friend to forgive
him — all these things and many others, came pouring
in upon him in a great wave of miserable self-pity.
No — she should not win. She should not triumph.
She should not enjoy the fruits of her victory — the
strong feminine animal! He would sooner kill her and
then kill himself to avoid the gallows. But killing was
a silly futile kind of revenge. Infants in the art of
hatred *killed* their enemies! But at any rate, if he
killed her she would never settle down in her nice new
house with her dear husband! But then, on the other
hand, she would be the winner to the end. She would
never feel as he was feeling now; she would never look
into his eyes and know that he knew he had beaten her;
he would never *see* her disappointment. No — killing
was a stupid, melodramatic, blundering way out of it.
Artists ought to have a subtler imagination! Well,
something must be done, and done soon. He felt he
did not care what suffering he caused Sorio, the more
he suffered the better, if only he could see the look in
those grey eyes of Nance that confessed she was de-
feated!

Quite quietly, quite calmly, he gathered together all
the forces of his nature to accomplish this one end.
His hatred rose to the level of a passion. He vowed
that nothing should make him pause, no scruple, no
obstacle, until he saw that beaten look in Nance's face.
Like all dominant obsessions, like all great lusts, his
purpose associated itself with a clear concrete image,
the image of the girl's expression when at last, face to

face with him, she knew herself broken, helpless and at his mercy.

He walked swiftly down the High Street, crossed the open space by the harbour and made his way to the edge of the waves. Surely that malignant tide would put some triumphant idea into his brain. The sea — the sterile, unharvested sea — had from the beginning of the world, been the enemy of woman! Warden of the Fishes! He laughed as he thought of Sorio's assuming such a title.

"Not yet, my friend — not quite yet!" he murmured, gazing across the stormy expanse of water. Warden of the Fishes! With a strong, sweet, affectionate wife to look after him? "No, no, Adriano!" he cried hoarsely, "we haven't come to that yet — we haven't come to that quite yet!"

By some complicated, psychological process he seemed to be aware, as he stared at the foaming sea-horses, of the head of his mute friend Flambard floating, amid the mist of his own woman-like hair, in the green hollows of the surf. He found himself vaguely wondering what he — the super-subtle Venetian — would have done had he been "fooled to the top of his bent" by a girl like Nance — had he been betrayed in his soul's deepest passion. And all at once it came over him, not distinctly and vividly but obscurely and remotely as if through a cloudy vapour from a long way off, from far down the vistas of time itself, what Flambard would have done.

He stooped and picked up a long leather-like thong of wet, slippery seaweed and caressed it with his hands. At that moment there passed through him a most curious sensation — the sensation that he had himself — he

and not Flambard — stood just in this way but by a
different sea, ages, centuries ago — and had arrived
at the same conclusion. The sensation vanished
quickly enough and with it the image of Flambard, but
the idea of what remained for him to do still hovered
like a cloud at the back of his mind. He did not drag
it forth from its hiding place. He never definitely accepted it. The thing was so dark and hideous, be-
longing so entirely to an age when " passional crimes "
were more common and more remorseless than at the
present, that even Baltazar with all the frozen malice
of his hate scrupled to visualize it in the daylight.
But he did not drive it away. He permitted it to work
upon him and dominate him. It was as though some
" other Baltazar " from a past as remote as Flambard's own and perhaps far remoter — had risen up
within him in answer to that cry to the inhuman waters. The actual working of his mind was very complicated and involved at that moment. There were moments of wavering — moments of drawing back into
the margin of uncertainty. But these moments grew
constantly less and less effective. Beyond everything
else that definite image of Nance's grey eyes, full of
infinite misery, confessing her defeat, and even pleading with him for mercy, drove these wavering moments
away. It was worth it, any horror was worth it, to
satiate his revenge by the sight of what her expression
would be as he looked into her face then. And, after
all, the thing he projected would in any case, come
about sooner or later. It was on its way. The destinies called for it. The nature of life demanded it.
The elements conspired to bring it about. The man's
own fatality was already with a kind of vehemence,

rushing headlong — under the fall of these Autumn
rains and the drifting of these Autumn leaves — to
meet it and embrace it! All he would have to do himself would be just to give the wheel of fate the least
little push, the least vibration of an impulse forward,
with his lightest finger!

Perhaps, as far as his friend was concerned, he would
really, in this way, be saving him in the larger issue.
Were Adrian's mind, for instance, to break down now
at once, rendering it necessary that he should be put,
as they say in that appalling phrase, "under restraint," it might as a matter of fact, save his brain
from ultimate and final disaster. It is true that this
aspect of what he projected was too fantastic, too
ironically distorted, to be dwelt upon clearly or log-
ically but it came and went like a shadowy bird hovering about a floating carcass, round the outskirts of his
unspeakable intention. What he reverted to more
articulately, as he made his way back across the littered sand-heaps to the entrance of the harbour, was
the idea that, after all, he would only be precipitating
an inevitable crisis. His friend was already on the
verge of an attack of monomania, if not of actual insanity. Sooner or later the thing must come to a
definite climax. Why not anticipate events, then, and
let the climax occur when it would save him from this
intolerable folly — worse than madness — of giving
himself up to his feminine pursuer? As he made his
way once more through the crowded little street, the
fixed and final impression all these thoughts left upon
his mind was the impression of Nance Herrick's face,
pale, vanquished and helpless, staring up at him from
the ground beneath his feet.

XXIV

THE TWENTY-EIGHTH OF OCTOBER

BALTAZAR was not long in carrying out what, in bitter self-colloquy, he called his Flambardian campaign. He deliberately absented himself from his work in the Mundham office and gave up all his time to Sorio. He now encouraged this latter in all his most dangerous manias, constantly leading the conversation round to what he knew were exciting and agitating topics and bringing him back again and again to especial points of irritation and annoyance.

The days quickly passed, however, and Adrian, though in a strange and restless mood, had still, in no public manner, given evidence of insanity, and short, of course, of some such public manifestation, his treacherous friend's plan of having him put under restraint, fell to the ground.

Meanwhile, Nance's preparations for her marriage and for their entrance into their new home advanced towards completion. It was within three days of the date decided upon for their wedding when Nance, who had had less time recently at her disposal for watching her sister's moods, came suddenly to the conclusion, as, on a wild and stormy afternoon, she led her home from the church, that something was seriously wrong. At first, as they left the churchyard and began making their way towards the bridge, she thought the gloom of the evening was a sufficient reason for Linda's despairing silence, but as they advanced, with the wind beating in their faces and the roar of the sea coming to them over the dunes, she came to the conclusion that the cause lay deeper.

But that night — it was the twenty-eighth of October — was certainly desolate enough to be the cause of any human being's depression. The sun was sinking as the sisters started for their walk home. A blood-red streak, jagged and livid, like the mutilated back of some bleeding monster, lay low down over the fens. The wind wailed in the poplars, whistled through the reeds, and sighed in long melancholy gasps like the sobbing of some unhappy earth-spirit across the dykes and the ditches. One by one a few flickering lamps appeared among the houses of the town as the girls drew near the river, but the long wavering lines of light thrown by these across the meadows only increased the general gloom.

"Don't let's cross at once," said Linda suddenly, when they reached the bridge. "Let's walk along the bank — just a little way! I feel excited and queer to-night. I've been in the church so long. Please let's stay out a little."

Nance thought it better to agree to the child's caprice; though the river-bank at that particular hour was dark with a strange melancholy. They left the road and walked slowly along the tow-path in the direction away from the town. A group of cattle standing huddled together near the path, rushed off into the middle of the field.

The waters of the Loon were high — the tide flowing seaward — and here and there from the windows of some scattered houses on the opposite bank, faint lights were reflected upon the river's surface. A strong smell of seaweed and brackish mud came up to them from the dark stream.

" What secrets," said Linda suddenly, " this old Loon could tell, if it could speak ! I call it a haunted river."

Nance's only reply to this was to pull her sister's cloak more tightly round her shoulders.

" I don't mean in the sense of having drowned so many people," Linda went on, " I mean in the sense of being half-human itself."

The words were hardly out of her mouth when a slender dusky figure that had been leaning against the edge of one of the numerous weirs that connect the river-tides with the streams of the water-meadows, came suddenly towards them and revealed herself as Philippa Renshaw.

Both the girls drew back in instinctive alarm. Nance was the first to recover.

" So you too are out to-night," she said. " Linda got so tired of practising, so we —"

Philippa interrupted her: " Since we *have* met, Nance Herrick, there's no reason why we shouldn't talk a little. Or do you think the people about here would find that an absurd thing for us to do, as we're both in love with the same man, and you're going to marry him? "

She uttered these words so calmly and in so strange a voice that Nance for the moment was too startled to reply. She recovered herself quickly, however, and taking Linda by the arm, made as if she would pass her by, without further speech. But Philippa refused to permit this. With the slow dramatic movement always

characteristic of her, she stepped into the middle of the
path and stopped them. Linda, at this, hung back,
trying to draw her sister away.

The two women faced one another in breathless silence. It was too dark for them to discern more than
the vaguest outlines of each other's features, but they
were each conscious of the extreme tension, which, like
a wave of magnetic force, at once united and divided
them. Nance was the first to break the spell.

"I'm surprised," she said, "to hear you speak of
love. I thought you considered all that sort of thing
sentimental and idiotic."

Philippa's hand went up in a quick and desperate
gesture, almost an imploring one.

"Miss Herrick," she whispered in a very low and
very clear tone, "you needn't do that. You needn't
say those things. You needn't hurt me more than is
necessary."

"Come away, Nance. Oh, please come away and
leave her!" interjected Linda.

"Miss Herrick, listen to me one moment!" Philippa
continued, speaking so low as almost to be inaudible.
"I have something to ask of you, something that you
can do for me. It isn't very much. It isn't anything
that you need suspect. It is a little thing. It's nothing you could possibly mind."

"Don't listen to her, Nance," cried Linda again.
"Don't listen to her."

Philippa's voice trembled as she went on, "I beg you,
I beg you on my knees to hear me. We two may never
meet again after this. Nance Herrick, will you, will
you let me speak?"

Linda leapt forward. She was shaking from head

to foot with fear and anger. " No," she cried, " she shall not listen to you. She shall not, she shall not."

Nance hesitated, weary and sick at heart. She had so hoped and prayed that all these lacerating contests were over and done with.

Finally she said, " I think you must see, you must feel, that between you and me there can be nothing — nothing more — nothing further. I think you'll be wise, I think you'll recognize it afterwards, to let me go now, to let me go and leave us alone." As she spoke she drew away from her and put her arm round Linda's waist. " In any case," she added, " I can't possibly hear you before this child. Perhaps, but I can't promise anything, but perhaps, some other day, when I'm by myself."

She gave one sad, half-sympathetic, half-reproachful glance, at the frail shadowy figure standing mute and silent; and then turning quickly, let herself be led away.

Linda swung round when they were some few paces away. " She'll never listen to you! " She called out, in a shrill vibrating voice, " I won't ever let her listen to you."

The growing darkness, made thicker by the river-mists, closed in between them, and in a brief while their very footsteps ceased to be heard. Philippa was left alone. She looked round her. On the fen side of the pathway there was nothing but a thick fluctuating shadow, out of which the forms of a few pollard-willows rose like panic-stricken ghosts. On the river itself there shimmered at intervals a faint whitish gleam as if some lingering relics of the vanished day, slow in their drowning, struggled to rise to the surface.

She moved back again to the place where she had

been standing at the edge of the weir. Leaning upon the time-worn plank rotten with autumn rains, she gazed down into the dense blackness beneath. Nothing could be seen but darkness. She might have been looking down into some unfathomable pit, leading to the caverns of the mid-earth.

A deathly cold wave of damp air met her face as she leaned over the plank, and a hollow gurgling roar, from the heavy volume of water swirling in the darkness, rose to her ears. She could smell the unseen water; and the smell of it was like the smell of dead black leaves plucked forth from a rain pool in the heart of a forest.

As she leaned forward with her soft breast pressing against the wooden bar and her long slender fingers clutching its edge, a sinister line of poetry, picked up somewhere — she could not recall where — came into her mind, and she found her lips mechanically echoing it. "Like a wolf, sucked under a weir," the line ran, and over and over again she repeated those words.

Meanwhile Nance, as they returned across the bridge, did her best to soothe and quiet her sister. The sudden appearance of Philippa seemed to have thrown the girl into a paroxysm of frenzy. "Oh, how I hate her!" she kept crying out, "oh, how I loathe and hate her!"

Nance was perplexed and bewildered by Linda's mood. Never had she known the girl to give way to feelings of this sort. When at last she got her into their house, and had seen her take off her things and begin tidying herself up for their evening meal quite in her accustomed way, she asked her point-blank what was the matter, and why to-day, on this twenty-eighth of October, she had suddenly grown different from her ordinary self.

Linda, standing with bare arms by the mirror and passing a comb through her heavy hair, turned almost fiercely round.

" Do you want to know? Do you really want to know? " she cried, throwing back her head and holding the hair back with her hands. " It's because of Philippa that *he* has deserted me! It's because of Philippa that he hasn't seen me nor spoken to me for a whole month! It's because of Philippa that he won't answer my letters and won't meet me anywhere! It's because of Philippa that now — now when I most want him "— and she threw the comb down and flung herself on her bed —" he refuses to come to me or to speak a word."

" How do you know it's because of Philippa? " Nance asked, distressed beyond words to find that in spite of all her efforts Linda was still as obsessed by Brand as ever before.

" I know *from him*," the girl replied. " You needn't ask me any more. She's got power over him, and she uses it against me. If it wasn't for her he'd have married me before now." She sat up on the edge of her bed and looked woefully at her sister with large sunken eyes. " Yes," she went on, " if it wasn't for her he'd marry me now — to-day — and, oh, Nance, I want him so! I want him so!"

Nance felt an oppressive weight of miserable helplessness in the presence of this heart-stricken cry. As she looked round the room and saw her various preparations for leaving it and for securing the happiness of her own love, she felt as though in some subtle way she had once more betrayed the unhappy child. She knew herself, only too well, what that famished and starving longing is — that cry of the flesh and blood, and the heart and the spirit, for what the eternal destinies have put out of our reach!

And she could do nothing to help her. What *could* she do? Now for the first time in her life, as she looked at that lamentable youthful figure, dumbly pleading with her for some kind of miracle, Nance was conscious of a vague unformulated indignation against the whole system of things that rendered this sort of suffering possible. If only *she* were a powerful and a tender deity, how she would hasten to end this whole business of sex-life which made existence so intolerable! Why could not people be born into the world like trees or plants? And being born, why could not love instinctively create the answering passion it craved, and not be left to beat itself against cruel walls, after scorching itself in the irresistible flame?

"Nance!" said the young girl suddenly. "Nance! Come here. Come over to me. I want to tell you something."

The elder sister obeyed. It was not long — for hard though it may be to break silence, these things are quickly spoken — before she knew the worst. Linda, with her arms clutched tightly round her, and her face hidden, confessed that she was with child.

Nance leapt to her feet. "I'll go to him," she cried, "I'll go to him at once! Of course he must marry you now. He must! He must! I'll go to him. I'll go to Hamish. I'll go to Adrian — to Fingal! He *must* marry you, Linda. Don't cry, little one. I'll make it all right. It *shall* be all right! I'll go to him this very evening."

A faint flush appeared in Linda's pale cheeks and a glimmer of hope in her eyes. "Do you think, possibly, that there's any chance? *Can* there be any chance? But no, no, darling, I know there's none — I know there's none."

"What makes you so sure, Linda?" asked Nance, rapidly changing her dress, and as she did so pouring herself out a glass of milk.

"It's Philippa," murmured the other in a low voice. "Oh, how I hate her! How I hate her!" she continued, in a sort of moaning refrain, twisting her long hair between her fingers and tying the ends of it into a little knot.

"Well, I'm off, my dear," cried Nance at length, finishing her glass of milk and adjusting her hat-pins. "I'm going straight to find him. I may pick up Adrian on the way, or I may not. It rather depends. And I *may* have a word or two with Philippa. The chances are that I shall overtake her if I go now. She can't have waited much longer down by the river."

Linda rushed up to her and clasped her in her arms. "My own darling!" she murmured, "how good you are to me — how good you are! Do you know, I was *afraid* to tell you this — afraid that you'd be angry and ashamed and not speak to me for days. But, oh, Nance, I do love him so much! I love him more than my life — more than my life *even now!*"

Nance kissed her tenderly. "Make yourself some tea, my darling, won't you? We'll have supper whenever I come back, and that'll be — I hope — with good news for you! Good-bye, my sweetheart! Say your prayers for me, and don't be frightened however late I am. And have a good tea!"

She kissed her again, and with a final wave of the
hand and an encouraging smile, she left the room and
ran down the stairs. She walked slowly to the top of
the street, her head bent, wondering in her mind whether
she should ask Adrian to go with her to the Renshaws'
or whether she should go alone.

The question was decided for her. As she emerged
on the green she suddenly came upon Sorio himself,
standing side by side with Philippa. They both turned
quickly as, in the flare of a wind-blown lamp, they perceived her approach. They turned and awaited her
without a word.

Without a word, too — and in that slow dreamlike
manner which human beings assume at certain crises
in their lives, when fate like a palpable presence among
them takes their movements into its own hand — they
moved off, all three together, in the direction of the
park gates. Not a word did any of them utter, till,
having passed the gates, they were quite far advanced
along that dark and lonely avenue.

Then Philippa broke the silence. " I can say to her,
Adrian, what I've just said to you — mayn't I? "

In the thick darkness, full of the heavy smell of
rain-soaked leaves, Sorio walked between them.
Nance's hand was already resting upon his arm, and
now, as she spoke, Philippa's fingers searched for his,
and took them in her own and held them feverishly.

" You can say what you please, Phil," he muttered,
" but you'll see what she answers — just what I told
you just now."

Their tone of intimate association stabbed like a
knife at the heart of Nance. A moment ago — in

fact, ever since she had left her by the weir — she had been feeling less antagonistic and more pitiful towards her vanquished rival. But this pronoun " she " applied mutually by them to herself, seemed to push her back — back and away — outside the circle of some mysterious understanding between the two. Her heart hardened fiercely. Was this girl still possessed of some unknown menacing power?

" What I asked Adrian," said Philippa quietly, while the pressure of her burning fingers within the man's hand indicated the strain of this quietness, " was whether you would be generous and noble enough to give him up to me for his last free day — the last day before you're married. Would you be large-hearted enough for that? "

" What do you mean —' give him up ' to you? " murmured Nance.

Philippa burst in a shrill unearthly laugh. " Oh, you needn't be frightened! " she exclaimed. " You needn't be jealous. I only mean let me go with him, for the whole day, a long walk — you know — or something like that — perhaps a row up the river. It doesn't matter what, as long as I feel that that day is *my* day, my day *with him* — the last, and the longest! "

She was silent, feverish, her fingers twining and twisting themselves round her companion's, and her breath coming in quick gasps. Nance was silent also, and they all three moved forward through the heavy fragrant darkness.

" You two seem to have settled it between yourselves definitely enough," Nance remarked at last. " I don't really see why you need bring me into it at all. Adrian is, of course, entirely free to do what he likes. I don't see what I have to do with it!"

Philippa's hot fingers closed tightly upon Sorio's as she received this rebuff. "You see!" she murmured in a tone that bit into Nance's flesh like the tooth of an adder. "You see, Adriano!" She shrugged her shoulders and gave a low vindictive laugh. "She's a thorough woman," she added with stinging emphasis. "She's what my mother would call a sweet, tender, sensitive girl. But we mustn't expect too much from her, Adrian, must we? I mean in the way of generosity."

Nance withdrew her hand from the arm of her betrothed and they all three walked on in silence.

"You see what you're in for, my friend," Philippa began again. "Once married it'll be always like this. That is what you seem unable to realize. It's a mistake, as I've often said, this mixing of classes."

Nance could no longer restrain herself. "May I ask what you mean by that last remark?" she whispered in a low voice.

Philippa laughed lightly. "It doesn't need much explanation," she replied. "Adrian is, of course, of very ancient blood, and you — well, you betray yourself naturally by this lack of nobility, this common middle-class jealousy!"

Nance turned fiercely upon them, and clutching Sorio's arm spoke loudly and passionately. "And *you* — what are *you*, who, like a girl of the streets, are ready to pick up what you can of a man's attentions and attract him with mere morbid physical attraction? *You* — what are *you*, who, as you say yourself, are ready to *share* a man with some one else? Do you call *that* a sign of good-breeding?"

Philippa laughed again. "It's a sign at any rate of being free from that stupid, stuffy, bourgeois respectability, which Adrian is going to get a taste of now! That very sneer of yours —'a girl of the streets'— shows the class to which you belong, Nance Herrick! We don't say those things. It's what one hears among tradespeople."

Nance's fingers almost hurt Sorio's arms as she tightened her hold upon him. "It's better than being what *you* are, Philippa Renshaw," she burst out. "It's better than deliberately helping your brother to ruin innocent young girls — yes, and taking pleasure in seeing him ruining them — and then taunting them cruelly in their shame, and holding him back from doing them justice! It's better than that, Philippa Renshaw, though it *may* be what most simple-minded decent-hearted women feel. It's better than being reduced by blind passion to have to come to another woman and beg her on your knees for a 'last day' as you call it! It's better than *that* — though it *may* be what ordinary unintellectual people feel!"

Philippa's fingers grew suddenly numb and stiff in Sorio's grasp. "Do you know," she murmured, "you 'decent-feeling' woman — if that's what you call yourself — that a couple of hours ago, when you left me on the river bank, I was within an ace of drowning myself? I suppose 'decent-feeling' women never run such a risk! They leave that to 'street-girls' and — and — and to us others!"

Nance turned to Sorio. "So she's been telling you that she was thinking of drowning herself? I thought it was sómething of that kind! And I suppose you believed her. I suppose you always believe her!"

"And he always believes *you!*" Philippa cried. "Yes, he's always deceived — the easy fool — by your womanly sensitive ways and your touching refinement! It's women like you, without intelligence and without imagination, who are the ruin of men of genius. A lot *you* care for his work! A lot *you* understand of his thoughts! Oh, yes, you may get him, and cuddle him, and spoil him, but, when it comes to the point, what *you* are to him is a mere domestic drudge! And not only a drudge, you're a drag, a burden, a dead-weight! A mere mass of 'decent-feeling' womanliness — weighing him down. He'll never be able to write another line when once you've really got hold of him!"

Nance had her answer to this. "I'd sooner he never *did* write another line," she cried, "and remain in his sober senses, than be left to *your* influence, and be driven mad by you — you and your diseased, morbid, wicked imagination!"

Their two voices, rising and falling in a lamentable litany of elemental antagonism — antagonism cruel as life and deeper than death — floated about Sorio's head, in that perfumed darkness, like opposing streams of poison. It was only that he himself, harassed by long irritating debates with Baltazar, was too troubled, too obsessed by a thousand agitating doubts, to have the energy or the spirit to bring the thing to an end, or he could not have endured it up to this point. With his nerves shaken by Baltazar's corrosive arts, and the weight of those rain-heavy trees and thick darkness all around him, he felt as if he were in some kind of trance, and were withheld by a paralysing interdict from lifting a finger. There came to him a sort of half-savage, half-humorous remembrance of a conversation he had once had with some one or other — his mind was too confused to recall the occasion — in which he had upheld the idealistic theory of the arrival of a day when sex jealousy would disappear from the earth.

But as the girls continued to outrage each other's most secret feelings, each unconsciously quickening her pace as she poured forth her taunts, and both dragging Sorio forward with them, the feeling grew upon him that he was watching some deep cosmic struggle, that was, in its way, as inhuman and elemental as a conflict between wind and water. With this idea lodged in his brain, he began to derive a certain wild and fantastic pleasure from the way they lacerated one another. There was no coxcombry in this. He was far too wrought-upon and shaken in his mind. But there was a certain grim exultant enjoyment, as if he were, at that moment, permitted a passing glimpse into some dark forbidden " cellarage " of Nature, where the primordial elements clash together in eternal conflict.

Inspired by this strange mood, he returned the pressure of Philippa's fingers, and entwined his arm round the trembling form of his betrothed, drawing both the girls closer towards him, and, in consequence, closer towards one another.

They continued their merciless encounter, almost unconscious, it seemed, of the presence of the man who was the cause of it, and without strength left to resist the force with which he was gradually drawing them together.

Suddenly the wind, which had dropped a little during the previous hour, rose again in a violent and furious gust. It tore at the dark branches above their heads and went moaning and wailing through the thickets on either side of them. Drops of rain, held in suspension by the thicker leaves, splashed suddenly upon their faces, and from the far distance, with a long-drawn ominous muttering, that seemed to come from some unknown region of flight and disaster, the sound of thunder came to their ears.

Sorio dropped Philippa's hand and embracing her tightly, drew her, too, closely towards him. Thus interlocked by the man's arms, all three of them staggered forward together, lashed by the wind and surrounded by vague wood-noises that rose and fell mysteriously in the impenetrable darkness.

The powers of the earth seemed let loose, and strange magnetic currents in fierce antipodal conflict, surged about them, and tugged and pulled at their hearts. The sound of the thunder, the wild noises of the night, the strange dark evocations of elemental hatred which at once divided and united his companions, surged through Sorio's brain and filled him with a sort of intoxication.

The three of them together might have been taken, had the clock of time been put back two thousand years, for some mad Dionysian worshippers following their god in a wild inhuman revel.

Inspired at last by a sort of storm-frenzy, while the wind came wailing and shrieking down the avenue into their faces, Sorio suddenly stopped.

" Come, you two little fools," he cried, " let's end this nonsense! Here — kiss one another! Kiss one another, and thank God that we're alive and free and conscious, and not mere inert matter, like these dead drifting leaves!"

As he spoke he stepped back a little, and with a swing of his powerful arms, brought both the girls face to face with one another. Nance struggled fiercely, and resisted with all her strength. Philippa, with a strange whispering laugh, remained passive in his hands.

"Kiss one another!" he cried again. "Are you kissing or are you holding back? It's too dark for me to see!"

Philippa suddenly lost her passivity, slipped like a snake from under his encircling arms, and rushed away among the trees. "I leave her to you!" she called back to them out of the darkness. "I leave her to you! You won't endure her long. *And what will Baptiste do,* Adriano?"

This last word of hers calmed Sorio's mood and threw him back upon his essential self. He sighed heavily.

"Well, Nance," he said, "shall we go back? It's no use waiting for her. She'll find her way to Oakguard. She knows every inch of these woods." He sighed again, as if bidding farewell, in one fate-burdened moment, both to the woods and the girl who knew them.

"*You* can go back if you like," Nance answered curtly. "I'm going to speak to Brand"; and she told him in a brief sentence what she had learned from Linda.

Sorio seized her hand and clutched it savagely. "Yes, yes," he cried, "yes, yes, let's go together. He must be taught a lesson — this Brand! Come, let's go together!"

They moved on rapidly and soon approached the end of the avenue and the entrance to the garden. As Sorio pushed open the iron gates, a sharp crack of thunder, followed by reverberating detonations, broke over their heads. The sudden flash that succeeded the sound brought into vivid relief the dark form of the house, while a long row of fading dahlias, drooping on their rain-soaked stems, stood forth in ghastly illumination.

Nance had time to catch on Adrian's face a look that gave her a premonition of danger. Had she not herself been wrought-up to an unnatural pitch of excitement by her contest with Philippa, she would probably have been warned in time and have drawn back, postponing her interview with Brand till she could have seen him alone. As it was, she felt herself driven forward by a force she could not resist. " Now — very now," she must face her sister's seducer.

A light, burning behind heavy curtains, in one of the lower mullioned windows, enabled them to mount the steps. As she rang the bell, a second peal of thunder, but this time farther off, was followed by a vivid flash of lightning, throwing into relief the wide spaces of the park and the scattered groups of monumental oak trees. For some queer psychic reason, inexplicable to any material analysis, Nance at that moment saw clearly before her mind's eye, a little church almanac, which Linda had pinned up above their dressing-table, and on this almanac she saw the date — the twenty-eighth of October — printed in Roman figures.

To the servant who opened the door Nance gave their names, and asked whether they could see Mr. Renshaw.

" *Mr.* Renshaw," she added emphatically, " and please tell him it's an urgent and important matter."

The man admitted them courteously and asked them to seat themselves in the entrance hall while he went to look for his master. He returned after a short time and ushered them into the library, where a moment later Brand joined them.

During their moment of waiting, both in the hall and in the room, Sorio had remained taciturn and inert, sunk in a fit of melancholy brooding, his chin propped on the handle of his stick. He had refused to allow the servant to take out of his hands either his stick or his hat, and he still held them both, doggedly and gloomily, as he sat by Nance's side opposite the carved fireplace.

When Brand entered they both rose, but he motioned them to remain seated, and drawing up a chair for himself close by the side of the hearth, looked gravely and intently into their faces.

At that moment another rolling vibration of thunder reached them, but this time it seemed to come from very far away, perhaps from several miles out to sea.

Brand's opening words were accompanied by a fierce lashing of rain against the window, and a spluttering, hissing noise, as several heavy drops fell through the old-fashioned chimney upon the burning logs.

" I think I can guess," he said, " why you two have come to me. I am glad you have come, especially you, Miss Herrick, as it simplifies things a great deal. It has become necessary that you and I should have an explanation. I owe it to myself as well as to you. Bah! What nonsense I'm talking. It isn't a case of ' owing.' It isn't a case of ' explaining.' I can see that clearly enough "— he laughed a genial boyish laugh —" in your two faces! It's a case of our own deciding, with all the issues of the future clearly in mind, what will be really best for your sister's happiness."

"She has not sent —" began Nance hurriedly.

"What you've got to understand — you Renshaw —" muttered Adrian, in a strange hoarse voice, clenching and unclenching his fingers.

Brand interrupted them both. "Pardon me," he cried, "you do not wish, I suppose, either of you, to cause any serious shock to my mother? It's absurd of her, of course, and old-fashioned, and all that sort of thing; but it would actually *kill* her —" he rose as he spoke and uttered the words clearly and firmly. "It would actually *kill* her to get any hint of what we're discussing now. So, if you've no objection, we'll continue this discussion in the work-shop." He moved towards the door.

Sorio followed him with a rapid stride. "You must understand, Renshaw —" he began.

"If it'll hurt your mother so," cried Nance hurriedly, "what must Linda be suffering? You didn't think of this, Mr. Renshaw, when you —"

Brand swung round on his heel. "You shall say all this to me, all that you wish to say — everything, do you hear, everything! Only it must and *shall* be where she cannot overhear us. Wait till we're alone. We shall be alone in the work-shop."

"If this 'work-shop' of yours," muttered Sorio savagely, seizing him by the arm, "turns out to be one of your English tricks, you'd better —"

"Silence, you fool!" whispered the other. "Can't

you stop him, Miss Herrick? It'll be pure murder if my mother hears this!"

Nance came quickly between them. "Lead on, Mr. Renshaw," she said. "We'll follow you."

He led them across the hall and down a long dimly lit passage. At the end of this there was a heavily panelled door. Brand took a key from his pocket and after some ineffectual attempts turned the lock and stood aside to let them enter. He closed the door behind them, leaving the key on the outside. The "workshop" Brand had spoken of turned out to be nothing more or less than the old private chapel of Oakguard, disassociated, however, for centuries from any religious use.

Nance glanced up at the carved ceiling, supported on foliated corbels. The windows, high up from the ground, were filled with Gothic tracery, but in place of biblical scenes their diamonded panes showed the armorial insignia of generations of ancient Renshaws. There was a raised space at the east end, where, in former times, the altar stood, but now, in place of an altar, a carpenter's table occupied the central position, covered with a litter of laths and wood-chippings. The middle portion of the chapel was bare and empty, but several low cane chairs stood round this space, like seats round a toy coliseum.

Brand indicated these chairs to his visitors, but neither Nance nor Sorio seemed inclined to avail themselves of the opportunity to rest. They all three, therefore, stood together, on the dark polished oak floor.

On first entering the chapel, Brand had lit one of a long row of tapers that stood in wooden candlesticks along the edge of what resembled choir stalls. Now, leaving his companions, he proceeded very deliberately to set light to the whole line of these. The place thus illuminated had a look strangely weird and confused.

Certain broken flower-pots on the ground, and one or two rusty gardening implements, combined with the presence of the wicker-chairs to produce the impression of some sort of " Petit Trianon," or manorial summerhouse, into which all manner of nondescript rubbish had in process of long years come to drift.

The coats-of-arms in the windows above, as the tapers flung their light upon them, had an air almost " collegiate," as if the chamber were some ancient dining-hall of a monastic order. The carpenter's table upon the raised dais, with some dimly coloured Italianated picture behind it, inserted in the panelling, gave Nance a most odd sensation. Where had she seen an effect of that kind before? In a picture — or in reality?

But the girl had no heart to analyse her emotions. There was too much at stake. The rain, pattering heavily on the roof of the building, seemed to remind her of her task. She faced Brand resolutely as he strolled back towards them across the polished floor.

" Linda has told me everything," she said. " She is going to have a child, and you, Mr. Renshaw, are the father of it."

Sorio made an inarticulate exclamation and approached Brand threateningly. But the latter, disregarding him, continued to look Nance straight in the face.

" Miss Herrick," he said quietly, " you are a sensible woman and not one, I think, liable to hysteric sentimentalism. I want to discuss this thing quite freely and openly with you, but I would greatly prefer it if your husband — I beg your pardon — if Mr. Sorio would let us talk without interrupting. I haven't got unlimited time. My mother and sister will be both waiting dinner for me and sending people to find me, perhaps even coming themselves. So it's obviously in the interests of all of us — particularly of Linda — that we should not waste time in any mock heroics."

Nance turned quickly to her betrothed. " You'll hear all we say, Adrian, but if it makes things easier, perhaps —"

Without a word, in mute obedience to her sad smile, Sorio left their side, and drawing back, seated himself in one of the wicker chairs, hugging his heavy stick between his knees.

The rain continued falling without intermission upon the leaden roof, and from a pipe above one of the windows they could hear a great jet of water splashing down outside the wall.

Brand spoke in a low hurried tone, without embarrassment and without any sort of shame. " Yes, Miss Herrick, what she says is quite true. But now come down to the facts, without any of this moral vituperation, which only clouds the issues. You have, no doubt, come here with the idea of asking me to marry Linda. No! Don't interrupt me. Let me finish. But I want to ask you this — how do you know that if I marry Linda, she'll be *really* any happier than she is to-day? Suppose I were to say to you that I would marry her — marry her to-morrow — would *that*, when you come to think it over in cold blood, really make you happy in your mind about her future?

" Come, Miss Herrick! Put aside for a moment your natural anger against me. Grant what you please as to my being a dangerous character and a bad man, does that make me a suitable husband for your sister? Your instinct is a common instinct — the natural first instinct of any protector of an injured girl, but is it one that will stand the light of quiet and reasonable second thoughts?

" I am, let us say, a selfish and unscrupulous man who has seduced a young girl. Very well! You want to punish me for my ill-conduct, and how do you go about it? By giving up your sister into my hands! By giving up to me — a cruel and unscrupulous wretch, at your own showing — the one thing you love best in the world! Is that a punishment such as I deserve? In one moment you take away all my remorse, for no one remains remorseful *after* he has been punished. And you give my victim up — bound hand and foot — into my hands.

" Linda may love me enough to be glad to marry me, quite apart from the question of her good fame. But will you, who probably know me better than Linda, feel happy at leaving her in my hands? Your idea may be that I should marry her and then let her go. But suppose I wouldn't consent to let her go? And suppose she wouldn't consent to leave me?

" There we are — tied together for life — and she as the weaker of the two the one to suffer for the ill-fated bargain! *That* will not have been a punishment for me, Nance Herrick, nor will it have been a compensation for her. It will simply have worked out as a temporary boredom to one of us, and as miserable wretchedness to the other!

" Is that what you wish to bring about by this interference on her behalf? It's absurd to pretend that you think of me as a mere hot-headed amorist, desperately in love with Linda, as she is with me, and that, by marrying us, you are smoothing out her path and settling her down happily for the rest of her life. You think of me as a cold-blooded selfish sensualist, and to punish me for being what I am, you propose to put Linda's entire happiness absolutely in my hands!

" Of course, I speak to you like this knowing that, whatever your feelings are, you have the instincts of a lady. A different type of woman from yourself would consider merely the worldly aspect of the matter and the advantage to your sister of becoming mistress of Oakguard. *That*, I know, does not enter, for one moment, into your thoughts, any more than it enters into hers. I am not ironical in saying this. I am not insulting you. I am speaking simply the truth.

" Forgive me, Miss Herrick! Even to mention such a thing is unworthy of either of us. I am, as you quite justly realize — and probably more than you realize — what the world calls unscrupulous. But no one has ever accused me of truckling to public opinion or social position. I care nothing for those things, any more than you do or Linda does. As far as those things go I would marry her to-morrow. My mother, as you doubtless know, hopes that I *shall* marry her — wishes and prays for it. My mother has never given a thought, and never will give a thought, to the opinion of the world. It isn't in her nature, as no doubt you quite realize. We Renshaws have always gone our own way, and done what we pleased. My father did — Philippa does; and I do.

"Come, Miss Herrick! Try for a moment to put your anger against me out of the question. Suppose you did induce me to marry Linda, and Linda to marry me, does that mean that you make me change my nature? We Renshaws never change and *I* never shall, you may be perfectly sure of that! I *couldn't* even if I wanted to. My blood, my race, my father's instincts in me, go too deep. We're an evil tribe, Nance Herrick, an evil tribe, and especially are we evil in our relations with women. Some families are like that, you know! It's a sort of tradition with them. And it is so with us. It may be some dark old strain of Viking blood, the blood of the race that burnt the monasteries in the days of Æthelred the Unready! On the other hand it may be some unaccountable twist in our brains, due — as Fingal says — to — oh! to God knows what!

"Let it go! It doesn't matter what it is; and I daresay you think me a grotesque hypocrite for bringing such a matter into it at all. Well! Let it go! There's really no need to drag in Æthelred the Unready! What you and I have to do, Miss Herrick, is, seriously and quietly, without passion or violence, to discuss what's best for your sister's happiness. Put my punishment out of your mind for the present — that can come later. Your friend Mr. Sorio will be only too pleased to deal with that! The point for *us* to consider, for us who both love your sister, is, what will really be happiest for her in the long run — and I can assure you that no woman who ever lived could be happy long tied hand and foot to a Renshaw.

"Look at my mother! Does she suggest a person who has had a happy life? I tell you she would give all she has ever enjoyed here — every stick and stone of Oakguard — never to have set eyes on my father — never to have given birth to Philippa or to me! We Renshaws may have our good qualities — God knows what they are — but we may have them. But one thing is certain. We are worse than the very devil for any woman who tries to live with us! It's in our blood, I tell you. We can't help it. We're made to drive women mad — to drive them into their graves! "

He stopped abruptly with a bitter and hopeless shrug of his shoulders. Nance had listened to him, all the way through his long speech, with concentrated and frowning attention. When he had finished she stood staring at him without a word, almost as if she wished him to continue; almost as if something about his personality fascinated her in spite of herself, and made her sympathetic.

But Sorio, who had been fidgetting with his heavy stick, rose now, slowly and deliberately, to his feet. Nance, looking at his face, saw upon it an expression which from long association she had come to regard with mingled tenderness and alarm. It was the look his features wore when on the point of rushing to the assistance of some wounded animal or ill-used child.

He uttered no word, but flinging Nance aside with his left hand, with the other he struck blindly with his stick, aiming a murderous blow straight at Brand's face.

Brand had barely time to raise his hand. The blow fell upon his wrist, and his arm sank under it limp and paralysed.

Nance, with a loud cry for assistance, clung frantically to Sorio's neck, trying to hold him back. But apparently beyond all consciousness now of what he was doing, Sorio flung her roughly back and drove his enemy with savage repeated strokes into a corner of the room. It was not long before Brand's other arm was rendered as useless as the first, and the blows falling now on his unprotected head, soon felled him to the ground.

Nance, who had flung open the door and uttered wild and panic-stricken cries for help, now rushed across the room and pinioned the exhausted flagellant in her strong young arms. Seeing his enemy motionless and helpless with a stream of blood trickling down his face, Adrian resigned himself passively to her controlling embrace.

They were found in this position by the two menservants, who came rushing down the passage in answer to her screams. Mrs. Renshaw, dressing in her room on the opposite side of the house, heard nothing. The steady downpour of the rain dulled all other sounds. Philippa had not yet returned.

Under Nance's directions, the two men carried their master out of the " workshop," while she herself continued to cling desperately to Sorio. There had been something hideous and awful to the girl's imagination about the repeated " thud — thud — thud " of the blows delivered by her lover. This was especially so after the numbing of his bruised arms reduced Adrian's victim to helplessness.

As she clung to him now she seemed to hear the sound of those blows — each one striking, as it seemed, something resistless and prostrate in her own being. And once more, with grotesque iteration, the figures upon Linda's almanac ticked like a clock in answer to the echo of that sound. " October the twenty-eighth

— October the twenty-eighth," repeated the church-almanac, from its red-lettered frame.

The extraordinary thing was that as her mind began to function more naturally again, she became conscious that, all the while, during that appalling scene, even at the very moment when she was crying out for help, she had experienced a sort of wild exultation.   She re-called that emotion quite clearly now with a sense of curious shame.

She was also aware that while glancing at Brand's pallid and unconscious face as they carried him from the room, she had felt a sudden indescribable softening towards him and a feeling for him that she would hardly have dared to put into words.   She found her-self, even now, as she went over in her mind with light-ning rapidity every one of the frightful moments she had just gone through, changing the final episode in her heart, to quite a different one; to one in which she herself knelt down by their enemy's side, and wiped the blood from his forehead, and brought him back to con-sciousness.

Left alone with Sorio, Nance relaxed her grasp and laid her hands appealingly upon his shoulder.   But it was into unseeing eyes that she looked, and into a face barely recognizable as that of her well-beloved.   He began talking incoherently and yet with a kind of ter-rible deliberation and assurance.

" What's that you say?   Only the rain?   They say it's only the rain when they want to fool me and quiet me.   But I know better !   They can't fool me like that. It's blood, of course ; it's Nance's blood.   *You*, Nance? Oh, no, no, no !   I'm not so easily fooled as that. Nance is at the bottom of that hole in the wood, where

I struck her — *one* — *two* — *three!* It took three hits
to do it — and she didn't speak a word, not a word, nor
utter one least little cry. It's funny that I had to hit
her three times! She is so soft, so soft and easy to
hurt. No, no, no, no! I'm not to be fooled like that.
My Nance had great laughing grey eyes. Yours are
horrible, horrible. I see terror in them. *She* was
afraid of nothing."

His expression changed, and a wistful hunted look
came into his face. The girl tried to pull him towards
one of the chairs, but he resisted — clasping her hand
appealingly.

"Tell me, Phil," he whispered, in a low awe-struck
voice, "tell me why you made me do it. Did you think
it would be better, better for all of us, to have her
lying there cold and still? No, no, no! You needn't
look at me with those dreadful eyes. Do you know,
Phil, since you made me kill her I think your eyes have
grown to look like hers, and your face, too — and all
of you."

Nance, as he spoke, cried out woefully and helplessly.
"I am! I am! I am! Adrian — my own — my
darling — don't you know me? I am your Nance!"

He staggered slowly now to one of the chairs, moving each foot as he did so with horrible deliberation
as if nothing he did could be done naturally any more,
or without a conscious effort of will. Seating himself
in the chair, he drew her down upon his knee and began passing his fingers backwards and forwards over
her face.

"Why did you make me do it, Phil?" he moaned,
rocking her to and fro as if she were a child. "Why
did you make me do it? She would have given me

sleep, if you'd only let her alone, cool, deep, delicious
sleep! She would have smoothed away all my troubles.
She would have destroyed the old Adrian and made a
new one — a clear untroubled one, bathed in great
floods of glorious white light!"

His voice sank to an awe-struck and troubled murmur. "Phil, my dear," he whispered, "Phil, listen to
me. There's something I can't remember! Something
— O God! No! It's *some one* — some one most precious to me — and I've forgotten. Something's happened to my brain, and I've forgotten. It was after
I struck those blows, those blows that made her mouth
look so twisted and funny — just like yours looks now,
Phil! Why is it, do you think, that dead people have
that look on their mouths? Phil, tell me; tell me what
it is I've forgotten! Don't be cruel now. I can't stand
it now. I *must* remember. I always seem just on the
point of remembering, and then something in my brain
closes up, like an iron door. Oh, Phil — my love, my
love, tell me what it is!"

As he spoke he clasped the girl convulsively, crushing her and hurting her by the strength of his arms.
To hear him address her thus by the name of her rival
was such misery to Nance that she was hardly conscious
of the physical distress caused by his violence. It was
still worse when, relaxing the force of his grasp, he
began to fondle and caress her, stroking her face with
his fingers and kissing her cheeks.

"Phil, my love, my darling!" he kept repeating,
" please tell me — please, please tell me, what it is I've
forgotten!"

Nance suffered at that moment the extreme limit of
what she was capable of enduring. She dreaded every

moment that Philippa herself would come in. She dreaded the re-appearance of the servants, perhaps with more assistance, ready to separate them and carry Adrian away from her. To feel his caresses and to know that in his wild thoughts they were not meant for her at all — that was more, surely more, than God could have intended her to suffer!

Suddenly she had an inspiration. "Is it Baptiste that you've forgotten?"

The word had an electrical effect upon him. He threw her off his lap and leapt to his feet.

"Yes," he cried savagely and wildly, the train of his thoughts completely altered, "you're all keeping him away from me! That's what's at the bottom of it! You've hidden Nance from me and given me this woman who looks like her but who can't smile and laugh like my Nance, to deceive me and betray me! I know you — you staring, white-faced, frightened thing! *You* don't deceive me! *You* don't fool Adrian. I know you. *You* are not my Nance."

She had staggered away, a few paces from him, when he first threw her off, and now, with a heart-rending effort, she tried to smooth the misery out of her face and to smile at him in her normal, natural way. But the effort was a ghastly mockery. It was little wonder, seeing her there, so lamentably trying to smile into his eyes, that he cried out savagely: "That's not my Nance's smile. That's the smile of a cunning mask! You've hidden her away from me. Curse you all — you've hidden her away from me — and Baptiste, too! Where is my Baptiste — you staring white thing? Where is my Baptiste, you woman with a twisted mouth?"

He rushed fiercely towards her and seized her by
the throat. "Tell me what you've done with him," he
cried, shaking her to and fro, and tightening his grasp
upon her neck. "Tell me, you devil! Tell me, or I'll
kill you."

Nance's brain clouded and darkened. Her senses
grew confused and misty. "He's going to strangle
me," she thought, "and I don't care! This pain won't
last long, and it will be death from *his* hand."

All at once, however, in a sudden flash of blinding
clearness, she realized what this moment meant. If she
let him murder her, passively, unresistingly, what would
become of him when she was dead? Simultaneously
with this thought something seemed to rise up, strong
and clear, from the depths of her being, something powerful and fearless, ready to wrestle with fate to the
very end.

"He shan't kill me!" she thought. "I'll live to save
us both." Tearing frantically at his hands, she struggled backwards towards the open door, dragging him
with her. In his mad blood-lust he was horribly, murderously strong; but this new life-impulse, springing
from some supernatural level in the girl's being, proved
still stronger. With one tremendous wrench at his
wrists she flung him from her; flung him away with
such violence that he slipped and fell to the ground.

In a moment she had rushed through the doorway and
closed and locked the heavy door behind her. Even
at the very second she achieved this and staggered
faint and weak against the wall, what seemed to her
rapidly clouding senses a large concourse of noisy
people carrying flickering lights, swept about her. As
they came upon her she sank to the floor, her last im-

pression being that of the great dark eyes of Philippa
Renshaw illuminated by an emotion which was beyond
her power of deciphering, an emotion in which her
mind lost itself, as she tried to understand it, in a deep
impenetrable mist, that changed to absolute darkness
as she fainted away.

XXV

BALTAZAR STORK

THE morning of the twenty-ninth of October crept slowly and greyly through the windows of the sisters' room. Linda had done her best to forget her own trouble and to offer what she could of consolation and hope to Nance. It was nearly three o'clock before the unhappy girl found forgetfulness in sleep, and now with the first gleam of light she was awake again.

The worst she could have anticipated was what had happened. Adrian had been taken away — not recognizing any one — to that very Asylum at Mundham which they had glanced at together with such ominous forebodings. She herself — what else could she do? — had been forced to sign her name to the official document which, before midnight fell upon Oakguard, made legal his removal.

She had signed it — she shuddered now to think of her feelings at that moment — below the name of Brand, who as a magistrate was officially compelled to take the initiative in the repulsive business. Dr. Raughty and Mr. Traherne, who had both been summoned to the house, had signed that dreadful paper, too. Nance's first impression on regaining consciousness was that of the Doctor's form bending anxiously over her. She remembered how queer his face looked in the shadowy candle-light and how gently he had stroked the back of

her hand when she unclosed her eyes, and what relief
his expression had shown when she whispered his name.

It was the Doctor who had driven her home at last,
when the appalling business was over and the people
had come, with a motor car from Mundham, and carried Adrian away. She had learnt from him that
Brand's injuries were in no way serious and were likely
to leave no lasting hurt, beyond a deep scar on the forehead. His arms were bruised and injured, Fingal told
her, but neither of them was actually broken.

Hamish Traherne had gone with the Mundham people
to the Asylum and would spend the night there. He
had promised Nance to come and see her before noon
and tell her everything.

She gathered also from Fingal that Philippa, showing unusual promptitude and tact, had succeeded in
keeping Mrs. Renshaw away, both from the closed door
of the chapel and from the bedside of Brand, until the
latter had recovered consciousness.

Nance, as her mind went over and over every detail
of that hideous evening, could not help thanking God
that Adrian had at least been spared the tragic burden
of blood-guiltiness. As far as the law of the land was
concerned, he had only to recover his sanity and re-
gain his normal senses, to make his liberation easy and
natural. There had been no suggestion in the paper she had signed — and she had been especially
on the look-out for that — with regard to *criminal*
lunacy.

She sat up in bed and looked at her sister. Linda
was sleeping as peacefully as a child. The cold morning light gave her face a curious pallor. Her long
brown lashes lay motionless upon her cheeks, and from

her gently parted lips her breath came evenly and calmly.

Nance recalled the strange interview she had had with Brand before Adrian flung himself between them. It was strange! Do what she could, she could not feel towards that man anything but a deep unspeakable pity. Had he magnetized her — her too — she wondered — with that mysterious force in him, that force at once terrible and tender, which so many women had found fatal? No — no! That, of course, was ridiculous. That was unthinkable. Her heart was Adrian's and Adrian's alone. But why, then, was it that she found herself not only pardoning him what he had done but actually — in some inexplicable way — condoning it and understanding it? Was she, too, losing her wits? Was she, too,— under the influence of this disastrous place — forfeiting all sense of moral proportion?

The man had seduced her sister, and had refused — *that* remained quite clearly as the prevailing impression of that wild interview with him — definitely and obstinately to marry her, and yet, here was she, her sister's only protector in the world, softening in her heart towards him and thinking of him with a sort of sentimental pity! Truly the minds of mortal men and women contained mysteries past finding out!

She lay back once more upon her pillows and let the hours of the morning flow over her head like softly murmuring waves. There is often, especially in a country town, something soothing and refreshing beyond words in the opening of an autumn day. In winter the light does not arrive till the stir and noise and traffic of the streets has already, so to speak, established itself. In summer the earlier hours are so long and bright, that by the time the first movements of humanity begin, the day has already been ravished of its pristine freshness and grown jaded and garish. Early mornings in spring have a magical and thrilling charm, but the very exuberance of joyous life then, the clamorous excitement of birds and animals, the feverish uneasiness and restlessness of human children, make it difficult to lie awake in perfect receptivity, drinking in every sound and letting oneself be rocked and lulled upon a languid tide of half-conscious dreaming.

Upon such a tide, however, Nance now lay, in spite of everything, and let the vague murmurs and the familiar sounds flow over her, in soft reiteration. That she should be able to lie like this, listening to the rattle of the milkman's cans and the crying of the sea-gulls and the voices of newly-awakened bargemen higher up the river, and the lowing of cattle from the marshes and the chirping of sparrows on the roof, when all the while her lover was moaning, in horrible unconsciousness, within those unspeakable walls, was itself, as she contemplated it in cold blood, an atrocious trick of all-subverting Nature!

She looked at the misty sunlight, soft and mellow, which now began to invade the room, and she marvelled at herself in a sort of bewildered shame that she should not, at this crisis in her life, *be able to feel more.* Was it that her experiences of the day before had so harrowed her soul that she had no power of reaction left? Or was it — and upon this thought she tried to fix her mind as the true explanation — that the great underlying restorative forces were already dimly but powerfully exerting themselves on behalf of Adrian, and on behalf of her sister and herself?

She articulated the words " restorative forces " in the depths of her mind, giving her thought this palpable definition ; but as she did so she was only too conscious of the presence of a mocking spirit there, whose finger pointed derisively at the words as soon as she had imaged them. Restorative forces? Were there such things in the world at all? Was it not much more likely that what she felt at this moment was nothing more than that sort of desperate calm which comes, with a kind of numbing inertia, upon human beings, when they have been wrought upon to the limit of their endurance? Was it not indeed rather a sign of her helplessness, a sign that she had come now to the end of all her powers, and could do no more than just stretch out her arms upon the tide and lie back upon the dark waters, letting them bear her whither they pleased — was it not rather a token of this, than of any inkling of possible help at hand?

It was at that moment that amid the various sounds which reached her ear, there came the clear joyous whistling of some boy apprentice, occupied in removing the shutters from one of the shop-windows in the street. The boy was whistling, casually and clumsily enough, but still with a beautiful intonation, certain familiar strophes from the Marseillaise. The great revolutionary tune echoed clear and strong over the drowsy cobble-stones, between the narrow patient walls, and down away towards the quiet harbour.

It was incredible the effect which this simple accident had upon the mind of the girl. In one moment she had flung to the winds all thought of submission to destiny — all idea of "lying back" upon fate. No longer did she dream vaguely and helplessly of "restorative forces," somewhere, somehow, remotely active in her favour. The old, brave, defiant, youthful spirit in her, the spirit of her father's child, leapt up, strong and vigorous in her heart and brain. No — no! Never would she yield. Never would she submit. "*Allons, enfants!*" She would fight to the end.

And then, all in a moment, she remembered Baptiste. Of course! That was the thing to be done. Fool that she was not to have thought of it before! She must send a cabled message to Adrian's son. It was towards Baptiste that his spirit was continually turning. It must be Baptiste who should restore him to health!

It was not much after six o'clock when that boy's whistling reached her, but between then and the first moment of the opening of the post office, her mind was in a whirl of hopeful thoughts.

As she stood waiting at the little stuccoed entrance for the door to open, and watched with an almost humorous interest the nervous expectancy of the most drooping, pallid, unhealthy and unfortunately complexioned youth she had ever set eyes upon, she felt full of strength and courage. Adrian had been ill before and had recovered. He would recover now! She herself would bring him the news of Baptiste's coming. The mere news of it would help him.

There was a little garden just visible through some iron railings by the side of the post office and above these railings and drooping towards them so that it almost rested upon their spikes, was a fading sunflower. The flower was so wilted and tattered that Nance had no scruple about stretching her hand to-

wards it and trying to pluck it from its stem. She did
this half-mechanically, full of her new hope, as a child
on its way to catch minnows in a freshly discovered
brook might pluck a handful of clover.

The sickly-looking youth — Nance couldn't help
longing to cover his face with zinc-ointment; why did
one *always* meet people with dreadful complexions in
country post offices? — observing her efforts, extended
his hand also, and together they pulled at the radiant
derelict, until they broke it off. When she held it in
her hands, Nance felt a little ashamed and sorry, for
the tall mutilated stem stood up so stark and raw with
drops of white frothy sap oozing from it. She could
not help remembering how it was one of Adrian's innocent superstitions to be reluctant to pick flowers.
However, it was done now. But what should she do
with this great globular orb of brown seeds with the
scanty yellow petals, like weary taper-flames, surrounding its circumference?

The lanky youth looked at her and smiled shyly.
She met his eyes, and observing his embarrassment,
obviously tinged with unconcealed admiration, she
smiled back at him, a sweet friendly smile of humorous
camaraderie.

Apparently this was the first time in his life that
a really beautiful girl had ever smiled at him, for he
blushed a deep purple-red all over his face.

"I think, ma'am," he stammered nervously, "I know
who you are. I've seen you with Mr. Stork."

Nance's face clouded. She regarded it as a bad
omen to hear this name mentioned. Her old mysterious
terror of her friend's friend rose powerfully upon her.
In some vague obscure way, she felt conscious of his

intimate association with all the forces in the world most inimical to her and to her future.

Observing her look and a little bewildered by it, the youth rambled helplessly on. "Mr. Stork has been a very good friend to me," he murmured. "He got me my job at Mr. Walpole's — Walpole the saddler, Miss. I should have had to have left mother if it hadn't been for him."

With a sudden impulse of girlish mischief, Nance placed in the boy's hand the great faded flower she was holding. "Put it into your button-hole," she said.

At that moment the door opened, and forgetting the boy, the sunflower, and the ambiguous Mr. Stork, she hurried into the building, full of her daring enterprise.

Her action seemed to remove from the youth's thoughts whatever motive he may have had in waiting for the opening of the office. Perhaps this goddess-like apparition rendered commonplace and absurd some quaint pictorial communication, smudgy and blotched, which now remained unstamped in his coat-pocket. At any rate he slunk away, with long, furtive, slouching strides, carrying the flower she had given him as reverently as a religious-minded acolyte might carry a sacred vessel.

Meanwhile, Nance sent off her message, laying down on the counter her half-sovereign with a docility that thrilled the young woman who officiated there with awe and importance.

"Baptiste Sorio, fifteen West Eleventh Street, New York City," the message ran, "come at once; your father in serious mental trouble"; and she signed it with her own name and address, and paid five shillings more to secure an immediate reply.

Then, leaving the post office, she returned slowly and thoughtfully to her lodging. The usual stir and movement of the beginning of the day's work filled the little street when she approached her room. Nance could not help thinking how strange and curious it was that the stream of life should thus go rolling forward with its eternal repetition of little familiar usages, in spite of the desperation of this or the other cruel personal drama.

Adrian might be moaning for his son in that Mundham house. Linda might be fearing and dreading the results of her obsession. Philippa might be tossing forth her elfish laugh upon the wind among the oak-trees. She herself might be " lying back upon fate " or struggling to wrestle with fate. What mattered any of these things to the people who sold and bought and laughed and quarrelled and laboured and made love, as the powers set in motion a new day, and the brisk puppets of a human town began their diurnal dance?

It was not till late in the afternoon that Nance received an answer to her message. She was alone when she opened it, Linda having gone.as usual, under her earnest persuasion, to practise in the church. The message was brief and satisfactory: " Sailing to-morrow *Altrunia* Liverpool six days boat Baptiste."

So he would really be here — here in Rodmoor — in seven or eight days. This was news for Adrian, if he had the power left to understand anything! She folded the paper carefully and placed it in her purse.

Mr. Traherne had come to her about noon, bringing news that, on the whole, was entirely reassuring. It seemed that Sorio had done little else than sleep since his first entrance into the place; and both the doctors there regarded this as the best possible sign.

Hamish explained to her that there were three degrees of insanity — mania, melancholia, and dementia — and, from what he could learn from his conversations with the doctors, this heavy access of drowsiness ruled out of Adrian's case the worst symptom of both these latter possibilities. What they called " mania," he explained to her, was something quite curable and with nearly all the chances in favour of recovery. It was really — he told her he had gathered from them — " only a question of time."

The priest had been careful to inquire as to the possibility of Nance being allowed to visit her betrothed; but neither of the doctors seemed to regard this, at any rate for the present, as at all desirable. He cordially congratulated her, however, on having sent for Sorio's son. " Whatever happens," he said, " it's right and natural that *he* should be here with you."

While Nance was thus engaged in " wrestling with fate," a very different mental drama was being enacted behind the closed windows of Baltazar's cottage.

Mr. Stork had not been permitted even to fall asleep before rumours reached him that some startling event had occurred at Oakguard. Long before midnight, by the simple method of dropping in at the bar of the Admiral's Head, he had picked up sufficient information to make him decide against seeing any one that night. They had taken Sorio away, and Mr. Renshaw had escaped from a prolonged struggle with the demented man with the penalty of only a few bruises. Thus, with various imaginative interpolations which he

discounted as soon as he heard them, Baltazar got from
the gossips of the tavern a fair account of what had
occurred.

There was, indeed, so much excitement in Rodmoor
over the event that, for the first time in the memory of
the oldest inhabitants, the Admiral's Head remained
open two whole hours after legal closing time. This
was in part explained by the fact that the two repre-
sentatives of the law in the little town had been summoned to Oakguard to be ready for any emergency.

It was now about four o'clock in the afternoon.
Baltazar had found himself with little appetite for
either breakfast or lunch, and at this moment, as he
sat staring at a fireplace full of nothing but burnt out
ashes, his eyes had such dark lines below them that one
might have assumed that sleep as well as food had lost
its savour for him in the last twelve hours. By his
side on a little table stood an untasted glass of brandy,
and at his feet in the fender lay innumerable, but in
many cases only half-smoked, cigarettes.

The impression which was now upon him was that of
being one of two human creatures left alive, those two
alone, after some world-destroying plague. He had
the feeling that he had only to go out into the street
to come upon endless dead bodies strewn about, in fantastic and horrible attitudes of death, and in various
stages of dissolution. It was his Adriano who alone
was left alive. But he had done something to him —
so that he could only hear his voice without being able
to reach him.

"I must end this," he said aloud; and then again,
as if addressing another person, "We must put an end
to this, mustn't we, Tassar?"

He rose to his feet and surveyed himself in one of his numerous beautifully framed mirrors. He passed his slender fingers through his fair curls and peered into his own eyes, opening the lids wide and wrinkling his forehead. He smiled at himself then — a long strange wanton smile — and turned away, shrugging his shoulders.

Then he moved straight up to the picture of the Venetian Secretary and snapped his fingers at it. "You wait, you smirking 'imp of fame'; you wait a little! We'll show you that you're not so deep or so subtle after all. You wait, Flambard, my boy, you wait a while; and we'll show you plots and counterplots!"

Then without a word he went upstairs to his bathroom. "By Jove!" he muttered to himself, "I begin to think Fingal's right. The only place in this Christian world where one can possess one's soul in peace is a tiled bathroom — only the tiles must be perfectly white," he added, after a pause.

He made an elaborate and careful toilet, brushing his hair with exhaustive assiduity, and perfuming his hands and face. He dressed himself in spotlessly clean linen and put on a suit that had never been worn before. Even the shoes which he chose were elegant and new. He took several minutes deciding what tie to wear and finally selected one of a pale mauve colour. Then, with one final long and wistful glance at himself, he kissed the tips of his fingers at his own image, and stepped lightly down the stairs.

He paused for a moment in the little hallway to select a cane from the stick rack. He took an ebony one at last, with an engraved silver knob bearing his own initials. There was something ghastly about the deliberation with which he did all this, but it was ghastliness wasted upon polished furniture and decrepit flies — unless every human house conceals invisible watchers. He hesitated a little between a Panama hat and one of some light-coloured cloth material, but finally selected the former, toying carefully with its flexible rim before placing it upon his head, and even when it was there giving it some final touches.

The absolute loneliness of the little house, broken only by an occasional voice from the tavern door, became, during his last moments there, a sort of passive accomplice to some nameless ritual. At length he opened the door and let himself out.

He walked deliberately and thoughtfully towards the park gates, and, passing in, made his way up the leaf-strewn avenue. Arrived at the house, he nodded in a friendly manner at the servant who opened the door, and asked to be taken to Mrs. Renshaw's room. The man obeyed him respectfully, and went before him up the staircase and down the long echoing passage.

He found Mrs. Renshaw sewing at the half-open window. She put down her work when he entered and greeted him with one of those *illumined* smiles of hers, which Fingal Raughty was accustomed to say made him believe in the supernatural.

" Thank you for coming to see me," she said, as he seated himself at her side, spreading around him an atmosphere of delicate odours. " Thank you, Baltazar, so much for coming."

" Why do you always say that, Aunt Helen? " he

murmured, almost crossly. It was one of the little long-established conventions between them that he should address his father's wife in this way.

There came once more that indescribable spiritual light into her faded eyes. "Well," she said gaily, "*isn't* it kind of a young man, who has so many interests, to give up his time to an old woman like me?"

"Nonsense, nonsense, Aunt Helen!" he cried, with a rich caressing intonation, laying one of his slender hands tenderly upon hers. "It makes me absolutely angry with you when you talk like that!"

"But isn't it true, Tassar?" she answered. "Isn't this world meant for the young and happy?"

"As if I cared what the world was *meant* for!" he exclaimed. "It's meant for nothing at all, I fancy. And the sooner it reaches what it was meant for and collapses altogether, the better for all of us!"

A look of distress that was painful to witness came into Mrs. Renshaw's face. Her fingers tightened upon his hand and she leant forward towards him. "Tassar, Tassar, dear!" she said very gravely, "when you talk like that you make me feel as if I were absolutely alone in the world."

"What do you mean, Aunt Helen?" murmured the young man in a low voice.

"You make me feel as if it were wrong of me to love you so much," she went on, bending her head and looking down at his feet.

As he saw her now, with the fading afternoon light falling on her parted hair, still wavy and beautiful even in its grey shadows, and on her broad pale forehead, he realized once more what he alone perhaps, of all who ever had known her realized, the unusual and almost terrifying power of her personality. She forced him to think of some of the profound portraits of the sixteenth century, revealing with an insight and a passion, long since lost to art, the tragic possibilities of human souls.

He laughed gently. "Dear, dear Aunt Helen!" he cried, "forget my foolishness. I was only jesting. I don't give a fig for any of my opinions on these things. To the deuce with them all, dear! To free you from one single moment of annoyance, I'd believe every word in the Church Catechism from 'What is your name?' down to 'without doubt are lost eternally'!"

She looked up at this, and made a most heart-breaking effort not to smile. Her abnormally sensitive mouth — the mouth, as Baltazar always maintained, of a great tragic actress — quivered at the corners.

"If *I* had taught you your catechism," she said, "you would remember it better than that!"

Baltazar's eyes softened as he watched her, and a strange look, full of a pity that was as impersonal as the sea itself, rose to their surface. He lifted her hand to his lips.

"Don't do that! You mustn't do that!" she murmured, and then with another flicker. of a smile, "you must keep those pretty manners, Tassar, for all your admiring young women!"

"Confound my young women!" cried the young man. "You're far more beautiful, Aunt Helen, than all of them put together!"

"You make me think of that passage in 'Hamlet,'" she rejoined, leaning back in her chair and resuming her work. "How does it go? 'Man delights me not nor woman either — though by your smiling you seem to say so!'"

"Aunt Helen!" he cried earnestly, "I have something important to say to you. I want you to understand this. It's sweet of you not to speak of Adriano's illness. Any one but you would have condoled with me most horribly already!"

She raised her eyes from her sewing. "We must pray for him," she said. "I have been praying for him all day — and all last night, too," she added with a faint smile. "I let Philippa think I didn't know what had happened. But I knew." She shuddered a little. "I knew. I heard him in the 'workshop.'"

"What I wanted to say, Aunt Helen," he went on, "was this. I want you to remember — whatever happens to either of us — that I love you more than any one in the world. Yes — yes," he continued, not allowing her to interrupt, "better even than Adriano!"

A look resembling the effect of some actual physical pain came into her face. "You mustn't say that, my dear," she murmured. "You must keep your love for your wife when you marry. I don't like to hear you say things like that — to an old woman." She hesitated a moment. "It sounds like flattery, Tassar," she added.

"But it's true, Aunt Helen!" he repeated with almost passionate emphasis. "You're by far the most beautiful and by far the most interesting woman I've ever met."

Mrs. Renshaw drew her hand across her face. Then she laughed gaily like a young girl. "What would Philippa say," she said, "if she heard you say that?"

Baltazar's face clouded. He looked at her long and closely.

" Philippa is interesting and deep," he said with a grave emphasis, " but she doesn't understand me. *You* understand me, though you think it right to hide your knowledge even from yourself."

Mrs. Renshaw's face changed in a moment. It became haggard and obstinate. " We mustn't talk any more about understanding and about love," she said. " God's will is that we should all of us only completely love and understand the person He leads us, in His wisdom, to marry."

Baltazar burst into a fit of heathen laughter. " I thought you were going to end quite differently, Aunt Helen," he said. " I thought the only person we were to love was going to be God. But it seems that it is man — or woman," he added bitterly.

Mrs. Renshaw bent low over her work and the shadow grew still deeper upon her face. Seeing that he had really hurt her, Baltazar changed his tone.

" Dear Aunt Helen!" he whispered gently, " how many happy hours, how many, how many! — have we spent together reading in this room!"

She looked up quickly at this, with the old bright look. " Yes, it's been a happy thing for me, Tassar, having you so near us. Do you remember how, last winter, we got through the whole of Sir Walter Scott? There's no one nowadays like *him* — is there? Though Philippa tells me that Mr. Hardy is a great writer."

" Mr. Hardy!" exclaimed her interlocutor whimsically. " I believe you *would* have come to him at last — perhaps you *will*, dear, some day. Let's hope so! But I'm afraid I shall not be here then."

"Don't talk like that, Tassar," she said without looking up from her work. "It will not be *you* who will leave *me*."

There was a pause between them then, and Baltazar's eyes wandered out into the hushed misty garden.

"Mr. Hardy does not believe in God," he remarked.

"Tassar!" she cried reproachfully. "You know what you promised just now. You mustn't tease me. No one deep down in his heart disbelieves in God. How can we? He makes His power felt among us every day."

There was another long silence, broken only by the melancholy cawing of the rooks, beginning to gather in their autumnal roosting-places.

Presently Mrs. Renshaw looked up. "Do you remember," she said very solemnly, "how you promised me one day never again to let Brand or Philippa speak disrespectfully of our English hymn-book? You said you thought the genius of some of our best-known poets was more expressed in their hymns than in their poetry. I have often thought of that."

A very curious expression came into Baltazar's face. He suddenly leaned forward. "Aunt Helen," he said, "this illness of Adrian's makes me feel, as you often say, how little security there is for any of our lives. I wish you'd say to me those peculiarly sad lines — you know the one I mean? — the one I used to make you smile over, when I was in a bad mood, by saying it always made me think of old women in a work-house! You know the one, don't you?"

The whole complicated subtlety of Mrs. Renshaw's character showed itself in her face now. She smiled almost playfully but at the same moment a supernat-

ural light came in her eyes. "I know," she said, and
without a moment's hesitation or the least touch of embarrassment, she began to sing, in a low plaintive melodious voice, the following well-known stanza. As she
sang she beat time with her hand; and there came over
her hearer the obscure vision of some old, wild, primordial religion, as different from paganism as it was
different from Christianity, of which his mysterious
friend was the votary and priestess. The words drifted
away through the open window into the mist and the
falling leaves.

" Rest comes at length, though life be long and weary,
    The day must dawn and darksome night be past;
Faith's journey ends in welcome to the weary,
    And heaven, the heart's true home, will come at last."

When it was finished there was a strange silence in
the room, and Baltazar rose to his feet. His face was
pale. He moved to her side and, for the first and last
time in their curious relations, he kissed her — a long
kiss upon the forehead.

With a heightened colour in her cheeks and a nervous deprecatory smile on her lips, she went with him to
the door. "Listen, dear," she said, as she took his
hand, "I want you to think of that poem of Cowper's
written when he was most despairing — the one that
begins 'God moves in a mysterious way.' I want you
to remember that though what he lays upon us seems
crushing, there is always something behind it — infinite
mercy behind infinite mystery."

Baltazar looked her straight in the face. "I wonder," he said, "whether it is I or you who is the most
unhappy person in Rodmoor!"

She let his hand fall. "What we suffer," she said, "seems to me like the weight of some great iron engine with jagged raw edges — like a battering-ram beating us against a dark mountain. It swings backwards and forwards, and it drives us on and on and on."

"And yet you believe in God," he whispered.

She smiled faintly. "Am I not alive and speaking to you, dear? If behind it all there wasn't His will, who could endure to live another moment?"

They looked into one another's face in silence. He made an attempt to say something else to her but his tongue refused to utter what his heart suggested.

"Good-bye, Aunt Helen," he said.

"Good night, Tassar," she answered, "and thank you for coming to see me."

He left the house without meeting any one else and walked with a deliberate and rapid step towards the river. The twilight had already fallen, and a white mist coming up over the sand-dunes was slowly invading the marshes. The tide had just turned and the full-brimmed current of the river's out-flowing poured swift and strong between the high mud-banks.

The Loon was at that moment emphasizing and asserting its identity with an exultant joy. It seemed almost to *purr*, with a kind of feline satisfaction, as its dark volume of brackish water rushed forward towards the sea. Whatever object it touched in its swift passage, it drew from it some sort of half-human sound — some whisper or murmur or protest of querulous complaining.

The reeds flapped; the pollard-roots creaked; the mud-promontories moaned; and all the while, with gurglings and suckings and lappings and deep-drawn, inward, self-complacent laughter, the sliding body of the slippery waters swept forward under its veil of mist.

On that night, of all nights, the Loon seemed to have reached that kind of emphasis of personality which things are permitted to attain — animate as well as inanimate — when their functional activity is at its highest and fullest.

And on that night, carefully divesting himself of his elegant clothes, and laying his hat and stick on the ground beside them, Baltazar Stork, without haste or violence, and with his brain supernaturally clear, drowned himself in the Loon.

XXVI

NOVEMBER MIST

BALTAZAR'S death, under circumstances which could leave no doubt as to the unhappy man's intention to destroy himself, coming, as it did, immediately after his friend's removal to the Asylum, stirred the scandalous gossip of Rodmoor to its very dregs.

The suicide's body — and even the indurated hearts of the weather-battered bargemen who discovered it, washed down by the tide as far as the New Bridge, were touched by its beauty — was buried, after a little private extemporary service, just at the debatable margin where the consecrated churchyard lost itself in the priest's flower-beds. Himself the only person in the place exactly aware of the precise limits of the sacred enclosure — the enclosure which had never been enclosed — Mr. Traherne was able to follow the most rigid stipulations of his ecclesiastical conscience without either hurting the feelings of the living or offering any insult to the dead. When it actually came to the point he was, as it turned out, able to remove from his own over-scrupulous heart the least occasion for future remorse.

The Rodmoor sexton — the usual digger of graves — happened to be at that particular time in the throes, or rather in the after-effects, of one of his periodic outbursts of inebriation. So it happened that the curate-in-charge had with his own hands to dig the grave of the one among all his parishioners who had remained most distant to him and had permitted him the least familiarity.

Mr. Traherne remained awake in his study half the night, turning over the pages of ancient scholastic authorities and comparing one doctrinal opinion with another on the question of the burial of suicides.

In the end, what he did, with a whimsical prayer to Providence to forgive him, was to *begin* digging the hole just outside the consecrated area, but by means of a slight northward *excavation*, when he got a few feet down, to arrange the completed orifice in such a way that, while Baltazar's body remained in common earth, his head was lodged safe and secure, under soil blessed by Holy Church.

One of the most pious and authoritative of the early divines, Mr. Traherne found out, maintained, as no fantastic or heretical speculation but as a reasonable and reverent conclusion, the idea that the surviving portion of a man — his " psyche " or living soul — had, as its mortal tabernacle, the posterior lobes of the human skull, and that it was from the *head* rather than from the *body* that the shadowy companion of our earthly days — that " animula blandula " of the heathen emperor — melted by degrees into the surrounding air and passed to " its own place."

The Renshaws themselves showed, none of them, the slightest wish to interfere with his arrangements, nor did Hamish Traherne ever succeed in learning whether the hollow-eyed lady of Oakguard knew or did not know that the clay mound over which every evening without fail, after the day of the unceremonious interment,

she knelt in silent prayer, was outside the circle of
the *covenanted* mercies of the Power to which she
prayed.

The "last will and testament" of the deceased —
written with the most exquisite care — was of so
strange a character, taking indeed the shape of something like a defiant and shameless "confession," that
Brand and Dr. Raughty, who were the appointed exec-
utors, hurriedly hid it out of sight. Everything Mr.
Stork possessed was left to Mrs. Renshaw, except the
picture of Eugenio Flambard. This, by a fantastic
codicil, which was so extraordinary that when Brand
and Dr. Raughty read it they could do nothing but
stare at one another in silent amazement, was be-
queathed, at the end of an astonishing panegyric, "to
our unknown Hippolytus, Mr. Baptiste Sorio, of New
York City."

Baltazar had been buried on the first of November,
and as the following days of this dark month dragged
by, under unbroken mists and rain, Nance lived from
hour to hour in a state of trembling expectancy.
Would Baptiste's ship bring him safely to England?
Would he, when he came, and discovered what her
relations with his father were, be kind to her and sympathetic, or angry and hurt? She could not tell. She
could make no guess. She did not even know whether
Adrian had really done what he promised and written
to his son about her at all.

The figure of the boy — on his way across the At-
lantic — took a fantastic hold upon her disturbed imagination. As day followed day and the time of his
arrival drew near, she found it hard to concentrate her
mind even sufficiently to fulfil her easy labours with the

little dressmaker. Miss Pontifex gently remonstrated with her.

" I know you're in trouble, Miss Herrick, and have a great deal on your mind, but it does no good worrying, and the girls get restless — you see how it is ! — when you can't give them your full attention."

Thus rebuked, Nance would smile submissively and turn her eyes away from the misty window.

But every night before she slept, she would see through her closed eyelids that longed-for boy, standing — that was how she always conceived him — at the bows of the ship, standing tall and fair like a young god; borne forwards over the starlit ocean to bring help to them all.

In her dreams, night after night, the boy came to her, and she found him then of an unearthly beauty and endowed with a mysterious supernatural power. In her dreams, the wild impossible hope, that somehow, somewhere, he would be the one to save Linda from the ruin of her youthful life, took to itself sweet immediate fulfilment.

Every little event that happened to her during those days of tension assumed the shape of something pregnant and symbolic. Her mind made auguries of the movements of the clouds, and found significant omens, propitious or menacing, from every turn of the wind and every coming and going of the rain. The smallest and simplest encounter took upon itself at that time a curious and mystic value.

In after days, she remembered with sad and woeful clearness how persons and things impressed her then, as, in their chance-brought groupings and gestures, they lent themselves to her strained expectant mood.

For instance, she never could forget the way she waited, on the night of the third of November, along with Linda and Dr. Raughty, for the arrival of the last train from Mundham, bringing Mr. Traherne back from a visit to the Asylum with news of Adrian.

The news the priest brought was unexpectedly favourable. Adrian, it seemed, had taken a rapid turn for the better, and the doctors declared that any day now it might become possible for Nance to see him.

As they stood talking on the almost deserted platform, Nance's mind visualized with passionate intensity the moment when she herself would take Baptiste to see his father and perhaps together — why not? — bring him back in triumph to Rodmoor.

Her happy reverie on this particular occasion was interrupted by a fantastic incident, which, trifling enough in itself, left a queer and significant impression behind it. This was nothing less than the sudden escape from Mr. Traherne's pocket of his beloved Ricoletto.

In the excitement of their pleasure over the news brought by the priest, the rat took the opportunity of slipping from the recesses of his master's coat; and jumping down on the platform, he leapt, quick as a flash, upon the railway track below. Mr. Traherne, with a cry of consternation, scrambled down after him, and throwing aside his ulster which impeded his progress, began desperately pursuing him. The engine of the train by which the clergyman had arrived was now resting motionless, separate from the line of carriages, deserted by its drivers. Straight beneath the wheels of this inert monster darted the escaped rat. The agitated priest, with husky perturbed cries, ran backwards

and forwards along the side of the engine, every now
and then stooping down and frantically endeavouring
to peer beneath it.

It was so queer a sight to see this ungainly figure,
dressed as always in his ecclesiastical cassock, rushing
madly round the dark form of the engine and at intervals falling on his knees beside it, that Linda could
not restrain an almost hysterical fit of laughter.

Dr. Raughty looked whimsically at Nance.

" He might be a priest of Science, worshipping the
god of machines," he remarked, assuming as he spoke
a sitting posture, the better to slide down, himself, from
the platform to the track.

The station-master now approached, anxious to close
his office for the night and go home. The porter, a
peculiarly unsympathetic figure, took not the least notice of the event, but coolly proceeded to extinguish the
lights, one by one.

The ostler from the Admiral's Head, who had come
to meet some expected visitor who never arrived, leaned
forward with drowsy interest from his seat on his cab
and surveyed the scene with grim detachment, promising himself that on the following night at his familiar
bar table, he would be the center of public interest as
he satisfied legitimate local curiosity with regard to
this unwonted occurrence.

Nance could not help smiling as she saw the excellent Fingal, his long overcoat flapping about his legs,
bending forward between the buffers of the engine and
peering into its metallic belly. She noticed that he
was tapping with his knuckles on the polished breast-
plate of the monster and uttering a clucking noise with
his tongue, as if calling for a recalcitrant chicken.

It was not long before Mr. Traherne, growing desperate as the oblivious porter approached the last of the station lamps, fell flat on his face and proceeded to shove himself clean under the engine. The vision of his long retreating form, wrapped in his cassock, thus worming himself slowly out of sight, drew from Nance a burst of laughter, and as for Linda, she clapped her hands together like a child.

He soon reappeared, to the relief of all of them, with his recaptured pet in his hand, and scrambled back upon the platform, just as the last of the lamps went out, leaving the place in utter darkness.

Nance, her laughter gone then, had a queer sensation as they moved away, that the ludicrous scene she had just witnessed was part of some fantastic unreal dream, and that she herself, with the whole tragedy of her life, was just such a dream, the dream perhaps of some dark driverless cosmic engine — of some remote Great Eastern Railway of the Universe!

The morning of the fourth of November dawned far more auspiciously than any day which Rodmoor had known for many weeks. It was one of those patient, hushed, indescribable days — calm and tender and full of whispered intimations of hidden reassurance — which rarely reach us in any country but England or in any district but East Anglia. The great powers of sea and air and sky seemed to draw close to one another and close to humanity; as if with some large and gracious gesture of benediction they would fain lay to rest, under a solemn and elemental requiem, the body of the dead season's life.

Nance escaped before noon from Miss Pontitfex's workroom. She and Linda had been invited by Dr.

Raughty to lunch with him and Hamish at the pastry-
cook's in the High Street. It was to be a sort of modest celebration, this little feast, to do honour to the
good news which Mr. Traherne had brought them the
night before and which was corroborated by a letter
to Nance herself from the head doctor, with regard to
Adrian's astonishing improvement.

Nance felt possessed by a deep and tumultuous excitement. Baptiste surely must be near England now!
Any day — almost any hour — she might hear of his
arrival. She strolled out across the Loon to meet
Linda, who had gone that morning to practise on the
organ for the following Sunday's services.

As she crossed the marsh-land between the bridge
and the church, she encountered Mrs. Renshaw returning from a visit to Baltazar's grave. The mistress of
Oakguard stopped for a little while to speak to her,
and to express, in her own way, her sympathy over
Adrian's recovery. She did this, however, in a manner so characteristic of her that it depressed rather
than encouraged the girl. Her attitude seemed to
imply that it was better, wiser, more reverent, not to
cherish any buoyant hopes, but to assume that the worst
that could come to us from the hands of God was what
ought to be expected and awaited in humble submissiveness.

She seemed in some strange way to *resent* any lifting of the heavy folds of the pall of fate and with a kind
of obstinate weariness, to lean to the darker and more
sombre aspect of every possibility.

She carried in her hands a bunch of faded flowers
brought from the grave she had visited and which she
seemed reluctant to throw away, and Nance never for-

got the appearance of her black-gowned drooping figure and white face, as she stood there, by the edge of the misty, sun-illumined fens, holding those dead stalks and withered leaves.

As they parted, Nance whispered hesitatingly some little word about Baltazar. She half expected her to answer with tears, but in place of that, her eyes seemed to shine with a weird exultant joy.

"When you're as old as I am, dear," she said, "and have seen life as I have seen it, you will not be sad to lose what you love best. The better we love them, the happier we must be when they are set free from the evil of the world."

She looked down on the ground, and when she raised her head, her eyes had an unearthly light in them. "I am closer to him now," she said, "closer than ever before. And it will not be long before I go to join him."

She moved slowly away, dragging her limbs heavily.

Nance, as she went on, kept seeing again and again before her that weird unearthly look. It left the impression on her mind that Mrs. Renshaw had actually secured some strange and unnatural link with the dead which made her cold and detached in her attitude towards the living.

Perhaps it had been all the while like this, the girl thought. Perhaps it was just this habitual intercourse with the Invisible which rendered her so entirely a votary of moonlight and of shadows, and so unsympathetic towards the sunshine and towards all genial normal expressions of natural humanity.

Nance had the sensation — when at last, with Linda at her side, she returned dreamily to the village — of having encountered some creature from a world differ-

ent from ours, a world of grey vapours and shadowy
margins, a world where the wraiths of the unborn meet
the ghosts of the dead, a world where the "might-have-
been" and the "never-to-be-again" weep together by
the shores of Lethe.

The little party which assembled presently round a
table in the bow-window of the Rodmoor confectioner's
proved a cheerful and happy one. The day was Saturday, so that the street was full of a quiet stir of people
preparing to leave their shops and begin the weekly
holiday. There was a vague feeling of delicate sadness, dreamy yet not unhappy, in the air, as though the
year itself were pausing for a moment in its onward
march towards the frosts of winter and gathering for
the last time all its children, all its fading leaves and
piled-up fruits and drooping flowers, into a hushed maternal embrace, an embrace of silent and everlasting
farewell.

The sun shone gently and tenderly from a sky of a
faint, sad, far-off blue — the sort of blue which, in the
earlier and more reserved of Florentine painters, may
be seen in the robes of Our Lady caught up to heaven
out of a grave of lilies.

The sea was calm and motionless, its hardly stirring
waves clearer and more translucent in their green
depths than when blown upon by impatient winds or
touched by shameless and glaring light.

A soft opalescent haze lay upon the houses, turning their gables, their chimneys, their porches, and
their roofs, into a pearl-dim mystery of vague illusive
forms ; forms that might have arisen out of the "perilous sea" itself, on some "beachéd margent" woven of
the stuff of dreams.

The queer old-fashioned ornaments of the room where the friends ate their meal took to themselves, as Nance in her dreamy emotion drew them into the circle of her thoughts, a singular and symbolic power. They seemed suggestive, these quaint things, of all that world of little casually accumulated mementoes and memories with which our troubled and turbulent humanity strews its path and fills the places of its passionate sojourning. Mother-of-pearl shells, faded antimacassars, china dogs, fruit under glass-cases, old faded photographs of long-since dead people, illuminated texts embroidered in bright wool, tarnished christening mugs of children that were now old women, portraits of celebrities from days when Victoria herself was in her cradle, all the sweet impossible bric-a-brac of a tea-parlour in a village shop surrounded them as they sat there, and thrilled at least two of their hearts — for Linda's mood was as receptive and as sensitive as Nance's — with an indescribable sense of the pathos of human life.

It was of " life "— in general terms — that Dr. Raughty was speaking, as the two young girls gave themselves up to the influence of the hour and played lightly with their food.

" It's all nonsense," the doctor cried, " this confounded perpetual pessimism! Why can't these people read Rabelais and Montaigne, and drink noble wine out of great casks? Why can't they choose from among the company of their friends gay and honest wenches and sport with them under pleasant trees? Why can't they get married to comfortable and comely girls and regale themselves in cool and well-appointed kitchens? "

He helped himself as he spoke to another slice of salmon and sprinkled salt upon a plateful of tomatoes and lettuce.

" Whose pessimism are you talking about, Fingal? " inquired Nance, playing up to his humour.

" Don't get it only for me," Mr. Traherne cried, addressing the demure and freckled damsel who waited on them. " I'm asking for a glass of ale, Doctor. They can send out for it. But I don't want it un- less —"

The Doctor's eyes shone across the table at him like soft lamps of sound antique wisdom. " Burton's," he exclaimed emphatically. " None of friend Renshaw's stuff! Burton's! And let it be that old dark ma- hogany-coloured liquor we drank once under the elm- trees at Ashbourne."

The waitress regarded him with a coquettish smile. She laboured under the perpetual illusion that every word the Doctor uttered was some elaborate and recon- dite gallantry directed towards herself.

The conversation ran on in lively spasmodic way- wardness. It was not long before the ale appeared, of the very body and colour suggested by the Doctor's memories. Nance refused to touch it.

" Have some ginger-pop, instead, then," murmured Fingal, pouring the brown ale into a china jug decor- ated with painted pansies. " Linda would like some of that, I know."

The priest held out his glass in the direction of the jug.

" A thousand deep-sea devils — pardon me, Nance, dear! — carry off these pessimists," went on the Doc- tor, filling up the clergyman's glass and his own with ritualistic solemnity while the little maid, the victim of an irrepressible laughing-fit, retired to fetch ginger-beer. "Let us remember how the great Voltaire served God and defended all honest people. Here's to Voltaire's memory and a fig for these neurotic scribblers who haven't the gall to put out their tongues!" He raised his glass to his lips, his eyes shining with humorous enjoyment.

"What scribblers are you talking about?" inquired Nance, peeling a golden apple and glancing at the misty roofs through the window at her side.

"All of these twopenny-halfpenny moderns," cried the Doctor, "who haven't the gall in their stomachs to take the world by the scruff of its neck and lash out. A fig for them! Our poor dear Adrian, when he gets cured, will write something — you mark my words — that'll make 'em stir themselves and sit up!"

"But Adrian is pessimistic too, isn't he?" said Nance, looking wistfully at the speaker.

"Nonsense!" cried the Doctor. "Adrian has more Attic salt in him than you women guess. I believe, myself, that this book of his will be worthy to be put beside the 'Thoughts' of Pascal. Have you ever seen Pascal's face? He isn't as good-looking as Adrian but he has the same intellectual fury."

"What's your opinion, Fingal," remarked Mr. Traherne, peering anxiously into the pansied jug, "about the art of making life endurable?"

Dr. Raughty surveyed him with a placid and equable smile. "Courage and gaiety," he said, "are the only recipe, and I don't mind sprinkling these, in spite of our modern philosophers, with a little milk of human kindness."

The priest nodded over what was left of his ale. "*De fructu operum tuorum, Domine, satiabitur terra: ut educas panem de terra, et vinum laetificet cor hominis; ut exhilaret faciem in oleo, et panis cor hominis confirmet*," he muttered, stretching out his long legs under the table and tilting back his chair.

"What the devil does all that mean?" asked the Doctor a little peevishly. "Can't you praise God in simple English? Nance and I couldn't catch a word except ' wine ' and ' bread ' and ' oil.' "

Mr. Traherne looked unspeakably ashamed. "I'm sorry, Nance," he murmured, sitting up very straight and pulling himself together. "It was out of place. It was rude. I'm not sure that it wasn't profane. I'm sorry, Fingal!"

"It's a beautiful afternoon," said Nance, keeping her eyes on the little street, whose very pavements reflected the soft opalescent light which was spreading itself over Rodmoor.

"Ah!" cried Dr. Raughty, "we left *that* out in our summary of the compensations of life. *You* left that out, too, Hamish, from your ' fructu ' and ' panem ' and ' vinum ' and the rest. But, after all, that is what we come back to in the end. The sky, the earth, the sea,— the great cool spaces of night — the sun, like a huge splendid god; the moon, like a sweet passionate nun; and the admirable stars, like gems in some great world-peacock's tail — yes, my darlings, we come back to these in the end!"

He rose from his seat and with shining eyes surveyed his guests.

"By the body of Mistress Bacbuc," he cried, in a loud voice, "we do wrong to sit here any longer! Let's go down to the sands and cool our heads. Here, Maggie! Madge! Marjorie! Where the deuce has that girl gone? There she is! Get me the bill, will you, and bring me a finger-bowl."

Mr. Traherne laid his hand gently on the doctor's arm. "I'm afraid we've been behaving badly, Fingal," he whispered. "We've been drinking ale and forgetting our good manners. Do I look all right? I mean, do I look as if I'd been drinking mahogany-coloured Burton? Do I look as usual?"

The doctor surveyed him with grave intentness. "You look," he said at last," "something between Friar John and Bishop Berkeley." He gave him a little push. "Go and talk to the girls while I buy them chocolates."

Having paid the bill, he occupied himself in selecting with delicate nicety a little box of sweet-meats for each of his friends, choosing one for Nance with a picture of Leda and the Swan upon it and one for Linda with a portrait of the Empress Josephine.

As he leant over the counter, his eyes gleamed with a soft benignant ecstasy and he rallied the shop-woman about some heart-shaped confectionary adorned with blue ribbons.

Before Mr. Traherne rejoined them Nance had time to whisper to Linda, "They're both a little excited, dear, but we needn't notice it. They'll be themselves in a moment. Men are all so babyish."

Linda smiled faintly at this and nodded her head. She looked a little sad and a little pale.

Dr. Raughty soon appeared. "Come on," he said, "let's go down to the sea"; and in a low dreamy voice he murmured the following ditty:

"A boat — a boat — to cross the ferry!
And let us all be wise and merry,
And laugh and quaff and drink brown sherry!"

Linda caught at Nance's sleeve. "I think I'll let you go without me," she whispered. "I feel rather tired."

Nance looked anxiously into her eyes. "I'd come back with you," she murmured, "but it would hurt their feelings. You'd better lie down a little. I'll be back soon." Then, in a lower whisper, "They did it to cheer us up. They're dear, absurd people. Take care of yourself, darling."

Linda stood for a while after she had bidden them all good-bye and watched them move down the street. In the misty sunshine there was something very gentle and appealing about Nance's girlish figure as she walked between the two men. They both seemed talking to her at the same time and, as they talked, they watched her face with affectionate and tender admiration.

"She treats them like children," said Linda to herself. "That's why they're all so fond of her."

She walked slowly back up the street; but instead of entering her house, she drifted languidly across the green and made her way towards the park gates.

She felt very lonely, just then — lonely and full of a heart-aching longing. If only she could catch one glimpse, just one, of the man who was so dear to her — of the man who was the father of her child.

She thought of Adrian's recovery and she thought vaguely and wistfully of the coming of Baptiste. "I hope he will like us," she said to herself. "I hope he will like us both."

Hardly knowing what she did, she passed in through the gates and began moving up the avenue. All the tragic and passionate emotions associated with this place came over her like a rushing wave. She stopped and hesitated. Then with a pitiful effort to control her feelings, she turned and began retracing her steps.

Suddenly she stopped again, her heart beating wildly. Yes, there were footsteps approaching her from the direction of Oakguard. She looked around. Brand Renshaw himself was behind her, standing at a curve of the avenue, bareheaded, under an enormous pine. The horizontal sunlight piercing the foliage in front of him shone red on the trunk of the great tree and red on the man's blood-coloured head.

She started towards him with a little gasping cry, like an animal that, after long wandering, catches sight of its hiding-place.

The man had stopped because he had seen her, and now when he saw her approaching him a convulsive tremor ran through his powerful frame. For one second he made a movement as if to meet her; but then, raising his long arms with a gesture as if at once embracing her and taking leave of her, he plunged into the shadows of the trees and was lost to view.

The girl stood where he had left her — stood as if turned to stone — for several long minutes, while over her head the misty sky looked down through the branches, and from the open spaces of the park came the harsh cry of sea-gulls flying towards the coast.

Then, with drooping head and dazed expressionless eyes, she walked slowly back, the way she had come.

XXVII

THRENOS

AFTER her encounter with Nance, Mrs. Renshaw, returning to Oakguard, informed both Philippa and Brand of the improvement in the condition of Adrian Sorio.

Philippa received the news quietly enough, conscious that the eyes of her brother were upon her; but as soon as she could get away, which was not till the afternoon was well advanced, she slipped off hastily and directed her steps, by a short cut through the park, to the Rodmoor railway-station. She had one fixed idea now in her mind — the idea of seeing Adrian and talking with him before any interview was allowed to the others.

She knew that her name and her prestige as the sister of the largest local landowner, would win her at any rate respectful consideration for anything she asked — and everything beyond that she left recklessly in the hands of fate.

Baltazar's death had affected her more than she would herself have supposed possible. She had felt during these last days a sort of malignant envy of her mother, whose attitude towards her friend's loss was so strange and abnormal.

Philippa, with her scarlet lips, her classic flesh, her Circean feverishness, suffered from her close association with this exultant mourner, as some heathen boy

447

robbed of his companion might have suffered from contact with a Christian visionary, for whom death was "far better."

At this moment, however, as she hurried towards the station, it was not of Baltazar, it was of Adrian, and Adrian only, that she thought.

She dismissed the fact of Baptiste's expected arrival with bitter contempt. Let the boy go to Nance if he pleased! After all, it was to herself — much more intimately than to Nance — that Adrian had confided his passionate idealization of his son and his savage craving for him.

Yes, it was to her he had confided this, and it was to her always, and never to Nance, that he spoke of his book and of his secret thoughts. Her *mind* was what Adrian wanted — her mind, her spirit, her imagination. These were things that Nance, with all her feminine ways, was never able to give him.

Why couldn't she tear him from her now and from all these people?

Let these others be afraid of his madness. He was not mad to her. If he were, why then, she too, she who loved him and understood him, was mad!

From the long sloping spaces of the park, as she hurried on, she could see at intervals, through the misty sun-bathed trees, the mouth of the harbour, with its masts and shipping, and, beyond that, the sea itself.

Ah! the sea was the thing that had mingled their souls! The sea was the accomplice of their love!

Yes, he was hers — hers in the heights and the depths — and none of them should tear him from her!

All the whimpering human crowd of them, with their paltry pieties and vulgar prudence — how she would love to strike them down and pass over them — over their upturned staring faces — until he and she were together!

Through the dreamy air, with its floating gossamer-seeds and faint smell of dead leaves, came to her, as she ran on, over the uneven ground, past rabbit-holes and bracken and clumps of furze, the far distant murmur of the waves on the sands. Yes! The sea was what had joined them; and, as long as that sound was in her ears, no power on earth could hold them apart!

She reached the station just in time. It was five minutes to five and the train left at the hour. Philippa secured a first-class ticket for herself and sank down exhausted in the empty compartment.

How long that five minutes seemed!

She was full of a fierce jealous dread lest any of Nance's friends might be going that very evening to visit the patient.

She listened to the conversation of two lads on the platform near her carriage window. They were speaking of a great bonfire which was to be prepared that day, on the southern side of the harbour, to be set alight the following evening, in honour of the historic Fifth of November. In the tension of her nerves Philippa found herself repeating the quaint lines of the old refrain, associated in her mind with many childish memories.

> " Remember, remember
> Fifth of November,
> Gunpowder Treason and plot.
> We know no reason
> Why Gunpowder Treason
> Should ever be forgot!"

And the question flashed through her mind as to what would have happened by the time that great spire of smoke and flame — she recalled the look of it so well! — rose up and drifted across the water. Would it be the welcoming signal to bring Baptiste to Rodmoor — to Rodmoor and to Adrian?

Two minutes more! She watched the hand upon the station-clock. It was slowly crossing the diminishing strip of white which separated it from the figure of the hour. Oh, these cruel signs, with their murderous moving fingers! Why must Love and Hope and Despair depend upon little patches of vanishing white, between black marks?

Off at last! And she made a little gasping noise in her throat as if she had swallowed that strip of white.

An hour later, as the November darkness was closing in, she passed through the iron gates into the Asylum garden. As she moved in, a small group of inmates of the Asylum, accompanied by a nurse, emerged from a secluded path. It was shadowy and obscure under those heavy trees, but led by the childish curiosity of the demented, these unfortunate persons, instead of obeying their attendant's command, drifted waveringly towards her.

A movement took place among them like that described by Dante in his Inferno as occurring when some single soul, out of a procession of lost spirits, recognizes in the dubious twilight, a living figure from the upper air.

For the moment Philippa wondered if Adrian was among them, but if he was he was given no opportunity to approach her, for the alert guardian of these people, like some Virgilian watcher of ghostly shadows upon the infernal stream, shepherded them away, across the darkened lawn, towards the corner of the building.

The Renshaw name acted like magic when she reached the house. Yes, Mr. Sorio was much better; practically quite himself again, and there was no reason at all why Miss Renshaw should not have an interview with him. A letter had, indeed, only that very afternoon been posted to Miss Herrick, asking her to come up to the place the following day.

Philippa inquired whether her interview with the patient might take the form of a little walk with him, before the hour of their evening meal. This request produced a momentary hesitation on the part of the official to whom she made it, but ultimately — for, after all, Miss Renshaw was the sister of the magistrate who had procured the unhappy man's admission into the place — that too was granted her, on condition that she returned in half-an-hour's time, and did not take her companion into the streets of the town. Having granted her request the Asylum doctor left her in the waiting-room, while he went to fetch her friend.

Philippa sank down upon a plush-covered chair and looked around her. What a horrible room it was! The shabby furniture, covered with gloomy drapery, had an air of sombre complicity with all the tragedies that darkened human life. It was like a room only entered when some one was dead or dying. It was like the ante-room to a cemetery. Everything in it drooped, and seemed anxious to efface itself, as if ashamed to witness the indecent exposures of outraged human thoughts.

They brought Sorio at last, and the man's sunken

eyes gleamed with a light of indescribable pleasure when his hand met Philippa's and clutched it with trembling eagerness.

They went out of the room together and moved down the long passage that led to the entrance of the place. As she walked by his side, Philippa experienced the queer sensation of having him as her partner in some diabolic *danse-macabre,* performed to the mingled tune of all the wild " songs of madness " created since the beginning of the world.

She couldn't help noticing that the groups of people they passed on their way had an air quite different from persons in a hospital or even in a prison. They made her think — these miserable ones — of some horrible school for grown-up people; such a school as those who have been ill-used in childhood see sometimes in their dreams.

They seemed to loiter and gather and peer and mutter, as if, " with bated breath and whispering humbleness," they were listening to something that was going on behind closed doors. Philippa got the impression of a horrible atmosphere of *guilt* hanging over the place, as if some dark and awful retribution were being undergone there, for crimes committed against the natural instincts of humanity.

A lean, emaciated old woman came shuffling past them, with elongated neck and outstretched arms. " I'm a camel! I'm a camel! I'm a camel! " Philippa heard her mutter.

Suddenly Adrian laid his hand on her arm. " They let me have my owl in here, Phil," he said. " We mustn't go far to-night or it'll get hungry. It has its supper off my plate. I never told you how I found it, did I? It was pecking at her eyes, you know. Yes, at her eyes! But that's nothing, is it? She had been dead for weeks, and owls are scavengers, and corpses are carrion!"

They crossed the garden with quick steps.

"How good the air is to-night!" cried Philippa's companion, throwing back his head and snuffing the leaf-scented darkness.

They were let out through the iron gates and turning instinctively south-wards, they wandered slowly down to the river — the girl's hand resting on the man's arm.

They passed, on their way, the blackened wall of a disused factory. A blurred and feeble street-lamp threw a flickering light upon this wall. Pasted upon its surface was a staring and coloured advertisement of some insurance company, representing a phoenix surrounded by flames.

Philippa thought at once of the bonfire which was being prepared for the ensuing evening. Would Adrian's boy really arrive in so short a time? And would Adrian himself, like that grotesque bird, so imperturbable in the midst of its funeral pyre, rise to new life after all this misery? Let it be her — oh, great heavenly powers! — let it be her and not Nance, nor Baptiste, nor any other, who should save him and heal him!

Still looking at the picture on the wall, she repeated to her companion a favourite verse of Mrs. Renshaw's which she had learnt as a child.

> "Death is now the phoenix' nest
> And the turtle's loyal breast
> To eternity doth rest.

> "Leaving no posterity,
> 'Twas not their infirmity,
> It was married chastity."

The rich dirge-like music of these Shakespearian rhymes — placed so quaintly under their strange title of " Threnos," at the end of the familiar volume — had a soothing influence upon them both at that moment.

It seemed to Philippa as if, by her utterance of them, they both came to share some sad sweet obsequies over the body of something that was neither human nor inhuman, something remote, strange, ineffable, that lay between them, and was of them and yet not of them, like the spirit-corpse of an unborn child.

They reached the bank of the river. The waters of the Loon were high and, through the darkness, a murmur as if composed of a hundred vague whispering voices blending together, rose to their ears from its dark surface.

They moved down close to the river's edge. A small barge, with its long guiding-pole lying across it, lay moored to the bank. Without a moment's delay — as if the thing had been prepared in advance to receive him — Adrian jumped into the barge and seized the pole.

" Come ! " he said quietly.

She was too reckless and indifferent to everything now, to care greatly what they did; so without a word of protest, or any attempt to turn his purpose, she leapt in after him and settling herself in the stern, seized the heavy wooden rudder.

The tide was running sea-ward, fast and strong, and the barge, pushed vigorously by Adrian's pole away from the bank, swept forward into the darkness.

Adrian, standing firmly on his feet, continued to hold the pole, his figure looming out of obscurity, tall and commanding.

The tide soon swept them beyond the last houses of the town and out into the open fens.

The night was very still and quite free from wind but a thin veil of mist concealed the stars.

Adrian, letting the pole sink down on the deck of the barge, moved forward to where she sat holding the rudder, and stretched himself out at her feet.

"Will they follow us?" he whispered in a dreamy indifferent voice.

"No, no!" the girl answered. "They'll never think of this. They'll wait for us and when we don't come back, they'll search the town and the roads. Let's go on as we are, dearest. What does it matter? What does anything matter?"

She lay back and ran her fingers gently and dreamily over his forehead.

Swiftly and silently the barge swept on, and willows, poplars, weirs, dam-gates, tall reeds and ruined rush-thatched hovels, passed them by, like figures woven out of unreal shadows.

The water gurgled against the sides of the barge and whispered mournfully against the banks, and, as they advanced, the mystery of the night and the brooding silence of the fens received them in a mystic embrace.

A strange deep happiness gradually surged up in Philippa's heart. She was with the man she loved; she was with the darkness she loved, and the river she loved. The Loon carried them forward, the pitiful friendly Loon, the Loon which had flowed by the dwell-

ing of her race for so many ages; the Loon which had
given Baltazar the peace he craved.

Just the faintest tremor of doubt troubled her, the
thought that it was towards Nance — towards her
rival — that the tide was bearing them; but let come
what might come, that hour at least was hers! Not
all the world could take that hour from her — and the
future? What did the future matter?

As to the brain-sick man himself, who lay at the girl's
feet, it were long and hard to tell all the strange dim
visions that flowed through his head. He took Philippa's hand in his own and kissed it tenderly but, had
the girl known, his thoughts were not of her. They
were not even of his son; of the son for whom he had
so passionately longed. They were not of any human
being. They circled constantly — these thoughts —
round a strange vague image, an image moulded of
white mists and white vapours and the reflection of
white stars in dark waters.

This image, of a shape dim and vast and elemental,
seemed to flow upwards from land and sea, and stretch
forth towards infinite space. It was an image of something beyond human expression, of something beyond
earth-loves and earth-hatreds, beyond life and also beyond death. It was the image of Nothingness; and yet
in this Nothingness there was a relief, an escape, a
refuge, a beyond-hope, which made all the ways of humanity seem indifferent, all its gods childish, all its
dreams vain, and yet offered a large cool draught of
" deep and liquid rest " the taste of which set the soul
completely free.

Many hours passed thus over their heads, as the tide
carried them down towards Rodmoor, round the great

sweeping curves made by the Loon, through the stubble-fields and the marshes.

It was, at last, the striking of the side of the barge against one of the arches of the New Bridge, which roused the prostrate man from the trance into which he had fallen.

As soon as they had emerged on the further side of the arch, he leapt to his feet. Bending forward towards Philippa, he pointed with an outstretched arm towards the shadowy houses of Rodmoor which, with here and there a faint light in some high window, could now be discerned through the darkness.

" I smell the sea! " he cried. " I smell the sea! Drift on, Phil, my little one, drift on to the harbour! I must leave you now. We shall meet by the sea, my girl — by the sea in the old way — but I can't wait now. I must be alone, alone, alone! '

Waving his hand wildly with a gesture of farewell, he clutched at a clump of reeds and sprang out upon the bank. Philippa, letting the barge float on as it pleased, followed him with all the speed she could.

He had secured a considerable start of her, however, and it was all she could do to keep him in sight in the darkness.

He ran first towards the church, but when he reached the path which deviated towards the sand-dunes, he turned sharply eastward. He ran wildly, desperately, with no thought in his whole being but the feeling that he must reach the sea and be alone.

He felt at that moment as though the whole of humanity — loathsome, cancerous, suffocating humanity — were pursuing him with outstretched hands.

Once, as he was mid-way between the church path

and the dunes, he turned his head, and catching sight
of Philippa's figure following him, he plunged forward
in a fury of panic.

As he crossed the dunes, at this savage pace, something seemed to break in his brain or in his heart. He
spat out a mouthful of sweet-tasting blood, and, falling
on his knees, fumbled in the loose sand, as if searching
for some lost object.

Staggering once more to his feet, and seeing that his
pursuer was near, he stumbled wildly down the slope
of the dunes and tottered across the sand to the water's
edge.

He was there at last — safe from everything — safe
from love and hatred and madness and pity — safe
from unspeakable imaginations — safe from himself!

The long dark line of waves broke calmly and indifferently at his feet, and away — away into the eternal
night — stretched the vast expanse of the sea, dim,
vague, full of inexpressible, infinite reassurance.

He raised both his arms into the air. For one brief
miraculous moment his brain became clear and an ecstatic feeling of triumph and unconquerable joy swept
through him.

"Baptiste!" he shouted in a shrill vibrating voice,
"Baptiste!"

His cry went reverberating over the water. He
turned and tried to struggle back. A rush of blood
once more filled his mouth. His head grew dizzy.

"Tell Nance that I — that I —" His words died
into a choking murmur and he fell heavily on his face
on the sand.

He was dead when she reached him. She lifted him

gently till he lay on his back and then pressing her hand to his heart, she knew that it was the end.

She sank beside him, bowing her forehead till it touched the ground, and clinging to his neck. After a minute or two she rose, and taking his hand in her own she sat staring into the darkness, with wide-open tear-less eyes.

She was "alone with her dead" and nothing mattered any more now.

She remained motionless for several long moments, while over her head something that resembled eternity seemed to pass by, on beautiful, terrible, beating wings.

Then she rose up upon her feet.

"She shall never have him!" she murmured. "She shall never have him!"

She tore from her waist a strongly-woven embroidered cord, the long tassels of which hung down at her side. She dragged the dead man to the very edge of the water. With an incredible effort, she raised him up till he leant, limp and heavy, against her own body.

Then, supporting him with difficulty, and with difficulty keeping herself from sinking under his weight, she twisted the cord round them both, and tied it in a secure knot. Holding him thus before her, with his chin resting on her shoulder, she staggered forward into the water.

It was not easy to advance, and her heart seemed on the point of breaking with the strain. But the savage thought that she was taking him away from Nance — from Nance and from every one — to possess him herself forever, gave her a supernatural strength.

It seemed as though the demon of madness, which

had passed from Adrian at the last, and left him free, had entered into her.

If that was indeed the case, it is more than likely that when she fell at last — fell backwards under his weight beneath the waves — it was rather with a mad ecstasy of abandonment that she drank the choking water, than with any hopeless struggle to escape the end she had willed.

Bound tightly together, both by the girl's clinging arms and by the cord she had fastened round them, the North Sea as it drew back in the outflowing of its tide, carried their bodies forth into the darkness.

Far from land it carried them — under the misty unseeing sky — far from misery and madness, and when the dawn came trembling at last over the restless expanse of water, it found only the white sea-horses and the white sea-birds. Those two had sunk together; out of reach of humanity, out of reach of Rodmoor.

THE END